Terror on Every Side!

THE LIFE OF JEREMIAH

VOLUME 6

That Broken Reed

Mark Morgan

Bible
Tales
www.BibleTales.online

Published in Australia by Bible Tales Online.
www.BibleTales.online

The series: Terror on Every Side! The Life of Jeremiah
Volume 1 – Early Days
Volume 2 – As Good As It Gets
Volume 3 – Darkness Falling
Volume 4 – The Darkness Deepens
Volume 5 – No Remedy
Volume 6 – That Broken Reed

This book: Volume 6 – That Broken Reed

ISBN (Paperback): 978-1-925587-18-0
ISBN (Hardcover) 978-1-925587-19-7
ISBN (eBook): 978-1-925587-16-6

Last updated: 5 February 2023.

Cover picture: Siout, Egypt (now called Asyut).
Painting by Sanford Robinson Gifford (1874).

Free Download

Paul in Snippets

A 109-page PDF novelette by Mark Morgan.

The life of Paul painted from the Acts of the Apostles.

Get your free copy of *Paul in Snippets* when you sign up for the Bible Tales mailing list. As well as the eBook, you will receive a weekly email newsletter with micro tales, informative articles and special offers.

Visit **https://www.BibleTales.online/free-pins**

www.BibleTales.online

To my ever-patient wife, Ruth.

Acknowledgements and thanks

Terror on Every Side! The Life of Jeremiah was originally published in five volumes, ending as Judah's surviving remnant fled the country after the assassination of Gedaliah, Nebuchadnezzar's appointed governor. Until then, the story is based on the many details recorded in the books of Kings, Chronicles, Jeremiah, Lamentations, Ezekiel, Daniel and other prophets, and some historical information from outside the Bible. At that point, however, most of the Biblical sources fall silent.

This sixth volume tells of Jeremiah's life from then on, something about which the Bible says very little – directly. However, many hidden nuggets of information help us to imagine Jeremiah's life in Egypt as he finished his work as Yahweh's prophet to the nations.

Particular thanks go to Ruth, my wife, who helps me find time to write, patiently reads it all, and humours me when I spend inordinate amounts of time on research into minute details. Once again, Cathy, my oldest daughter, has proof read the entire manuscript more than once. Thanks.

Thanks also to serial subscribers who have greatly improved the book through their feedback. No manuscript is flawless, but these early readers helped eliminate most errors.

The map of Egypt and Judah in about 580BC was derived from a map of the Middle East[1] by Yiyi[2] with a CC BY 3.0 licence.[3] The "derivative work" in this book is released under the same CC BY 3.0 licence.

---

[1] https://commons.wikimedia.org/wiki/File:
Near_East_topographic_map_with_toponyms_3000bc-pt.svg
[2] https://commons.wikimedia.org/wiki/User:Yiyi
[3] https://creativecommons.org/licenses/by/3.0/deed.en

A request

I have a request to make of all readers: if you find any typos, spelling errors, poor grammar, unkempt use of vocabulary, or, most importantly, errors of fact where the story misrepresents the Bible, please let me know. I can't correct printed books, but electronic versions and new printed editions can be fixed.

VOLUME SIX

That Broken Reed

Contents

Terror on Every Side!

For I hear the whispering of many —
terror on every side! —
as they scheme together against me,
as they plot to take my life.

A psalm of David: Psalm 31:13

For I hear many whispering.
Terror is on every side!
"Denounce him! Let us denounce him!"
say all my close friends,
watching for my fall.
"Perhaps he will be deceived;
then we can overcome him
and take our revenge on him."

Jeremiah 20:10

Map

After Jeremiah was taken to Egypt, God gave him messages for the people of Judah spread throughout Egypt and for Egypt itself. The locations mentioned are shown in the map below.

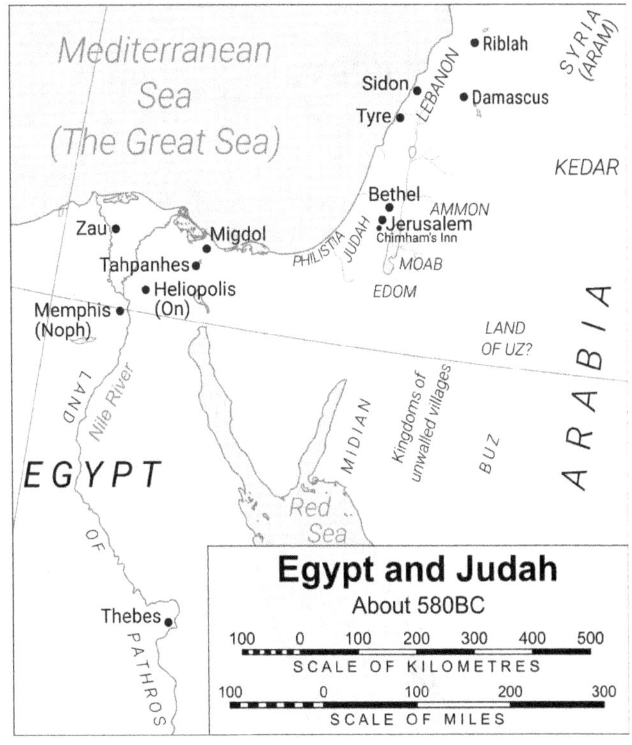

Chapter 1

Leaving

March 585BC

"Off to Egypt today, Jeremiah," said Baruch with a crooked smile as we met outside the inn.

It was just after dawn on a fine morning in early spring, less than a day since the remnants of Judah had rejected God's command and decided to escape to Egypt.

We stood in the same place where I had confronted the crowd the day before and told them that God's answer to their question – the answer they had promised to abide by – was that they should stay in Judah.

"Egypt! Egypt! Egypt!" had been the response, and Baruch and I were going along whether we liked it or not.

That evening, Johanan had made it clear that if we cooperated we could go along in relative freedom, but if we resisted we would suffer. To make sure that we understood, we were forced to collect our belongings and were taken to separate dormitories in the inn where his men could keep a watchful eye on us. In that crowded room, I began writing my prophet's diary. Finally, after several hours, I was told to stop, and lay down to sleep under the watchful eye of some of his men.

We were given no opportunity to escape.

I returned Baruch's smile with a wry smile of my own and sighed. Neither of us knew quite what to expect. Once again, life was uncertain, and we knew that some of our countrymen would be very happy to find any excuse to make us suffer.

"Yes, off to Egypt. The very journey God told our fathers we would never need to make again once he led them out of there."[4]

"Oh, you prophets," said Johanan, who had come out of the inn in time to hear my words. "You keep harping on things. Just let it go. The decision is made."

"We could still change our minds. Even now, we could have a time of prayer and thought. We could…"

"Shut up, you old fool!" said Johanan in an angry voice. For a moment, I thought he was about to strike me, but he took a deep breath and continued with a little more control, "Oh, I suppose that I shouldn't speak to a prophet – a priest – like that, but you just won't accept when you're beaten. Everyone has agreed. We're not talking about it any more. So, just leave it. Do you understand?"

"Yahweh is the one you are abusing, Johanan, I'm just a prophet. He has told you what to do, and…"

Johanan held up his hands. "Stop!" he commanded. "Not another word from you, or you'll be coming along with us tied up and with a bag over your head."

I closed my mouth.

ℭℜ

Almost everyone got up early that day, but that didn't mean they were ready to leave!

---

[4] Deuteronomy 17:16; 26:68

Men and women hurried to and fro, shouting – often at each other. Children played with the goods already packed for transport, sometimes carrying them away or leaving them mixed up with other stacks of goods. Noise was the overwhelming result, but there was also an underlying feeling of urgency. With the passing of winter, the survivors' dread of Nebuchadnezzar and his army had returned in full force. What if the Chaldeans had heard about the assassination of Gedaliah and the soldiers? A detachment of soldiers might already be bearing down on them from the north, approaching from Jerusalem as the sun climbed above the horizon!

Few oxen and even fewer asses were available to pull the limited number of carts that had survived the Chaldean invasion. Most of the refugees would have to walk all the way to Egypt, just as their relatives and friends had recently walked to Babylon.

I stood near the inn and listened to the words of the would-be refugees. Some spoke only of the things they needed to take with them to Egypt, while others reflected on the past or the future.

"It will be good to get away from this cursed place," said one man to his companion.

"Yes, a curse has been on it ever since our fathers came here."

"If only they had never left Egypt."

I couldn't help myself. "Are you serious?" I interrupted. "Our fathers were *slaves* in Egypt! We've had hundreds of years of freedom in this land, although it hasn't always been as good as it would've been if only we'd obeyed God's commands!"

They looked at me in that "here he goes again" way that 40 years of delivering God's messages has forced me to get used to.

I suppose it is desperation that makes people paint in such gloomy colours something they have decided to abandon. After all, Judah was the only country most had ever known, and now they were leaving it to walk into the unknown. And fear was driving them. God had warned that we would meet terror on every side, and now that terror was outweighing God's assurance of his care.

Without faith in God, only terror remained.

No soldiers came, however, and the sun was high in the cloudless sky before the trumpet sounded to start the ragtag caravan travelling south.

℞

King Solomon ruled over a kingdom that extended from the Euphrates to the border of Egypt during a time of unparalleled prosperity for Israel.[5]

But empires crumble, and this was no exception. The grandeur and extravagance of its peak were matched by the suddenness of its fall: within five years of Solomon's death, the kingdom he ruled had split in two and Egypt, that hovering vulture, had descended on its defenceless victim. Riches beyond the wildest dreams of most nations had been carried back to Egypt and the divided seed of Jacob were left to count their losses.

Count their losses they did, but regretting the godlessness that had caused them was still beyond them. God had led them out of Egypt and told them to keep away from there. Solomon had flouted those rules,[6] trading with Egypt in horses and chariots, and even taking the daughter of Pharaoh as his wife. Egypt had been well

---

[5] 1 Kings 4:21
[6] 1 Kings 10:26-29; 1 Kings 3:1

aware of the vast riches that sat so temptingly to their north!

Never again would two-tribe Judah, or even ten-tribe Israel to the north, be free of the influence of Egypt. God's commands had been discarded, and his care along with them. Egypt became the rod of God's judgement, bruising the backs of his people on many occasions in repeated, but vain, attempts to gain their repentant attention.

It would be unfair to dismiss the 350 years that followed as simply the prolonged death-throes of the nation Jacob had fathered: indeed, there were some shining lights among the kings of Judah, kings who did their best to guide the nation in the footsteps of David their forebear. Not only so, but there were hundreds, even thousands, of prophets who did their utmost to help, but it was all too little in the face of so much idolatry. Reforms were limited and short-lived, and the overall trajectory of the nation was downhill. The reforms were no more than temporary upward blips on a fatal, inevitable collision course with judgement that had ended with Nebuchadnezzar's destruction of Jerusalem.

Those of us who lived through that final siege and saw its aftermath were still numbed by the horrors we had witnessed. We had endured hunger and plague, the disorientation of starvation and the terror of uncertainty as the final hours passed slowly over the survivors of the siege.

By that time, many were almost too tired to care. The defenders too weak to defend, the mothers too hungry to do what mothers always do: care for their children.

Words cannot adequately describe what we all witnessed, and many still endure screaming terrors every night as they helplessly relive the deaths of their loved ones.

Eventually, Nebuchadnezzar and his army returned to Babylon, leaving Gedaliah the son of Ahikam to manage the few people left in the land. Mostly this was the poor and the weak, the sick and the hopeless, but there were also those who fled the land when Nebuchadnezzar invaded and returned once the fighting was over and the victors had left. Guerrilla bands who had avoided excessive involvement in the war reappeared, and many foreigners grasped at an opportunity to take over an empty land.

There were few who could lead, and fewer still who would lead with Judah's best interests at heart. Gedaliah was one such, but he didn't last long. Just a few weeks after Nebuchadnezzar's army left, he was assassinated – along with the Chaldean soldiers left behind to support him.

Once Gedaliah was gone, all instincts suggested flight. When those weak but arrogant leaders decided to ask for guidance from God, I hoped it was a positive sign, but it wasn't. I have thought it over so many times now, and my conclusion never changes: don't ask God for guidance if you won't listen to his answer. They asked, but by the time God gave an answer, they had already decided what they were going to do – whatever the answer was. Of course, I explained all of this earlier in my diary, but I can't stop reliving it: it is so upsetting.

I was called a liar – well, I'm used to that. But they're also ignoring God's words and we are all going back to Egypt. Egypt! A place God said we would never have to go to again, and now we're going by our own choice!

Assyria did away with Israel, Babylon has done away with Judah, and now the tiny remnant of Judah is going to Egypt.

∞

We went south from Bethlehem along the road to Hebron, seeing very few people along the way. Most of those we saw had already heard about the assassination of Gedaliah, and many joined our pitiful caravan from fear of Nebuchadnezzar's expected reprisals.

We passed the ruins of Hebron, staying the night nearby, and next day continued south. Beersheba was reached during the third day's march and then left behind as we went on through the Negev towards the boundaries of the land God had promised to Abraham.

The next morning was cloudy with a little rain. I don't know if God was sending us a message, but it was particularly dark in the south and west, while the sky towards the north seemed cloudless and lovely. Was God giving us one last chance?

If he was, we ignored it and marched south towards Egypt.

Once we left the land of our fathers, Johanan and the other leaders decided that Baruch and I could be freed. It was good to be free of the ropes we had been bound with. Nevertheless, they made it clear that we must still come with them, and that any attempt to escape would be punished severely. I'm sure that some of them hoped we would give them an excuse to take their revenge on us: revenge for giving them God's answer.

That night, my mind was full of conflict. Should I do my best to escape and return to Judah? God had said that we should stay there, but our leaders would not listen. Should I?

Baruch and I could probably have found a way to escape. There were guards stationed near the tents, but I think we could have crept away to safety in the depths of the night.

But I was tired; morose; depressed. Escape didn't seem worthwhile.

God had told my fellow refugees not to leave Judah, but what about me? Should I be struggling to return to an empty land or was my next task opening up before me in Egypt?

Over the years I had spent long periods of time travelling through many different nations – including Egypt. I was, after all, a prophet to the nations. It was only in recent years that I had spent the majority of my time in Jerusalem – unwelcome and often locked up.

I had no clear direction from God. No message that gave me a confident direction or purpose. I didn't know what to do.

Energetic escape and a lonely journey north felt beyond me. I wondered if my work was just petering out, wandering to an uncertain end. I couldn't help remembering how my father had died – when he was a little younger than I was – just fading away. Would I follow his path? I desperately wanted to write my diary, but exhaustion had stolen my enthusiasm.

In the darkness of the desert night, keenly aware of being outside the Promised Land, I fell into a disturbed sleep.

Chapter 2

Into the Desert

If my companions thought the journey to Egypt would be easy, it didn't take them long to realise their error.

People often complain about the heat of the day in Jerusalem, even during winter, but the fierce midday heat of the desert is quite different. The road stretches out before you like an endless ribbon, shimmering in the heat, and there is nowhere to hide from the glare of the sun.

It was five days since we had left Bethlehem and, paradoxically, I was feeling much better. The temporary feeling of melancholy had left me and I was able to look forward to the future once more with optimism and happy expectation, although cold logic told me that I had little to look forward to in Egypt.

Sweat trickled down my face and into my beard. I could feel it running down my back as well, but really, I was not finding the dry heat of the desert too unpleasant.

However, those around me seemed to be finding the conditions rather more difficult. In Judah, we would often have rested at that time to avoid the heat of the day, but here the lack of shade or cover had made people decide to keep walking. There were no cooling breezes and it would be several hours before the temperature would start to drop. We had enough water with us for survival, but none to spare for cooling us down. To many, the middle of the day seemed like an unending torment. I tried to encourage them by reminding them that the full heat of the day didn't last long in early spring, but they weren't convinced.

The road we were following would lead us directly to Egypt, and there were enough of us that our leaders believed we would be safe from robbers. Johanan and the other commanders were all armed, as were their men, so it would take a strong force to threaten us. It was the weather and the terrain that were likely to prove our strongest opponents.

Much of the track was firm and clear, but in places, shifting sand made it hard for people and carts alike, while in other places, large scattered stones made the passage of carts awkward.

However, every step towards Egypt reduced the fear of Nebuchadnezzar and his men overtaking us, so, step by step, we crossed the desert.

Baruch and I walked together, pondering what might happen and when. We knew God's judgement on our fleeing caravan:

"Hear the word of the Lord, O remnant of Judah.
'Thus says the Lord of hosts, the God of Israel:
If you set your faces to enter Egypt and go to live there,
then the sword that you fear shall overtake you
there in the land of Egypt,
and the famine of which you are afraid
shall follow close after you to Egypt,
and there you shall die.' "[7]

What we knew nothing about was the timing of this judgement.

---

[7] Jeremiah 42:15-16

" 'Close after you' is what God said," reflected Baruch. "Can that mean anything other than 'soon'?"

"I don't *think* so," I answered, "but don't forget that God's idea of 'soon' is not always the same as ours. I was sure that Yahweh's judgement was coming 'soon' back in the days of Josiah – 40 years ago. Even now, I often expect God to act more quickly than he does, but I have learned a bit of patience."

"I suppose you're right. It's not really worth guessing at the timing, is it?"

"No. It might be today or it might be another 40 years."

We stopped talking and walked for some time in silence. Apart from our slow-moving caravan, nothing disturbed the emptiness of the desert. From horizon to horizon, all we could see were the yellows, browns and reds of sand and rocks. We passed very little that grew, and what there was reached no great height.

"Did you ever think you would see Israel going back to Egypt by choice?" I asked.

"Of course not!" he replied. "You know the scriptures, and you know how much the idea of us living in the Promised Land has been part of our national psyche for almost a thousand years."

"Yet now we've left."

"Yes."

"And sometime, God's judgement will follow us, and then we'll all see again the sights we saw in Jerusalem."

"Yes: the sword, famine and death." Baruch sighed.

A soldier who walked near us as a guard had been listening to our conversation, and now he interjected, "But Egypt is a powerful nation. We'll find peace and safety there. They'll look after us."

"Have you ever heard the saying, 'You are trusting in Egypt, that broken reed of a staff, which will pierce the hand of any man who leans on it'?"[8] asked Baruch.

"No," said the soldier. "Who said that?"

"One of the army commanders of Sennacherib, the king of Assyria," said Baruch.

"Not a man you'd normally quote as wise, Baruch," I remarked.

"True," he admitted, "but that time he was right."

"Maybe so," said the soldier, "but Nebuchadnezzar hasn't been able to beat Egypt, has he?"

"He hasn't even tried yet. However, last time they met in battle, up at Carchemish about 20 years ago, Nebuchadnezzar won."

"But he's had a long time since then to attack Egypt at home and he hasn't done so. He's scared. Egypt is the power around here."

"Well, Pharaoh hasn't helped us much, has he? Remember just two years ago when we heard that he'd come out to attack Nebuchadnezzar? What came of that?"

"The Chaldeans had to leave us to go and face the Egyptians," he argued. "They went and left us alone."

"For a few weeks!" I said.

"And then they came back," added Baruch.

"And the next time they left Jerusalem, they took thousands of our people with them as captives," I said.

"So much for Egypt's help!" Baruch concluded.

"But they have to be better than Babylon," protested the soldier.

"Perhaps, but what if Babylon comes to Egypt?"

"It can't happen," said the soldier confidently. "They would be too far from home. Their supply chains would

---

8 Isaiah 36:6; 2 Kings 18:21

be too long and too fragile. An army can't win in that situation."

"I don't know anything about supply chains," I answered, "but I do know that we won't find peace in Egypt."

We couldn't convince the soldier. He was too sure of military theory and the difficulties of waging war across the vast distances that separated Babylon from Egypt.

Our caravan trudged slowly across the desert, and gradually the shadows lengthened. Eventually, the temperature began to drop, reminding us that when night came, we would all be shivering, wishing for some of the heat of the day!

There, in the middle of the desert, we stopped for another night. Everyone did what they could to keep warm, but the treeless desert deprived us of the pleasure of roaring campfires. It was a strangely quiet scene as our small cooking fires burned low and died out. Guards surrounded the camp. I would have liked to go outside the camp to pray, but they wouldn't let me, so I sat outside my tent while I prayed and thought over the discussions of the day. Above me, the splendour of the stars was spread across the dome of the sky from horizon to horizon.

God's message of condemnation had been so clear and simple. I tried to put myself in the position of the refugees, but even when I tried hard, I couldn't understand how they could have made the choices they had. True, I had personally seen so much proof that Yahweh was in control, but everyone had seen the destruction of Jerusalem, the captivity of our nation, the taking away of Zedekiah! Surely these and many other things must convince everyone that Yahweh was the God of Israel and of the whole world. How could people ignore this proof?

It was only a week since God's simple, frighteningly clear message had been given to me, but so much had changed in that time. It had offered the battered nation so much – such gentle, loving care *if only we would stay in the land he had given us*. Yet from the beginning, God had made it clear that he knew the people were not going to listen, and I was still finding it hard to believe – or understand.

The cold, flickering stars gave me no answers, and nor did God, so eventually, I gave up and went to bed.

Chapter 3

Surprise

Two days later, our rearguard saw a small cloud of dust behind us in the distance. It quickly grew larger until it was obvious that we were being pursued by a group of mounted men, travelling much faster than we were.

Johanan and the other military leaders quickly sent all of the available mounted men to the rear of our column while the caravan began to form into a circle.

Women and children were hurriedly placed in the centre, but the carts were still being moved to complete the circle when the mounted men caught up with us. There was no time to wait, no opportunity to try peaceful negotiations. If this group of riders meant us no harm, they were making no attempt to show it.

Our guards were not well armed, but some had bows and all had slings. Johanan's right-hand-man held a ram's horn trumpet and when Johanan gave him the signal, he blew it loudly.

The urgent, raucous sound split the air, and in a moment, the sky was filled with a cloud of slingstones and arrows. Yet again, as I have done so often over the years, I stood and watched a conflict in which I had no part. The projectiles swooped down on the pursuing force, inflicting a surprising number of casualties.

As soon as our pre-emptive defence was launched, the galloping party showed that sudden attack had always been their plan. Bows were drawn from their places of concealment where they had presumably been hidden in the hope that we would allow them to approach without resistance. Even as our projectiles continued to land among them, their answering salvo was already being loosed towards us. Presumably they were experienced at mounting such attacks, but, surprisingly, that first salvo left us completely unscathed.

The attackers fanned out to surround us, threatening us from all directions and no longer presenting the defenders with a clustered target. Some of our fighters were obviously expert slingers, and they continued to find the fast-moving enemy targets despite the distance.

Even so, our situation was serious enough.

Though the defenders outnumbered our attackers, they were hampered by the need to protect a helpless array of families who were slow even to follow shouted instructions, let alone to assist with the resistance. The thundering of hooves and the screams of terrified men, women and children made so much noise that none of the leaders of either side could communicate with their men.

Nevertheless, by the time the mounted men had surrounded us, about twenty of them had already been killed or injured, while only one of Johanan's men had been injured – an arrow suddenly sprouting grotesquely from his lower arm.

Once they had encircled us, our attackers had the advantage that even if they missed the defenders they were targeting, there was still a good chance that they would hit some other target that would weaken the defence.

Had there been enough carts to surround the caravan, we could all have hidden behind them and defence would have been easy, but we had few carts, and that left gaping holes in our defence. After surrounding us, the attackers withdrew a short distance to make sure that our slingers had little chance of hurting them, then stopped and sat quietly for a while, looking for weaknesses in our defence and waiting for a signal from their leader.

Suddenly, the signal came. Waving their bows above their heads, they all shouted and charged.

Baruch and I were bunched up in the centre with the members of the caravan who were not fighters – mostly women, children and old men. Nobody had demanded that we join the defence, and we wouldn't have done so if they had. I had decided this question in my mind many years ago, and when Baruch began to work for me as a scribe, we had discussed it and he agreed with my decision – which had quite encouraged me at the time. Although the situation had changed a little with the destruction of Jerusalem, it was still fundamentally the same: I had to be on God's side, not on the side of my nation. First and foremost, my loyalty was to God.

I had tried to explain how I felt to Johanan as we travelled, saying that it wouldn't make any sense to tell everyone that God had ordered us not to travel to Egypt and then to support the journey by helping to defend the party. After all, God had said that the sword would pursue us to Egypt, so it couldn't really be a surprise if we were attacked!

Johanan had dismissed my argument, suggesting that it was just cowardice instead. However, when the crunch came, at least he didn't try to argue.

The attackers galloped for the wide openings between the carts, and it was a terrifying sight as they hurriedly drew and loosed arrows towards us. The arrows weren't aimed accurately, but some came close enough to have everyone ducking for any cover they could find. Johanan's men replied with arrows and slingstones, and their aim was better. In my field of view, another three or four attackers screamed and one fell from his donkey, rolled a short distance and lay still.

Johanan and his men were obviously gaining confidence, but the situation changed as our attackers got closer. Arrows that had at first gone wide of us now began to land among us. Two old men screamed as arrows struck them, and several women and children were hit soon afterwards.

This was not the first time that I'd been nearby when warfare became very personal. I'm no doctor, but as a priest I've grown very familiar with blood and flesh through making animal sacrifices. I moved quickly across to help one of the injured old men, who was not being cared for by anyone else. The arrow was embedded in his shoulder and he was screaming with the pain as he tried to pull it out. I was glad to have something to concentrate on beyond the fighting. Quickly I removed the arrow, tore some material off my outer garment and made it into a pad that I tied over the wound to stop the bleeding. Looking after wounded people is quite different from sacrificing an animal, but at least the sight of plenty of blood is nothing new to me.

From that time on, I know very little of what happened in the skirmish: I was busy helping the wounded. Baruch didn't have the past experience as I had, but he could calmly follow instructions, which was a great help. If we had not been there, I believe that several more would have died, but even so, the death toll was horribly high.

The attackers never made it within the circle of carts, but it was a near-run thing. Johanan's men were hard-pressed and several were badly injured. At times, the attackers were only metres from me, near enough for me to hear their shouts and unconsciously recognise the Edomite language.

Some time later, I realised that most of the noise had died down and that the remaining shouts were shouts of victory. At the time, I was caring for a young child who had been hit in the chest by an arrow. It seemed obvious that he had little chance of survival, but the small chance he had depended on me stopping the heavy bleeding. Compressing the area around the wound didn't seem to help and the folded pad of material I had applied was already soaked with blood. The boy's mother was doing her best to help with the treatment, while weeping quietly as his movements weakened. It wasn't long before they stopped altogether.

If only the people of Judah had followed God's instructions and remained in the land! In all probability, if they had, this little child would now be playing happily in the fields near his parents' home instead of lying lifeless in the desert on the forbidden path to Egypt.

What a tragic waste!

Will my people never learn that obeying God gives peace and happiness, while disobedience leads to disaster?

"I told you so!" is one of the most unwelcome things anyone can ever say. Yet if it is not said, will anyone ever recognise that it is true? As a nation, God has given us this unwelcome message many times before, but I don't think we've ever listened. Should I say it? Should I remind them of God's warning that the sword would pursue them? Would there ever be a right time to tell them that this was just the first sortie in their hopeless fight against the promised destruction? I mulled over the matter as I slowly smoothed away the look of pain from the boy's dead face.

In the past, seeing this pointless tragedy would have made me very angry with those who had caused it, but I have learnt to accept that pointless tragedy is a typical part of human life – rarely intended, but not avoided, even when the information that makes it avoidable is freely available.

As I stood up and looked around, it was clear that the skirmish was over and the attackers had gone. Plenty of fallen donkeys lay scattered about, mostly unmoving, though two or three still writhed in pain. Of the bodies of the attackers that I had seen fall from their donkeys, there was no sign.

Everyone who needed care was now being looked after, and I was not needed. Baruch was helping some of Johanan's men collect the arrows left lying outside the defensive circle, so I went out to join him.

"Can you tell me what happened while I was busy, Baruch?" I asked.

"Not really. I was busy myself, though I don't have any skill for that sort of work." He smiled wryly. "Now, if they wanted me to write a report about it, that would be different!"

"I know how you feel," I said.

"We could ask one of Johanan's men."

"Yes, if they'll talk to us."

"Let's find out."

We approached a man who stood watching a donkey that was squirming on the ground with an arrow in its chest. I recognised him as Jezaniah the son of Hoshaiah, one of those who had derided me when I delivered God's answer to the crowd beside the inn near Bethlehem.

"What happened at the end of the fight?" I asked.

"Weren't you watching? Too busy hiding under the baggage, hey?"

I ignored his question and waited for him to answer mine. He didn't answer for some time: it was clear that he was upset and struggling to contain his emotion.

Baruch and I looked at each other, puzzled. "What's wrong?" I asked.

"Azariah, my brother," Jezaniah said, beginning to weep quietly. "He's dead."

There it was again. The face of humanity: suffering from pointless, avoidable tragedy.

"I'm sorry," I said.

"No wonder you're upset. Death can be such a shock," said Baruch.

"Oh, I'm used to death," sighed Jezaniah. "My father died in battle when Nebuchadnezzar first invaded twenty years ago, back in the time of King Jehoiakim. I had two other brothers, and they're both dead. My mother is dead too. I'm the only one left."

Once again I was left bemused. Everybody knows that some plants are poisonous, so nobody eats them. Yet despite God's warnings that worshipping other gods will kill people just as effectively, nobody really believes him or is willing to change their behaviour to stay alive. People want to be "in control" and follow their own desires, so society ends up in this sort of tragic mess. As Jezaniah spoke I remember thinking, "…and now he'll blame God for all of this…"

Sure enough, he continued, "How can you believe in a God who lets these things happen? What have I done to him to deserve all of this?"

If I had a silver shekel for every time I have been asked this question I would be buried under a mountain of silver. Yet it's just not rational. The answer is so simple and obvious if only people would accept that our creator has the right to set the rules for his creation. Many of the rules seem to emphasise just how the world goes wrong. Murder begets murder. Theft begets theft. Adultery begets adultery. Cruelty begets cruelty. When someone breaks God's rules and does something nasty to me, I feel a strong desire to get my own back. Yet if no-one breaks his rules in the first place, the problem doesn't arise.

A vicious circle.

That afternoon, Jezaniah was suffering the effects of mankind's evil and blaming God for it all.

It hurts when the God you know to be loving and forgiving is criticised because he doesn't *force* us to do good.

Enough reflection on our human folly.

"Is there anything we can do for this donkey?" I asked.

"Yes, that's right, worry about the animals and ignore the people," said Jezaniah, bitterly. "I suppose it would be best to kill the poor beast."

I ignored his first comment and reached out my hand towards the suffering animal. Her eyes opened wider, her lips curled back and she tried to bite me. This was no surprise and I was easily able to avoid her teeth.

"Calm down, don't worry," I said soothingly in Edomite. The fear in the donkey's eyes seemed to lessen a little and I tried again to stroke her neck, speaking calmingly as I did so. After a while, I was able to convince the poor animal that I meant her no harm, and then it was just a matter of patient persistence to examine the wound and finally remove the arrow which was embedded in her chest. It didn't seem likely to be a fatal wound since there was no blood in the flecks of foam around her mouth and no blood surging from the wound. As I worked, Jezaniah sat morosely on the ground and watched.

"What language were you speaking then?" he asked.

"Edomite," I replied.

"Do you always speak to donkeys in Edomite?"

I laughed and the tension suddenly relaxed. "No, but the group that attacked us spoke Edomite, so this donkey will understand it more than Hebrew."

"How do you know Edomite?"

"When God first spoke to me, he told me that I was to be a prophet to the nations, not just Judah. Over the last 40 years, particularly early on, I've spent a lot of time in places like Edom, giving them God's messages. I've learned quite a few languages, too. Ones like Edomite are quite like Hebrew, so they're easier."

"Do you find languages easy to learn?"

"No, but with God's help they're not impossible. The first one was hardest – and it just happened to be Edomite! Jacob and Esau were brothers, so God sent me with messages to Edom several times."

"How did they like having a foreigner telling them what to do?"

"Sometimes they were more willing to listen than my own people. One thing I do have a particular gift for is imitating accents, so I was always able to make the most of what I did know of the different languages."

"How did you learn a new language?"

"Whenever I arrived in a new country, I kept my eye out for a Jew who could speak both Hebrew and the local language. Then I stayed with him for as long as it took to learn enough of the language to be able to get by."

"You mean just saying hello and goodbye – that sort of stuff?"

"God's warnings are often very simple, but not always. In fact, some of his explanations are quite complex, so it really took a lot more than just a simple understanding of a language. But God always helped me by giving me the messages directly in the language of the place I was going to, and because I could hear the words in my mind, I knew the pronunciation and accent to use. It made my work so much easier."

"How often has God spoken to you?"

"That's a good question! I haven't counted, but I could work it out if I needed to. You see, I can remember every message he has ever given me."

During this conversation, I continued to stroke the donkey, doing my best to calm her down while I held a pad of material against her wound to staunch the bleeding. As I stopped speaking, I took away the pad and examined the wound. I would have liked to have washed it properly, but this was the desert and we had no spare water for looking after injured donkeys.

Baruch had been listening to our conversation, and now asked, "You've talked about seeing the words written in your mind. But if God gave you messages in the language of the people you were talking to, did he use their script too? After all, the Edomite script isn't the same as our Hebrew script."

"Isn't it?" asked Jezaniah, surprised.

"No, it's not the same," I confirmed, "but when God wrote these things in my mind, he wrote them in the local script. The Edomite script is quite similar to that used by the Phoenicians of Tyre and Sidon and quite a few other nations."

"So you had to learn a different way of writing as well as learning different words?" Jezaniah was looking at me with more respect than ever before.

"Yes," I laughed, "but a new script is much easier to learn than an entire language."

"So how many different scripts have you learned?" asked Baruch.

"I don't know, really. Quite a few."

Despite spending so much time working together, this subject had not come up before, and Baruch too was looking at me with new respect. I had always concentrated more on using the languages, but I suddenly realised that for a scribe, the script would be very important.

The donkey interrupted our conversation by rolling over and trying to stand up. It was clearly painful, but after a few attempts and with a little help, she stood, shaking a little but looking surprisingly well.

"Are you like Elijah?" asked Jezaniah with wonder in his eyes. "Do you work miracles too?"

"No," I said, surprised in my turn. It was the first time anyone had ever suspected me of doing miracles like that! "There was no need. The poor beast wasn't too badly injured, and I hope that she will recover fully."

We led her slowly back to the caravan and joined the ongoing efforts to tidy up the mess and repair the damage caused by the Edomites' attack. Jezaniah went to where the body of his brother Azariah lay and took a few personal effects by which to remember his brother.

I watched and wondered again at the paradox that is human life. Just one week earlier, Jezaniah had abused me, shouting that I had not been sent by God, and yet this afternoon we had sat and discussed my work as a prophet and he had listened carefully to my explanations as few had listened for years. It was too late for his brother – he could never listen to me or hear God's words again – but would Jezaniah take the opportunity to reverse his chosen direction in life?

Chapter 4

Brotherhood

Gradually, the wounded were helped and the dead buried. Four injured Edomites had been captured, and Johanan and his men were interrogating them to find out why we had been attacked.

However, they had little success and after a while, Johanan came and found me. "Jezaniah says you can speak Edomite," he said. "Can you do some translating for us?"

I nodded and he led me over to where one of the Edomites was being "interviewed". I quickly saw that it was a brutal process. A badly wounded man was being asked questions in a language he did not understand and then beaten when he didn't answer, or gave an answer that his interrogators did not understand. Since Edomite is not far from Hebrew as a language, he was able to understand some of the questions, and some of his answers could be partly understood by those listening. Nevertheless, by the time I approached, he was lying on the ground, slipping in and out of consciousness. His face was covered with blood.

"Ask him why they attacked us," said Johanan. "He's refusing to answer."

Despite Johanan's obvious impatience, I crouched down and tried to clean up the man's face a little. After a while he began to look better and struggled to stand up. I let him, standing up myself at the same time.

"Why did you attack us?" I asked him. He looked at me in relief, glad to hear words he understood.

"We are one of the mobile military forces of the kingdom of Edom. We assess possible enemies and attack those we are sure have attacked our nation or are likely to do so." Despite his injuries, he spoke with an arrogant confidence that bordered on contempt.

I reported his answer to Johanan, who responded with an angry look, "So a group of families travelling to Egypt is a threat to Edom? We have travelled from Judah and have already passed Edom. We made no attacks on your kingdom."

I translated for the Edomite and he stood up straight and looked proud.

"Judah has been our enemy for many years," he said. "All Jews are enemies, a danger to our kingdom. They dominated us for generations and we are still inflicting retribution."

This time I did not translate immediately for Johanan, but asked the man, "But were not Jacob and Esau twins? They are our fathers: should not we as nations be brothers?"

"No. Never! Judah has been destroyed by Nebuchadnezzar and we have rejoiced. We will take any parts of her land that we can. We will make the Jews our slaves, and any treasures they still have will be ours. While Nebuchadnezzar is away, we will take out our hatred on your people. May your dead fill the land and your blood run in rivers."

"Do you know what will happen to you if I translate your words to Johanan here?"

"Of course I know. I am willing to die for my nation!"

"You are not dying for your nation. You will die in a way that doesn't help your nation at all!"

"Heroes always help to make a nation great."

I shook my head and translated the man's words for Johanan. I had not got very far before his growing look of anger transformed into action. He lifted his sword and killed the man. As the body fell to the ground, Johanan hacked off its head, then walked away without a backward glance.

The other three Edomites were interviewed in turn, and the first two interviews finished in the same way as the first had, with the wounded prisoner hacked to death after a similar arrogant outburst.

As we approached the fourth, I prayed that this would be a different experience. After all, Jacob and Esau *were* brothers, and this hatred and malice was not how brothers should behave. This time I didn't wait for Johanan to ask questions, but asked my own.

"Who are you and how old are you?"

"My name is Dishon, the son of Mezaheb," he said proudly. "I am 21 years old."

"Have you ever fought against Nebuchadnezzar and the Chaldeans?"

"No."

"Have you ever fought against the army of Judah?"

"No."

"So you hate the Jews but are afraid to fight them?"

"No, that's not how it is," he said angrily. "We have small forces and make effective pinpoint attacks on our enemies." The words sounded rehearsed.

"Like this one? Attacking a group of families who were not threatening you at all?"

"All Jews are our enemies. We take any opportunity we can to defeat and kill them."

"How did you know that we were Jews?"

"Some travellers told us."

"Did you kill them too?"

"No, they were Arameans and not doing us any harm."

"But you always attack Jews whether they are harming you or not? Yet you are so weak and ineffective in battle that you couldn't even defeat a poorly-equipped caravan like ours."

"If I met you by yourself," he snarled, "I would kill you."

"Maybe," I answered. "But why? Why do you hate us so much?"

"We need to pay back the Jews for how they have treated us for hundreds of years."

This was getting nowhere new or helpful, so I decided to change the subject. "What god do you worship?"

"We mostly worship the god of our father Esau."

"Was he a god of war?"

"He helps us to win our battles."

"Is he different from Yahweh, the God of Israel, who was known as El Shaddai when our forefathers were born?"

"I am not a priest."

"I am. And I know that El Shaddai – Yahweh – is not a god who loves war. Nor is he a god who likes pride and hatred. Your nation and mine are brothers and should act as brothers. You should go back and tell your nation that God will never reward you for hating your brothers. All you will receive is suffering. Your entire nation will be destroyed just as the kingdom of Judah has been."

" 'Go back'," he scoffed. "You intend to kill me. You talk about brothers, but you and your men plan to kill me."

"If we let you go, will you go back to your people and give them the message that they must stop their hatred, stop rejoicing at the suffering of their brother, Judah? If your party hadn't attacked us, more people would be alive now on both your side and ours. Hatred and war will lead to your utter destruction."

"Why does Edom's attitude matter so much to you? Wouldn't you like to pay back the Chaldeans for what *they* have done to Judah?"

"They have done the work of God," I replied. "True, they have pursued it with cruelty and hatred. They have enjoyed our suffering, just as your people are doing. In time to come, they will suffer, just as Edom will if your nation does not repent."

"Oh, this is just nonsense. War has always been with us. War is natural. Hatred is natural. Death is natural too."

"But wouldn't you like something better? God promised that Abraham our forefather would be a blessing for all nations. He promised peace, not hatred. Blessing, not fighting. Wouldn't you like that?"

"I suppose so, but we didn't start the trouble. Israel attacked us first. We know all about your vicious king, David, and how many of my people he killed."

"And does your history remember that when the Israelites entered their Promised Land they did not attack Edom? We left your Promised Land to you and went to live in our own Promised Land. God gave Edom to you and Canaan to us, yet you will not leave us alone to enjoy it."

By this time Johanan was tired of all this discussion that he could not understand. He wanted to get on with killing this Edomite so that we could continue our journey to Egypt, leaving the man's body to the birds and beasts.

"Have you got any useful information from him, Jeremiah, before we kill him?"

"All I have learned is that he hates us in just the same way as you hate him. If you were in his position and he in yours, he would kill you."

"So let's kill him now, then," said Johanan, lifting up his sword once again.

"Why don't we let him go?"

"Are you serious?"

"I am. Let him go with a message to his people that we do not want to kill them all. We want peace and brotherhood between Jacob and Esau."

"Do we?"

I smiled at his look of surprise. "We should. Remember that God stopped us from invading Edom when our fathers arrived in Canaan. God wanted us to treat them like brothers."

"But look how they have treated us in return."

"I'm sure that they too could list many times when we have treated them as enemies instead of brothers. Do we always have to pay everyone back?"

"If we don't fight our enemies, they take advantage of us more and more. Jacob's children will all be destroyed."

"If we trust God, *he* will look after Jacob's children. The reason we're in our current situation is because we thought we were in control and could choose our own way. We boasted of our strength in battle instead of boasting of the strength of our God. We boasted that God had promised to stay in Jerusalem and then did all we could to drive him away by our idolatry. Seventy years of desolation is overtaking our country, and it has only just begun. Why make it worse?" I didn't mention his decision that we should go to Egypt, or how that choice would bring even heavier judgement on us from God.

For a moment, Johanan had a yearning look in his eye, as if he had glimpsed an alluring scene of peace and comfort, but he quickly cleared it from his mind and returned to his wonted way of thinking.

"No," he said firmly. "War has always been with us, and so has hatred. If *we* give up war, our enemies won't – and we'll be the ones who suffer." He waved his hand at the Edomite. "People like him will attack us," he said. "If we let him go now, the next time we meet him he'll have his sword at our throats. Death is the best thing for him."

I gave up and walked away. I knew what was going to happen and didn't want to see it.

Chapter 5

Blame

The next morning, there were still injured people to care for and bodies to bury.

Wailing filled the desert air as our dead were buried; buried, then quickly left to the care of the shifting sands. Dust to dust.

Four young children had been killed, and now their parents consigned their hopes and dreams for the future to a land of heat and hopelessness. An entire generation had perished between Egypt and Israel during the exodus due to the same sin: rebellion against God.

At that time, Moses was blamed by many for the deaths, although he had not caused them and had, in fact, been vocal in his prayers of intercession before God.

Blame is not always apportioned fairly.

Around midday, with the last of our dead buried, and the injured patched up and found places on carts as necessary, we resumed our journey, but the weeping and mourning did not stop. Those who had survived the terrible disaster of Jerusalem had now lost even more: parents had lost children and children their parents, wives had lost husbands and husbands their wives.

Tragedy and grief had overtaken our caravan, and where there is grief, there is always a wish to blame someone.

After we set up camp that night, Baruch and I were sitting around our cooking fire preparing our evening meal when a young woman approached us. Her eyes were red with weeping, her hair untidy, her clothes dishevelled. Yet her eyes were fixed on me and filled with purpose as she approached.

Just before our fire she stopped and stood with arms akimbo. "You murderer!" she spat out in an anger fuelled by despair. "You killed my child." Her voice broke.

"What happened to your child, young lady? And what did I have to do with it?" I tried to speak kindly.

"We *had* to go to Egypt to escape the Chaldeans. Everyone knew that, but you wouldn't let us. Now you've used Yahweh your God to kill my son, you murderer."

For a moment I couldn't answer. I was utterly at a loss for words. As if *I* could direct God to punish her son! God had made it clear to me that his judgement of Judah was to be more harsh than I would ever have been – except in my moments of indignant anger. Yahweh had even forbidden me from praying for my people. After hundreds of years of rebellion, he would not listen to any more requests for clemency. I quickly asked Yahweh to give me the best words to use.

"I do not control Yahweh," I said, as gently as I could. "Yahweh is the judge; Yahweh is our master. He warned us all of what would happen if we went to Egypt. I am his messenger, not his commander."

"So my son must die just because we are travelling to Egypt?"

"God gives life and God takes it away. Yet he also shows love and kindness to the whole nation if only we will obey. It was not your son who chose to disobey. Yet we as a group have chosen to disobey God's commands and ignore his warnings, and your son and others have died as a result. Yahweh warned us. He tried to keep us away from this suffering, but we wouldn't listen. For you and your son and our nation, this is a tragedy."

"Oh, don't try to sound all sympathetic with me!" she said with loathing. "You killed my son and now you try to put the blame on to everyone else." Her last words were muffled by heart-wrenching sobs, and I sat beside the fire in silence, looking sadly into its glowing depths as I waited for her to regain control.

She didn't stay. Instead, she turned and walked blindly away, wailing as she went.

I shook my head then looked down and closed my eyes. I spent some moments in prayer, upset that I had not been able to achieve anything. My words had not soothed her sorrow, nor had they seemed to convince her that the problem was our disobedience, not cruelty on the part of Yahweh or me.

When I looked up, Baruch was tending the fire, but it wasn't long before our eyes met and we exchanged a look of shared perplexity. How could anyone really be so willing to blame me in the face of all evidence? Was it self-justification or self-delusion?

It wouldn't have been difficult to simply dismiss her arguments as ridiculous and her as a fool. Yet despite the foolishness of her attack on Yahweh, I couldn't completely ignore her suffering and sorrow. At the same time, I could never agree with her arguments or excuse the disobedience that had led to the tragedy she so deeply resented.

How simple it all is: God's laws are not given to cruelly frustrate us or take away our enjoyment of life; they are given because only a life guided by his principles can ever achieve long-term happiness.

I was glad at least that Jezaniah did not seem to blame me for the death of his brother Azariah.

I sat and stared into the dancing flames as they slowly consumed the two small branches that were all we could afford to burn each night as we crossed this treeless waste. At the edge of the fire, small flames rippled among the glowing embers, their warmth and beauty unaffected by the ugly coldness of human hatred and death.

How often our hopes turn to ashes. And how often we are to blame.

Chapter 6

Companionship

"Did you ever get your message mixed up because of language problems?" Jezaniah asked.

In the three days since the Edomite attack, he had spoken to me quite a lot about my work as a prophet. He seemed particularly fascinated by the question of language. As a member of one of the small groups that made up Judah's Forces in the Open Country, he was used to carrying out covert operations in the border areas of Judah, sometimes spilling across into neighbouring countries. Thus, he was very familiar with the fact that people spoke many different languages, but he had always dismissed it as one of life's little problems. Hearing of my need to learn and use other languages had prompted him to consider what sorts of awkward situation might arise. He was also used to the difficulties caused by differing accents and dialects of the *same* language, astutely observing that at times it was almost impossible to understand the so-called Hebrew used by people from the north of Israel!

Although he hadn't thought much about language before, Jezaniah was quite observant and had noticed that words can have different meanings in different geographical areas, and this had prompted his unusual question. He wanted to know if I had ever mixed up the message I was delivering because I learned a language in one place and then delivered a message in the same language somewhere else.

I laughed, recalling one mortifying case. It had been a particularly busy time when I had been travelling from nation to nation talking to many leaders about the cup of God's anger. Tyre and Sidon both spoke a Phoenician language which I first learned from an Israelite who had lived in Tyre for many years. He taught me the language, including – although I didn't realise it at the time – plenty of local usage that was specific to Tyre. When I moved on to Sidon I was in a hurry. Confident in my knowledge of the language, I had approached a guard near the king's palace to find out who could help me arrange a meeting with the king.

"I have come to see the king," I said, confidently, in my clearest Phoenician.

"What about?"

"I must tell the king about the cup of God's anger."

The guard had smiled when I first spoke, but when I said those words, he broke into laughter and it took him a while to control himself. "You don't come from here, do you?" he said. "Fortunately, your accent is terrible, or I would have thought you were mad. Where did you learn to speak our language so badly?"

This was quite a letdown, of course, so I tried to explain how I had learned the language – which was difficult now that he had destroyed my confidence!

He asked a few more questions, then smiled again and said, "Ah, now I understand. There are two problems. In Tyre they use the word 'tickle' to mean 'tell' or 'speak to', maybe with the idea of tickling somebody's ear or something like that. They also have a peculiar pronunciation of the word 'cup' which makes it sound very much the same as the word we use for the young of a small octopus common in these parts. We pronounce the two words carefully so that people don't get them mixed up, but with your terrible accent, there was no chance I could understand what you meant. So, with those two mix-ups, what you said was, 'I must tickle the king with a baby octopus'. Can you see why I laughed?"[9]

I recounted this incident to Jezaniah and he laughed, seeing how easily such a situation could occur.

At the time, I found the harmless incident deeply embarrassing rather than funny. I left the guard and learnt how to speak Phoenician the Sidonian way. After that, I never forgot the dangers of dialects and accents, and always tried to make it clear as early as possible that I was a foreigner – and to apologise in advance for my mistreatment of their language! Most people are very patient and understanding if one tries to speak their language.

To speak a language well you need confidence, but having too much confidence will *always* get you in trouble. When I was giving God's messages it was easy because I followed the words he had given me, but when expressing my own ideas I have always wanted to express myself concisely, using the one best way to say something. Nevertheless, I have learned that it is better to restate a message several times in different ways if my audience does not use my mother tongue. Sometimes my efforts made my audience laugh, but I could normally get my message across given a few attempts. I've concluded that if I can't think of several ways to express the same idea in a language, then I'm not ready to use it.

---

[9] This entire episode is made up, but reflects some of the problems that can arise with accents, dialects and learning languages.

We walked on towards Egypt, heading west now, and my spirits continued to rise. One evening after the sun had set, Baruch and I were discussing the exodus of our ancestors from Egypt as the sky darkened to sable and the stars began to shine in their myriad glory. Our small cooking fire was little more than a few glowing embers and the temperature was quickly dropping. The caravan's food supply was running low and we couldn't help wishing that we were able to go out each morning and collect manna from the desert floor.

"The journey would be much easier if we didn't have to carry food, wouldn't it?" said Baruch.

"Yes. Just imagine: wake up and walk a few steps to pick up your breakfast."

"Did some pieces of manna look nicer than others? Did people choose pieces they liked the look of?"

"I've no idea," I said, "but I know that if they looked for manna on the Sabbath, they didn't find any however far they walked. Lazy on Friday meant hungry on Saturday."[10]

"Wouldn't it have been amazing to have such a clear proof every day that God was looking after them – and a reminder every week that he also has rules for us to obey. Such simple proofs. Do you think that everyone would believe in Yahweh more if we had the same thing now?"

"Frankly, I doubt it."

"But how could anybody deny it?" asked Jezaniah, who was sitting with us as he had done often since the Edomite attack.

"I have found that people come up with 'logical' explanations for anything they don't want to accept," I said.

"Jeremiah began warning people that Babylon would attack Judah a long time ago, Jezaniah. Everyone laughed

---

[10] Exodus 16:23-30

at him until it happened, and then they said it was just bad luck," said Baruch.

"That's true," I said. "Do you remember how people freed their slaves after the Chaldeans began besieging Jerusalem?[11] I presume they obeyed God's law just because they were desperate, but then when they heard that the Egyptians were coming and saw the Chaldeans leaving, they thought they were safe! God told me that the Egyptians would go back home and the Chaldeans would return to finish the siege and destroy Jerusalem. But nobody would believe what God said, so they cruelly reclaimed the slaves they had just freed. Then, when the Chaldeans returned, they told me it was just chance. Yet at the same time, they blamed me for the fact that it happened!"

"I suppose that's how I felt at the time," said Jezaniah, "though now I can see that it doesn't make much sense."

"I've always found it very hard," I said, "because everybody – even my family – has always said that what I said were *my* words, *my* thoughts, but they weren't. If it had been up to me, I would have predicted completely different things – and most of them would have been wrong."

"So how can you ever convince people?" asked Jezaniah.

Baruch laughed. "That's what I was about to ask!"

"Over the years I've learned that it's impossible to convince anybody of *anything* they have decided not to accept. Seriously, some people will not believe things that their eyes have told them, just because they don't want them to be true. Yet God doesn't give up just because people won't listen. I don't have anything like the patience he has."

"But there's an end to his patience, isn't there," observed Baruch, soberly. "And you warned us of that, too."

---

[11] Jeremiah 34:8-16

"Yes," I answered, sadly. "My family were priests, but now they're all gone. When my forefathers travelled through this wilderness on the way to Canaan, they chose to be on God's side and were given a perpetual priesthood as a reward, but now they're all gone."

I stared at the flickering embers, remembering some of the disasters that had befallen my family since I had become a prophet. My father and my two brothers, all dead at an early age. My nephew, Seraiah, the last High Priest, killed by Nebuchadnezzar. I had heard that Jehozadak his son was taken away to Babylon. No more priests in Jerusalem. In fact, no more temple, no more city. It would be seventy years before the nation would return. What would happen then?

Suddenly, my rising spirits were crushed again. The beauty of the flickering embers could not touch me and the cold stars seemed to freeze my heart. Jehozadak was my great-nephew and, apart from me, he was the oldest of my close family still alive.

Why would they not listen to God?

My two companions sat in silence for some time, seeming to share in my suffering, and I appreciated their sympathy. Then, suddenly, I remembered that they were in very similar situations, as were most of the survivors. Baruch's family was gone too, and Jezaniah had lost his sole remaining close relative just a few days ago.

"I'm sorry," I said. "I'm feeling sorry for myself, yet you're both suffering the same way. We've each lost our family, and I suspect that none of them really believed God's words through his prophets. Isaiah warned more than a hundred years ago that Babylon would attack, and so did other prophets. Yet our people would not believe it."

"Jezaniah," said Baruch, "we were talking about proof before, and I can offer you one extra bit of proof. After I wrote out Jeremiah's messages from God, God sent him a message especially for me, saying that I would survive the destruction of Jerusalem.[12] And I did. No-one else in my family did, but *I* did."

"And the same thing happened for Ebed-melech," I agreed.[13]

"Ebed-melech? Was that the Cushite servant of King Zedekiah?" asked Jezaniah. "I heard someone talking about him. What happened to him?"

"Almost a year ago, when I was thrown into an empty cistern by some of the king's friends and left to die in the mud, Ebed-melech told the king that what they had done was evil and insisted that he wanted to get me out."[14]

Jezaniah was looking a little shocked, so Baruch nodded and answered his unspoken question, "Yes, a foreign servant told the king that his friends were being evil."

"Wow. That's brave."

"It was. And it saved my life," I said.

"Amazing."

"Yes, and God's response was to send him a personal message that he would survive the siege of Jerusalem."

"Oh… was he the Cushite at Chimham's Inn?"

"Yes, that was Ebed-melech."

"So what happened to him?"

"He'd been given a farm after Jerusalem was destroyed and he wanted to go back to it. I warned him to go secretly without telling anyone, and that's what he did. He was glad to be staying in the Promised Land."

"So God helped a foreigner?"

"Yes, a foreigner who knew right and wrong and trusted the God of Israel."

---

[12] Jeremiah 45:1-5
[13] Jeremiah 39:15-18
[14] See Volume 5 – No Remedy, Chapter 3

"And he was just a servant."

"Yes – just a servant."

Jezaniah sighed and the three of us again sat in silence for a while. The embers were glowing more dimly now and the wondrous glory of the stars showed even more clearly and beautifully above us. But the stars no longer seemed cold. Instead, I felt in them the warmth of a vast and infinitely powerful God who works even in the small things like the pinpricks of light we could see above us. Yet he also works in the big things of the world and guides the nations of the world in the directions he wants.

God is in control of everything.

"I'm reminded of a prayer that I wrote almost two years ago, Baruch. Do you remember when I bought the land from my cousin Hanamel and gave you that deed of purchase?"[15]

"Yes, I remember – and you mentioning just how hard you found it to understand the whole episode. Do you remember the prayer?"

"Word for word, and it fits well with our discussions and the display above us," I said, waving my hand toward the sky. They both looked up at the stars as I continued, "I wrote: 'Ah, Lord God! It is you who has made the heavens and the earth by your great power and by your outstretched arm! Nothing is too hard for you. You show steadfast love to thousands, but you repay the guilt of fathers to their children after them, O great and mighty God, whose name is the Lord of hosts, great in counsel and mighty in deed, whose eyes are open to all the ways of the children of man, rewarding each one according to his ways and according to the fruit of his deeds.'[16] There was quite a lot more, because I really was struggling to understand why I would buy a property in a land doomed

---

[15] Jeremiah 32:9-15
[16] Jeremiah 32:17-19

to destruction. But it's fascinating just how much it relates to where we are going. A little bit further on, I wrote, 'You brought your people Israel out of the land of Egypt with signs and wonders, with a strong hand and outstretched arm, and with great terror. And you gave them this land, which you swore to their fathers to give them, a land flowing with milk and honey. And they entered and took possession of it. But they did not obey your voice or walk in your law. They did nothing of all you commanded them to do. Therefore you have made all this disaster come upon them.' "[17]

"Egypt has always had a fascination for our people, hasn't it?" commented Baruch. "Solomon with Pharaoh's daughter, chariots and horses; King Josiah fighting Pharaoh Neco; King Jehoahaz deposed by him and replaced with Jehoiakim; Zedekiah asking Pharaoh for help against Nebuchadnezzar."

"And now, we're going back there," said Jezaniah. "Does anyone know whether they will welcome us or throw us all in prison?"

"A good question," I answered, gazing once more into the embers of the dying fire. "A good question."

"I think Jeremiah means that we don't know," said Baruch, sardonically.

CR

Although Jezaniah was still one of the military leaders of the caravan, he was spending a lot of time with Baruch and me. Having been thrown into a mire of dislocation and personal suffering by the death of his brother, Jezaniah was more susceptible to influence when he met Baruch and me – contacts from outside his ordinary set of

---

[17] Jeremiah 32:21-23

acquaintances – allowing us to open his eyes to truths about his nation that he had never recognised.

Since Johanan was also wondering about our reception in Egypt, he used Jezaniah to sound me out about it.

"You've been to Egypt before, haven't you?" he asked me one evening. We were almost there – I expected us to reach the border the following day.

"Yes, several times."

"When was the last time?"

"Quite a few years ago. In fact, it was probably around the fourth or fifth year of Jehoiakim."

"So, sixteen or seventeen years ago?"

"Yes, I suppose so. A lot has happened since then, hasn't it?"

"Whereabouts in Egypt did you go that time?"

"I had to find my way to Zau,[18] where Pharaoh Neco had his favourite palace. I believe that both of the Pharaohs since then[19] have ruled from the same place, rather than changing their main city as seems to have been so common through Egypt's history. Anyway, when you want an audience with the king as I did, it's best to enter the country in an official way. To do that, I had to talk to the guards at the border stations. They have men at the border along all the major roads. I'd been told that getting into Egypt wasn't too hard, but I was also given the warning that every frequent traveller learns: be careful what you say."

"Good advice in life," said Baruch, smiling, "but what exactly does it mean for border crossings?"

---

[18] Also known as Sais (https://en.wikipedia.org/wiki/Sais,_Egypt), in the west of the Nile delta of Egypt.

[19] Pharaoh Neco died in 595BC. His son Psamtik II (also known as Psammetichus) ruled from 595-589BC and his son Hophra (Jeremiah 44:30), also known as Apries, ruled from 589-570BC.

"Simple things: don't speak unless you are spoken to; only answer questions you are asked; never denigrate the country you are entering; don't try to make jokes – that sort of thing. And they're true everywhere. A little bit of quiet humility goes a long way at a border post."

"What about language?" asked Jezaniah.

"It's always best to speak their language if you can do it well, but that can be a sword with two edges. People like you using their language, but you can easily make bad mistakes if you're not expert. Not only that, but if you use *any* of their language, they'll assume you're fluent in it and use all sorts of colloquialisms you've never heard before.

"In general, if you're not fluent in their language, it's better to stick to the language you know best and hope that they'll be able to understand you. If you can get through to them that way, using their language a little just as you finish talking to them is a good idea. It tends to give them a good feeling about you if anyone asks them later."

"So, in your experience, what will we be up against at the Egyptian border posts tomorrow?" asked Jezaniah.

"The guard will ask what you are going into Egypt for, and that's the first opportunity to get things wrong. Countries always have certain things that they're sensitive about, but the things vary from country to country. However, absolutely every country is on the lookout for foreign attacks and internal rebellions, so showing any military interest or background is a no-no. Tax is normally the next most important thing. They'll be on the lookout for items they can charge you import duty or some other tax on."

"Safety first, money next," said Baruch, nodding. "I suppose that makes sense."

"I've been in the army for almost 20 years," said Jezaniah. "I've never done anything else. Does that mean I could have problems getting into Egypt?"

"I'm not sure how Egypt will feel about a group this size wanting to come to stay anyway. We're a bigger group than Joseph took into Egypt, and there are already many Jews in Egypt.[20] It's funny, but despite the fact that we were slaves in Egypt and eager to leave, there have been lots of Jews in Egypt for most of the time since. The Egyptians find that our people are generally hardworking and clever, and that they benefit from having us around. That's true for many of the countries I've visited. I've met Jews everywhere."

"I wonder why?" mused Baruch. "If I had the choice, I'd be staying in Judah. Why would anyone be looking for another country to live in?"

"What if you don't like the religion of Judah?" asked Jezaniah. "I don't want to upset you, Jeremiah, but your family really has had things set up rather nicely for themselves. You were talking about taxes and charges before – well, that's why the priests were rich and so many others were poor. The tithes they took, the maintenance collections for the temple, the fees for special animals, health inspections and all of the other charges: they were all just taxes. Religious taxes."

Talking to people from different backgrounds has often helped me to get a different slant on familiar situations. God had spoken to me of his priests in very critical terms, and much of Jezaniah's criticism was similar. "Hmm," I said thoughtfully. "I know you're right about the money, Jezaniah. When I was young, I didn't know any of the detail and assumed it was all the will of God. But once I thought about it more, I remembered that God directed the people to build the tabernacle in the wilderness mostly using donations, not tithes.[21] Tithes were meant to be used to care for the poor as well as the priests, but that's

---

[20] Jeremiah 24:8 contains a hint of this.
[21] Exodus 25:1-9

not how it worked. Instead, the poor went hungry and became slaves while the priests grew rich and fat.[22] But do you really think it was our religion that drove people away from Judah? That idea has never occurred to me before. None of the Jews I've met in other countries have suggested it; but then again, I haven't asked – and they might be a little loth to say it to me, knowing that I was a priest." I paused for a moment in thought. "You know, that would be even worse. Not only did we Levites badly mislead people in the worship of God in Judah, we may even have driven people right away from God and his land."

"I wouldn't worry about it now," said Jezaniah. "The temple, the priests and everything else to do with our religion are gone now. They aren't likely to come back."

"Oh, they'll come back all right," I said confidently. "God said that after 70 years the nation would return.[23] My grand-nephews Jehozadak and Ezra have gone to Babylon. Perhaps they will return as very old men,[24] or maybe it will be their children[25] and grandchildren who will come. Our people will return – but I'm afraid that we who are going to Egypt won't."

"I still can't get used to the idea that you really believe the things you say and that they actually come from God," said Jezaniah. "All my life I've believed that you made it all up – after all, that's what everyone told me."

"Do you still feel that way?"

"I don't think so, but… well, if I do still have doubts, how would you convince me that you are speaking God's words?"

"Most of my proof is based on the prophecies God made through me that have been fulfilled. There are lots

---

[22] 1 Samuel 2:29; Jeremiah 6:13
[23] Jeremiah 29:10
[24] Ezra returned as an old man (Ezra 7: 1, 6).
[25] Jehozadak's son Joshua returned (Haggai 2:2; Zechariah 6:11).

of those, like the death of King Jehoiakim, whose body was dumped outside the gates of Jerusalem and left to rot;[26] that King Zedekiah would be taken away to Babylon rather than being killed as everybody expected;[27] the destruction of Jerusalem and the temple...[28] and so many other details, including ones about how Egypt would lose to Nebuchadnezzar in what people now call the Battle of Carchemish.[29] What else can I use?"

"Well, what about you, yourself?" asked Baruch.

"What do you mean?" I asked, puzzled.

"*You're still alive.* Most – perhaps all – of the people who've tried to kill you are dead, but *you* are still alive. Kings, nobles, princes, priests, idolaters and many other people. Even your own relatives. And remember Hananiah the prophet?"

"Yes."

"He tried to out-prophesy you – but with false prophecies. God judged him and said he would be dead before the end of the year. Jezaniah, he was dead within two months!"[30]

"I knew that he died, but I was told that Jeremiah killed him."

"Who did you hear that from?" I asked, shocked to hear that I had been openly accused of killing him. *God* had killed him – and none of the doctors he asked to help could cure him. I had not seen him from the day I had passed on God's condemnation until his death. Who could have suggested that I had killed him?

"I can't really remember, but it might have been one of the gatekeepers."

---

[26] Jeremiah 22:18-19; Jeremiah 36:30
[27] Jeremiah 38:17-23; 32:3-5; 34:3-5
[28] Jeremiah 21:10; 32:29; 34:22; 37:8
[29] Jeremiah 46:1-12
[30] Jeremiah 28:1-17

"Irijah?" I asked.

"It might have been," he said thoughtfully, stroking his beard. Then he looked suddenly confident, "In fact, yes, it *was* Irijah. I remember now: he said he had made sure you were thrown into prison."

"He did indeed," I said. "Did he tell you why?"

"Well, I assumed it was because you had killed Hananiah, although he didn't say how you had killed him."

"Did he mention that Hananiah was his grandfather?"

"No, he didn't."

"Or that he wouldn't believe I was a prophet at all, but somehow he still blamed me when my prophecy came true?"

"Ah," said Jezaniah. Once again, he looked thoughtful, and after a few moments continued, "I really have had lots of details wrong. And many of them were deliberately told to me wrongly. I suppose that most of the others here will be in the same situation."

"Probably," I agreed.

"Is there anything that we can do to straighten people out? I'm sure people would believe you if they knew the truth!"

"I'm not so sure," I said, pessimistically. "After all, if that were so, how could the malicious lies have spread in the first place?"

Chapter 7

At the Border

Our concerns about entering Egypt were not unreasonable. Moving between countries is very common, often to escape war or persecution, but it is also common for people to be detained at a border. Individuals and families can often make their way across national borders in wild areas far from main roads, avoiding official notice and living for generations on the fringes of society in their adopted home – but our party was too large for this to be practical. We would have to face up to the border guards and their probing questions, seeking permission to enter Egypt.

We saw the border post from some distance away. It was quite an imposing stone building, built grandly in the Egyptian style, forcefully announcing Egyptian sovereignty to all who approached.

When we arrived, the small garrison of guards looked a little concerned. It was understandable: we significantly outnumbered them and our group included armed men who looked as if they knew how to use the arms they carried.

Johanan asked me to come with him in the hope that I would be able to speak to the guards in their own language. I had already warned him that being able to speak the language almost 20 years ago was quite different from knowing it now. However, I had been practising using my Egyptian as we walked. The road was not busy, but we had met quite a few travellers since our battle with the Edomites. Many of them were Egyptians and I had greeted all those that I could, asking them about their families, assuring them that we intended no harm, and many other mundane discussions. I had practised denying any intention to avoid taxes, and proclaimed my complete ignorance of the political situation in Egypt. The travellers seemed to understand what I was saying, which was encouraging.

By the time we approached the chief of the guard, therefore, I felt that I should be able to carry on a conversation as long as nothing too unexpected happened.

Naturally, it did.

"More troublesome mercenaries from Greece, hey?" remarked the chief of the guard, clearly irritated. "Why didn't you follow the instructions to come by sea? And why didn't you arrive by the third of the month?" he asked, waving his finger at us.

This was exactly what I didn't need. Surprisingly, perhaps, I understood all he said, but in the stress of the moment, any ability to speak Egyptian abandoned me. I just stood there, opening and closing my mouth and probably looking guilty.

"The instructions were clear," he continued, firmly. "I saw them myself. You mercenaries think you are the saviours of Egypt and can do whatever you want."

He looked as if he was going to continue, so I held up an apologetic hand.

"I'm sorry," I said in a stumbling voice that wasn't completely assumed. "We are Jews travelling from Bethlehem in Judah. We are not mercenaries. Our leaders are officers from the armed forces of Judah – Johanan here is their chief."

The man looked completely baffled. I might as well not have spoken at all.

"Where are your documents?" he asked, peremptorily. "You were all sent letters to present when you arrived. Where are they?" He held out his hand and Johanan looked at me questioningly.

I tried again, speaking slowly and trying to copy his accent, but it was no good. He understood nothing of what I said.

This unsuccessful interchange went back and forth for a time before I made a last desperate attempt at communication. "We are Jews," I said in Hebrew.

A sudden smile of comprehension spread across his face and he said, "Jews? Why didn't you say so before? So you aren't those hopeless Greek mercenaries that we're waiting for? Maybe that's all to the good. What language were you speaking before?"

"I was trying to speak your language," I said, rather crestfallen.

The commander looked at me for a few moments and then began to laugh, quietly at first, but soon he was laughing uproariously. His men joined in and Johanan smiled too, although he had very little idea of what was going on. Laughter is infectious, so I suppose I smiled too, but I certainly didn't find it very funny. This man couldn't even recognise that I was trying to speak his language! Would I have to start learning it all over again? I felt too old to begin such a task.

Eventually the laughter died down and the commander said, "Now that I know you are speaking my language, please go back to what you started with."

I repeated my introductory speech and he listened carefully. He began to show signs of limited comprehension, and when I finished, he said, "Ah, yes. Now that I know what to listen for, I can recognise small fragments of our language. But where did you get that atrocious accent? I thought you must be speaking Greek, and I don't speak Greek very well. Hebrew is alright though – we have many Jews passing through here. Let's speak Hebrew, shall we? That way we'll be able to understand each other."

With that, my usefulness was at an end. Johanan could handle the negotiations himself – but I stayed and listened anyway.

It soon became obvious that the commander was trying to delay us. Such a large group of foreigners could not be allowed to enter the country straight away. I guessed that he wanted confirmation from his superiors, but he never said so. He just made it clear – very diplomatically – that although we would be welcome in the country, he needed to go through various formalities first, which would take a while with so many of us. He talked about the need to examine all goods being brought into the country and hinted at the payment of import duties for saleable goods. He asked if we were bringing large quantities of gold, silver, spices or other valuable commodities. And, of course, he wanted all of our names, not to mention plenty of other details about those who were members of Judah's army.

It went on and on, and eventually I left, sure that we would not be passing the guard post before the next morning at best. Ah well, Johanan and the others had wanted to come to Egypt, so they could look after the paperwork!

I returned to Baruch, but I hadn't been with him long before a messenger from Johanan arrived requesting Baruch's skill as a scribe to help fill out the paperwork demanded by the Egyptian guards.

Baruch considered refusing – after all, he had never wanted to come to Egypt either – but in the end his generous nature won out and he went off to help. Possibly helping in such ways would be the best way to get our people to accept him again. Nevertheless, my imagination couldn't stretch to picturing Johanan thanking him sweetly and humbly apologising for the false accusations made at Chimham's Inn.

Darkness fell and the immigration process was still not complete. It would begin again in the morning, said the commander, but in the meantime, we were welcome to camp by the road for the night and drink all the water we wanted – as long as we kept off the road and didn't make too much noise.

СᎡ

When I woke the next morning, a large detachment of soldiers was marching up the road towards us: the border post had called for reinforcements.

Now we were outnumbered and the road with its flanking stone guard-post was crowded with Egyptian soldiers looking at us suspiciously. As their leaders met the border guards, there was much discussion and plenty of gesticulations in our direction. For a moment, I was afraid that we were going to be rounded up and marched away, but then it became clear that they weren't pointing at us. Instead, another party was approaching along the road: a second group of soldiers, this time surrounding a column of brightly-coloured palanquins and chariots. Somebody important was arriving.

It didn't seem likely that this could have anything to do with us, but we might get caught up in it anyway. Were we going to be delayed by some state occasion?

The leading troops marched swiftly towards the now-crowded border post, resplendent in their bright uniforms, each carrying a shield. As they got closer, I saw their weapons and protective leather helmets too. A grim-faced bunch of soldiers they were. As they approached, the dust raised by their tramping feet obscured the scene and I saw little of the grand personage they were escorting. When the column stopped, there was a lot of saluting and bowing, but we had no idea what was going on.

We sat waiting near the border post while the dust settled, trying not to attract unwanted attention from the Egyptian soldiers. Although it was still early morning, the temperature was rising quickly, but we left the little shade there was to the waiting soldiers. An hour passed and Johanan and Jezaniah were at last called into the border post. Apparently, with reinforcements to support him, the commander's tone was much more militant. However, it wasn't long before Johanan sent Jezaniah to ask me to come in and join the discussions. As we walked towards the elegant stone border post, Jezaniah explained that I had been asked for by name by an important Egyptian. I couldn't think of any important Egyptians who would know me, so it was with some puzzlement that I entered the cool darkness of the hall.

As my eyes adjusted to the gloom, Jezaniah led me towards a table. Several Egyptians sat at one end while Johanan stood at the other.

"This is Jeremiah, the prophet of Yahweh," said Johanan in Hebrew. "He has visited Egypt before, although it was many years ago." He addressed a man dressed in simple Egyptian clothes who sat slouched in a chair in the shadows. From the unspoken deference accorded him by every other man in the room, including the senior officer who had arrived with the first batch of troops, it was clear that he was a notable figure.

"Heremyo," he said in a powerful voice that I recognised instantly, "do you remember me?"

"Amasis!" I exclaimed with pleasure. "It's a long time since we met."

"Yes. I taught you our language when I was just a poor soldier, eager to earn a little extra money by teaching a foreigner our wonderful tongue. Do you remember any of it?"

"Oh, yes, although until a few days ago I hadn't used it out loud for years."

"I remember that I was disappointed at the time because you learned so quickly – I didn't earn as much as I'd hoped. Your ability with accents was amazing. After only a little practise it was almost as if you were an Egyptian. Perfect intonation, delightful pronunciation."

"Well, I must have forgotten that part," I said, smiling. "The commander here described my accent as 'atrocious' yesterday."

"Oh?" he turned and looked at the commander, raising his eyebrows. "But then again, Baufre is from upper Egypt where they speak like savages. Their vowels are horrific. Yours were much better – once upon a time. Tell me what you said yesterday and I'll be the judge."

I repeated the sentences I had spoken and, after the first few words, Amasis began to smile. When I finished, he turned to the commander and said, "Baufre, you ignorant savage, how could you criticise such beautiful pronunciation? This man speaks our language better than you do! You expose the painful accent of a back-country boy, while he uses the cultured enunciation of the royal court."

"I speak as I learned at my mother's knee," said the commander, stiffly. "I do not try to put on airs or act above my station."

"No, nor do I," said Amasis jovially. "But I was born in the delta, and in the delta, it isn't putting on airs to speak as Pharaoh does."

"Well, sir, I suppose I can understand him better now. It is a help knowing that he is speaking our language."

"Are you suggesting that you can't tell that I am speaking our language, young man?" This was spoken in Egyptian, using the accent I felt most at home with. Cultured, apparently.

"Of course not, sir. Your speech is beautifully clear."

Amasis smiled again and turned back to me, continuing in Egyptian, "I never thought that I would see you again, Heremyo. When I asked about you before, I didn't seriously expect to hear that you were with the party. What are you doing?"

Did I dare answer in his language, or should I make the most of the fact that he spoke Hebrew beautifully? In some trepidation, I responded in his language, and it was worth the risk. He looked pleased and seemed to understand most of what I said. Even Baufre appeared to comprehend my speech, now that he knew my background and what to expect in my accent.

Johanan was not referred to again for some time. Instead, I explained where we were from, who we were, and what our party hoped to do by moving to Egypt.

"Your enemy is our enemy," said Amasis, "so maybe we can work together. Of course, Nebuchadnezzar is not likely to attack us here in Egypt. He will realise that we are more powerful than he, particularly in our own land where we know the conditions so much better than he does. Nevertheless, if he is foolish enough to attack, having some soldiers who have fought him before would be useful."

I turned and asked Johanan in Hebrew, "Would you be willing to fight for the Egyptians against Nebuchadnezzar if he attacked?"

"Yes, of course," he replied. "We want to make Egypt our home and will provide any help we can."

"A company your size will need approval from Zau to enter Egypt," Amasis told Johanan in Hebrew, "but if I write the report, I expect approval will be given. The main question is where you would stay. There are a few towns in the delta with sections set aside for foreigners, particularly for the Greeks at the moment – mercenaries. Maybe Tahpanhes would suit. How does that sound to you?"

Johanan answered that it would be wonderful; being able to live in peace in Egypt was what they had hoped for. There was a gleam in his eye as he gave this answer. No doubt he was having a dig at me, seeing an opportunity to disprove the curse I had delivered from God.

Amasis reverted to Egyptian as he continued, thoughtfully: "Pharaoh Apries, or 'Hophra' as many of you foreigners call him, has a small palace in Tahpanhes. Naturally, it's not his main palace – that's the one you visited in Zau, Heremyo. Nevertheless, if he let you all live in Tahpanhes, it would be a powerful sign of Pharaoh's approval, and that would make your life in Egypt more comfortable."

"Just remember what I said to Pharaoh Neco, Amasis. It was two years after Nebuchadnezzar had defeated our king, Jehoiakim, and Judah had become subservient to Babylon. I warned Pharaoh that the cup of God's anger

was coming to Egypt also.[31] Don't forget: Nebuchadnezzar will come here too."

"I hadn't forgotten your warnings, Heremyo, but
surely *you* remember that Pharaoh Neco wasn't convinced
– and I wasn't either. Bear in mind that Egypt is a superpower. Nebuchadnezzar has tried attacking us before and
gone home with his tail between his legs."

"Nevertheless, the last time your Pharaoh had a
chance to meet Nebuchadnezzar in battle he withdrew.
King Zedekiah of Judah would have dearly loved the support of Apries of Egypt against Nebuchadnezzar at that
time."

"Strategy is important in international affairs. Pharaoh knew that Nebuchadnezzar wouldn't be able to push
his attack into Egypt and that all Pharaoh had to do was
feint, then withdraw and wait for Nebuchadnezzar to go
away. Nebuchadnezzar has never invaded Egypt yet, and
he's never likely to."

"Yahweh doesn't get things wrong, Amasis," I said
earnestly. "He wanted me to warn Egypt and encourage
you to submit to Nebuchadnezzar. If you resist him, you
will suffer just as Judah has. Yahweh is giving you a
chance to minimise the damage. Nebuchadnezzar is not
a forgiving king."

"I think Pharaoh will take his chances in this matter.
Egypt is a powerful nation. All over the world we are
known for our ancient culture and irresistible power. We
are great. We are Egypt!" Amasis' powerful voice rose as
he spoke and his closing sentence was delivered with the
conviction of an inspiring orator.

"Yes, you are Egypt, and Yahweh is God," I replied;
"famous because he led his people out of Egypt with terrible plagues and mighty miracles. We've been through this

---

[31] Jeremiah 25:15-19

before, haven't we, Amasis? In fact, I remember that you used your argument to teach me a special construct in your language that I was finding hard to understand – and I used my counter-argument to teach you about the use of superlatives in Hebrew. For what it's worth, I still find that construction in your language hard to understand, and I find the logic you used hard to understand too. Taking a chance in the face of an omnipotent God has left Judah in ruins. We should talk about it more when we have a chance, to see if I can convince you."

"Perhaps I will convince *you*, Heremyo," said Amasis smoothly, but the veneer of patience in his voice showed some cracks.

Johanan and Jezaniah understood little of what passed between us. Had they done so, Johanan at least would have worried that I was ruining our chances of being accepted into Egypt. Yet I couldn't remain silent, leaving Egypt without the warnings God wanted to give them.

Chapter 8

Into Egypt

That morning Amasis and Baufre sent messengers to Zau, and within just two days the messengers had returned with papers giving us permission to enter Egypt and settle there. By that time, Amasis and his retinue had left to continue his inspection of Pharaoh's border forces. Nevertheless, the speed and positive nature of the reply convinced me that Amasis really had become an important man.

We packed up our goods and gratefully left the border post, taking the road that would lead us eventually to Tahpanhes.

"People are remarkably inventive when it comes to charging taxes," commented Baruch.

I laughed and agreed. "Yes – never let down your guard when you're dealing with a tax collector! They'll always catch you out when you least expect it."

Most of the refugees in our caravan left the border post significantly poorer than they approached it. As everyone had left Judah with no intention of ever returning, they had all brought any money they had been able to hide from the Chaldeans. Altogether it added up to quite a sizeable sum, and Pharaoh claimed entitlement to a significant portion of it. Animals like donkeys helped to facilitate trade, but they were also items of trade themselves – and a trade in which Egypt considered herself prominent – so bringing animals into Egypt attracted a fee. Even the Edomite donkey from which I had removed the arrow was included, even though she was not yet well enough to carry much of a load. Wheat was similar, and the caravan had brought quite a lot of wheat with it after the bumper crop of last summer. Spices were luxury goods, and luxury goods were taxed heavily since this was an impost the market could bear.

All in all, the cost of entering Egypt had been unexpectedly high, and some goods had to be left at the border post in exchange for being allowed to keep the remainder.

But the joy the company felt at being offered sanctuary in Egypt was only slightly tempered by the unexpected cost of entry. Nebuchadnezzar could do his worst: we were, everyone was convinced, safe.

The sun was hot and there was not a cloud in the sky as we walked. It was a beautiful morning and something about it reminded me of that first day when I travelled north from Anathoth into Israel to begin my work as a prophet beyond the borders of Judah. I remembered my uncertainty and ignorance; my naive hope that the nation of Israel would listen to God's words and return to him with all their heart.

Nostalgia frames the past in attractive colours, but although a mixture of emotions filled my mind as I thought of my early work as a prophet, the overall feeling was one of sorrow. Of opportunities lost, not because God had not given countless openings and innumerable nudges along the way, but because people were too busy with their own ways to listen.

Yet the beauty of creation did take me on a flight of appreciation, remembering the times spent admiring that beauty. And suddenly I saw in my mind's eye an innocent, serious face framed with long, dark hair. A smile that, when it came, was enchanting, and a voice that sang with a beauty and richness I have never heard matched.

I began to sing some words of King David, the first words I had ever heard Maacah sing as she worked in the kitchen of her mother's inn in Bethel:

> "This is the day that the Lord has made;
> let us rejoice and be glad in it."[32]

My voice was never sweet or gentle, but singing the psalm reminded me of that morning, of Maacah and the times of opportunity that were past. Yet still the words rang true, and the disasters that have filled the years since could not overcome the joy that a new day in God's creation can bring.

At first I sang quietly, but even singing like mine can be infectious. Soon those near me were humming or singing along, and after a while, the voices of many throughout the party were lifted in praise to God:

> "Save us, we pray, O Lord!
> O Lord, we pray, give us success!
> Blessed is he who comes in the name of the Lord!
> We bless you from the house of the Lord."[33]

The chorus quieted a little as we sang of the temple of Yahweh that was no more. It was clear that doubt was rising in people's minds, and many were asking themselves whether we could still sing such words. I saw many surreptitious looks directed at me, and it occurred to me that people were looking to me for guidance: I was a priest; I was expected to teach the people.

I tried to think. Did the words matter, or was it the intention? True, the temple was gone, but then again, it hadn't even been built when David wrote those words!

---

[32] Psalm 118:24
[33] Psalm 118:25-26

And when I thought further back, I remembered that Moses spoke in a few places about what was to be done with the house of the Lord – yet it was not built until hundreds of years later.[34] Now that the temple had been destroyed, I wondered if it was fair to say that "the house of the Lord" was anywhere where people worshipped him? – at least until the temple was established again in Jerusalem. It seemed to me a better choice than avoiding all references to our attachment to God's house. Really, it was a good sign that people had noticed the words enough for it to raise the question in their minds!

Sadly, for the time being, the temple was only a place in our memories, or a home for our dreams of the future. It had been destroyed because we had treated it as a 'den of robbers',[35] rather than the house of God.

"God's temple is a ruin, within a ruined city," I called out, "but God will bring back his people and his house will be rebuilt. Let's sing about his house as we remember it, and as it will be again. Let's think of his house with repentance as well as with thankfulness for his daily blessings."

Not everyone joined in, but many did, sparking a hope that the refugees would turn to God as Solomon had suggested they could in his prayer of dedication for the temple.[36] Yet I couldn't help thinking that Solomon's prayer had been for those carried into captivity against their will, not for those choosing to leave the land because their fear outweighed their faith.

---

[34] Deuteronomy 12:5, 11, 18; 16:6, 11, 15, 16
[35] Jeremiah 7:11
[36] 1 Kings 8:46-50; 2 Chronicles 6:36-39

Bland. Smooth. Level. Flat.

We walked across Egypt's delta and, once again, I was struck by its never-ending flatness. My old home near Anathoth gave a breathtaking view of the mountains of Moab across the deep valley of the Jordan. From early childhood I had enjoyed the depth of that vista, yet here there were none of the hills and valleys that add character and beauty to the land of Israel. True, there was a mighty river that the Jordan could never match for size, not even in spring, but its sluggish, torpid, languorous movement almost gave it the appearance of a slow-moving tongue of land.

Maybe I am overstating the nostalgic spirit of the place, but I think of Egypt as a land living on the grandeur of the past – a power that has already flowed, like the Nile, out to sea.

Tahpanhes was our final destination, as Amasis had suggested it might be, but first we had to march on past it to the Nile. The leaders of the party had been ordered to visit Zau while the rest waited at the Nile. As the only one with any skill in the language, I accompanied them as they crossed the Nile in papyrus boats.

Those who remained behind would have to fend for themselves for the best part of a week, finding a place to camp and food to eat without upsetting the local population. Maybe it was a test.

As we approached the royal city of Zau, we met plenty of soldiers and had to show our letter of entry several times. Our Judean clothing attracted attention, but since the spring weather was still warming up, we had no trouble with the heat. Within two months, the fierce summer heat would be properly upon us, and then it would be very clear why most Egyptians do not wear many clothes in summer.

Zau lies sprawled beside a major branch of the Nile River, but while we were still a long walk away, we passed more and more grand buildings. Egyptian architecture is very solid, but much of it is painted with bright colours and covered with pictures of people, which is not common in Judah's art.

I've often heard people comment on the tawny colour of Jerusalem, where walls and buildings reflect the colour of the commonly-available stone, but Zau was filled with splashes of many colours. Various types of stone hauled from quarries far away adorned the streets and glorious buildings, while many of the ubiquitous bricks in the less-grand buildings were covered with paint, presenting a colourful, almost festival atmosphere.

We made our way to the lesser palace which housed the department of immigration and presented our letter to one of the guards at the entrance. He looked us over with scant respect and told us to wait in the street while he took our letter to the relevant secretaries. We stood in the sun and waited for quite some time before he returned and told us all that we had been granted an audience. He seemed a little surprised at that, and we found out why when he took us to the immigration inspectors.

"Who are these men?" asked the man sitting at a table. "Haven't they any letter of permission?"

He spoke in the Egyptian language, so I answered him in the same tongue, "Yes, we have a letter, but we were told to present it here."

"But if a letter has been given, we don't need to see you. Just go wherever you were told to go."

"I'm sorry sir, but we were told to go to Tahpanhes, but to come here first."

"Oh, are you Greek mercenaries?" he asked. "Where are your letters of commission?"

"No, we are Jewish immigrants," I said.

"Jewish immigrants," he repeated, as if the words were a little distasteful to him. "I see. Why are you being sent to Tahpanhes? Pharaoh has a glorious palace in Tahpanhes – yet now we're filling up the city with Greeks and Jews." He sniffed, and said, "Where is this letter?"

I asked Johanan for the letter and handed it over to the secretary.

He scanned it quickly, his eyes widening a little when he saw who had written the recommendation. "Amasis," he said, thoughtfully. "Well, well, well. You've made a good friend there."

He read on, and after a while his eyes widened again and he looked up at me in some amazement. "You are to see Pharaoh? This is extraordinary. A scruffy bunch of runaway Jews, and Amasis asks for one of you to be presented to Pharaoh."

This was news to all of us. I had not tried to read the letter because it was written in an old script that I had not learned, and no-one else in the party could have done any better. Was this some trick from Amasis, or was he trying to help? I couldn't help thinking about Joseph's brothers and the difficult position Joseph had put them in when they visited Egypt to find food. Were we being hoodwinked as they had been?

"Which of you is Heremyo?" asked the secretary.

It took a few moments for me to work out that he probably meant me. The pronunciation of names between languages can be difficult, but Amasis had called me Heremyo throughout our acquaintance.

"I suppose it's me," I said.

"Did you meet Pharaoh Neco, may his soul fly swiftly, during his illustrious reign?"

"Yes, I did. Almost 20 years ago in this very palace."

Respect grew in his eyes, although I could tell that he wondered how I had ever managed to get an audience with the Pharaoh.

"Very well, sir," he said. "My name is Senenmut. I will submit the paperwork and a meeting shall be arranged for you. In the meantime, please come with me." He stood and began to walk away.

I started to follow him, then stopped and called after him, "But what about my companions?"

"They will be looked after, but you don't need to worry about them. I will return with a translator who speaks Hebrew and explain the situation to them."

I explained this to Johanan – as much as I could in two sentences – then followed Senenmut. He led me into another building within the palace complex. Guards were everywhere, but everyone seemed to wave us through without question. If only my first attempt to visit a Pharaoh had been so easy! Yes, I did finally manage to see him, but it had taken quite some time and many careful explanations to protective lower-level functionaries. In short, it had been hard work – although I'm sure it would have been completely impossible without God's help.

This time, every door seemed to open in front of me, and after a while I found myself in a room that was clearly intended for sleeping. It was well lit, and many of the pictures that make up their old hieroglyphic script decorated the upper reaches of the walls. I couldn't read the writing, but I recognised some of the Egyptian gods standing around the walls. I felt uncomfortable in their colourful presence, but decided that it didn't matter since they were simply dead idols, the imaginations of skilful artists.

The secretary explained that I would be provided with all the necessary equipment for sleeping and helped to prepare for a meeting with Pharaoh Hophra. The meeting would probably be in the morning and a barber would attend me first – this last with a somewhat disgusted look at my hair. Now I am not young and my hair is rather thin on top, but in Egypt, most men shave off their hair completely. They will never admit it, but it's easier than trying to cope with fleas and lice. We in Judah pay more attention to cleanliness and thus avoid such unpleasant problems. Maybe there's also a difference in the climate or conditions, I'm not sure. I do know that it took me quite a while after my last visit to Egypt to get rid of the fleas that seemed so ubiquitous and the lice that caused me to almost completely shave my head quite early on.

He looked at my clothes and I could tell that they had been condemned also.

"A dresser will attend you in the morning and provide appropriate clothes for your interview," Senenmut added, drily.

"What about washing?" I asked, remembering that finding water for washing was not always easy in Egypt.

"Washing?" he asked. "Washing. Hmm. Yes. Well, we will try to help you with your cultural requirements if you must. Washing…" He pursed his lips and frowned. "Washing. Ah, well, never mind. We will do something."

I had obviously upset his train of thought, so I prompted him, "And food?"

"Yes, food," he said. "We will provide you with food and the facilities in which to eat privately. This will be later this afternoon and again in the evening. Tomorrow morning you will receive another meal. Egypt is generous with food. Exotic food, too."

"Thank you, Senenmut, but I don't need exotic food. Bread and wine are all I need – and, in fact, what I prefer. Some honey would be a nice treat, but if it's not readily available, I don't need it."

"Of course honey is available, and honey shall be provided. Bread, however, may be a little more difficult in the afternoon. Nevertheless, we will satisfy your needs, although they may be different from ours. Are you sure that wine is all you would like? No beer? We also have other fermented drinks that tickle the palate and relax the mind."

"Wine would be ideal. A simple wine, new or old. But I don't need any strong drinks: I like my mind to remain clear."

"Clear? Ah. Very well. If that is all then, sir, I will chase up all of your needs."

"Thank you."

"And, sir, what is Amasis like? I believe that he is a magnificent soldier, but I have never met him." He spoke in an almost conspiratorial manner, adding, "He is my hero."

It was clear that my friend Amasis was now a great man in Egypt and that I needed to find out what had brought him such fame.

"Amasis is a brave and courageous man who is a true and loyal friend. He did a thorough job of teaching me your language so that I could meet Pharaoh Neco."

"He taught you well. And you are right that he's courageous. Five or six years ago he led an attack on the Cushites beyond the borders of upper Egypt. In fact, there are all sorts of stories about his personal bravery in battle, yet I'm told that he just brushes them off as everyday work. If we had more people like him, Egypt would be great again."

"Five years ago," I said thoughtfully. "That was before your current Pharaoh began to reign, wasn't it?"

"Yes, Psamtik was Pharaoh then, may his soul fly swiftly. He was present with the army, which was very important, but it was Amasis who made the courageous decisions and led the charges that were so decisive. He's a very popular man in Egypt."

That night I ate what Egyptian food I could while maintaining God's strict laws of cleanliness. I enjoyed more variety of food than I had tasted for some time.

Having spent most of the last 10 or 15 years in Judah, I had done without the variety of diet I had sometimes enjoyed and sometimes endured in other lands over the years. I thought wistfully of my mother's dire warnings about the food that foreigners ate and the pleasure with which she had fed me well on home food whenever I spent time in Judah. I still missed her reliable support and guidance.

Most of the evening I spent in prayer. Since I was being provided with an opportunity to speak to Pharaoh, it seemed likely that God would have something specific for me to say. The evening passed and still I had no guidance from Yahweh. It left me feeling a horrible uncertainty. Although I had been taken away from Judah against my will, God was not answering my prayers. Had he expected me to escape from the caravan and return to Judah?

As the evening passed and my prayers became increasingly desperate, I began to make tentative plans to escape from Egypt. Obviously God did not want me here, so I must find a way out.

I had just settled into more detailed planning when the familiar presence of God began to slowly fill the room. There in Pharaoh's palace, I was given a message for Pharaoh. It was brief, very brief, but it reminded me that Egypt was not a place of safety – neither for the exiles from Judah nor for the people of Egypt.

God told me:

> "Declare in Egypt, and proclaim in Migdol;
> proclaim in Memphis and Tahpanhes;
> Say, 'Stand ready and be prepared,
> for the sword shall devour around you.' "[37]

---

[37] Jeremiah 46:14

Although the word of God burns inside me like a fire, causing pain and often profound tiredness, it was a very welcome return of his presence. It made me feel at home, even in a foreign land. More than 40 years ago, God told me that he had chosen me before my birth to be a prophet to the nations, and he was still using me in that way now. It was a true delight, a confirmation of God's presence, and I was filled with grateful thanks.

Finally, exhausted, I slept.

Chapter 9

An Interview

Breakfast was waiting for me when I awoke. Being deep inside the palace, there was no natural light, and the tiredness that often comes from being close to the infinite power of God had left me sleeping deeply.

Nevertheless, breakfast was ready and I was eager to eat. Egyptian bread is different from ours, not least because it sometimes hides nasty surprises for your teeth. They tell me it is necessary to add small amounts of certain sands and gravel when grinding the particular grains they grow. Without these additives, the grain grinds very slowly and wears out the millstones instead. So whichever path they choose, they end up with gravel in their bread. It's no wonder that the Egyptians have such terrible teeth!

I assume they know what they're doing, but it makes me cautious when eating Egyptian bread. Nevertheless, the flavour is nice and their cooking methods give the bread a pleasant texture.

However, I don't like their water. Judah is not a wet land, but we can normally get what I would call "fresh" water. Water that flows, and water I can see through! I don't like water with wriggly things in it. My mother warned me about water whenever I left Israel, and I've always done my best to find clean water to drink when travelling. That morning, however, there was no chance of getting anything other than Pharaoh's standard-issue Egyptian water. I drank it in my own room and wished for water from the pools in Jerusalem or the Gihon Spring, water that has a sweet taste and includes far less dirt!

Obviously, although Egyptians find the eating habits of other races repulsive, Senenmut had been keeping enough of an eye on me to notice when I had finished my meal. Within moments, he was tapping on the wall near my doorway to get my attention.

I looked up and he greeted me with a smile of satisfaction. "I have found water for you to bathe in," he said. "Come with me and I will show you."

He took me to a cistern that had been damaged recently so that the water inside had been contaminated with dirty water from a drain. Senenmut explained this to me quite unashamedly as we walked, saying that I was welcome to use the cistern for bathing to satisfy my cultural norms.

After hearing his explanation, I was no longer so eager to wash! In the end, the water didn't look too bad, so I thanked him and washed. I was careful not to drink the water, but I think that I was probably cleaner afterwards than I had been at the start.

My washing completed, Senenmut explained to me that Pharaoh Hophra was eager to see me just before noon. Apparently, he wanted to hear words from another god. Egyptians are really quite religious – when you have so many gods, spending just a little time with each adds up to a lot of time!

My morning was spent being prepared for my audience with Pharaoh. They really wanted me to shave and have my hair trimmed, and I agreed to it on the proviso that they didn't twist my hair into any of the styles that acknowledge their gods. Senenmut wrung his hands over that, but in the end he agreed. As long as I would accept a very close-cropped head and face, all would be well. That satisfied both my objections to their worship and God's rule that priests were not allowed to create bald patches on their heads.[38] True, my time to work as a priest had passed because of my age, and in any case the destruction of the temple had taken away any opportunity to be a priest, but I still wished to follow God's rules.

A barber was called and instructed regarding the peculiar requirements of this strange visitor. He did his work quickly and efficiently, although he did try suggesting by means of hand signs that he could shave off all my hair if I would let him. I said, "No, thank you," firmly in his language and he seemed satisfied with that.

As noon approached, I was led into Pharaoh Hophra's throne room. It was very grand, with gold covering almost every visible surface. Pharaoh himself wore a gold-trimmed floor-length linen garment that would have helped to keep out the cool of the spring morning. As on earlier visits, I was struck by the thought that, in Pharaoh's court, it seemed that the more important people were, the more clothes they wore. I was dressed in clothes very similar to Pharaoh's, although without the golden decorations. On the other hand, the male and female servants who attended him wore almost nothing. I wasn't sure whether this reflected an opinion that modesty was only for the great or to make sure servants had nowhere to hide any weapons to use against their monarch. Whatever the reason, I was glad to be part of the privileged group allowed to be properly dressed.

"Heremyo, the prophet of Yoveh from Hudyah."

The herald announced my name, albeit with an interesting pronunciation, and a guard led me close to Pharaoh.

---

[38] Leviticus 21:5

"Heremyo," he said. "You spoke with my grandfather many years ago."

"Yes sir, I did."

"Did you deliver a special message from the gods?"

"Yes, I had a special message from Yahweh, the God of gods and Lord of kings."

"I believe that the message was written down at the time and stored somewhere in the archives, but it seems to have been lost." Pharaoh laughed and continued, "It didn't seem worth scouring every shelf in every room just to find a message that you could repeat for me anyway."

I couldn't put my finger on it, but there seemed something significant in that approach to finding a document.

Nevertheless, I agreed to repeat the message from Yahweh in which he demanded that all the kings in the area drink of the cup of his anger.

"Did you offer my grandfather this cup? Was it a literal cup or just a symbolic one?"

"I was told to offer a cup to each leader and give a particular message to any who refused to accept it and drink."

"Did my grandfather drink from this cup you offered him?"

"No. So I passed on Yahweh's message to him. However, now, my lord, I have a message from Yahweh specifically for you."

Pharaoh Hophra looked pleased and eager to hear his own special message from God, so I repeated the words I had been told during the night:

"Declare in Egypt, and proclaim in Migdol;
   proclaim in Memphis and Tahpanhes;

Say, 'Stand ready and be prepared,
for the sword shall devour around you.' "[39]

As he heard the message, Pharaoh's eagerness disappeared. This was not the message he had expected or hoped for! I could almost read his thoughts from the expressions flitting across his face. How dare this visiting foreigner suggest that Egypt could be attacked and invaded?

Being a prophet of Yahweh has placed me in front of many kings, delivering messages that would ordinarily have warranted the immediate execution of such an upstart foreigner! Yet no king has executed me. Rarely have I even been imprisoned, for however short a time, and very few kings have ever told me to leave and never return. In fact, the kings who have reacted the most threateningly have been the kings of Judah.

Why didn't Pharaoh Neco execute me for my temerity all those years ago, and why wouldn't Pharaoh Hophra do so now? My only logical answer is that God didn't want them to. And once a few kings chose not to execute me, I suppose other kings heard the reports and no longer considered it a viable option. I became part of the scenery of international diplomacy and religion. For about 30 years, I was known by nations and their rulers everywhere. I travelled around with disrespectful messages for all of the most important people in the world! And with God's blessing, I got away with it.

Pharaoh Hophra showed the same anger as his grandfather had, but he also showed the same restraint. I was not immediately dismembered or disembowelled for my effrontery. I was not dragged away to be sold as a slave or fed to the denizens of the Nile; rather, my message was heard and paid at least some attention.

---

[39] Jeremiah 46:14

Pharaoh Neco had not accepted God's message any more than he had accepted the cup I offered him. Nor would his grandson accept that time was running out for Egypt; but both of them had heard God's word and considered it.

"Nebuchadnezzar will not attack Egypt," Hophra responded with confidence, leaning back comfortably on his throne. He took a date from a waiting attendant and popped it into his mouth. "He knows our strength and his own limitations. Babylon will never set foot in our palaces or temples."

"I will have more messages for you later, my lord," I said. "This is all for the present, but I warn you that there will be more."

"You hear that, my advisors?" said Hophra to the group of men who stood nearby, ready to give the king answers whenever he wanted them. "A foreign prophet warns me that he will have more messages to deliver to me. Messages from a foreign god who cannot even protect his own land from destruction."

"Pharaoh, you know that Yahweh predicted the attacks of Nebuchadnezzar and his destruction of the kingdom of Judah. And he didn't just predict those events, he *caused* them. Yahweh is in control. This is what I told your grandfather when he advised me that I should concern myself with saving Judah from attack. I told him that Judah would be punished by Yahweh before Egypt, but that in the end, Egypt would not escape unless he listened to God's commands."

His advisors would never have heard anyone speak to Pharaoh like that before, yet I did it as respectfully as I could. The words were simple, even blunt, but the delivery was not arrogant or rude. My words were matter of fact, although they would, no doubt, be irritating to a king who believed himself in control.

I made no effort to either prolong the interview or cut it short. My task was done and I was available for Pharaoh to question if he chose to do so.

After a few minutes, I was thanked for my message and led out of the throne room.

Senenmut was waiting for me and led me back to the room I had slept in. Quickly I was fed once more, then I changed back into my own clothes.

Before I left, Senenmut had one last question for me: "When you first met Amasis, how did you communicate with him? I understand that he taught you our language, but how did he do that?"

"We both spoke Aramaic, so he taught me in Aramaic."

"Did you use any other languages?"

"Well, Amasis was very good with languages, so we exchanged knowledge about a few languages. I taught him some Hebrew and he taught me some of the language of Cush, which was very useful later."

"Ah, the language of Cush. No wonder he was able to get so much intelligence from the Cushites when we invaded the area."

Senenmut led me out to the entrance where we had parted from my companions the day before. We crossed the road to another grand building and were taken to a dormitory where the others had spent the night. For once, they were pleased to see me – being eager to leave as soon as possible. Our hosts had treated them well, but they were nervous that the situation could change very quickly if my words upset Pharaoh.

That possibility hadn't even occurred to me.

Before we left, we were given another letter that we were told would make finding somewhere to stay in Tahpanhes much easier, so it seemed that our time in Zau had not been wasted.

As we hurried back to the rest of the caravan, we were all concerned about what we would find when we arrived. We scanned the far bank as we crossed the river, but there was no sign of the crowds of Jews we had expected to see. It was a slow crossing, punctuated with all sorts of suggestions regarding the whereabouts of our companions. Johanan, however, had a sharp eye and spotted a young man from the company reclining on the bank. He shouted and waved, and soon the young man jumped up and hurried to the jetty to meet us.

We had scarcely greeted each other before he breathlessly began telling us what had happened while we were away. Unfortunately, on the third day after our departure, a group of soldiers had arrived at the river looking for a way to cross. Some of them were drunk, and when they saw our party sitting in the shade of the few trees that bordered the river, they began to complain about the selfish collection of foreigners who were taking their shade.

The situation quickly deteriorated, with abusive shouts from both sides and just enough comprehension for the hotheads in each group to get annoyed. Had Baruch not intervened and convinced Johanan's men to sheathe their swords and move away from the riverbank, we could have returned to the site of a massacre. Even so, the drunken trouble-makers might well have pressed the fight had not a large wooden boat arrived at the bank at that moment, its crew shouting for passengers who wished to cross. Quickly, the Egyptians began to board, probably hoping that they were taking berths from our people and yelling abuse as they did so. Fortunately, most of it was in their own language, so it was not understood by those they were trying to abuse. At the same time, Baruch was attempting to herd our countrymen away, hoping to completely disengage the two groups and avoid major conflict. It worked, mostly because one of the drunken soldiers missed his footing as he boarded the boat and fell into the river, with lots of shouting and splashing. The rest of the soldiers had to rescue him, and while they were distracted, Baruch led the caravan safely away. He even convinced some excitable hotheads not to cheer!

After that incident, the group stayed away from the road, camping in a quiet field that was not visible from the road. However, Baruch had insisted that the men must take turns waiting at the river crossing so as not to miss us when we returned from Zau. His plan worked and we were united again, a little subdued by the reminder of just how quickly one can get into trouble in a foreign land. After exchanging greetings and news, we were ready to retrace our steps to the road that would lead us to Tahpanhes.

Chapter 10

Tahpanhes

April 585BC

We met the road to Tahpanhes at a crossroads and turned to follow it. Our caravan travelled quietly, doing our best not to draw attention to ourselves.

Tahpanhes was home to one of Pharaoh's palaces, but also to a growing population of Greek mercenaries. I began to wonder if it might be better to find somewhere more remote where we could slowly learn to fit into Egyptian society. However, the authorities' gracious permission to enter Egypt included instructions to settle in Tahpanhes. Going somewhere else would probably be seen as disobedience, and might completely invalidate our permission to remain in Egypt.

Anyway, everyone was eager to find a place to settle down, so the question of going elsewhere was deferred for the time being. Tahpanhes would be a good place to start.

We had only a few kilometres to go when Johanan appeared quietly beside me.

"What do you think?" he asked. "Should we go ahead to Tahpanhes and find someone to show our letters to? I don't like the idea of walking into the centre of Tahpanhes with a large group of people when we don't know where we're going."

"I agree," I said. "It will be easier if we two can find the right officers. They'll tell us what to do first."

"We were very lucky to meet that soldier you knew," said Johanan.

"Lucky?" I asked, wryly.

"Yes, lucky. After all, you keep telling us that God is going to send judgement on us, so he wouldn't bless us with that sort of opportunity."

"We can talk about that as we go," I said, "but in the meantime, why not let everyone know what's happening?"

Johanan accordingly gave instructions for the people to keep moving towards Tahpanhes, but not too quickly. When they arrived at the city limits, they were to halt beside the road, and we would rejoin them when everything had been sorted out.

Johanan and I hurried on ahead, and as we walked, I returned to Johanan's comment. "I don't claim to understand how God works," I said, "but I do know that he is very patient and forgiving. He also deals with us as both individuals and as part of a nation."

"What do you mean?"

"He deals with people as individuals in that he treats us all differently. For example, God told Zedekiah that he would go into captivity, yet he told Ebed-melech that he would *not* go into captivity."

"I can see what you mean about personal treatment – at least in theory. To be honest, I don't know how you can be so confident about what God says. After all, he doesn't talk in public, and I never hear him talking to me, but we'll ignore that for the moment."

"I agree that God doesn't talk to everyone, but he *has* spoken to me. Do you believe that?"

"Why should I believe it? You keep telling me that there are false prophets, so why should I believe that you are a true prophet and the others are frauds? How can I tell who is a fraud and who is a real prophet?"

"If I tell you that God has said something will happen and it happens, particularly if it's an unlikely thing, isn't that a good indication that I'm telling the truth?"

"I guess so, but do you have any examples?"

"Do you remember Hananiah, the man I said was a false prophet?"

"Yes. I heard that you killed him."

"Did you hear that from Irijah? He certainly had it in for me! *I did not kill Hananiah.* I didn't even see him again after I told him that God had said he would die before the end of the year. He just died – and it wasn't in battle or anything like that. He died exactly as God said he would. That's just one proof that God really has been talking to me. And that you can believe God."

"Very well then, I'll concede that point for the moment, but what about your other point: you said that God also treats us as part of a nation. What do you mean by that?"

"God judges entire nations and rewards or punishes them based on their behaviour as a nation. If a nation obeys his commands, they will be blessed, even if there are some individuals who aren't so good. Good crops, good health, happiness, and so on. All these things are given to nations that are good as a whole."

"Like a good army can win a battle and even the bad soldiers will benefit?"

"Yes," I agreed, "I suppose that's much the same."

"But is the reverse true too? If a bad army loses a battle, even the good soldiers can suffer and die?"

"Yes. And God manages that balance of individual and national rewards and punishment, although I don't know how he decides it. When David fought Goliath, one person brought victory to an entire nation."

"Got it," said Johanan. "I suppose that makes sense."

By this time, we were within sight of the walls that surrounded Tahpanhes and could see guards standing above the gate.

"How are we going to handle this?" I asked.

"Can I use you as a translator? When I say things, you translate for them and then tell me what they say. What I want to do first is to find out where we need to go to present that letter."

We approached the gates and four guards made their way out towards us.

"What's your business?"

I translated the question for Johanan, who answered, "We have a letter from the immigration department in Zau. We were told to deliver it to certain officers in the municipal offices here."

I translated the message into Egyptian and was gratified to see that the guards clearly understood what I was saying. That proved to be the case throughout the conversation, in which I was just a mouthpiece.

"The municipal offices are near Pharaoh's palace, opposite the large courtyard and next to the temple that is still under construction. Pharaoh likes his building projects, particularly upgrading temples. He does a good job too, and shows off Egypt's grandeur to anyone who visits."

"We saw his work in Zau," said Johanan. "Amazing architecture. Enormous buildings."

"True. We're good at building and have been for a very long time. No-one else builds like we do."

Johanan seemed to be genuine in his comments, and it was the first time I had heard him show much interest in anything other than military matters. However, whether he was genuine or not, he had certainly said the right thing to keep the guards happy! Leaving them on friendly terms, we followed their instructions, progressing along a wide street that led eventually to the buildings they had described. As we entered the municipal buildings, my uncertainty as to the outcome increased. After all, how likely was it that a group of our size could appear in a crowded town and be provided with satisfactory dwellings? Even if we were willing to use all the gold and silver that many had brought from Judah, would there even be enough dwellings available?

We had already been told that the town was filling up with Greek mercenaries, so we would be just another burden on the town's infrastructure.

However, I was wrong. At first our frosty reception matched my expectations, but as soon as we presented our letter, we were welcomed with surprising generosity.

"Jews?" mused the senior officer named in the letter in a puzzled voice.

"Yes," responded Johanan as I took up my translator's job again.

"Yet you have letters from the department of immigration, and specifically from the notable Senenmut."

"Yes. These come at the request of Amasis."

"You mean the great General Amasis?"

"Yes."

"You have amazing connections in Egypt."

"I don't have connections, it is Jeremiah here, the prophet of Yahweh."

"You mean this is Heremyo the prophet?" The man looked at me wide-eyed and then acknowledged in fulsome terms that he had heard much about me. I was not used to this notoriety, and the officer's words suggested that it was widespread in other nations also. How could this be so? My own nation paid me no attention at all —

except to drag me to Egypt because they were worried that I might tell Nebuchadnezzar where they were.

"Why is Jeremiah so famous?" asked Johanan, but I refused to translate his question. There had already been far too much talk about me and I was not going to cooperate any more. I don't mind if people talk about the importance of God's messages, but I don't want them talking about *me*.

Instead, I asked, "What does the letter request of you?"

"I'll read it to you," he offered.

As usual, the letter was full of flowery phrases, but it also had some unexpected content.

We were to be given free access to a group of houses in Tahpanhes that had been intended for a new group of Greek mercenaries – possibly the group that people kept mistaking us for. However, it had now been confirmed that they were not coming for at least six months, and possibly not at all. We were to be given free use of the houses in the meantime, and by then it was expected that more houses would have been built and these ones would not be required anyway!

There were a few pieces of legally limiting language, saying that if we did not use any of the houses or moved elsewhere as a group, we must give up all access, provide vacant possession and so on. In short, we could only benefit from this gift while we used it. It was not something we could on-sell to others or make money from directly. Knowing the joy we Jews get from buying and selling, I thought this a wise condition to add.

Nevertheless, I was amazed by the generosity that was being shown. As far as I was concerned, I had never done anything to deserve such treatment, and this was amazing treatment not only for me but also for all of my fellows. It was equivalent to a very significant gift in gold.

I was given another letter to present to the guards who patrolled the area around our new houses, along with instructions for finding them. This concluded the interview and Johanan and I left the municipal offices and went to find the guards.

As we walked, I summarised for Johanan the letter we had delivered. He was as astonished as I had been.

"You mean we have been given houses to live in free of charge?"

"Yes," I said.

"In Tahpanhes itself – a royal city?"

"Yes."

"With no long-term demands on our citizenship, loyalty or anything like that?"

"No, none."

He shook his head in disbelief.

"Apparently the houses are in quite a good part of town, too. Not the best part, you understand – after all, you don't put mercenaries in the very best parts of town!"

"It will suit us better not to be in the best part of town anyway. A pleasant, quiet area where we won't be noticed will be ideal and allow us to live in peace and safety." He shook his head again and smiled in deep satisfaction. Maybe he caught the gleam in my eye, though, because he hurriedly added, "Yes, I know, you've already told us that we aren't going to have peace and safety here. But you also acknowledged that you don't understand everything God does and that he is very generous and forgiving. Maybe he will forgive and forget what we did."

"Maybe he will," I agreed, "if we repent and try to worship him better here than we did in Judah. There are lots of grand temples around here, and God won't want to see any of us in them or learning anything about the Egyptian ways of worship."

"Look, Jeremiah, things really weren't as bad as you're saying. After all, the priests in Jerusalem were happy with our ways of worship. It was just you who stood out as the one who was always grumbling."

"I was not 'grumbling'," I said, irritated. "I was saying what Yahweh told me to say. Anyway, let's find these houses and then bring our people to see their new homes."

℈℈

Tahpanhes was set out in a grid, with different quarters of the city being separated by wide avenues. The flatness of the terrain made it easy to construct huge buildings on a single level – a luxury we never had in Judah – and one quarter of the city was full of such grand buildings. This was the quarter we had visited first, the area which contained the municipal offices, Pharaoh's palace and several temples.

Our new houses were in the foreign quarter of the city, and our new neighbours were the Greek mercenaries we had heard so much about, as well as other foreign workers who kept the palace clean and performed many of the lowly tasks around the city.

We led our fellow refugees into the city and along an avenue to the houses we had been allocated. As we stopped, Johanan showed them the closest houses and described the boundaries of our area. I rejoiced at the wonder and amazement that spread across all faces. Smiles broke out everywhere and cheers rose into the air. No-one could find words to express their joy at this quite unexpected bounty that had come their way. The news that we had been given free use of these houses had already diffused through the group as we made our way into the city, but now they could actually see them, their tentative hope was transformed into pure pleasure.

Their reaction was balm to my soul; enough to bring tears to my eyes. Although it is easy to say – and true – that their own behaviour had been the cause of all their suffering, they had, nevertheless, suffered enormously in the past three years. There was not a person among us who had not lost at least one close friend or family member in that time, and most had also suffered in many other ways.

I am not a particularly sympathetic man by nature, but seeing smiles on faces that had not worn them for so long was enough to fill me with hope. Surely such an unexpected benefit must be accepted as a gift of God's grace?

Rows of neat, whitewashed houses spread out in front of us, and all we had to do was assign each family a house; then we could move in and really start to live again.

Johanan and the other leaders chose a committee to assess the housing needs, and each family head went to them to report the number, ages and capabilities of their family members. Another committee dispatched its members to collect information about the available housing, which they then presented to a third committee which assigned families to houses. The results of their deliberations were reported to the people in a remarkably short period of time, and then the fun began.

"We have been given a house with only two rooms," I heard one man saying, "while my cousin has been given a house with three rooms. It's not fair."

I knew nothing about his personal situation, but I did know that he was being given a house to live in with no requirement for effort or payment on his part. Perhaps I should have kept quiet, but I was, quite frankly, disgusted.

"How many rooms did you have in your house in Judah?" I asked.

"Two."

"So what is the problem?"

"My cousin will have three!"

"You don't have to stay in the house you have been assigned," I said. "Other houses are available for rent elsewhere in the city. Go and find one, pay the rent and live there. You can rent a house with three rooms, or even four if you want to."

"And how will I afford that? From what I've heard of prices in Tahpanhes, I couldn't even afford a house with two rooms!"

"If you can't afford a house with two rooms, why are you complaining when you are offered a house with two rooms at no cost to you at all?"

"I've already told you. My cousin has been given a house with three rooms. It's not fair. Can't you see that?"

And so it went on. The man grew increasingly angry with his cousin, with me, and with the committee which had assigned him his utterly unacceptable two-room house. And he was far from being the only one complaining.

The houses, greeted such a short time before with tears of joy and thankfulness, were now the cause of deep resentment because of utterly self-centred attitudes. Nothing had changed.

Baruch and I, both being without family, were kindly assigned a small house with two rooms that would make it easy for us to pursue our different interests where necessary. Baruch would probably be seeking work as a scribe once things settled down, while I would have to see what I could do to get food to eat. I had little left of the gift given me by Nebuzaradan, the captain of the guard,[40] and unless I found some way of earning my daily bread, I would soon be going hungry. Working as a scribe wasn't

---

[40] Jeremiah 40:5

an option for me: my writing was so bad that people would take one look at it and refuse to pay me!

I was too old to work as a priest, and we had no temple anyway. As a Levite, I was entitled to tithes, but who would pay them? If the gift of a very adequate two-room house rent-free could generate such jealousy, anger and hatred, what hope was there of obedience to God's laws?

I made a mental note to consider any tithes I myself might owe. I had been living for so long at the beck and call of others that I had not earned a proper living for quite a while. The king had fed me while I was imprisoned – at least until the food ran out. After that, the Chaldean army had provided my food and a generous gift that was still keeping me alive. I must consider what tithes I owed – and what to do about them.

Baruch and I moved into our new house and it was a joy for both of us. Although we knew that trouble would come, our new-found peace and comfort felt like a gift from God, however temporary.

Chapter 11

Worship

A sense of responsibility niggled at me. As a priest, I should be doing my best to guide my nation in the worship of Yahweh.

But how could I do it when I was confident that nobody wanted to hear about worship?

In the end, I decided to promote a few symbols of worship that I was sure would be important in a foreign land. Some were things I had used myself when I was travelling as a prophet to the nations for long periods of time. They had helped to keep my own worship alive when I couldn't visit the temple – surely they must help others too?

Reading God's word was one, and in this my "smelly scroll"[41] was my constant companion, though far from my only source. By that time, I knew the words of Isaiah, my predecessor as a prophet of God, pretty much by heart. His words help to bring me near to God wherever I am, and I find having the physical scroll to read important even though the words are already firmly fixed in my mind.

---

[41] See Volume 1 – Early Days, Chapter 12.

Another was prayer. King Solomon the Wise prayed a marvellous prayer when he dedicated his newly-built temple, and I was sure that his suggestion for our exiles to pray toward the temple was right, although that temple was now reduced to rubble. I had already begun to do so myself and had suggested it to others. Now I wanted to install it as a national habit until we could return to our homeland.

My persistent concern that this group of refugees had left the land *by their own choice* rather than through enforced captivity gave me some qualms, but, on balance, I concluded that it was best to act as Solomon had advocated captives should behave.

Teaching and explaining God's law were essential too. Although the captivity had come because of disobedience, we must never stop looking for, and working toward, the next revival. Priests and kings had always been the source of any drive for revival, and it was my responsibility never to give up – despite the fact that I had never succeeded yet! God's work was still there to be done, and maybe I had now learned enough wisdom to be able to do a better job than ever before.

Never give up, I told myself. Then I tried to act on it.

I had a plan, a collection of actions and attitudes that must be promoted if this little outpost of Israel was to maintain the religion of our fathers. Once again, I suppressed the memory of God's warning that he would destroy everyone who came into Egypt.

God was a forgiving God, I argued to myself. If we followed his ways in Egypt, surely *some* would be forgiven and allowed to return to the land of their fathers?

That night I spent several hours in prayer, looking for confirmation from God that my goals were right.

I didn't get any specific answer, but I did gain greater confidence that my conclusions were correct. And I found a specific target to aim for, based on words God had spoken to me many years before.

I would begin with the Sabbath.

I'm a little embarrassed to admit that it took considerable thought to work out what day of the week it was. I had been so much out of my normal routine since leaving Chimham's Inn that working out when the week started and ended was surprisingly difficult – certainly no one in our group had done anything to mark specific days of the week. Indeed, keeping the Sabbath had not been popular in Judah for generations.

Sabbaths were inconvenient. They curtailed trade. They limited opportunities for enjoyment, for feasting and celebration.

God had spoken to me about the Sabbath on just one occasion, but don't let that mislead you into thinking that he did not consider it important. His command was that the people must keep the Sabbath, and he finished with the uncompromising warning:

"But if you do not listen to me,
to keep the Sabbath day holy, and not to bear a burden
and enter by the gates of Jerusalem on the Sabbath day,
then I will kindle a fire in its gates,
and it shall devour the palaces of Jerusalem
and shall not be quenched."[42]

It goes almost without saying that they did not listen. Burdens were still carried on the Sabbath and traders went in and out through the gates of Jerusalem every day of the week, making the most of any opportunity for making money.

It also goes without saying that a fire had indeed been lit in the gates of Jerusalem that had burned to destruction, just as God had promised.

---

[42] Jeremiah 17:27

Yes, I was certain that the Sabbath was the place to start.

And the Sabbath was only one day away.

If I was going to start the process at all, I had to start today – and that meant both making arrangements and inviting people to the worship I was going to arrange.

When morning arrived, I would have only twelve hours to make my plans known to everybody.

With such a limited time, the intensity of my prayer redoubled. Before dawn, I had to decide on a form of worship and the best way to spread the word to everyone who would listen.

In such situations, faith is really shown to be faith. I had no doubt that God would help me, and as I chewed over the problem, I felt his guidance.

Only a rough framework of worship was required by dawn. Furthermore, the methods of spreading the word and convincing people that it was important had only to be well enough defined to allow me to begin.

Of course, realistically, the entire project was impossible, and it was silly to force such a tight deadline on myself. Yet I felt that there was no choice. Revivals are begun by seizing the moment and relying on God to drag everyone along. Josiah had shown me how it worked when I was young, and I must follow his example. I had also read of Hezekiah opening the doors of the temple at the very start of his reign. Not a day had been wasted, and he was successful because he seized the opportunity with such faith, urgency and determination that nobody could resist him. And those are the situations in which God's help can always be completely relied on without the need for any explicit instructions. Goliath died and the Philistines became subservient to Israel because David seized a non-existent opportunity and made victory inevitable. Of course, I'm really preaching to myself here!

My thoughts were so utterly convincing that my excuses and doubts were unable to make any impression on them. Memories of great men who had succeeded in the past seemed to be inspiring me to make the leap of doing my best to spark a reformation.

By the time the night began to ease its hold on Tahpanhes, I had plans and a determination to follow them through.

I left my bed before dawn and went to look for a place where I could watch God's recreation of the day once more and share that uplifting time with my maker. Outside, a rim of light was spreading around the horizon, but so much of the horizon was hidden by buildings! Noticing a ladder near the door of our house, I climbed it and found a small flat area on the roof, presumably intended for spreading out items to dry in the sun. From my new vantage point, more of the horizon was visible, and in the darkness I could sense a broad flat land spread out about me. No notable hills were visible, and it was only when I looked towards the palace quarter that large buildings obscured my view. These buildings had many torches burning on their ramparts and entryways: I could see them flickering in the early morning breeze.

But they were away to the west, and the light I was waiting for would come from the east. The light of the sun, appointed by God to rule the day. And this was the light that was imperceptibly spreading across the land, revealing to me its foreign contours and strange geography.

This would be a very busy day and only God's help could make it a successful one. I plunged once more into prayer, helped in my concentration by the exquisite unfolding of God's gift of sunrise.

Dawn was lighting the sky more distinctly in the east now, and a focus of the light began to glow. With characteristic suddenness, the first rays of the sun flashed over the horizon. Despite being entranced by its captivating beauty, however, I was abruptly reminded that time marches on and that my time was already running short. Without waiting for the sun to climb any further above the horizon, I hurried down the ladder and back into the house.

Baruch had just risen from sleep and we greeted each other with the traditional Jewish greeting, "Peace." Egypt could not take that away from us.

"Did you know that tomorrow is the Sabbath?" I asked.

"Yes," he said.

I wondered how he knew it so easily when I had had to think so hard! Nevertheless, his knowledge made it more likely that he would be a useful helper in my urgent task.

"God made the Sabbath a special day for our people when we left Egypt during the Exodus," I pointed out.

"True, but it hasn't been very special for a long time."

"We need to make it special again. The temple is gone and we've left our homeland; what can we do to worship Yahweh except to use his old forms of worship to form a new tradition here in Egypt?"

"What old forms can we maintain? Sacrifice? The priesthood?"

"No. God spoke only of making sacrifices in the place he chose, and that place was the temple in Jerusalem, not here in Tahpanhes. Most of the work of the priesthood was to maintain the service in the temple, particularly in offering sacrifices, and that is no longer appropriate."

"But priests weren't only meant to offer sacrifices. They were meant to teach God's law too."

"True, yet so much of God's law includes sacrifices. Imagine if someone came to me saying that they have recovered from leprosy: various sacrifices are commanded before they can be pronounced clean."

"You're right," said Baruch. "But it's God who has taken away our ability to offer those sacrifices. It's been his choice to change how we can keep the law."

"God punished us because we weren't interested in worshipping him, so if we want to worship him now, we'll have to work out how to do so. Not everything in the law depended on sacrifices or the temple. Keeping the Ten Commandments doesn't require us to have a temple, but they do command us to keep the Sabbath."

"And didn't you mention sometime that God had said that while the nation was in captivity, the land would enjoy its Sabbaths? Or something like that?"

"Yes. So Sabbaths are important to God. We should be keeping the Sabbath here in Egypt. The sword is following us into Egypt and we don't know when it will arrive."

"Does that mean it's not worth trying to please God because we'll all be killed by the sword anyway?"

"Of course not! God often seems to change threatened punishments if we fix the behaviour that warranted the punishment. Nineveh proved that when they listened to Jonah and repented. God forgave them – yet he hadn't even suggested that was a possibility beforehand."[43]

"I know what you mean," said Baruch, "but it does leave me unsure which of God's prophecies are, shall we say, immutable, and which can be changed if the situation changes."

"No man can answer that question for you, I'm afraid. I've been delivering prophecies from God for 40 years and yet I still don't know with certainty myself. What I have learned, however, is never to give up on God's mercy. After all, if God has promised that punishment will come upon me and I repent and change my life, I'm sure that

---

[43] Jonah 3:4-10

my reformed life will be better, even if God decides not to forgive me. A life focused on serving God is always better than a life that works against him."

"I suppose so, but it would be nice to understand it all better!"

"True," I answered, smiling. "Just let me know when you work it out, will you?"

We sat together in silence for a few moments before Baruch asked, "You talked about the Sabbath. What are your plans for tomorrow? I'm willing to keep the Sabbath with you."

"My plans are much grander than that," I said. "I want every Jew here to keep a Sabbath to God every week."

"I see. You don't start with small ambitions, do you?"

"If we aim low, there's nothing to achieve and no need for God's help to achieve it. We need a major reformation, and now is the time to start it."

"Wouldn't it be better to tell people this week that we're starting next week? That gives you a chance to make sure that everyone hears about it."

"It also gives them a week to get used to *not* keeping a Sabbath in Tahpanhes. If I give them that week now, they'll never give it back to God. And I'm convinced that they'll never give any other Sabbaths to him either."

"So you think it's now or never?"

"Yes."

"Very well. Do you need any help in organising this?"

"I do. I need people like you who know what the law says about the Sabbath, even if you haven't been keeping it any more than anyone else has. Are you willing to keep it from now on?"

"I think so. As you say, the Ten Commandments tell me that I must, so I suppose I must. Do you really think that life will be better if we keep the Sabbath?"

"Yes. God promised that if we keep his Sabbaths and his feasts, he will look after us and we won't lose anything by dedicating that time to him. Remember that he said our enemies would never attack us during the feasts if we went to Jerusalem to keep them?"

"I remember. What happens about feasts now? We can't go to Jerusalem."

"No. We'll have to think more about that."

"Well, I'm willing to try out keeping the Sabbath properly."

"Thank you, Baruch. I needed that support from you, and I'm sure you won't regret it."

"We shall see."

"However, that's not all I need from you," I added, earnestly. "I need you to go around and talk to our fellow Jews. I'll be talking to anyone I can too: our leaders, as well as individual men, women, and even children, to make sure that everyone hears about what's happening tomorrow."

"What *is* happening tomorrow? It's fine to talk about keeping the Sabbath, but what do you mean by it?"

"I intend to find people who are willing to hold meetings in their homes or outside in courtyards or squares. I don't know exactly how they'll work yet, but I plan to have meetings that will include reading from scripture, the Law, the Psalms and the words of the prophets, and then have some explanation of the words read. Can I count on you to be willing to help with that?"

"Yes – but don't forget, I'm not a priest, I'm only a scribe."

"Better 'only a scribe' who knows God's word than a priest who doesn't know it at all!"

"How many priests or Levites are here with us?" asked Baruch.

"Altogether, I believe there are almost a hundred people from the tribe of Levi, counting men, women and children."

"I see. That's more than I thought."

"It *should* give us enough knowledge to work with, but if I thought that was really the case, I wouldn't be needing to ask 'only a scribe', would I?"

"How many Sabbath meetings do you plan?"

"I want one for about every 20 or 30 adults."

"All at the same time?"

"Yes. At least, more or less. Otherwise, people will distract each other, and the meetings will keep getting interrupted."

"You talked about readings from Scripture, which raises two questions: firstly, where do we get the scrolls from – I'm not sure that we have enough available – and secondly, what passages will we read?"

"They're good questions, Baruch. I'll be asking about the scriptures as I talk to people today. I made sure that I have a full set myself, and I suspect that you must have the same or something pretty close to it."

"Yes, I have a full set of scrolls written in small text. It meant that I didn't bring much else with me, though, and it was exhausting carrying them – scrolls are quite heavy when you have enough of them, as you must know!"

"Definitely. We'll have to see whether others thought the word of God was worth the effort of carrying. I know that at least two sets of large, ornate scrolls were brought by some priests – they were able to arrange for them to be carried on a cart."

"That would have made it easier."

"Yes, but the cart was hit by an arrow when the Edomites attacked. It did quite a bit of damage to the ornate Book of the Law they'd brought."

"Anyway, it sounds as if we need to get on with the work," said Baruch.

"You're right. Let's finish our meal quickly and find people to talk to. We're quite close to the middle of the block of houses we've been given. If you head south and I head north, we shouldn't waste time talking to the same people twice."

"So, just to confirm: you want meetings of 20 to 30 adults in any place where we can fit that many people and people to lead them. For this first Sabbath, each group will need a scroll that includes the Ten Commandments, so I'm to check that they can get one."

"That's right. Everyone needs to know the reason behind keeping the Sabbath, and we need to hear it from God's word. Not only that, but we need to highlight the fact that there are many other laws we must still obey although we do not have a temple anymore."

"I'll do my best. But before we go, can we pray for God's help in this work?"

CR

"No," said the woman, flatly.

"Could I speak to your husband please?"

"No, he will not be interested either."

"If you aren't interested in God's commands, that's your prerogative – but you are choosing death."

"God has already chosen death for us. You know he killed our youngest son. And at your instigation!"

I had been working my way north through the block of houses we had been allocated in Tahpanhes. Some of the responses were positive, but in this house I met the woman who had confronted me after the death of her child during the Edomite attack.

She was not willing to listen to me in any way. Instead, she blamed me for everything from the death of her son to the loss of the jewellery taken during the Chaldean invasion.

Not only so, but she was not willing to let her husband listen either.

"I will spend my time worshipping other gods," she said defiantly. "Gods that don't destroy everything I've ever worked for."

"Don't forget that sometimes we are the ones who should accept blame, madam. If you'd stayed in Judah, do you have any reason to think that the Edomites would have killed your son?"

"How would I know?"

"Then don't blame Yahweh. He warned you what would happen if you left Judah. And don't reject him now when he gives you another chance. Choose life. Obey Yahweh's commands – they help you live a life that is the best, happiest, most fulfilling life you and your family can live."

"My father was killed by the Chaldeans when Jeconiah was taken captive. All Yahweh has ever done for me is to make me suffer."

"I'm sorry to hear about your father. I knew many people who died then, but I do not blame Yahweh for it."

"If Yahweh is in control of the nations as you say, who else can we blame for the disasters that come?"

"God is in control of the nations, just as he is in control of you and me. Yet he doesn't control our every action, does he?"

"I don't believe he controls anything."

"Then why do you blame him for everything? You can't have it both ways."

"My little boy is dead. If your God is in control, then your God killed him. And if you say that God answers prayers, then you must have prayed to God to kill my son."

"You're just looking for a scapegoat, not for truth."

"And your God is looking for victims! He's never done anything good for me. Why should I worship him?"

"And what have you ever done for him?"

Maybe I should have asked that question first, because it was the only one that stopped her. For once she didn't answer immediately, and for once she really seemed to be thinking about the question instead of just what her next argument should be. Yet how bad would she feel if she did decide that all of the disasters that had befallen her were her own fault? – or, at least, the combined responsibility of herself and her society.

Accepting responsibility for our failures is never easy: it's much easier to avoid the failures in the first place. Yet none of us ever completely avoids blunders and sin, and facing up to them is terribly difficult.

I have always done my best to avoid sin and worked hard to be on God's side whenever there was a choice to be made. Yet around the time of the fall of Jerusalem, I had gradually begun losing my faith, my direction, my obedience, and everything else I treasured. It was not until God finally told me that if I returned to him he would accept me[44] that I realised how seriously I had failed. At that point, I suddenly saw clearly that if we ever stop putting God first and foremost in our life, we are making a choice to leave him.

---

[44] Jeremiah 15:19-20

God is good. That seems obvious to any godly person, but it understates the situation: God is *all* there is, and without him, nothing is worth having.

I kept trying to convince this woman of what God meant when he urged his people to choose life, but I failed – for the moment at least. She had had more tragedy than she could handle without using others as scapegoats.

Neither she nor her husband would be with us to celebrate the Sabbath.

Yet my visits were receiving more positive responses than I had expected. The number of people who said they would come to celebrate the Sabbath was proving to be a big surprise.

Even Johanan said that he would join us and that we could have a meeting in the courtyard in front of his house. I hadn't asked for that, as I wasn't sure that I wanted his help in the organisation. His attitude in first asking for God's guidance and then ignoring it when it didn't suit him was not encouraging. Nevertheless, he assured me that he felt that worship of Yahweh was very important and that we should pay close attention to our worship in this foreign land.

His words sounded right, but I wasn't convinced that his thinking matched his words. Or maybe he meant something different from what I understood. After all, he had "paid close attention" to our worship in Judah and done his best to control it.

However, by nature, I always tend to think the best of people and their motives, so I accepted his offer and moved on.

By the end, Baruch and I had received commitments to run worship in ten different congregations, and we were elated.

The meetings were planned for the morning of the Sabbath. Was there anything else that we could do to prepare for our worship?

℞

Baruch and I met for lunch and decided to spend the afternoon talking to others, trying to encourage the reformation I was hoping for.

Older people are always open to reminiscing, so in my visiting, I prompted quite a few of them to remember King Josiah and the spectacular fire of reformation that he had lit in Judah in his eighteenth year.[45] Many of them recalled with pleasure the reading of the Book of the Law when the king himself had stood and led the nation in worship.[46]

That was a time of genuine greatness for the kingdom of Judah – a time when the entire nation was elevated to seek God, every man and woman seeming to stumble on a conviction that there were greater possibilities within them that the worship of God could unleash. Josiah had presented a picture of godliness that struck a chord and hollowed out a welcoming home in the normally hard hearts of the nation. For a time, people outdid themselves in living the law in all its generosity and greatness.

Using Josiah's glorious reformation to inspire another seemed the method most likely to succeed.

Many younger people listened to the reminiscing, and I was astounded just how few had even heard of Josiah's inspiring behaviour! We older ones could recall the special Passover that followed and describe the crowded streets and houses of Jerusalem and the joy that filled the

---

[45] 2 Chronicles 34:8-21. See also Volume 2 – As Good As It Gets.
[46] 2 Chronicles 34:29-30

city.[47] In trying to appeal to the aged, God had led me to retell a story that was guaranteed to intrigue and attract the young!

I remembered how King Josiah had inspired me as a young man and shown what a young man could do for his nation if he wanted to work hard enough.

I also took the opportunity to describe what a Sabbath of rest should look like. Food preparation was to be done before nightfall, so I urged them all: Start now! God doesn't want us concentrating on cooking during the Sabbath.

The women seemed to be almost evenly divided in their opinions on this. Some liked the idea of preparing twice as much food today with the benefit of avoiding any preparation tomorrow, but others felt it was just extra hard work being loaded onto them.

I encouraged the former and argued against the latter.

The men were divided too. Some looked forward to the idea of rest, pleased at the thought of their family resting together and worshipping together. Others thought they should be busy organising their new dwelling, their family or their business, or doing whatever was needed to make sure they could survive in Tahpanhes.

If nothing else, we had certainly got the people talking about worship and the Sabbath. That was a triumph worth celebrating, whatever happened on the morrow.

As sunset approached, many were finishing cooking the family dinner and the food for the Sabbath.

Never had I seen my nation paying so much attention to the Sabbath, and I was excited to see what the next morning would bring!

---

[47] 2 Chronicles 35:1-19

❦

As the sun set, Baruch and I discussed the results of our efforts. I was excited and hopeful, Baruch a little more restrained. Perhaps he would have said he was being more realistic.

However, to me, the prospect of ten groups of people gathering to read the Ten Commandments was a triumph. How many would finally attend, I could not tell, but I hoped and believed that the numbers would be high.

Once again, I spent several hours of the night in prayer. God had to be thanked for the success that we had already had. That day I had seen priests and Levites shaken out of their apathy and moved to open their scrolls. In the morning, scripture would be read out loud in Tahpanhes, perhaps for the first time!

It was a long night; not without some uncertainty, but generally a happy, joyous time of prayer.

Chapter 12

Keeping the Sabbath

Once more I climbed up to the roof in the darkness before dawn. I watched the horizon brighten, saw the pink light spread to all corners of the sky and enjoyed the gradual lightening of the streets and corners. However, again, I could not wait for the sun to rise. The day had arrived and the work of the Sabbath must begin.

Why do I refer to the *work* of the Sabbath? Because, on Sabbaths, those who do God's work are meant to be busy. Not for them the rest that God commanded for the remainder of the nation: they must help the people in their worship. That was to be my work for the day.

C3

When the third hour of the day arrived, we began celebrating our first Sabbath in Tahpanhes. By that time, I had visited each of the places where a Sabbath meeting was to take place, to check that everything was ready. As I prepared for our own meeting, I couldn't help thinking of Shobai, the faithful servant of God from Bethel, and the Sabbath-day meetings he had arranged with fellow worshippers of Yahweh all those years ago. While others in

Bethel had been busy with the calf-worship instituted by Jeroboam the son of Nebat, or with the worship of Baal, Asherah and many other idols, Shobai had gathered together a congregation to worship Yahweh and to read from the Book of the Law, the Psalms and the Prophets.

This morning, many in Tahpanhes would be pursuing their own comfort or worshipping the multitude of Egyptian gods, but we would be able to worship God and enjoy his Sabbaths, even in this foreign city.

Although – after so many disappointments – I scarcely dared admit it even to myself, I was hoping that we could develop our religion into something that would form the centre of our community. Surely God would forgive if we diligently tried to worship him as best we could?

I was to be part of a congregation that met right in front of the house that Baruch and I had been allocated. A well was there, in the centre of an open area that could easily seat 50 people, particularly with the way the shadows fell before the heat of the day fully came.

People assembled in dribs and drabs as they do, many looking tentative or sheepish. Yet there was also a sense of anticipation in the crowd that filled me with hope.

I had arranged for a Levite to lead the meeting of worship and I was to read. He had asked me to lead instead, but I wanted to take the opportunity to read the chosen scripture to the people.

Once we had prayed with the words of a Psalm of David, we sang a Psalm also. It was one of the new Psalms written in Babylon by the exiles there and sent to Jerusalem for us to include in the nation's songs of worship.

I had chosen it because of its connection with our position as exiles, although it was particularly associated with Babylon. It was a sad psalm with a haunting melody. I found it hard to sing without having my voice crack with emotion:

"By the waters of Babylon, there we sat down and wept,
when we remembered Zion.
On the willows there we hung up our lyres.
For there our captors required of us songs,
and our tormentors, mirth, saying,
'Sing us one of the songs of Zion!'
How shall we sing the Lord's song in a foreign land?"[48]

I wanted the people to make the connection with our countrymen in that far distant land, but it also had a section that seemed irresistibly relevant for us:

"Remember, O Lord, against the Edomites
the day of Jerusalem,
how they said, 'Lay it bare, lay it bare,
down to its foundations!' "[49]

Many did not know the Psalm, but both I and the Levite who was leading the meeting did, so we sang it together first and then he encouraged the rest of the people to join in. As a singing performance it was far from rivalling the singing of the Levites when Josiah had read from the Book of the Law, but it was a good start.

At times, music can unlock emotion in a way that allows our consciences to work more freely. And on that bright spring morning as we sat around a well in Tahpanhes, surrounded by undeserved blessings from God, it certainly did for me. I hoped that it would do the same for others. We had much to regret in the way our nation had lived, and our very presence in Egypt was something of a slap in the face of God. I felt guilty for everyone and prayed silently for the mercy we all need in the face of a holy God.

I was then invited to come forward and read from the Law of Moses, and I stood and unrolled my scroll in front

---

[48] Psalm 137:1-4
[49] Psalm 137:7

of them all. I read a section that introduced the Ten Commandments, and then read the commandments themselves as loudly and clearly as possible. I went on to read the response of the nation at Sinai and concluded with the words:

> "Moses said to the people,
> 'Do not fear, for God has come to test you,
> that the fear of him may be before you,
> that you may not sin.' "[50]

There was no doubt that everyone was listening. God's leading of his nation out of Egypt and the demonstration of his power at Mount Sinai are exciting narratives and describe a people utterly convinced of the presence of God and terrified that they were in mortal danger.

After reading the words of God, I was asked to teach the assembly. The Ten Commandments are simple but demanding laws. They demand control over our behaviour, our emotions, our worship, and even our thoughts.

I reminded them that what God was asking of his people was faithfulness and obedience. He promised us life if we obeyed and death if we did not. Yet he also promised a land in which we could live in peace and safety.

We needed to start all over again, I insisted. We were in a disastrous situation because we had failed to obey, but we could still return to God and try again. God was merciful, and he would show us loving kindness if only we would repent.

After we had all sung another Psalm, the Levite asked me to finish our Sabbath worship with the priests' blessing. It was an unexpected but delightful request: those words have always been some of my favourite words of scripture. I stood and looked around at the people as they sat about me in many different positions, some with eyes glued to

---

[50] Exodus 20:20

my face, others with eyes closed in contemplation. The morning was warming up quickly and the intense brightness of the sunshine seemed fitting as I recited:

"The Lord bless you and keep you;
the Lord make his face to shine upon you
and be gracious to you;
the Lord lift up his countenance upon you
and give you peace."[51]

Our first meeting of worship in Egypt was over, and how wonderful it had been! I sensed that we had begun a new chapter in the history of our nation, and my dreams immediately raced far ahead of reality. I saw this small collection of disobedient Jews turning to God with their whole heart. I dreamed of God reversing his threat to destroy everyone who had come down to Egypt and instead leading us gently back to his land as a shepherd would care for defenceless lambs.

Our time of worship that morning began a different sort of worship from that which the land of Judah had known. No temple, no sacrifices, no grand ceremonies – instead, the worship of a nation offered just because we wanted to worship. Low-key and quiet. I hoped it was genuine.

One small part of me pointed out bitterly that it was more likely to be genuine because there were no priests on the take; no fraudsters who promoted the worship of God as long as it lined their pockets, but never lived it themselves!

Many remained after we finished simply to chat. I couldn't help smiling when I noticed some of those I knew as tireless workers looking a little lost. With the Sabbath in progress, the tasks that busied their daily lives were forcibly put on hold. A discussion of God's love for Israel over the centuries was one way to use their time, but few

---

[51] Numbers 6:24-26

were in the habit of such conversation. Instead, they looked lost. Moses had told parents that one of their most important tasks was to teach their children about Yahweh,[52] and that times of worship were perfect opportunities to do this, yet there were few children present. Of course, I have never been a father, but it seemed obvious to me that the teaching Moses had commanded was for daily life and intended as an addition to the worship of the nation experienced through feasts and other special times. What a perfect time the Sabbath should be for this sort of teaching, when the time was already set aside and dedicated to God!

Many smiles surrounded me, yet people seemed uncertain what to do.

"Sharing worship together in a strange land is an opportunity for us to build community," I observed to the leader of the service. I took full advantage of the powers of penetration God put in my voice, doing my best to give people a hint. "The people here today are the ones with whom we can discuss the differences between the people of Yahweh and the people of Egypt. We're not looking for conflict, just trying to understand and maintain the separation between a living God and the masses of dead and powerless gods worshipped in Egypt."

A man I knew only by sight unwittingly gave me the help I needed.

"You read from the Ten Commandments, and I have a question about the last one. What is wrong with coveting? Everyone always says that we need to have a plan; goals for the future. We're encouraged to be aware of the things we're working for, and that seems to make sense, don't you think?"

"Some of the earlier commandments seem to be connected with that last commandment," I answered. "For

---

[52] Deuteronomy 6:7

example, it seems clear to me that 'do not commit adultery' is connected with one of the examples of what you should not covet: your neighbour's wife. Adultery is clearly wrong, but so is the desire that leads to adultery. Allowing yourself to covet your neighbour's wife makes you much more likely to commit adultery with her."

"That make sense, I suppose," replied my questioner.

" 'Do not steal' is closely linked to the other examples of coveting too," added the Levite. "If you want your neighbour's goods so much that you keep thinking about them and coveting them – whether his servants or his animals or his house or anything else – you are much more likely to steal them."

"That's right," I agreed. "And to go one step further, if I covet my neighbour's goods, I may end up killing him to get them, or telling lies about him in court to get him into trouble in the hope that I can win his goods."

The man who had asked the question looked thoughtful and the Levite said to him, "I hadn't seen it all so clearly before myself, so thanks for asking the question. Although it's the last commandment, if you break it, you are much more likely to break the previous four as well."

The discussion continued, and many of the group listened for a while before gradually breaking up into smaller groups to talk among themselves. Some left, but most stayed and joined in discussions about the Ten Commandments.

For me, the crowning joy of the time of worship was when various men and women, and even some of the older children, came and said that they had enjoyed the time of worship and would come again the next week.

I tried to pass the afternoon writing the diary I had begun on the day the survivors had rejected God's commands, claiming that God had not spoken to me at all.

I had not got very far, but beginning the task had nudged my memory. My life as a teenager filled my mind and I relived the beginning of my work as a prophet. My father has been dead for many years, but I thought over the times we had spent together. The times of peace that I preferred to remember were far less common than the times of conflict, but he did set me some good examples and it was pleasant to think of them.

I remembered my brother Azariah, who viewed me as an upstart and a trouble-maker. I didn't want to be either, but I did desperately want to know God and his ways, and God told me that I was to be a prophet to the nations. If I wanted to please God, I had no choice.

Azariah never believed me and nor did his son, Seraiah. Both are dead now, and that made me sad, too.

Baruch was in the house and obviously read the distress on my face. He knew about my task of writing the diary and guessed what made me upset.

To distract me, Baruch brought out a scroll of all the words God had given me, from the first words in the thirteenth year of Josiah until the answer God gave when the leaders asked whether we should travel to Egypt. I had told him of God's latest words about Egypt, but they had not yet been added to the scroll. He asked if he could write them down straight away so that nothing would be lost.

Thankful for the offered distraction, I dictated God's words to him. He wrote them down on a small piece of parchment, then asked me where he should include them in the record of my work. I suggested that they should go with other prophecies of Egypt and we looked through the scroll to find an appropriate place.

"Will God have more words for you?" asked Baruch.

"I don't know for certain," I answered cautiously, "but these words ended with a very strong feeling that more would be coming."

"Should I cut up the scroll and add in a new sheet to fit this section and anything else that comes?"

How easy a simple narrative is compared with this task! God had instructed me to record all of his messages and I had done so, but many of the messages have been repeated through the years and delivered to many different people. I'm afraid that producing an organised, collated written record will never be easy!

Once the dictation was finished and I had instructed Baruch where to insert the new text, I went back to my diary.

Straight away, my despondency returned.

What had happened to the optimism that had filled me during and after our new and novel meeting of worship?

I was sure that if I did not find a way to overcome this sadness, I would never complete my diary or be able to pursue the reformation I was so much hoping for.

I tried to turn my thoughts in different directions, but whatever direction I chose, they soon led me into another avenue of memories down which I didn't want to walk.

Praising God for a few moments took my thoughts to the Psalms, but rehearsing the Psalms filled my mind with a tuneful voice and a lovely face that I had had to leave behind. Reading the Scripture reminded me of the attempts of the scribes to rewrite the Book of the Law to match human preferences. Their efforts were thwarted on that occasion, but what would happen in the future?

Every direction my mind pursued led me into sadness or hopelessness. The joy of the morning simply could not be reclaimed.

In the end, I gave up all attempts to write and began to talk to Baruch, who, by that time, had finished his work on the scroll.

Our discussion ranged far and wide, exploring the history of our people. We couldn't do that without acknowledging the failures of our fathers, but they merely highlighted the amazing blessings of a faithful creator who had cared for our people through good times and bad. If God only treated us kindly when we had *earned* it, our nation's outlook would be bleak indeed, but there was so much evidence in our history that God went a long way beyond what we deserved when showering blessings upon us.

By the time dusk came, I had managed to recover my happiness and hopefulness.

I made a mental note for myself that next Sabbath I might be wise to avoid my diary! In any case, it was perhaps too much like the "ordinary work" that should be avoided on the Sabbath.

A beautiful sunset completed the day and, tired, I was able to fall into a happy sleep. The Sabbath had really been a blessing.

Chapter 13

Families

Over the next few days, an idea that had occurred to me during the Sabbath came back to trouble me several times.

Moses gave a simple command that families should speak about God's law not just in times of worship, but at *all* times. Thinking that it would be a helpful passage to read during one of our meetings for worship, I searched it out.

The idea occurs a few times in Moses' writings, but it is explained most clearly in two particular places. These passages tell any reader who will listen, that God's laws should be in the mouths of families *all the time*. Not only that, but one of them pairs the idea with a reminder to the people that Israel has only one God, Yahweh. That thought too would be worth studying one Sabbath in Egypt, a land of many idols.

"Hear, O Israel: The Lord our God, the Lord is one.
You shall love the Lord your God
with all your heart
and with all your soul
and with all your might.
And these words that I command you today

shall be on your heart.
You shall teach them diligently to your children,
and shall talk of them when you sit in your house,
and when you walk by the way,
and when you lie down,
and when you rise.
You shall bind them as a sign on your hand,
and they shall be as frontlets between your eyes.
You shall write them on the doorposts of your house
and on your gates."[53]

Love of God must completely fill us, and for parents, that must show in the topics of conversation in the home. There was also the challenge of understanding exactly what was meant by 'a sign on your hand', 'frontlets between your eyes' and writing 'on the doorposts'. Were these intended to be taken literally?

Reading these words forced me to review the topics of conversation in my own home as I grew up. In retrospect, I wondered: did the talk at the High Priest's meal table match the requirements God had laid down for his nation?

And as I thought, I must admit that I was disappointed with the answer. We did talk about God's law at home from time to time, but my memory suggests that much more of our time was spent on other topics of conversation than was spent discussing God and his law.

I don't want this diary to become an attack on my father. He is not here and cannot defend himself, and in any case, memories are notoriously unreliable, particularly if there is a conflict of character – which I think there was between my father and me. He could not understand me and I could not really understand him either. My mother was stuck in the middle between us, which made

---

[53] Deuteronomy 6:4-9

her life very difficult at times. In temperament and preferred approach to worship, she was much closer to me, yet she must honour her husband, particularly as he was also the High Priest. As I grew up and was chosen by Yahweh as his prophet, I had to learn to honour my father without allowing his attitudes to lead me away from God. At least, that was how I viewed it. God came first and honour for my father must come second to that.

My father spoke often about the temple, and I'm sure that he thought he was honouring God in so doing. Yet I did not find his comments satisfying. Administrative questions were common topics, as was the need to fit the worship of God around what he called the "realities of life". The paramount importance of there being only one God was pushed to one side or twisted. The fact that God was one was acknowledged in word, but other gods must nevertheless be tolerated because they were so popular, and one never knew when the tides of popular opinion might turn. Having grown up during the reign of Manasseh, when priests either cooperated with false religion or perished, my father and his family had learned to collaborate rather than confront. Tolerance and careful words were my father's greatest delights. Ensuring that, as High Priest, he did not upset those who did not worship Yahweh was more important to him than almost anything else.

It was a tightrope of compromise. If you had asked my father directly, he would always have said that Yahweh was his master – and he believed it utterly. Yet King Manasseh was also his master, and, of course, he struggled to satisfy both at once! To truly satisfy either was to anger the other.

My father and my grandfather; my brother and my nephew; all chose a path that angered Yahweh. Yet both my father and my brother had been High Priest in a time when our king was Josiah – a righteous man who would have supported them in fearlessly walking the right path. In fact, Josiah did his best to lead *them* in service to God, though they should have been the ones providing spiritual leadership for the king and the nation.

So where did Josiah gain his spiritual strength? Where did he learn to love Yahweh with all his heart, all his soul and all his strength? Certainly not from his father Amon! He was an intrinsically evil king whose behaviour was so bad that his own servants assassinated him while he was still a young man.[54]

Did Josiah's godliness come from his mother in the same way as height or beauty or intelligence often seem to come from one or both parents? Or was it from the active teaching he received as a young child? King Amon was married to Queen Jedidah, the daughter of Adaiah of Bozkath,[55] a small town near the Philistine border. They were both very young when they married – as has been true for most of the royal family over several centuries. But though Amon was just 15 years old and Jedidah even younger, she was a godly young girl who had done nothing to deserve the substandard husband she got!

Amon was convinced to marry her because of her beauty and quietly delightful character, and fortunately he left Josiah's upbringing almost entirely to the queen and the nurses she chose. Of course, one could argue that no king can have enough time to both reign over a kingdom and lead his family, but I am increasingly convinced that the bringing up of his children is an essential part of being a king. After all, a good and righteous king who does *not* bring up his heir to live a righteous life will normally bequeath his kingdom to an evil son who will quickly undo all his father's good work.

---

[54] 2 Kings 21:19-23
[55] 2 Kings 21:25-2:1

Sadly, this is precisely what happened after the death of Josiah – but I'll get to that later.

As I said, Jedidah was a beautiful woman, but she was also godly, and it was her godliness that helped the kingdom most amazingly. I was not a member of the royal household, but I heard from my father, and later from Shaphan and Ahikam, that it was common for the queen to sit with Josiah on her lap telling him stories of the great history of Israel. He learned of Abraham, Isaac and Jacob *from his mother*, just as I did from mine.

It seems that she was literally keeping God's command to talk about him and his laws in the house while sitting, eating and drinking. In fact, King Josiah himself once mentioned to me that his mother had taught him many stories about his ancestor King David as she put him to bed at night – including the inspiring tale about him killing Goliath the giant.

Yes, Josiah was a good example of a man who was taught godliness as a child, and chose to make it his own at an early age.

If only he had been able to give the same gift to his sons who reigned after him!

However, Josiah's wives were not of the same quality as his mother. Though beautiful in form and features, their characters were not so attractive.

Three of Josiah's sons reigned after him, and not one of them was good – either in the quality of his reign or in his moral standing. Jehoahaz was the first to reign and he reigned for only three months before being taken away captive to Egypt. Though not the oldest son, he was appointed king by the people of the land because he was less objectionable than his older brother Eliakim. Unfortunately, when Jehoahaz was taken away by Pharaoh Neco, Eliakim was made king anyway, and renamed Jehoiakim.

Two kings from two different mothers: Hamutal, the daughter of Jeremiah of Libnah, was the mother of Jehoahaz;[56] and Zebidah, daughter of Pedaiah of Rumah, was the mother of Jehoiakim.[57]

Were they evil women? I don't really know, but the hints I have heard suggest that they were more likely to care about their own comfort than to talk to their sons about God. After all, a king's wives can make up their own minds whether to care for their children themselves or leave it all to nurses. My mother never left *me* to be brought up by nurses, although our family was rich enough to have as many servants and nurses as my mother might have wanted. I was blessed that she chose to look after me herself.

King Zedekiah was a full brother of Jehoahaz, but he was far too easily led by his friends. And anyone could see that he didn't choose good friends! Could his mother have made a difference if she had spent more time talking to her sons – the two future kings – about God and what he expected of a king?

I can't judge, but I can observe the results. Hamutal had two sons who ruled over Judah,[58] but neither will be held up to future generations as a king to emulate. Both were taken away as captives – Jehoahaz to Egypt[59] and Zedekiah to Babylon[60] – and it was prophesied of each that they would die in captivity.[61]

Briefly I wondered whether there was any way to find out if Jehoahaz was still alive in prison, somewhere in

---

[56] 2 Kings 23:31

[57] 2 Kings 23:36

[58] 2 Kings 23:31; 24:18

[59] 2 Kings 23:34

[60] 2 Kings 25:6-7; Jeremiah 39:7; 52:11

[61] Of Jehoahaz: Jeremiah 22:11-12 (where he is called Shallum); Ezekiel 19:3-4. Of Zedekiah: Jeremiah 32:3-5; 34:3-5; Ezekiel 12:13.

Egypt. It's about 23 years since he was taken away, which would be a long time to survive in an Egyptian prison.

In some ways, this result is symbolic of the failure of the descendants of Jacob as a whole. As a nation, we have taken the path of idolatry and rebellion instead of passing on the laws and love of God to our children and our children's children.

Some of Zedekiah's daughters have come with us to Egypt, but none of them ever even met their grandfather Josiah, let alone sat at his feet to learn about Yahweh.

What a colossal failure of family can be seen among the descendants of Abraham, Isaac and Jacob!

Chapter 14

Pharaoh's Palace

March 583BC

One day, for no particular reason that I could think of, I went to have a look at Pharaoh's palace in Tahpanhes. He was not there at the time – in fact, he ordinarily spent little time there. Zau was his chosen royal city, and that was where most of the machinery of government was maintained.

Yet even when a palace is not graced by the reigning monarch, that doesn't mean it is empty. Different members of the royal family spend extended times there throughout the year, while others pass through on journeys and stay for days or weeks.

And a palace, however full or empty it may be, needs maintaining. Pharaoh's palace in Tahpanhes was always being worked on! Existing walls needed repairing from time to time. Paint was touched up or completely redone. Cracked and worn out pavements were patched, replaced or even completely redesigned, and as I studied the imposing building, I saw workmen doing precisely that.

I was glad that the responsibility of *paying* for the upkeep of the palace was not mine! Rich though my family was, I'm sure that our fortune would have been consumed in days if we'd had to pay the bills to maintain that palace!

Looking at the palace, I marvelled at the marble and other expensive materials used in its construction. I saw the huge obelisks near the entrance and was utterly amazed by the idea that such massive stones had been transported from a great distance, and for what? This entire edifice was maintained for the pleasure of just one man, so that he could visit it when the fancy took him. And not only was this grand palace mostly unused by its owner, but I knew that there were several other, equally grand, palaces spread throughout Egypt that were likewise kept in constant readiness, yet spent most of their time unoccupied by the Pharaoh.

A king can spend his nation's money in any way he chooses, but I couldn't help trying to calculate how many of the inhabitants of besieged Jerusalem, those who died of hunger, could have been kept alive with the food that filled the stomachs of the servants who maintained Pharaoh's empty palaces!

After observing the palace and studying the nearby temples, I returned home, wondering why I had wasted my time on idle sightseeing.

That night, I learned why.

My prayers to God were drawing to an end and I was beginning to feel drowsy when suddenly I noticed that the sounds of the city were beginning to recede. Having experienced this once before in our house in Anathoth, I understood what was happening a little more quickly than I had on that occasion. The room was in complete darkness – I had no money to spare for burning a lamp during my prayers! – yet as the silence and deep calm seemed to cut me off from the surrounding city, light began to spread through the room. I know that this sounds strange, but it was a light that was dim yet intense; white, but filled with all the colours of the rainbow.

I knew that I was in the presence of Yahweh and I waited for him to speak. His voice did not seem to echo at all, yet it filled me, and filled the room, in a way that must be experienced to be understood:

"Take in your hands large stones
and hide them in the mortar in the pavement
that is at the entrance to Pharaoh's palace in Tahpanhes,
in the sight of the men of Judah."[62]

As God spoke, I saw, in the dim light, pictures of Pharaoh's palace in Tahpanhes. Were they in my mind's eye or somehow presented in the room? I don't know, but they showed me the pavement I had been looking at that afternoon. Workmen had been removing both the paving stones and the underlying mortar in which they were set. Several deep holes were left in the pavement where larger stones had been removed, and as I watched, God gave me instructions about that pavement.

I must take stones and put them in the pavement, or maybe under the pavement. It seemed a peculiar request, and the awkwardness of obedience struck me again, as it has so many times before. Would the workmen allow me to? God has commanded me to do many things that have been impossible in any practical or logical manner. Yet each time I have set about obeying, events have worked out just as God said they would. Unlikely, but inevitable, you might say. Here was another unlikely command: after all, who would allow some unknown Jewish prophet to come along and place large stones in the king's pavement? How could it possibly work?

Yet I knew that it would – somehow. The vision continued:

"…and say to them,
'Thus says the Lord of hosts, the God of Israel:
Behold, I will send and take Nebuchadnezzar

---

[62] Jeremiah 43:9

the king of Babylon, my servant,
and I will set his throne
above these stones that I have hidden,
and he will spread his royal canopy over them.
He shall come and strike the land of Egypt,
giving over to the pestilence
those who are doomed to the pestilence,
to captivity those who are doomed to captivity,
and to the sword those who are doomed to the sword.
I shall kindle a fire in the temples of the gods of Egypt,
and he shall burn them and carry them away captive.
And he shall clean the land of Egypt
as a shepherd cleans his cloak of vermin,
and he shall go away from there in peace.
He shall break the obelisks of Heliopolis,
which is in the land of Egypt,
and the temples of the gods of Egypt
he shall burn with fire.' "[63]

As God's words continued, I sat up and began to feel more and more uncomfortable. You see, we had heard rumours that Pharaoh would soon be visiting Tahpanhes. Imagine if Pharaoh Hophra was there when I went to put on this show! Firstly, there was the possible conflict over putting large stones into his special pavement; but even assuming that part worked out successfully, what would happen when Pharaoh heard this message about Nebuchadnezzar? He'd already dismissed the warning I delivered in Zau, and this was much more detailed.

Put yourself in the position of Pharaoh, perhaps inspecting the work around his palace, only to hear a foreigner delivering a message of coming disaster for Egypt to an audience of foreigners on his very doorstep. Wouldn't he think that I was treating his palace as a spectacle, a venue for my own religious presentations? Not

---

[63] Jeremiah 43:10-13

only so, but he would no doubt remember that he had generously welcomed these particular foreigners into his country, even to the extent of providing them with lodgings!

I shook my head as the struggle in my mind continued. If you were Pharaoh, wouldn't such a series of events convince you that these foreigners were extremely ungrateful? I was sure that would be my attitude, and confident how I would respond! Would my delivery of this prophecy be the beginning of the promised pursuit by the sword of my people in the land of Egypt?

Those were my thoughts, and I hope you will excuse my lack of faith in God. I got very little sleep that night. I would obey – but I was worried.

In the morning, I returned to the palace, praying for guidance and planning to make a few observations prior to following God's instructions. Pharaoh's palace was served by a grand avenue that swept through the centre of Tahpanhes and paid homage to its grandeur. Spread out before the imposing palace lay a large courtyard which rose slowly above the avenue, narrowing gradually so that its design inevitably filled any visitors with an appropriate sense of awe as it led them, finally, to the massive palace doors. An enormous column stood on each side of the courtyard and the magnificent doors formed a fitting entrance to Pharaoh's palace. The picture of royal elegance was almost perfect – except that the construction of the broad, sweeping pavement was still in progress.

Work was progressing rapidly under the guidance of the royal architect, so how could I follow God's instructions and put large stones under the pavement?

Viewing the site again didn't help: no obvious way to proceed came to mind. Prayer still appeared to be my only way forward, so I continued to ask God for guidance while looking around for practical answers. Yet I knew that I couldn't keep on delaying: if nothing obvious arose,

I would have to begin to make arrangements and see what happened; see how the situation worked out.

Where would I get large stones from? There were some smoothed paving stones lying around, but the workmen would not want me to take their prepared paving stones and bury them under the pavement! In the end, I gave up and went back home. I would have to collect my audience first and take them to the palace to see the display, trusting that God would arrange it as he wanted. It reminded me of the time when I had been told to collect some elders and act out a parable for them near the Potsherd Gate. Recalling the beating I received immediately afterwards, I hoped that *that* wouldn't happen again!

For the rest of the day, I went around talking to or leaving messages for the men of Judah. I advised that I would show them a message from God at the entrance to Pharaoh's palace at noon the next day, and that they should attend to hear Yahweh's words. Some made it brutally clear that they would not be attending. A few even referred to the time at Chimham's Inn when I had last given them a message, and scoffed at the idea of listening to me again.

Fortunately however, others were equally definite in the other direction, so I expected that at least some people would be there to hear. Whether or not they would listen could not be told.

A little before noon on the following day, I went around again and reminded some of the leaders that God wanted them to come and listen to his words; then I went to Pharaoh's palace in trepidation because I still wasn't sure what I would be doing about those stones.

When I arrived, several men of Judah were already waiting.

"What's the show this time, Jeremiah?" asked Rapha, a man known for his laziness. He had probably come early to avoid work, but at least he was there.

"You'll find out once more people have arrived," I said.

"Well, Jeremiah, you told us how bad it would be coming to Egypt. You've been wrong, haven't you?"

"Was it *good* to have the Edomites attack us and kill people?" I asked. "I'd call that bad enough, and that is just a starter."

"Why do you keep working as a prophet?"

"I love Yahweh, so I do what he tells me – it's that simple."

"But why only you? Surely you could get him to share the work around with others?"

"He does share the work around. That's why I don't have to go to Babylon any more: Yahweh is using other people there to do his work. The important part is that *he* chooses who to use as a prophet. Not me. Not you."

While we talked, several more of our countrymen joined us in front of the palace. I quickly estimated the numbers and decided that there were enough there to begin the presentation.

Turning back towards the entrance, I saw a line of men staggering out of the palace. Each was struggling under the weight of a large stone, which they piled just outside the door. Were those the 'large stones' I needed? I hurried across and asked the men if the stones were being disposed of.

"Yes," answered one. "Not only are they a little too small for what we need for the decorative bath we're building, they're also the wrong colour. They really can't be used in the palace at all. They don't quite match the basic colours, but they don't provide enough contrast either."

"Do you mind if I use some of them?" I asked.

"Feel free. Then we won't need to get rid of so many."

Requirement number one was suddenly satisfied.

Amazingly, as we spoke, the other tricky question was also in the process of being answered. As I walked back towards my waiting audience, I had to pass the group of men working on the pavement. They had stopped work and were looking frustrated as they talked to a man dressed in formal clothes. I overheard enough of their discussion to understand that there was a question about the final height of the pavement.

"We can't raise the level without having to get in more fill. And that will blow your budget."

"The chief architect has revised the drawings. He wants the level of the pavement to begin to rise a little earlier than was proposed in the original design. The slope needs to be introduced immediately, right at the joint between the road and the pavement. The architect is convinced that it will improve the appearance – and the drainage as well."

"But raising the level so soon requires fill that we don't have. And getting extra fill will delay the completion of the pavement by at least a week. It'll be three weeks before we can finish, but we were told we had to finish within two. Isn't Pharaoh coming in two weeks' time? Just imagine how happy he'll be when he arrives and sees a worksite instead of the newly finished pavement he's been promised!"

I felt that I knew enough to make it worthwhile to interrupt. "Excuse me," I said, "I hear that you need to raise the level of the pavement and don't have enough fill to do so." Both the workman and the architect's representative nodded their heads in confirmation. "Well, there's a pile of stones near the door that can't be used inside. Could they be used here as fill? There are only a few stacked there at the moment, but I believe that there are still quite a lot more inside that can't be used."

The reaction was tentative, but positive.

"That could be useful," said the chief worker, "but where did you get the information from?"

"Workers started bringing out the stones a few moments ago. Look, there are some more coming now."

"How about I go and talk to them and see what we can work out," said the architect's man, marching off to the entry where workers were piling more stones near the doorway.

"Can I leave it up to him?" mused the chief worker. "I'm concerned that if we don't get everything confirmed officially, we'll finish the pavement and then have to rip it up again. Or I'll get blamed for wastage and lose my job."

Making up his mind, he too walked across to the doorway and joined in the discussion.

After a short while, he returned and told his workers to collect some of the stones. He was content that he had authority to use at least *some* of the stones, enough to start his men working where the pavement met the roadway.

The men crossed to where the stones were stacked near the doorway and began to carry them to where they would be used as fill to raise the level of the new pavement.

"Can I help you?" I asked.

The worker looked surprised. "Why?" he asked.

"I am giving a message to my countrymen from Yahweh, our God. These stones would be just right for my message, since I could bury them under the pavement. I want to lift some of the pavement stones you've already placed and put a few of these stones underneath. I'll bury them in the existing fill so that the level should be pretty close to what you need. If you want, you can use your mortar to make sure that the path profile is exactly what you want. After that, I'd put the pavement stones back on top of the mortar. You could finish the work by fitting them properly in place if I don't get it right."

He didn't look completely convinced, so I hurried on, "It won't slow you down, and it might even speed your work up a bit. And don't forget, it was I who gave you the solution to your problem with levels and fill."

"I suppose so. Are you a mason?"

"No," I laughed, "I'm a prophet – but I'll be careful!"

The man still looked doubtful, but responded, "Well, we'll keep collecting stones and bringing them across. You can start your prophesying if you want. Just don't forget that if you're messing up the work we need to do, I'll have to stop you. Nothing against you personally, but we need to get on with this. Even with these stones as fill, we'll still have more work to do than was planned. And some work we'll have to redo." He looked around in disgust and grumbled, "Oh, why can't these architects get things right in the first place?"

All of this remarkable arrangement had taken very little time to come together, but in that time, more of my audience had arrived. Everything was working out amazingly well – not that I should have been surprised with God involved! I returned to the start of the pavement and called the men of Judah to me. Since I was speaking in Hebrew, it was as if we were having a private meeting, despite being at the junction of a busy road and an important construction site.

"Yahweh has a message for you to hear," I began. "But first, I have a sign to show you." I walked across to where the workers had stacked some of the stones I was to bury, as well as the paving stones that were to be laid on top. One worker was mixing mortar nearby and everything was ready for my display. All prepared ideally for me by God's coordination.

Everything went well. I took the large stones in my hands and hid them in the mortar of the pavement at the entrance to Pharaoh's palace in Tahpanhes. Everything went according to plan in exact detail.

With the demonstration complete – the part I had worried so much about – I was able to deliver the verbal message as well:

" 'Thus says the Lord of hosts, the God of Israel:
Behold, I will send and take Nebuchadnezzar
the king of Babylon, my servant,
and I will set his throne
above these stones that I have hidden,
and he will spread his royal canopy over them.' "[64]

Normally when I speak to an audience it becomes very clear very quickly what the majority response is. In this case, it was no surprise that my audience was not happy. They had had experience with Nebuchadnezzar, and they had also made it clear that they were afraid of him. After all, it was fear of him that had driven them to flee to Egypt.

I knew that the next words I had to speak would be even worse:

" 'He shall come and strike the land of Egypt,
giving over to the pestilence
those who are doomed to the pestilence,
to captivity those who are doomed to captivity,
and to the sword those who are doomed to the sword.
I shall kindle a fire in the temples of the gods of Egypt,
and he shall burn them and carry them away captive.
And he shall clean the land of Egypt
as a shepherd cleans his cloak of vermin,
and he shall go away from there in peace.
He shall break the obelisks of Heliopolis,
which is in the land of Egypt,

---

[64] Jeremiah 43:10

and the temples of the gods of Egypt
he shall burn with fire.' "[65]

I was right. My audience had seen Nebuchadnezzar breaking down *our* cities and burning *our* temple with fire. Egypt had seemed like a safe haven, but now I was presenting them with God's dire warning that it would not be a haven at all. I had told them that the sword would follow them to Egypt, and now God was saying that Nebuchadnezzar would give to the sword all those who were doomed to the sword. If my audience believed God's word at all, this was a restating of their doom.

Perhaps God's choice of location for delivering this particular message was intended to protect me. No-one in my audience was willing to attack me in front of the palace or the workmen who watched us blankly whenever they didn't have to concentrate on their paving work.

Had we been in the temple in Jerusalem, before the city fell, perhaps the outcome would have been different.

---

[65] Jeremiah 43:11-13

Chapter 15

A Visit to Migdol

April 583BC

Pharaoh's new pavement was ready before he arrived, and the workers and the architect were very pleased. So was Pharaoh. He made his way along it, walking slowly but with a swagger, until he reached the imposing entrance of his palace and disappeared inside.

I had made the opportunity to see his arrival, wondering whether anything of interest would arise, and I was glad that I had.

As I stood watching Pharaoh's grand entry from behind the line of soldiers that separated him from us onlookers, suddenly a loud voice caught my attention.

"Heremyo!"

Amasis waved above the crowd and then walked towards me. The soldiers were clearly uncertain what to do; though they opened a path for him to pass through, they also watched me worriedly to see what they should do to protect their general. Amasis made his way through the crowd as it opened up, sometimes pushing soldiers out of the way when they didn't move quickly enough and giving them no chance to defend him had there been a need.

I wasn't sure what I should do, but it was clear that Amasis was determined to greet me, so I accepted the inevitable.

"Amasis," I said, as he wrapped me in a bear hug. It was our normal way of greeting each other, despite the differences in nationality and habits. We had always enjoyed each other's company, and the contrasts seemed to matter little.

"Heremyo, my old friend!" he said, and, despite our shared good will, I wondered why he was quite so fulsome in his greeting.

"What brings you to Tahpanhes?" I asked. "And why are you so overjoyed to see me? What do you want from me?"

It was a good guess, and Amasis smiled broadly.

"You see through my happiness, friend." He looked around and switched to Hebrew. "The fact is, I do need some of your knowledge. Your religious knowledge."

"I'll be happy to give it. The more you listen to the words of Yahweh, the better. Our God is much greater than all of your gods put together." It was an ongoing, familiar argument between us. Amasis was not a particularly religious man, but he was still attached to the gods of his fathers. My mocking of his gods was often gentle but pointed, and we each knew where we stood with the other.

"You're still on about that, Heremyo? Surely fifty powerful gods working together add up to more than one god! Our gods develop their power in their own specific areas. They are masters of what they do. You have a god who must do everything himself. Better an expert than a jack of all trades!"

Amasis had used this argument before, and I suppose that I could have got upset at his description of the creator of the universe as a 'jack of all trades'; yet, used in the right way, that is exactly what Yahweh is. He can do *anything* and has no limit to his areas of expertise. Egyptian gods were said to work in small, carefully delineated areas of the business of life, and all Egyptians had to constantly balance their attention to each god with the attention demanded by other gods whenever the events of life fell within their supposed purview.

However, Amasis had only ever once added "and master of none" to his figure of speech about Yahweh. On that occasion, my horror had been unmistakeable, and my shocked explanation as to why he should *never* deride Yahweh like that was apparently sobering enough. From then on, he had made sure that he tempered his words – at least when I was around. After all, he had heard of the ten plagues[66] and was willing to acknowledge the amazing power that had allowed the people of Israel to cross the Red Sea while Pharaoh and his men had drowned. He explained the incident to himself as a one-off event, a case where at that particular time, Yahweh had been more powerful than Egypt's gods. Yet he had always been quick to remind me that Egypt was now a superpower, while Judah was a third-rate nation and Israel nothing but a captive failure. And now Judah was captive also.

Amasis smiled again and deferred our discussions. "Never mind, I'll talk to you about what I need later. In the meantime, what's this I hear about you interfering with Pharaoh's pavement?"

"Where did you hear that from?" I asked, amazed.

"We have our methods," he said, laughing at my surprise.

"I buried some stones in the mortar beneath the pavement."

---

[66] Exodus 7-11

"Yes, so I heard, but nobody could tell me why. All they could tell me is that you were speaking in some language they didn't understand."

"Yes, in Hebrew. If you'd been there, you would have known. It would have done you good to hear some more Hebrew again," I teased. "It's a much better language for expressing complex ideas."

"Then what was it you were saying?"

"I'll have to take a column from your scroll here, Amasis. I'll explain it all when we discuss your other questions."

I had been so engrossed in our conversation that I hadn't noticed until then that we were now surrounded by some fifty of Pharaoh's guards, all of whom were watching me carefully.

Amasis seemed to think little of the situation – I suppose a general has to be very used to being surrounded by soldiers! Yet it made me feel uncomfortable. One, who seemed to be an officer, stepped forward respectfully and spoke quietly to Amasis. It was obvious that he was being asked to leave this strange prophet and follow Pharaoh into the palace. I tried to make it easy for him.

"Where shall we meet, Amasis?" I asked.

"I am not expecting to stay in Tahpanhes for long," he said. "Where are you living?"

"I live in what people are now calling the Jewish quarter. It's nothing like a quarter of the city, but it's a section in which almost everyone is Jewish. It is the area you arranged for us to be given."

"I could find you there, then, but I think it might shock your countrymen less if you came and met me at the barracks instead."

I wasn't completely happy with the idea, but decided that an opportunity to talk to an Egyptian general about Yahweh might help my people – not to mention helping

Egypt, the nation that had welcomed us and offered us a place to live, even in the face of the probable anger of King Nebuchadnezzar.

"Tomorrow evening, then, Heremyo," he said. "At the gates of the barracks, at sunset."

The sun was touching the horizon as I approached the barracks gates of the city garrison the next day. As usual, it was still hot, but it was beginning to cool down. Seeing many guards surrounding the entrance, I hung back, standing on the far side of the avenue as I waited to see if Amasis would come.

While I waited, I watched the guards on their beat, noting that they paid little attention to any of the people who passed their barracks on the crowded thoroughfare. To be sure, the soldiers were present in large numbers, but their lack of attention to their surroundings wouldn't have satisfied *me* as a leader of the army. Each guard seemed to be concentrating more on maintaining his part of a carefully choreographed presentation than on providing a dependable guard. It fitted my picture of Egypt as an empire. *Appearance* seemed more important than practical reality, and nothing mattered more than highlighting the grandeur of the kingdom – the inherent greatness of Egypt.

As I watched, Amasis came through the gate and greeted the guard. He had a very familiar way of conversing with his subordinates, and they seemed to appreciate his interaction.

Maybe he was simply chatting or maybe he was asking about me, but either way, the guards did not give him any information about me. Indeed, I considered it unlikely that any of the guards had even noticed me, and that didn't seem quite right to me – although I am no soldier.

Amasis began to scan the street himself, spotted me in mere moments and walked across to meet me.

Once again, the guard was slow to respond, and he had crossed the avenue and greeted me before any of the guards followed him. Had my intentions been hostile, I could have dispatched their general without difficulty, and they could have done nothing to prevent it. "Egypt the do-nothing," I thought.[67]

"Heremyo," was Amasis's familiar greeting.

"Shalom," I responded.

"That's one thing we aren't expecting," he said wryly, referring to my salutation of "peace". "Why don't you come into the barracks now and answer my questions?"

"I don't think it will do your career much good if you're seen interviewing a Jewish prophet too often."

"Don't worry. Although there are soldiers and guards everywhere, most of them don't notice what's going on. I became a general because I paid more attention to the little details than anyone else. Pharaoh likes to be thought of as a man of action, so he wants people like me around, but not too many of us. Let's go inside."

We entered the barracks and crossed the open courtyard. Up a set of stairs to the second storey we went and then along a passageway, until Amasis paused before a closed door. The door was immediately opened to us, so obviously someone had been watching for Amasis to arrive.

"Come in," he said to me.

We passed through the doorway and entered a room which held a large table.

---

[67] Isaiah 30:7

"Leave us alone, Dedu," said Amasis as we sat down at the table. "I'll call you when I need you."

Dedu left the room.

"He may have left the room, but one way or another, he'll still hear everything we say. He's a remarkably reliable secretary, but he hears a little too much at times. If the rest of the army was like him, we would never be in danger of an unexpected attack such as we're worried about at the moment."

"Who might be attacking Egypt?" I asked.

"Who is attacking everyone at the moment?"

"Why, Nebuchadnezzar, of course, but I thought Egypt was a superpower? Won't your many gods look after you?"

Amasis looked at me in a worried manner and said, "As you say, Nebuchadnezzar, of course. He doesn't seem to understand the fundamentals of international power or logistics. He should understand that attacking Egypt is beyond him!"

"But what if it *isn't* beyond him?" I asked gently.

"What do you mean?"

"What if he is going to mount an overwhelming attack on Egypt, overrunning your defences, or perhaps even going around them?"

"But that's not possible! Do you know how far it is from Babylon to here? Have you considered the difficulty of making sure that his army has enough consumable items available? How many cartloads of arrows or bow strings? How many servants to look after the food? Just be practical!"

"Can't an army live off the land? Nebuchadnezzar and his army stripped Judah bare while they were attacking. I doubt that there was any food coming from Babylon to feed them. And they control all the nations along the roads from Babylon too. It's true that Judah was the end of the line, but it was a line that Nebuchadnezzar controlled, every step of the way from Babylon."

"He wouldn't rely on bowstrings from Syria."

"Why not?"

"What if the Syrians deliberately make them badly? Make them to… break during battle? Or make arrows with feathers that fall off?"

"Surely his men can inspect whatever they take from their captive nations? It can't take too much skill to inspect a bowstring, can it?"

Amasis looked at me with surprise. "You could be right," he said slowly. "But that's against all of our doctrine of warfare. Logistics, logistics, logistics, they say. And they're right too!"

"Then sit down and don't worry!" I said.

"No, I don't necessarily mean that they're *completely* right, but the principles are correct. We had a hard time attacking Cush because of the huge distance over which we had to maintain our lines of communication and supply. Just picture what happens if you're attacking your enemy and suddenly they cut your supply lines through some unexpected move. Your army calls for more arrows, but they can't get any. Your troops are tired and need a rest, but no more reserves can come up because the roads are blocked by the enemy. Your army just starves to death or runs out of weapons or fresh troops. In the end, you have to surrender."

"You know that I'm not a military man," I said, "but I can tell you what is going to happen with Babylon attacking Egypt."

"Well, that's what I came to you for."

"Nebuchadnezzar will attack Egypt and defeat you."

"But that's ridiculous. Ask all of our military advisors."

"Then sit on your hands and do nothing. It won't make any difference in the end, anyway."

"Hmm. Your answers are just what I expected, I suppose, although they presuppose that Nebuchadnezzar would be so stupid as to extend his supply lines all the way through Judah, and then stretch them further across the desert. By the time his army gets here, they'll be exhausted and demoralised."

"I don't know anything about that. But I do know that when the Chaldeans were attacking Jerusalem, God told me that even if all the Chaldean soldiers were lying in their tents exhausted and wounded, they would still get up, defeat Jerusalem, and burn it with fire.[68] They did, too."

"Yes, yes. But there wasn't much of a defence against them. It wasn't as if they were attacking a mighty nation like Egypt!" He waved his hand to dismiss the army of Judah like so many small ants and continued, "Yet that is not really the point. An attack from Nebuchadnezzar is impossible, but Pharaoh is still asking for my advice about it. What I need to know from you is when the attack will come." He looked at me expectantly.

"I don't know," I said, simply.

Amasis looked crestfallen. "So twenty years ago you warned us about an impossible attack. Twenty years later, it still hasn't happened, and you can't tell us when it will come?" He turned up his eyes to the heavens and said, "Why don't the gods just leave us alone to work out our own problems?"

"Yahweh cares about people. He made them and he wants to look after them. The people of Israel are his chosen people, but that doesn't mean that he ignores everyone else. He wants all nations to know him and live his way."

---

[68] Jeremiah 37:9-10

"So how do these prophecies help? What is the point of warning all the nations that Babylon will attack them and they'll have to submit to him – and then having nothing at all happen for twenty years?"

"You can't say that nothing has happened: after all, Syria has been defeated, and Jerusalem lies in ruins. The events God warned about are happening. And Egypt was given the same warning."

"But can't we have a timeline? I'm an army commander. Already twenty years have gone by with nothing to show for it – I can't have my men lining the border for the next twenty years!"

"No, and you shouldn't anyway. Fighting against Yahweh doesn't work. If you learn nothing else from what happened to Judah, learn that!"

Amasis listened and argued; agreed and disputed. It was like talking to King Zedekiah had been – and I was just as successful in guiding his behaviour!

CR

That was the first of several discussions I had with Amasis in Tahpanhes. When I first met him, he was a poor but very ambitious young soldier, dreaming of leadership of the Egyptian army – and this was exactly what he had achieved. Most of his achievements he ascribed to being in the right place at the right time, but he had a singleness of purpose that had enabled him to take advantage of those opportunities in a way that others could not.

Pharaoh considered him a gifted commander, and I suppose he was. He was good at listening to advice, but once decisions were made, he was also good at single-mindedly pursuing the chosen option. He got on well with his men and was an unusually considerate commander in how he looked after his men.

As Pharaoh's favourite general, he had been selected to maintain the north-eastern frontier, by which Nebuchadnezzar would have to approach Egypt. As part of his desire to defend the border, he wanted to know when he could expect Nebuchadnezzar to attack, and he continued to hope that I could help him with this question. He didn't want a hopelessly demoralising campaign of sitting on the border waiting for an army that never came.

Yet I couldn't help him. I knew no more than he about when Nebuchadnezzar would arrive at Egypt's border. The main difference was that I was certain it would happen, while Amasis thought only that it was *possible*, perhaps even *likely*, but far from certain.

Nevertheless, he still wanted to discuss all these things with me – possibly because I was not Egyptian and he hoped that my Hebrew way of thinking might give him some different ideas.

When I look back on it, it still feels strange to have an Egyptian general talking to a Judean prophet about what was needed to defend Egypt!

After two weeks, he and his men moved on to Migdol, the town further to the east from which he would command the defence of the border. Large numbers of troops would be following him in a short time, but he would set up his staff in the town first.

With his departure, my life in Tahpanhes returned to normal and I busied myself doing my best to support my people in their worship. There was little other work that I could do, for all of my working life had been centred around the work of a priest and Levite.

Just two weeks later, however, I received a message from Amasis. It was written in an Egyptian script which Amasis knew I had never learned, so he had arranged for it to be delivered by a servant from Pharaoh's palace who could read the message to me.

An imperative rap on my door demanded that I open it, and when I did, I wondered why an impressively dressed scribe was visiting me.

"Are you Heremyo, the prophet of Yahweh?" he asked in an aloof voice, giving me the impression that he did not seriously expect me to understand his language.

"Yes," I answered, and he looked a little surprised.

"I have a message for you from Pharaoh's great general, Amasis. Do you understand Egyptian?"

"Yes, I do," I said.

"Then I will read you his letter: 'Amasis, commanding general of Pharaoh's hosts stationed at Migdol, to Heremyo, the prophet of Yahweh, currently residing in Tahpanhes, Greetings.' " The scribe paused. "Do you really understand what I am reading?" he asked again.

"I do," I confirmed, "and it was your general who taught me the language, although he never taught me to read your script."

"General Amasis taught you our language? Amazing. He is a gifted man indeed to teach a foreigner our tongue."

I ignored the implication that foreigners must be stupid and agreed. Amasis seemed to be appreciated by the common people.

"I will continue," said the scribe. " 'Your assistance would be appreciated in the preparation of an important strategic plan. If you can do so, please come to Migdol by the day of the new moon. You will be provided with lodgings and sustenance.' That is all. The new moon is in three days. When will you be leaving?"

This time I ignored the assumption that if Amasis asked, I would automatically obey; instead, I responded, "I will first engage in prayer to see whether Yahweh has other plans for me, but if not, I will leave the day after tomorrow. Tomorrow is a Sabbath."

What could Amasis want, I wondered.

❧

Two days later, I made the thirty-kilometre[69] journey to Migdol and arrived late in the afternoon. The following morning, I found Amasis in the army barracks. He thanked me for coming.

He began by speaking more generally about the state of international affairs, but quickly focused on his task of guarding the border of Egypt against Chaldean attack.

"What do you know about Nebuchadnezzar's movements?" I asked.

"Very little," he said with a frustrated frown. After a moment's pause, he tried to explain his difficulties, while carefully avoiding any criticism of his monarch. The problem seemed to be that Pharaoh was convinced that a superpower had no need to constantly keep an eye on the surrounding nations. Snooping around trying to find out what Nebuchadnezzar was doing was admitting that he was a threat, and Pharaoh was unwilling to acknowledge that at all.

"We know that he went back to Babylon after destroying Jerusalem," I said, "but we don't know anything beyond that. Ah… except that he hadn't returned to Judah before we left to come to Egypt. Where do you think he is now?"

"Some say he is busy fighting the Medes, others suggest that he has returned to Assyria to exterminate the Assyrians. Some even suggest that he has taken a fleet of ships to cross the Great Sea to Tarshish." He stood up and paced the room in frustration before sitting down again with a sigh. "If only I could read his mind!"

---

[69] Twenty miles.

"I can't do that either," I said sympathetically. "All I can do is what I have already done: assure you that he *will* come, and that when he does, none of your defensive manoeuvres will save Egypt from defeat."

"Yes, Heremyo, I understand just how convinced you are, but it flies in the face of all military experience and expertise. Egypt has *never* been defeated from the north; it just can't happen!"

"If it can't happen, then why are you asking about Nebuchadnezzar?"

"Well, naturally, it is foolish to ignore any possibility, even such a faint possibility as this. We Egyptians are methodical and thorough."

He explained that he was still finding it difficult to get any good information about Nebuchadnezzar. Merchants seemed to have some information, and they were suggesting that Nebuchadnezzar was getting ready to attack the Phoenicians, probably the city of Tyre, but possibly Sidon.

"Are you sure that you cannot tell me when Nebuchadnezzar will come?" Amasis asked, yet again.

"I cannot tell you at all. I was a prophet in Judah for forty years before the destruction Yahweh had promised came about."

"You mean that I may have to wait forty years? If that's the case, I might as well abandon the entire enterprise right now. Perhaps Pharaoh would do better to plunder Cush again or find some other place to pillage."

"I didn't say it *would* be forty years. It *might* be. Or it might be forty days. What I'm saying is that I don't know. Yahweh is the one who is in control, not me."

"So we'll have to make up our own minds how best to handle this threat?"

"Ah, well, you already know my answer to that question. In fact, you've heard it several times: you will not be able to handle the threat. If you want my recommendation, it is that when Nebuchadnezzar does attack, you ask for terms of peace. Submit to his demands. Do not fight him. That will be the best solution for Egypt, causing the least death, destruction and plundering."

"Pharaoh would never accept that idea – and I wouldn't be foolish enough to suggest it. We'll have to take our own steps, and I'll have to find some way to collect the information we need. This brings me to my reason for asking you to come."

Why will people never learn? Why do we always believe that we are in control? As I was mulling over this folly of human pride, Amasis made a suggestion that came as a complete shock to me.

He wanted me to visit the areas north of Israel and work for him as a spy! Of course, he didn't express it in those terms: no, he assured me that he knew I had often travelled widely outside Judah, and wondered if I could do so again and send him reports from time to time about what I saw in those areas. For him, knowledge of the actions of his enemies was vitally important, but difficult to obtain. Pharaoh was not convinced that Nebuchadnezzar would attack at all, and Amasis believed that if no attack happened in the next year or two, he was unlikely to be able to maintain his credibility with Pharaoh.

In the meantime, having a foreigner collecting the information would at least avoid the suggestion that he was questioning Pharaoh's judgement.

I understood Amasis's problem, but I was not willing to offer my allegiance either to him or to Pharaoh. How could I deny that allegiance to a king of Judah and then offer it to Pharaoh?

Chapter 16

For all the Jews in Egypt

That night in Migdol, as I was praying in the room Amasis had provided for me, God spoke to me and gave me a message for all the Jews who lived in the land of Egypt: those in Migdol, Tahpanhes, Memphis, and in the land of Pathros on the Nile River.

I was surprised how my heart leapt at Yahweh's instruction. It felt like old times again: being given a message for a widespread audience that I must deliver in several places. True, it did spark a little bit of a feeling of "that's going to be hard work" – after all, I'm not as young as I used to be – but overall, the feeling was good!

My earlier work as a prophet had taught me that not all of God's people felt the importance of living in the Promised Land, and some had found much greater success or happiness in other lands. In fact, I found Jews in almost every kingdom I ever visited.

I had always felt that God considered these people to be outcasts, exiles who would, even should, someday return to Israel. I'll try to remember to say more about that later in this diary.

Some Jews had fled to Egypt before the Chaldeans attacked Judah and had lived in Egypt for many years. Indeed, some had moved far earlier, and their families had been there for hundreds of years. As a result, there were many Jews spread throughout Egypt.

Adding to this, some of those who came (or who, like me, were forced to come) from Judah had left Tahpanhes as soon as they could and moved up the Nile into upper Egypt, or even further. This area was called the Land of Pathros – the 'southern land'.

My task of conveying God's message to these far-spread places would take some time.

Since I was already in Migdol, the next morning I found where the Jews lived and delivered the message in a few of the local open areas.

After a second meeting, Amasis grudgingly accepted my refusal to gather information for him, so I was free to return to Tahpanhes the next day. The following day, I delivered God's message to as many people as I could in the city. Yes, it was just like old times: travelling around telling people a message that nobody wanted to hear!

One thing, however, had changed: God's prophecies *had* been fulfilled. Jerusalem *was* ruined. The temple *was* burned with fire. King Zedekiah *had* gone to Babylon in chains.

Surely, I thought to myself, I must have some credibility now! The terrors I had warned of years ago had come to pass. Surely people must listen when everyone had seen the charred evidence that I was speaking the words of God, and smelled the foul smell of rotting flesh that none of us who had lived through those horrors could ever forget?

Yet that same supposed credibility had got me nowhere just a short time later when it had come to passing on God's command that the survivors should not leave the land to come to Egypt.

In the end, I concluded that it probably *would* be just like old times! Nevertheless, if I didn't try, I would never know, so I stood in the open square in front of the house in which I lived and began to speak to the men and women resting there in the heat of the day. I told them that these were words God had given to me just a few days before. This was not old news, it was God's current opinion of our nation:

"Thus says the Lord of hosts, the God of Israel:
You have seen all the disaster
that I brought upon Jerusalem
and upon all the cities of Judah.
Behold, this day they are a desolation,
and no one dwells in them,
because of the evil that they committed,
provoking me to anger,
in that they went to make offerings
and serve other gods that they knew not,
neither they, nor you, nor your fathers.
Yet I persistently sent to you
all my servants the prophets, saying,
'Oh, do not do this abomination that I hate!'
But they did not listen or incline their ear,
to turn from their evil
and make no offerings to other gods.
Therefore my wrath and my anger were poured out
and kindled in the cities of Judah
and in the streets of Jerusalem,
and they became a waste and a desolation, as at this day.
And now thus says the Lord God of hosts,
the God of Israel:
Why do you commit this great evil against yourselves,
to cut off from you man and woman, infant and child,
from the midst of Judah,
leaving you no remnant?"[70]

---

[70] Jeremiah 44:2-7

As I spoke, a few pointedly stood up and walked away, unwilling to listen at all. Others seemed to pay polite attention to the ageing prophet as he delivered his usual message of doom and gloom. Some looked angry, some looked bored, and some went quietly off to sleep.

It was very much like old times. All that was missing were the responses threatening my life. I reflected that it had been quite some time since I had delivered such a tirade of condemnation; if I repeated it frequently, maybe the threats to my life would return too!

It was a disheartening experience. Later in the day, though, it occurred to me that God has this same disheartening experience all the time. Yet he still keeps sending prophets!

℃

March 582BC

Through the winter, I delivered God's message in several other locations in the Jewish quarter of Tahpanhes, then, early in the spring, I packed up my travelling pack and set off upriver.

Memphis is some 120 or 130 kilometres[71] upstream, and all the Egyptians I spoke to suggested that I travel by boat. There are roads beside the river, but they are difficult and, at times, dangerous. Egypt was famous in Judah for the crocodiles that lounge along the Nile, but the locals referred to another enormous animal, the hippopotamus, that is apparently even more aggressive than the crocodiles. I learned that hippopotamuses kill many people in Egypt each year, most of them near the banks of the river, so it is safest to travel in boats that keep to the middle of the stream.

---

[71] 75-80 miles.

The Nile is a vast river that flows sluggishly but powerfully towards the sea. I had seen boats being carried irresistibly downstream by the current, but when I asked how boats could overcome the current to travel upstream, no-one could answer my question except to say that people travelled upstream all the time without trouble.

Based on this advice, I walked to the Nile River and found a place where boats could be boarded to travel upstream. I asked whether it was better to go by boat or simply walk to Memphis. The boatmen laughed at my question and one told me that I could walk if I wanted to, but I would find walking so far exhausting – Egypt is a hot, dry country. Sailing would, he said, be swift and easy by contrast. When I asked obliquely about the current, they all just smiled and said, "Wait and see!"

Accordingly, I made arrangements to travel to Memphis, paid the fare and boarded the boat. Shortly afterwards, the sailors cast off and hoisted the sails. They filled with wind, and under their propulsion we made our way out into the current.

The pilot kept out from the shore enough to have clearance under the hull of the boat, but not too far, to avoid the full strength of the current. Remembering the comments I had heard about hippopotamuses, I asked about them and was told that the pilot would take us further out into the river when there was a need, but that most of the time we would hug the bank of the mighty Nile.

Time passed and the wind blew us steadily upstream. After a while I began to understand that the trick to travelling up the Nile is the consistent wind – without which it would be utterly impossible. When you wish to travel downstream, of course, the current hurries you downstream easily.

On my earlier visits to Egypt I had always walked to my destinations – which had all been in the delta area –

but this time I was gaining quite a different picture of the country, and from a comfortable, relaxed position, too. The banks slid by, and I watched with interest the panorama of reeds, trees and fields that lined the river.

Yet even from the river, there were many places where the desert sand could be seen, and it was clear just how narrow a ribbon of green was formed by the Nile River. Beyond its banks and flood plains, the land was more or less untouched by the vast flood of water that surged past on its way to the sea.

One afternoon, Memphis finally came in sight on the west bank of the river. The jetties that lined the bank led up to elegant avenues that showed the remarkable character of the place. Memphis was an ancient city and its white walls showed a delightful patina of age.

I had already asked the sailors where the Jewish part of the city was, mostly in hope that there were enough Jews there for them to be easy to find. Having received directions, the next day I searched for the outcasts of Israel living in this amazing city.

When I found the Jewish quarter, it was clear that these people had been in Egypt for a very long time, but that they still had not completely lost their Jewish heritage. The houses fitted in well with the houses in the surrounding suburbs, but there were a few simple Jewish touches that almost made me feel at home. The houses had parapets around the roofs as commanded in our law,[72] which the houses nearby did not. Doorways often had quotes from the law, written in Hebrew.

I passed through the Jewish area until I met an old man sitting beside the door of his house in the late afternoon sun.

"The Lord bless you," I greeted him.

---

[72] Deuteronomy 22:8

"The Lord keep you," he responded.

It really did feel like a little bit of Judah tucked away in an ancient foreign city.

"I am Jeremiah, one of the priests from the city of Anathoth," I said.

"A priest?" he asked. "Do we still have priests when the temple has been destroyed?"

"Oh yes," I said. "God appointed priests before there was a temple. He even chose them before there was a tabernacle in the wilderness. Priests represent Yahweh to the people of Israel, and we can do that even without a temple."

"I suppose so. But what about everything else that has been destroyed? Does the city of Anathoth still stand?"

"No. It too has been destroyed. Did you know Anathoth?"

"Yes, in my youth, although I have only ever passed through it – and that not very often."

"How long have you been here in Egypt?"

"I came to Egypt when Nebuchadnezzar first attacked Jerusalem in the time of King Jehoiakim. That was about… ah… 19 years ago, when I was not young, but not so old as I am now. I brought my wife and children, and we have made our home here in the safety of Egypt. I found an enclave of Jews already living in Memphis, and we have lived here happily ever since."

"How many of you are there?"

"There are only two of us now," he said, misunderstanding my question. "The children have all married and left home. Our habits are different here. In a rich town like Memphis, children find their own homes. We have worked hard, and our children work hard too, but the rewards are good. Better than they ever were in Judah. Life is good. We are safe from the Chaldeans."

"Do you miss Judah at all?"

"I miss the food, and I miss our relatives. I used to miss the temple, but now it's been destroyed. There isn't much else to miss. I'm not even sure if any of our relatives are still alive. We've had some newcomers arriving in the last few months – people who were in Judah when Gedaliah was assassinated and the remnant of the people decided to leave the land and escape to Egypt before Nebuchadnezzar tracked them down and wiped them all out. Here they will be safe. But they don't have news of many other survivors."

"How many of you live in this enclave?" I asked, trying again.

"About 250 people," he said. "It is not many, but we help each other and the Egyptians leave us in peace. We provide some skills that they don't have themselves, so we all benefit from it."

"What skills do you provide?"

"We work well with money. We lend money, we trade, we turn money into more money and help our clients to do the same thing."

"Had you worked that way in Judah before you left?"

"No, it was something that I learned when I came here. In Judah there was never enough money to go around and we spent all our time working the fields just to get enough to live on. Here, things are different. We have no fields and there are few opportunities to get work that we have experience with. Many of the Jews who were living here when I arrived worked as shoemakers, weavers, and makers of clothes and other items of material, and were able to help me find work that I could do. But many had found work in the money industry like I ended up doing. I'm not sure why, but we seem to have a gift for working with money and making it multiply. At first, we worked for Egyptians who wanted others to deal with their

Egyptian customers who needed loans, short term or long. The rich liked gathering up more money, but they didn't want to deal with the unpleasant matters of demanding repayments, pressuring people into signing agreements committing themselves to unpleasantly large repayments and other unsavoury things like that. I learned how to turn my master's money into more and more money, and kept enough of it myself over time to begin lending out my own money to help the needy achieve their goals."

"Does dealing with money like that make you popular?"

"No, not really, but we mostly keep to ourselves, so what the rest of the people think of us doesn't matter all that much. It would be nice to be popular, but they all consider us foreigners anyway."

"Do they exclude you from their society?"

"Many people do," he said, then added in a sarcastic tone, "but only until they want to get some money. Then we're suddenly their best friends."

"And what about their worship?"

"Well, that's one of the problems, as you might expect. They don't like it if we keep separate and worship Yahweh – they say we think we're different from them, above them maybe. But if we ask to join in their worship, they don't really want that either, although they probably dislike it less, if you know what I mean. As a result, most of us just dabble in their worship, you understand, to keep them happy. And we maintain our traditional worship as well."

"Does that include Baal and Asherah?"

"For some of us, yes. People choose the gods they like for whatever reason."

"Are there many temples here in Memphis?"

"Yes, lots: for Ptah, Astarte, and many others. And having a temple to worship in makes it much easier to worship. Yes, indeed. Worshipping Yahweh with no idols and no temple is rather taxing. In fact, hearing that the temple in Jerusalem has been destroyed has been rather depressing. We could always picture the temple in our minds, see those enormous columns and the broad court-yards. But now the temples here are so much more real. Even so, I prefer to worship Yahweh."

"So do I," I agreed heartily.

"You said that you come from Anathoth. The high priests came from Anathoth, didn't they? What happened to them when Nebuchadnezzar destroyed the temple?"

"Azariah would have been High Priest when you left. He died just before Nebuchadnezzar attacked for the last time, and his son Seraiah became High Priest. When the city was sacked, Seraiah was taken away to Riblah and killed. His young sons Jehozadak and Ezra were taken away into captivity, and lots of other priests and Levites went with them."

"So what is left of our religion?"

"Yahweh still remains, and while he remains, our religion will never end. His scripture is still with us too, so we know what pleases him – and what doesn't! Abraham our father worshipped Yahweh before there was a temple, and we can do the same now without a temple, even with-out priests or Levites."

"But Abraham worshipped by himself, and we've been worshipping together as a nation. What should we do now?"

"In Tahpanhes, we've been meeting on the Sabbath day to read the scriptures and to worship Yahweh to-gether. We sing Psalms, pray and remember Jerusalem and the temple."

"Some of us do that sort of thing here, although not normally on the Sabbath. The Sabbath is always a busy day in my line of work."

"Everyone will always be busy on the Sabbath unless they decide not to be, my friend. As a priest, I've spent many of my Sabbaths working harder than on any usual day, but the difference is that it is work for Yahweh, not for putting food on the table."

"I'll have to think about that. I don't want to worship God in a way that he doesn't want, but at the same time, we do need to put food on the table, as you say."

Another man approached us and greeted my companion, then looked at me with interest.

"One of us, Phinehas?" he asked.

"Yes, this is Jeremiah, a priest from Anathoth."

"A priest, hey?" He laughed. "There are lots of priests around here."

"Yes, Eliezer," said my companion, "but he is a priest of Yahweh."

"Ah, a rich man." Eliezer was obviously a bit of a wit.

"I'm not starving," I said mildly.

"Were you there when Jerusalem fell?" he asked.

"Yes, I was."

"Did you get any of the loot from the temple?"

"What do you mean?" I asked, taken aback.

"I assume that once it was obvious that the city would fall to the Chaldeans, you priests arranged for all the valuable items to be hidden. You know, for protection."

"I know that there was some hiding of valuables, but most of the priests were sure that God would continue to protect the city, even when it was obvious to everyone else that Nebuchadnezzar was going to break through the walls."

"So, did you get your share then?"

"No and yes."

"What do you mean?"

"I got nothing, but that was all that was *my share*. I have no right to any of the treasures of the temple. They were dedicated to Yahweh, they're not for me to steal. Anyway, Nebuchadnezzar took most of them to Babylon. Some were melted down and taken as bullion, others were taken as the priceless works of art they are. He'll probably use them in his own temples in Babylon."

"You sound far too strait-laced to be a priest as I knew priests," said Eliezer. "What gives?"

"I can't really answer your question. Instead, I'll ask you one: Do you think that Aaron would have helped himself to any of the golden implements made for the tabernacle?"

"No, of course not. But he lived in the old days when God chose the priests because they had morals."

"And you don't think there are any priests like that now?"

"I've never met one. Unless you're like that – and if you are, then I have a question or two for you."

"You'll have to judge for yourself whether I live up to the expectations God had of his priests. All I can say is that I try, and when I realise that I've failed, I repent."

"Can I ask you two questions then?"

"Ask away."

"Which family of priests do you come from?"

"I am a son of Hilkiah."

The man looked at me in surprise. "Well, that doesn't fill me with much hope that you're a good priest. He was the richest of them all."

I remained silent. I could not defend my father, but nor would I criticise him. After hearing my answer, Eliezer seemed to have decided that one question was all he needed to ask. I was curious what the second question was, but was not willing to ask.

After a while, Phinehas broke the awkward silence that had fallen, saying, "Come on, Eliezer, what was your second question for Jeremiah?"

"I was going to ask where he was when the city fell."

"I was in the court of the guard," I answered. "Locked up at the command of the king and his friends."

"Ah, so you couldn't have got to the treasures anyway!"

"No, I couldn't."

"Then your protestations of honesty weren't even tested anyway. You couldn't have helped yourself even if you had wanted to."

"No, that's true – but so what? Why are you so sure that I would have stolen things from the temple if I could have done so?"

"Look, I don't want to get into a fight, Jeremiah, but my experience with priests is that they're all in it for the money."

"And yet you admit that Aaron, their ancestor, wouldn't have been like that."

"I do, but that just shows that the family has gone downhill. They *were* faithful, but now they're rich instead."

"Was King David rich?"

"Yes, and he left most of his wealth to be used in the temple. Yet even his family has gone downhill. You'd have to admit that."

"Our whole nation has gone downhill. In that you're right. That's why Jerusalem was destroyed and the temple burned with fire. Yet none of us *has* to follow that way. None of us has to take the bad path. We have good examples from the past – all we have to do as individuals is to copy those examples. If we think Aaron wouldn't steal and that this was a good thing, then all we have to do is refuse to steal ourselves. It's really important to do those things, but it's also really simple."

"So are you claiming that the priests are good?" asked Eliezer, trying to defend himself.

"Haven't you heard of Jeremiah?" interrupted Phinehas. "If you knew who he is and what he's been doing for the last forty or fifty years, you wouldn't be asking all these questions."

"What do you mean?"

"Jeremiah, the son of Hilkiah, is a prophet of Yahweh," said Phinehas. "He was in prison when Jerusalem fell because he had upset the king, the princes, the nobles, the priests, the Levites and most of the people with what he said. In fact, if it hadn't been for God protecting him, he would've been dead a long time before that."

I looked at him in surprise. From our earlier conversation, I had assumed that he did not recognise my name and knew nothing about me. The extent of my notoriety still shocks me at times.

Eliezer was also looking at me in surprise. "So you're *that* Jeremiah," he said. Phinehas laughed and I joined in.

"Yes, I'm *that* Jeremiah." My smile suddenly slipped and I added harshly, "I am the Jeremiah that everyone hated, from the king down to the poorest slave in the palace. But now most of them are dead."

"Yet you aren't," said Phinehas, "and I suspect that's one of the best proofs that you're telling the truth."

"I am telling the truth, yet it's not I who is telling the truth but Yahweh. He's been warning us that destruction would come since the time of Isaiah, and even earlier." I sighed and spread out my hands towards them. "Can anyone explain to me why people won't listen to Yahweh? Do they love death?"

"No, Jeremiah," said Phinehas soberly, "it's because they love life. Their *own choice* of life. They want to be able to choose what they do. We all do that. Even the best people I've known, all of them still want to live life their own way. After all, don't you want to do the same?"

"I want to be a prophet for God," I said. "That means doing things that he wants, not what I want."

"Yes, but if he didn't *command* you to talk to his people, would you keep doing it? The point I'm trying to make is that we all try to do what *we* want. We do two kinds of things in life: things we have to do because we can't get out of them, and things that we choose to do."

"I suppose so," I said, slowly. "I hadn't thought of it that way. I'd always looked at what I did for God and thought that it was good work." I laughed and continued a little ruefully, "To be honest, I suppose I've always felt that I should be admired and honoured for it. Hmm."

My mind was racing. Did I do work for God because I loved the work or because I *had* to do it? It was one thing to do what God told me because I needed his guidance to do it the best way, but quite another to need him to tell me because otherwise I wouldn't even want to do his work. Was I a grudging servant or a willing, eager slave?

Chapter 17

The Land of Pathros

April-September 582BC

Memphis sits at the entrance to the Nile Valley, where the Nile River escapes the constraints of its surrounding hills and spreads out across the plains of Egypt to form the vast delta for which Egypt is famous. Memphis is the meeting place of the two parts of Egypt. Upriver to the south, in what some call Upper Egypt, the land and the river are completely different from what we see in Lower Egypt where I had been living. Lower Egypt is low and flat, and the Nile River spreads far and wide, meandering and diverging. Each year, the flooding river deposits more of the silt that makes Lower Egypt so fertile, able to support a large population despite its very low rainfall.

My final destination, however, was much further up the Nile Valley, beyond the first cataract. Here the Land of Pathros began, and even here there lived Jews.

Not only did they live there, but I had reason to believe that some of them had left Tahpanhes and travelled south *because of the word of Yahweh*.

Let me explain.

Several years before, not long after we had arrived from Judah, I had warned the men of Judah in Tahpanhes that Nebuchadnezzar would set up his throne at the entrance to Pharaoh's palace in Tahpanhes, just as he had set up his throne in the gate of Jerusalem when he conquered that city.

I believe that many were hoping to avoid this impending doom. Of course, they would probably deny that there was any connection between their relocation and God's threats – after all, they had told me that they didn't believe I spoke for God anyway – but what other reason could there be?

Significant numbers of Jews had travelled well beyond the cataracts of the Nile, up to the areas where control of the land was a little more fluid and uncertain. Amasis, my teacher of old, had led Pharaoh's army into that area and beyond, vanquishing the Cushites with outstanding success. It was into these areas that many of my countrymen were now relocating in the hope of avoiding God's judgement. Yet with each step they took to avoid it, the more they invited that punishment.

If you were a king who had commanded his subjects not to leave the country, would you be pleased when they ignored your orders and left anyway? Imagine that you then followed them into the foreign land and warned them that punishment would follow them there and they could not escape it. How would you respond if they then travelled even further away in an attempt to hide from your punishment? Would you let them get away with it, or treat them even more harshly? I know how *I* would feel and what I would do, but God is much more merciful than I.

I passed the first cataract and continued to travel south. As I went, the signs of Egyptian civilisation became less clear and even the architecture began to change.

I wasn't sure where I would find my countrymen, so I had to visit many towns to inquire. Some towns held one or two Jews and I delivered God's message to them, but most of these were people who had spent many years in Egypt and for whom some of God's message was not relevant. After all, they had not set their faces to come to Egypt in opposition to God's command – except insofar as they had returned to Egypt despite the fact that God had said his people would never need to make that journey again. Whether or not they considered the message applied to them was up to them, but with each person I told, the weight of responsibility that I felt decreased slightly.

A few of the larger towns had more Jews, and in some I found people that I recognised. These were the ones I particularly suspected of leaving Lower Egypt to escape the threat of Nebuchadnezzar.

Strangely – at least in my eyes – one of these was Johanan, one of the commanders who had insisted that I was not speaking the words of God. When I saw him in the street, the first Jew I had seen in the town, I greeted him enthusiastically, while he showed somewhat less enthusiasm.

"Johanan, the Lord bless you."

"The Lord keep you, Jeremiah. What are you doing here?"

"I am here with tidings. News from God that you need to hear."

"I'm sick of your news, Jeremiah. Part of my reason for leaving Tahpanhes was to get away from your holier-than-thou attitude."

"Well, you're going to hear God's message anyway. You are a son of Jacob, one of God's chosen people, and you cannot avoid it."

"We left Judah by choice, and then we left Tahpanhes as well. We have travelled far, far away from the land of our fathers. We are still Jews, but we are not Jews that *you* can order around. The temple is gone, the kingdom is gone, and your power over us is gone too."

"How many Jews are in this town?" I asked.

"About three hundred – more if you include all the little children."

This was clearly the largest outpost of Judeans that I would find anywhere in the area.

"I must speak to them," I said. "God has told me to give his message to *all* of the people of Judah in this area."

"I'm not going to force them to listen to you, Jeremiah, but I can tell them that you're here and want to speak to everyone."

"Thank you. Tomorrow is the Sabbath. Do you work on the Sabbath now that you are so far from Judah?"

"Some of us do and some don't. There are still some who worship God carefully, even though you may say they've done their best to run away from him. But not everyone wants to serve Yahweh as you say we should. Some want more flexibility, not your rigid stuck-in-the-mud traditions."

"I'll cover that in the message God wants me to communicate to you. God redeemed us out of Egypt in the time of Moses. We are his people and we can't escape the responsibility which comes with that.

"I want to see everybody tomorrow, a while before noon. Until then, I have nothing in particular to do. Are there any of our countrymen whom I should visit? Any who are sick or dying? Any with needs that I could assist with? Any young men or women who need help in learning about Yahweh and his ways?"

"Come with me and I'll introduce you to some people who might welcome you."

That afternoon, I spent several hours talking to a number of my countrymen in this place so far removed from the land God had promised us. Sadly, the conversations did not fill me with hope for my announcements the next day! The men appeared to be throwing off much of the restraint they had grown up with, not that they seemed to view it like that. The women were also casting off restraint, but in a different way: they openly stated their preferences for other gods. I wondered uneasily what would happen the next day.

I hate to say it, but I got up the next morning hoping for no more than to get through the day alive and unharmed, rather than hoping to trigger a much-needed reformation.

As noon approached, I walked to an open area that Johanan had described to me, ready to speak to my people, but found few there. Based on the numbers Johanan had mentioned, it appeared that there were many people who weren't coming to listen.

I waited for a while, greeting some whom I knew and being introduced to others who were long-time residents of this out-of-the-way spot. Some of the latter even came over to introduce themselves, eager to hear some words from a prophet of Yahweh after several years of silence. Would they still feel the same by the time I'd finished?

More people trickled into the square as we waited, and at last it was time to start.

I began with the warning that some of Yahweh's words were targeted at the people who had left the land of Judah after the assassination of Gedaliah:

"Thus says the Lord of hosts, the God of Israel:
You have seen all the disaster
that I brought upon Jerusalem
and upon all the cities of Judah.
Behold, this day they are a desolation,
and no one dwells in them,
because of the evil that they committed,
provoking me to anger,

in that they went to make offerings
and serve other gods that they knew not,
neither they, nor you, nor your fathers.
Yet I persistently sent to you
all my servants the prophets, saying,
'Oh, do not do this abomination that I hate!' "[73]

A deliberately bored-sounding voice interrupted me: "We've heard all this before, Jeremiah. And we know that Jerusalem was destroyed: we don't need you to tell us again."

A woman laughed a high-pitched laugh and called out, " 'Persistently' is right. We've heard this sort of thing from you so many times that we can tell you what you're going to say before you even start."

"You may *know* what God will say, but are you doing it? You may know what I will say, but Yahweh knows what you are like too, so he continues:

"But they did not listen or incline their ear,
to turn from their evil
and make no offerings to other gods.
Therefore my wrath and my anger were poured out
and kindled in the cities of Judah
and in the streets of Jerusalem,
and they became a waste and a desolation,
as at this day."[74]

They continued to interject from time to time, but I continued anyway, and my voice was able to overwhelm all except a very few with particularly powerful voices. Not only so, but the words of God discouraged ridicule from anyone but the most hardened of rebels.

Next came God's attack on their worship:

---

[73] Jeremiah 44:2-4
[74] Jeremiah 44:5-6

"Why do you provoke me to anger
with the works of your hands,
making offerings to other gods
in the land of Egypt where you have come to live,
so that you may be cut off and become a curse
and a taunt among all the nations of the earth?
Have you forgotten the evil of your fathers,
the evil of the kings of Judah, the evil of their wives,
your own evil, and the evil of your wives,
which they committed in the land of Judah
and in the streets of Jerusalem?"[75]

There was silence. The audience had not anticipated such a direct attack. The women who were obviously promoting themselves as being able to lead the community were shocked at being singled out as targets of Yahweh's judgement.

Quickly I continued, presenting God's words with all the power and conviction I could muster:

"They have not humbled themselves even to this day,
nor have they feared,
nor walked in my law and my statutes
that I set before you and before your fathers.
Therefore thus says the Lord of hosts, the God of Israel:
Behold, I will set my face against you for harm,
to cut off all Judah."[76]

This was more familiar territory for my audience. It was very much the same message as I had delivered to them before we left Chimham's Inn, and their restlessness rose again. I hurried on before anyone could interrupt:

"I will take the remnant of Judah
who have set their faces
to come to the land of Egypt to live,
and they shall all be consumed.

---

[75] Jeremiah 44:8-9
[76] Jeremiah 44:10-11

In the land of Egypt they shall fall;
by the sword and by famine they shall be consumed.
From the least to the greatest,
they shall die by the sword and by famine,
and they shall become an oath,
a horror, a curse, and a taunt."[77]

At this point I stopped. One person at a time, I looked around the crowd, challenging them to respond, to say that they truly didn't care. No-one spoke, although there were many sneering looks and expressions that showed neither respect nor concern.

I continued the words of God, speaking slowly as I scanned the faces of my audience.

"I will punish those who dwell in the land of Egypt,
as I have punished Jerusalem,
with the sword, with famine, and with pestilence,
so that none of the remnant of Judah
who have come to live in the land of Egypt
shall escape or survive or return to the land of Judah,
to which they desire to return to dwell there.
For they shall not return,
except some fugitives."[78]

God's message was complete, so I stopped. It was a heart-rending curse to be calling down on the heads of my countrymen. As I spoke to them, I mulled over the meaning in my mind. None of those I was speaking to would ever return. They might wish to return to Judah, but they never would. Only a few fugitives would survive.

As I pondered the words, so did those listening, and the mood grew decidedly angry. My audience had continued to increase as stragglers arrived while I spoke, and now there really was a large crowd. Indeed, Johanan later reported that there were no Jews he knew of in the land of

---

[77] Jeremiah 44:12
[78] Jeremiah 44:13-14

Pathros who were not there – or had at least sent a representative.

Then all the men who knew that their wives made offerings to other gods began shouting at me, and the women who stood by joined in. It was a completely disorganised rabble which flatly denied God's right to command them.

One man with a particularly loud voice declared: "We will not listen to any of the words you have spoken to us in the name of the Lord." There were cheers, and arms were waved in the air. It was as if this statement gave everyone the freedom they had been fighting for: freedom to abandon all restraint.

When the cheering died down a little, he continued, "We will do everything that we have vowed. We will make offerings to the queen of heaven. We will pour out drink offerings to her, just as we did in the cities of Judah and in the streets of Jerusalem. It wasn't just us, either – it was our fathers, our kings and our officials too."

Another called out, "You know, Jeremiah, at that time we had plenty of food, and we prospered. We didn't see disasters. Life was good."

"You're right," confirmed the first. "But since we stopped making offerings to the queen of heaven and pouring out drink offerings to her, we've lost everything."

"Yes, we've been consumed by the sword and by famine since we stopped making those offerings," called another.

"All of you goody-goodies stopped us – you and Josiah, even Zedekiah at times. If only we'd never stopped!"

One of the women added in a sharp voice, "When we made offerings to the queen of heaven and poured out drink offerings to her, we didn't do it without our husbands' approval. They knew that we were making cakes for her bearing her image and pouring out drink offerings to her."

Many of the women cheered and made it clear that they agreed with her words. There were many other comments, both hostile and sneering. Most of the crowd was against me and many of them were eager to tell me exactly what they thought.

For a few moments it was tempting to just stop talking and walk away, leaving them to the trouble they were courting – but then I remembered the examination of my motives that I had been encouraged to undertake in Memphis. Was I only doing this job because God had told me to, or was it the work of my life; the joy of my life; my reason for living?

So I didn't walk away, and I didn't keep quiet. Instead, I stepped forward and asserted my authority. Of course, I had none, but often simply asserting authority is all that is required.

I held up my hands, demanding silence. It worked, and I replied to those who had given me these answers, both men and women: "As for the offerings that you offered in the cities of Judah and in the streets of Jerusalem, you and your fathers, your kings and your officials, and the people of the land, does not the Lord remember them? Do you think that he didn't notice them or see what you were doing? The Lord could no longer bear your evil deeds and the abominations that you were committing. Therefore your land has become a desolation and a waste and a curse, without inhabitant, as it is this day.[79]

"It is not because you *stopped* your offerings to these idols, but because you *made them in the first place*, and because you sinned against the Lord and did not obey the

---

[79] Jeremiah 44:21-22

voice of the Lord or walk in his law, his statutes or his tes-timonies that this disaster has happened to you, as at this day."[80]

Even as I spoke, I felt the fire of God spreading through me. I heard the voice of the Almighty and felt a new message from Yahweh being written in my mind. Having taken God's work as my own work, now he had worked further with me.

Then I said to all the people including all the women who were eager to have the leadership in their families and were not willing to leave their opinions unspoken: "Hear the word of the Lord, all you of Judah who are in the land of Egypt. Thus says the Lord of hosts, the God of Israel: You and your wives have declared with your mouths, and have fulfilled it with your hands, saying, 'We will surely perform our vows that we have made, to make offerings to the queen of heaven and to pour out drink offerings to her.' Then confirm your vows and perform your vows! Therefore, hear the word of the Lord, all you of Judah who dwell in the land of Egypt: Behold, I have sworn by my great name, says the Lord, that my name shall no more be invoked by the mouth of *any man of Judah in all the land of Egypt*, saying, 'As the Lord God lives.' Behold, I am watching over them for disaster and not for good. All the men of Judah who are in the land of Egypt shall be con-sumed by the sword and by famine, until there is an end of them. And those who escape the sword shall return from the land of Egypt to the land of Judah, few in num-ber; and all the remnant of Judah, who came to the land of Egypt to live, shall know whose word will stand, mine or theirs.

"This shall be the sign to you, declares the Lord, that I will punish you in this place, in order that you may know that my words will surely stand against you for harm: Thus

---

[80] Jeremiah 44:23

says the Lord, behold, I will give Pharaoh Hophra king of Egypt into the hand of his enemies and into the hand of those who seek his life, as I gave Zedekiah king of Judah into the hand of Nebuchadnezzar king of Babylon, who was his enemy and sought his life."[81]

It was nothing particularly new – in fact, the message was very much the same as what God had already given me to say – but for me it was a breakthrough. No longer was this a work that I did because it was my job. Instead, it was my life's work. It was what I had lived for and the work I wanted to do. I wanted to represent God to this people and I wanted to make sure that the people would hear anything God wanted them to hear.

Nevertheless, the fact that it was a breakthrough for *me* didn't seem to make any difference to my audience. They rejected my words utterly. They despised the God who had led their fathers out of Egypt, just as they had rejected his love in providing a Promised Land for his chosen people.

---

[81] Jeremiah 44:24-30

Chapter 18

Responses

As I finished speaking to that unyielding crowd, I noticed two people I recognised beginning to thread their way through the press towards me from different directions.

The first was the woman whose young son had been killed when the Edomites attacked us in the desert. Seeing her made me realise for the first time that she must have left Tahpanhes. Since she'd never attended our Sabbath discussions, I hadn't noticed her absence, and I certainly hadn't felt the loss of her unreasonable criticism!

There was a determined look on her face and I wasn't surprised when, without any greeting, she began berating me.

"You can't take a hint, can you! We left our comfortable houses in Tahpanhes just to get away from you, and now you follow us all the way up the Nile!"

"Pardon?"

"You made life unbearable for so many people, pestering us with prophecies and demands that we attend your Sabbath meetings. And now you track us down here to remind us of everything we suffered in Judah and on the way to Egypt because of Yahweh, your God!"

She had a young child standing next to her, clinging to her legs and looking anxious. After some quick calculations, I decided he was too young to have been born before we came to Egypt.

"You have another son?" I asked, trying to change the subject.

"Yes. Another son to replace the one you killed."

Changing the subject wasn't going to work against such venom. I'd have to fall back on head-on confrontation again. "You and your nation killed your son through your stubbornness and disobedience. Now that God has blessed you with another son, have you thanked him?"

"*Thanked* him! When you and he killed my firstborn? And according to you, your God was also the one who killed so many of my family and friends and destroyed our nation. Why would I thank him?"

"Woman, stop hating and *think*. When you were born, it was Yahweh who gave you life. When you were not killed in the siege or the pestilence, it was because God graciously kept you alive. He gave you a son who survived that terrible siege, and he also told us how we could have a happy life in Israel. You ignored everything he said and took your son somewhere he shouldn't have been, yet when he died you accepted no blame for that – instead, you blamed God. After the death of your son, God blessed you with another son, but all you do is curse. Have *you* been worshipping the so-called queen of heaven?"

"Yes."

"What can I say? At every step, in every way, you have resisted your maker who gave you life. Yet when things go wrong, you blame him as if they're his fault. If he behaved towards *you* as you do towards him, you would never have lived to adulthood. Do you love your son?"

She looked at me suspiciously. "Why do you ask? Are you going to kill him too?" Fear blossomed in her eyes.

"Stop it!" I said, angrily. "Stop this nonsense! I've never done *anything* to you *or* your family. Even God hasn't punished your stubborn rebellion as you deserve – yet you respond with nothing but hatred and cursing. You should be ashamed of yourself! How would you feel if this son of yours treated you the way you treat God? You feed him, you clothe him, you show him love, and any discipline you apply is because you love him and want to keep him safe. Would you consider it fair if he resisted you every step of the way, blamed you for anything he didn't like – even when it was his own fault – and hated you for any trouble that his own stubbornness caused?"

"You're exaggerating."

"I am not. Try thinking of God as your father and then think how you're treating him. How would you feel if your son grew up and treated you like that?"

"But why should I believe in God at all?"

At this point, the second person whom I had earlier seen heading my way interrupted to answer the woman's question.

"Because of the amazing things he has done in the past and the way he accurately tells the future," said Jezaniah.

I had noticed him as I was speaking to the defiant crowd and wondered briefly what he now thought of me and my message. This answer lit a fire of hope in me. Jezaniah had left Tahpanhes not long after we arrived, looking for adventure, and I had not heard from him since. Now here he was sounding like a man of faith in the middle of a crowd that had laughed at faith!

"You're right, Jezaniah," I said, probably sounding a little surprised.

"Are you another prophet of Yahweh?" spat out the woman, bitterly.

"Oh no," said Jezaniah, smiling. "Don't you remember me? I was a leader of a detachment of guerrilla fighters in Judah. I was one of the men who opposed Jeremiah when he said we should stay there after Gedaliah was assassinated."

"So why are you supporting him now?"

"I was wrong."

"Why do you say that?"

"Are you never wrong… ah, I'm sorry, I don't know your name."

"I am Zillah, the wife of Shemaiah, and this is our son Benjamin."

"Are you never wrong, Zillah?"

"Why should I be wrong?"

"Have you ever believed you were right, but later found that you'd been wrong?"

"I don't remember."

"Did you believe Jeremiah when he said that Nebuchadnezzar would destroy Jerusalem and that people would fill up the Valley of Ben Hinnom with dead bodies?"

"You mean the Valley of Slaughter?" Zillah cringed, whispering the words in horror. No doubt Jezaniah's reminder had brought to her mind's eye the same sort of hideous atrocities as it had to mine.

"Yes! That is exactly what I do mean. It was filled with dead bodies because everywhere else in the city was already full of dead bodies. Jeremiah predicted that.[82] But did you believe it?"

---

[82] Jeremiah 7:32-33

"Of course not." She had recovered her poise.

"It always used to be called Topheth. Did you believe it would be called 'the Valley of Slaughter' as Jeremiah predicted, and as you just spoke of it?"

"You're trying to trap me," said Zillah.

"No, I'm not trying to trap you. Just trying to get you to admit that you've been wrong about what Jeremiah's said in the past. Will you admit it?"

"Never."

"Then you're not interested in truth, in which case you can't expect truth or justice from anyone else. You've got no right to argue with Jeremiah unless you're willing to admit that he was right in what he said about Jerusalem, and you were wrong," said Jezaniah.

"So what if he was?" she answered, aggressively.

"Well, if he was right in that, and you were wrong, why would you refuse to believe him now, unless it's just because you don't like what he says? You don't care whether what he says is right or wrong; you aren't going to listen either way."

"I'm not the only one who says he's wrong – everyone else agrees with me."

"So according to you, if the majority of people don't like something that is said, it's wrong – even if it's right? Are you serious?"

"Stop treating me like a fool!" she ranted.

Jezaniah threw his hands in the air and sighed. "I take people as I find them," he said simply.

As the conversation grew more heated, at least at Zillah's end, I had noticed a quiet-looking man making his way through the crowd towards us. He hadn't seemed in too much of a hurry to arrive, but now at last he reached Zillah's side.

"Zillah," he said, "let's go." His voice matched his mien.

"Not yet. He called me a fool, Shemaiah!"

"Who did?"

"That man there," she said bitterly, pointing at Jezaniah. Things were looking as if they might get out of hand.

"I did not," said Jezaniah, "but if you think the description applies, perhaps you're right."

"See," she shrieked at her husband, "he called me a fool. Punish him!"

I had never seen Shemaiah before. Whenever we had met in the past, Zillah had been alone, probably feeling no need to have her husband around. Clearly Jezaniah had got through to her more than I ever had!

"I'm sure he didn't mean it, my dear. Let's go."

"You're meant to look after me, Shemaiah. Don't let this man abuse me."

"What were you saying to her, sir?" asked Shemaiah of Jezaniah, reluctantly.

"I was ridiculing her absurd logic. She's determined to reject everything Jeremiah says even when it's obviously true. That is foolish."

"Excuse me, sir, my wife can choose her own way in life. She doesn't need you to instruct her."

"She needs *someone* to instruct her if she can't think properly for herself! You should take her home and teach her how to think."

Eventually, Shemaiah and Zillah left, a poor, frightened-looking Benjamin trailing along behind, but they were no more interested than they had been in listening to truth! Shemaiah tried to excuse Zillah's continued ranting and raging whenever he could get a word in edgeways, but it was clear that it was she who made the decisions for the family, and that she had no intention of correcting her paganism.

☙

"Thanks for your support, Jezaniah," I said as Zillah and Shemaiah left.

"Have you really had people responding like that for more than 40 years?" he asked.

"Zillah is an extreme case, but yes, much like that."

"Well, no thanks are necessary. I still have some catching up to do. I've been doing a lot of thinking since I came up here from Tahpanhes. In fact, that's why I came. I wanted to get away from all the influences I've known over so many years: away from my army comrades, from the few friends I have left, and even from you; because I wanted to stop and think, and I didn't seem to be able to do it there.

"Since I came here, I've even started reading the law – imagine that! An ignorant, uneducated soldier like me starting to compete with the scribes and priests by reading the law! You and Baruch started me thinking, but I felt that I had to check things for myself. I didn't plan the reading when I came, but fortunately, quite a few of the Israelites who have made their home here have also brought copies of the law and the prophets with them. I was amazed to find that there are even some of your words in a scroll here!"

"My words – here?"

"Yes. It's a small scroll with an introduction saying it was a letter you had sent to Babylon to our surviving countrymen there. It talks about the exile lasting 70 years and tells them to live ordinary lives in Babylon while they wait for the 70 years to pass."[83]

"I did send a letter about that, back when Jeconiah was taken into captivity and Zedekiah had just become king. But how did it get here, so far from Babylon?"

"Rekem, the man who owns the scroll, is a rich man with a large collection of scrolls, both scripture and other things. He bought this one from a man called Tobijah who copied it in Babylon soon after it arrived there. Later, Tobijah had to escape from Babylon and wanted to get as far away as he could. By the time he ended up here, he needed money, so he sold the scroll to Rekem."

"Is Tobijah a scribe?"

"Yes. When I told Rekem that I was interested in your writings, he suggested that I go and talk to Tobijah – apparently there's quite an exciting story about this letter and his escape from Babylon. I would have been looking for him now if I hadn't been distracted by seeing you!"

"Perhaps the story of his escape will be more interesting than most of the information in that letter. It was intended for the exiles in Babylon."

"I hope the story will be good. I've done a lot of reading since I started trying to check on your prophecies, and reading is hard work. So I leapt at the idea of getting some information just by talking to someone. I'm a soldier, not a scribe."

"You must be very determined to find answers, Jezaniah, if you're willing to do so much reading."

"I suppose so. It would have been easy to dismiss your words – as everyone else does – but I've got to know you enough that I felt inclined to trust you. After a while, when I was almost convinced, I could have gone back to

---

[83] Jeremiah 29:1-10

Tahpanhes and talked to you and Baruch, but I decided to finish checking it all myself, talking to people and listening to their explanations as to why I should ignore your words."

"Just don't forget that they're not my words. They're God's words."

"Sorry. I should have put it that way, but it still slips out sometimes."

"That's all right. Well, there doesn't seem to be anyone else wanting to speak to me here, so why don't we go and look for this Tobijah? Was he here today when I spoke?"

"I saw him early on, but I think he left while you were talking. Anyway, I know where to start looking, so let's go and track him down."

Leaving the open square, Jezaniah led me through the streets until we reached the area where he hoped to find Tobijah. Locals helped us with more information until at last we stood outside the door of a small house.

Jezaniah knocked, and after a while the door opened, revealing a small man with greying hair who looked enquiringly at Jezaniah. His clothes, his hair, his beard and everything else about him were neat.

"The Lord bless you," said Jezaniah.

"The Lord keep you," replied the man in a pleasant, cultured voice.

"Are you Tobijah the scribe?" asked Jezaniah.

"I am," he answered. "And who are you?"

"I am Jezaniah, formerly one of the commanders of the mobile forces of Judah, and this…" he stepped to one side so that Tobijah could see me clearly, "is…"

"…Jeremiah the so-called prophet," finished Tobijah, looking far from pleased with finding me at his door.

"I came to ask you about a letter you sold to Rekem," said Jezaniah.

"One of Jeremiah's letters."

"One of them?" Jezaniah looked at me doubtfully. "You mean he wrote other letters?"

"At least one other that I know of."

"The one Rekem has talks about how long the captivity will be."

"Yes; the other was a personal attack on a few of our countrymen in Babylon."

"Was the attack warranted?"

"Maybe. But it caused a lot of trouble."

"Do you mean the letter I wrote a few months later about Ahab the son of Kolaiah, Zedekiah the son of Maaseiah and Shemaiah of Nehelem?"[84]

"Yes."

"God told me that they would be punished for what they were doing. Wasn't I right to warn them? Give them a chance to repent?"

"Well, I don't know if God punished them, but I do know that they're all dead."

Jezaniah looked at me, perhaps a hint of fear in his eyes. "Like with Hananiah the prophet in Jerusalem?"

"He claimed to prophesy from God, but he was lying," I said. "So were Ahab, Zedekiah and Shemaiah."

"Yet you are still alive, Jeremiah. Is that proof that you have always been telling the truth from God?"

"Or just proof that some people die earlier than others?" countered Tobijah. He clearly wasn't convinced that I was a prophet of God.

"But surely you know that Hananiah died very soon after Jeremiah said he would," said Jezaniah. "Jeremiah

---

[84] Jeremiah 29:21-23, 30-32

said he would die before the end of the year and he was dead within two months – well and truly before the end of the year."

"An interesting coincidence," observed Tobijah in a precise voice.

"Was there anything special about the deaths of Ahab, Zedekiah and Shemaiah?" asked Jezaniah.

"Ahab and Zedekiah were burned in Nebuchadnezzar's furnace," admitted Tobijah, reluctantly.

"Were they?" I asked in excitement. "God told me Nebuchadnezzar would roast them in the fire!"

"Well, it wasn't exactly roasting them – he wasn't planning to eat them!"

I laughed exultantly, though rather bemused by this strange attempt to play with words. Until then I hadn't known the outcome of God's promise, and it was another outstanding confirmation of God's power.

"Was their death a coincidence, too, Tobijah?" asked Jezaniah.

"There were quite a few people killed around then. It was a dangerous time – I only just got away myself!"

"Tell us what happened," coaxed Jezaniah.

"I lived in Babylon near both Ahab and Zedekiah, and when Jeremiah's letter arrived – the one I sold to Rekem – they were vocal in their opposition to what the letter said. They prophesied that we would return to the land of Judah much earlier than the pessimistic 70 years Jeremiah suggested. Everyone listened eagerly and liked their message."

"I didn't suggest 70 years," I interrupted. "*God* said that's how long the captivity will be."

"You may be right. We'll have to wait and see. Anyway, Shemaiah of Nehelem wrote a letter and sent it back to Jerusalem, which obviously upset Jeremiah, because a few months later another letter arrived condemning Ahab, Zedekiah and Shemaiah."

"Who are all now dead," I interposed, still a little amazed myself at the news.

"Yes, yes, I'll get to that," said Tobijah, tartly. "Anyway, just before that letter arrived, Ahab saw an opportunity to get some fame by lampooning Jeremiah's letter, so he commissioned me to copy it for him. I copied it faithfully and gave him the copy, but he never paid me for it. You see, Ahab and Zedekiah were enjoying life as popular prophets but they overdid it. They were playing around with other men's wives, and they made prophecies that got them into trouble with the king. Nebuchadnezzar is a touchy customer. When he learned about their prophecies and their immoral behaviour, he threw them into his fiery furnace, and that was the end of them. Personally, I think it was Daniel and his friends who told Nebuchadnezzar and incited him to do it all. They didn't like Ahab and Zedekiah, and Daniel can pull strings in court. If only he'd use his power to help his nation instead of kowtowing to a vicious murderer like Nebuchadnezzar!"

"Who's Daniel?" asked Jezaniah.

"One of the captives taken away when Jehoiakim was king. He's done rather well for himself in Babylon. A brilliant scholar, they say, but ever so strait-laced. Second in the kingdom when I last heard. The king leaves him in command when he goes out on military campaigns."

This fitted with the little news I'd heard about young Daniel, the son of Zaccai and Abigail, and his three friends, although I hoped that Tobijah's report was somewhat biased. The Daniel I had known would always have held God first in his heart. I hoped and prayed that this was still the case.

"Why were you in danger, Tobijah?" I asked.

"I was at Ahab's house trying to collect my payment when the king's men came for him. I had to do some fast talking to convince them that I had nothing to do with him and had just come to get my money. They were going to come and interview me the next day, but when I heard that Ahab and Zedekiah had been killed out of hand, I ran away that night. I didn't get my money, but at least I got the letter back. When I finally arrived here, Rekem paid me handsomely for it – and by then I needed the money badly!"

"You obviously don't believe Jeremiah at all," said Jezaniah, going back to the main point. "But why? It seems to me that you've seen and heard all sorts of proof that what Jeremiah says are the true words of God. If Hananiah or these others had been right in their prophecies, we'd be back in Judah already. Instead, they're all dead and no-one's back in the land, which is just what Jeremiah said would happen. Why won't you believe Jeremiah?"

"We're not all superstitious soldiers, you know," said Tobijah, a trace of contempt entering his voice. "We can't let mere coincidences change our entire outlook on life."

"How can you believe these were coincidences? Treating them that way ignores the fact that they happened exactly as prophesied. That's no coincidence! Sure, if I said vaguely that someone would die, and 20 or 30 years later they died of old age, I wouldn't have much credibility as a prophet. But if I said that a perfectly healthy man would die before the end of the year, that's a reasonable test. And if I said that another two men would be roasted in the fire, and not long afterwards they were thrown into a fiery furnace and burned to death, that would be another good test. Good proof, in fact, that I could tell the future."

It was the first time in my career as a prophet that I had ever had anyone support me like this, and to have it come from a man who had started as a vocal opponent was amazing. Jezaniah had given God a chance and God really had worked on him to open his eyes.

"Some strange things happen in this world," said Tobijah defensively. "These men knew of Jeremiah's prophecies, so that made them more likely to come true. Hananiah was probably scared to death, and Shemaiah too. And Ahab and Zedekiah weren't as careful as they should have been because they knew of Jeremiah's prophecies. It's just a combination of chance and you seeing something that confirms your existing bias."

"*My* bias? Tobijah, you're so wedded to your own bias that you can't see simple proofs that you're wrong," said Jezaniah. "I've thought a lot about this question recently. Have you ever asked yourself what it would take to convince you that Jeremiah *is* right? What would you need to see? It seems to me that there's *nothing* that you would ever allow to convince you that you're wrong. You'd always explain everything away with fancy words."

Chapter 19

Back to Memphis

October 582BC-April 581BC

I learned several lessons during my visit to the land of Pathros. Although I had already met Jews in many different parts of the world, I was still surprised by just how far we have spread and how many of us there are in foreign countries. Had God wanted me to go further upstream, apparently I could have found Jews the entire way up the Nile River, all following the religion of their fathers to varying degrees. I learned that some of my countrymen are very devout and dedicated to the worship of Yahweh, albeit with some local peculiarities or customs. Others, though, have completely abandoned the faith of their fathers except for a few lingering religious customs. They consider that the nation has suffered unreasonably because of that faith. However, since most people view religion as a part of their inherited culture rather than a personal, living relationship with their creator, Jews still tend to follow most of Moses' laws. Unfortunately, with little to command or control their beliefs, I fear that their religion will gradually move further and further away from God's commandments.

One night, shortly before I began to travel back down the Nile again, I indulged in the fruitless exercise of trying to guess where their beliefs would wander. The comments about the so-called queen of heaven made me fear that many in this area will soon join Yahweh to an imaginary wife-god!

Making up your own religion: that's what it really is – and how anyone can justify it I don't know!

Jezaniah and I spent a lot of time together, and the change in his attitude was like a drink of cold, refreshing water to a man lost in a scorching desert. While others were trying to stretch their religion to incorporate their own preferences, Jezaniah was searching for God's guidance to improve his religion and focus it more exactly on Yahweh and his ways.

I learned that he had never been completely godless, but that his family had not been devout. Priests and Levites had earned precious little respect from him and he had never known the scriptures at all. Although he had always felt that life should have more meaning, it had taken the loss of his entire family to prod him to investigate further.

It was a joy to present Yahweh our God to someone who genuinely wanted to hear more about him! Jezaniah and I often visited Rekem, who kindly allowed us to read from his large collection of scrolls. I say 'us', but really, I did most of the reading. Though Jezaniah was able to read, he found it hard work, so when he learned that I loved to read scripture out loud, he begged me to do so. He reluctantly agreed to my suggestion that he should follow along in the scroll as I read, and he genuinely tried to do so, despite the difficulty. He confided in me that as a field commander, he had always asked his second in command to read him any written messages that came from army commanders. Within his own squad, he had always given verbal instructions – "for security," he told me, laughing. This made me realise again just how much some people are forced to depend on others for their religious understanding. That in turn emphasised for me the huge responsibility that has been placed, throughout Israel's history, on priests and Levites, appointed to teach God's ways.

I was able to teach him, reading from scripture, including showing him God's own description of himself to Moses on Mount Sinai:

"The Lord passed before him and proclaimed,
'The Lord, the Lord,
a God merciful and gracious, slow to anger,
and abounding in steadfast love and faithfulness,
keeping steadfast love for thousands,
forgiving iniquity and transgression and sin,
but who will by no means clear the guilty,
visiting the iniquity of the fathers on the children
and the children's children,
to the third and the fourth generation.' "[85]

"Can I ask a question?" enquired Jezaniah when I finished.

"Of course."

"I read that passage a few weeks ago and I've been thinking about it since. If God both forgives and punishes, how does he decide which to do? Surely if I break the law, I'm guilty, aren't I?"

Well, that started me off! We talked for a long time about God's willingness to forgive anyone who genuinely repents. I used King David as an example of genuine repentance leading to forgiveness, even for a sin like adultery.[86] He lapped up the lesson, but I was shocked to discover that it was the first time he had ever heard of David's sin!

---

[85] Exodus 34:5-7
[86] 2 Samuel 12:13

As I got to know Jezaniah better and understood just how difficult reading was for him, it made me realise how determined he had been to discover the truth. Before I arrived, he had read much of the law – some of it several times – as well as parts of the prophets and some of the Psalms.

How blessed I had been in childhood, finding reading easy and growing up in a family where scripture was always available to read!

CR

After a few months in the land of Pathros, I felt that it was time to leave. I had passed on God's words to everybody I could find, and most of them were not interested. It was time to return the way I had come, giving the message to others as I made my way back down the river.

Jezaniah decided to come with me and I was delighted. I still had to do God's work in talking to large groups, but having an opportunity to teach one man who was so open to listening was marvellous.

We travelled down beyond the first cataract and some of my fears that Jews living in foreign countries would gradually depart from the law were realised. Landing on an island called Elephantine, we met a group of Jews. They had hit on the idea of building a temple to Yahweh, and none of them seemed to know God's statement that Jerusalem was the one and only place he had chosen for a temple. There was already a large temple to an Egyptian god on the island, and the Jews were planning to match it. If they had argued that God had abandoned Jerusalem for the duration of our 70-year exile, I could have excused it more, but their plan made no reference to God whatsoever.

I spoke to them and seemingly convinced them to give up on the idea at least for the time being, but only time will tell whether the effect is permanent.

We made our way past Thebes and all the way down to Memphis, speaking to many Jews as we went. Sadly, Jezaniah had several opportunities to witness the negative and dismissive responses that have greeted God's word throughout my career as a prophet.

We arrived in Memphis in the late afternoon. Climbing out of the boat, we followed a broad avenue away from the jetty and found the Jewish area that I had visited on my way upstream. There I looked for Phinehas, the old man I had met on that occasion, sitting outside his house in the afternoon sunshine. Once again he was sitting there, but this time he was asleep, so we walked on. I wanted to thank him, but it would have to wait. Instead, I looked for his friend Eliezer and, with some help from passers-by, soon found his house.

I knocked on his door and he opened it, looking enquiringly at us. After a few moments, he recognised me and said, "Ah, Jeremiah, the honest priest! Welcome back. Did they welcome you in the land of Pathros?"

"The Lord bless you, Eliezer. Some welcomed me. Most didn't."

"Do you expect it to be any different here?"

"I don't know. I'm here to find out."

"Oh, no!" said Eliezer, putting his hand to his mouth in mock fear.

"Would *you* welcome me and God's message?" I asked, finding that I really cared. It isn't that I haven't cared in the past, but I have to admit that at times, my concern has been more about my personal safety than about whether my audience will listen and be saved from idolatry or rebellion. Was this another step in truly making my job my own? True, it was mostly a matter of degree, but I believed that since my last visit to Memphis, I had gradually begun to care more consistently about *my audience* and how they could benefit from God's work through me.

"I would welcome you as a brave man."

"I don't want that. I want you to welcome me because you hope to hear God's word from me. That's what matters."

Evidently uncomfortable, Eliezer changed the subject. "If you don't mind me asking, who is your companion?"

"This is Jezaniah. He truly is a brave man."

"You mean because he's willing to travel with you?"

"Partly. Jezaniah was one of our field commanders in Judah. He led our men in guerrilla warfare against the Chaldeans. Does that convince you that he is a brave man?"

"Yes. But is that why *you* say he's brave?"

"No. What he did as a field commander required great bravery, but what he's started to do recently requires even more."

"What is that?"

"He's begun to listen to God and is doing his best to find out what God wants of him."

"What's brave about that?"

"Accepting God's rules for life means handing over control of your life to someone else. Have you ever done that?"

"I'm married," answered Eliezer, smiling. He obviously still considered himself a wit.

"Well, Jeremiah isn't," said Jezaniah bluntly. "And that's because God told him he couldn't. That's what handing over control to God can mean."

The next morning, I went and found Phinehas, taking Jezaniah with me. When I explained who Jezaniah was, Phinehas showed a great deal of interest in the defence of Judah and the guerrilla warfare in which Jezaniah had been involved, particularly during the siege of Jerusalem as Judah tottered towards defeat. Jezaniah described how the Chaldeans had invaded with overwhelming force and the small army of Judah had been quickly defeated. From then on, there were no more pitched battles.

The Chaldean army had subsequently split into several parts, attacking and defeating all the fortified cities of Judah one by one. That simplified description gives the impression that the only resistance came from within walled cities, but such was not the case. Despite their continuing victories and superior military capabilities, the Chaldean army still had to be cautious, as the defenders refused to give up. Like dogs nipping at the heels of a much larger foe, Jezaniah and his fellows continued to make life as difficult as they could for the Chaldeans. Yet it was a dangerous business. If the harrying dogs grew too brave or too careless, the foe turned on them, cornered them and tore them to shreds. And by that time, Judah's forces were so few in number that such losses significantly reduced their ability to fight.

"We kept fighting, and we kept losing," said Jezaniah. "At the time, I didn't realise that we could never win, no matter what we did."

"Why?" asked Phinehas.

"It wasn't Jeremiah's fault," said Jezaniah, waving at me, "but what he'd been telling us all along was true: fighting against God doesn't work. Jeremiah once told King Zedekiah that even if the Chaldean soldiers were all lying wounded in their tents, they would still get up and burn Jerusalem with fire.[87] It was the same for us outside the cities. Whatever we did, things went unexpectedly wrong, and each time we lost more men. However much time we spent planning, however clever our plans were, we always lost more of our men than we killed of theirs."

"And they had more men to spare than you did," observed Phinehas.

"Exactly," said Jezaniah. "By the time Nebuchadnezzar left with the captives, I only had thirteen men left – and most of the time we had to hide in caves and tombs." He stopped, putting a hand over his eyes and bowing his head. "Thirteen men, when only two years earlier I had commanded more than two hundred!"

I said nothing. It was a sad story – if you forgot that it was rebellion against God that had caused it. Even so, it was sad that Jezaniah had fought so hard against God only to regret it when he finally understood.

"God has not been kind to us, has he?" mused Phinehas.

"Not kind?" asked Jezaniah, blankly. He seemed to shake himself, trying to understand what Phinehas meant.

"Oh, Phinehas," I said, "how can you say God has not been kind when Jezaniah is alive, you are alive, and our nation has not been exterminated despite our rebellion?" I sighed. "King David said in a Psalm, 'God does not deal with us according to our sins or repay us according to our iniquities'.[88] If he did, we'd all be dead."

"But we are his people," objected Phinehas. "The sheep of his hand. Yahweh said he would look after us."

"Then why are you here?"

---

[87] Jeremiah 37:10
[88] Psalm 103:10

"We needed to escape from Nebuchadnezzar's invasion."

"Escape from God's discipline? You came back to Egypt where God said we would never need to go again!"

"Should we have stayed and died like everyone else?"

"What if you had stayed and repented instead?"

"I wasn't as bad as most of the people around."

"Of course you weren't," I said wearily. "And nobody who is sure of that can ever repent."

Jezaniah joined in the argument then, trying to convince Phinehas that it wasn't that God had failed us, but that we had failed God. He was no more successful than I had been. Yet Phinehas clearly did not want to send us away as enemies, and in the end, he said that we would have to agree to disagree. I have heard this expression many times from the more polite of my opponents. It is intended as an olive branch to end an unproductive argument, but I can never accept the tacit agreement on which it is founded, that I will not bring up the subject again. From the beginning, God told me to be like an immovable iron pillar for him, and agreeing to tolerate their views and avoid the same confrontation in the future is to water down God's message in a way he has never allowed me to.

Naturally, this never goes down well with my opponents, who often respond with bitter words or worse. Phinehas, however, responded quite gently, saying that he would not argue that point either. I think he was eager to hear what we had been doing upstream, and it turned out that he also had some important news to pass on. Together, these desires were strong enough for him to tolerate my intolerance.

So we continued to talk, describing what we had done and what ardent idolatry we had met in the south, particularly among the women. I also mentioned my concerns that our religion would gradually be reshaped to fit with the surrounding religions – a fear Phinehas shared.

We talked of the scriptures and the scrolls that many Jews had brought with them, and Jezaniah described the copy of the letter I had sent to Babylon and my surprise at finding it so far from there.

"It's the only way we can keep our scriptures intact," said Phinehas: "if people make faithful copies of the scripture and keep on making faithful copies. Did you know that our people are making copies of the words of God's prophets in Babylon too?" His eyes were bright, and suddenly, I knew that this was what he had wanted to tell me about all along.

"Who are these prophets?" I asked doubtfully, thinking of the many false prophets in Babylon about whom I had written to warn the exiles. "How do you know about them?"

"I'll answer your questions soon, and those answers would be news enough, but first, some even more amazing news!" Phinehas looked so excited that I wondered how he had waited so long to tell us. "A few weeks ago, a man arrived here from Tahpanhes. He said that Baruch, the son of Neriah, told him to come here in the hope of finding you. There, I knew that would get your attention!"

"Of course. Why did Baruch tell him to look for me?"

"Well, this man was living in Moab but returned to Judah after everyone was taken into exile and your party had come here following the assassination of Gedaliah. He lived there, apparently quite happily, for about four years – then Nebuchadnezzar returned."

"Nebuchadnezzar returned to Judah?"

"Yes, with Nebuzaradan, the Captain of the Guard, and quite an army. He was angry about the death of Gedaliah and his soldiers, and took more captives away to

Babylon.[89] This man managed to avoid being taken away again and stayed on in Judah for another two or three years."

"But we heard that Nebuchadnezzar was laying siege to Tyre!"

"Apparently his army was doing so – still is – but Nebuchadnezzar himself has gone back to Babylon. Well, this man decided to leave Judah and come to Egypt, and he brought some amazing news with him, just arrived from Babylon. It makes your predictions about Nebuchadnezzar attacking Egypt rather unlikely."

"What is it?"

"King Nebuchadnezzar has gone mad!"

---

[89] Jeremiah 52:30

Chapter 20

News and Scrolls

"Mad?" I said, blankly.

"So they say," answered Phinehas, a hint of glee in his voice.

"It's probably just a rumour spread by his enemies, or an exaggeration. I expect that all great empire-builders are a bit mad."

"Maybe, but it sounds worse than that. Apparently he's been put out to pasture, quite literally. He's been living out with the wild animals and birds for the last few months – or he had been when the news left Babylon."

"Who brought the news?"

"Well, when Nebuzaradan came from Tyre four years after they destroyed Jerusalem and took away more prisoners, he set up a garrison of Chaldean soldiers in Mizpah. About two or three months ago, new soldiers arrived from Babylon to relieve half the garrison, and Uzal, that countryman I mentioned, decided to invest some of his wine in improving relationships with the new Chaldean soldiers, hoping to gather some news from Babylon. When some of the soldiers had imbibed freely, one of them joked that if he didn't stop drinking he'd be as under the weather as Nebuchadnezzar. The soldiers all looked at each other and laughed, but they refused to explain what was so funny. Once they'd drunk a whole lot more, though, one got confidential and revealed that Nebuchadnezzar has gone raving mad and is living out in the fields. Apparently none of the others denied it, so I guess it must be true."

"Nebuchadnezzar, mad?" I mused. "I wonder what happens next?"

"Anyway, after that, Uzal decided that being in a captive country with a new king could be risky. So he came to Egypt."

"I suppose it makes sense that a nation wouldn't want a king who's gone mad," said Jezaniah.

"True," I agreed, "but God named Nebuchadnezzar as the king who would attack Egypt, so it has to happen."

"You really think Babylon is crazy enough to keep a king who's raving mad?" asked Phinehas.

"Could it mean a descendant of Nebuchadnezzar?" I wondered.

"You've had more experience with God's prophecies than I have," said Jezaniah, "but that doesn't sound likely to me. You told me yourself about a prophecy that named King Josiah more than 200 years before he was born, and showed me two prophecies of Isaiah that named a king called Cyrus who will rebuild the temple. Surely God must mean Nebuchadnezzar!"

"Yes," I said, slowly and a little doubtfully.

"Oh, come on!" said Phinehas, curling his lip. "Can you imagine a foreign king going to Babylon to see Nebuchadnezzar and being told, 'He's down near the river, but… be careful, he might peck your eyes out.' No nation would keep a king who's gone mad. They'll dump him. Nebuchadnezzar is their great warrior-king – they can't keep him in a paddock when he should be leading the army!"

"But Jezaniah is right," I said, thoughtfully. "God said *Nebuchadnezzar* would attack Egypt, so that will be what happens."

"But how?" asked Jezaniah. "Phinehas has a point. Could there be another King Nebuchadnezzar?"

"I don't know," I said. "If Nebuchadnezzar has gone mad then someone must have taken over as leader, even if he's not called the king."

"Not yet, anyway," said Phinehas. "But once someone gets a taste of running a kingdom, they're never likely to give it up."

A sudden thought occurred to me. "I wonder if Daniel or one of his friends might take over?"

"Daniel?" said Phinehas, blankly.

"An important man in Nebuchadnezzar's court," said Jezaniah. "He's a Jew, but more popular with Nebuchadnezzar than with other Jews, from what we've heard."

"I don't know how things are now," I said, "but Daniel originally became famous because when he arrived as an exile in Babylon, he refused to eat Nebuchadnezzar's special food.[90] Then he came top in the university in Babylon and interpreted a dream for the king that no-one else could even describe, let alone interpret.[91] Nebuchadnezzar seems to appreciate him because he's brilliant, hardworking and honest – although the king doesn't always like what he says about religion."

As I finished, I saw Eliezer coming toward us, accompanied by another man.

"Eliezer and Uzal," called Phinehas, beckoning to them. As they approached, he said to us, "Uzal is the recent arrival in Egypt I mentioned to you." To Uzal, he said, "We were just talking about your news."

---

[90] Daniel 1:8-16
[91] Daniel 2:31-45

Eliezer introduced Jezaniah and me to his companion, then said, "Uzal's news must have knocked your confidence about, Jeremiah."

"It gave me a shock," I admitted, "but don't worry, God can still work, even with a mad king."

Eliezer turned to Uzal with a laugh, "You see the problem everyone's always had with Jeremiah? Nothing fazes him. Nothing makes him see reason. Nothing can ever make him admit that his expectations are absurd."

"So what's he got wrong so far?" asked Jezaniah. Once again, he was bent on defending me and I wasn't used to it.

"Well, this invasion thing's obviously wrong, isn't it? Nebuchadnezzar won't be going anywhere – unless they put him in a cage on wheels!"

"Let's wait and see," insisted Jezaniah. "Don't forget that everyone dismissed what Jeremiah said about Judah, Jerusalem and the temple. I did myself! But who was right in the end?"

"Very well, I won't argue with you about the past," said Eliezer, "but this time, Jeremiah's obviously got it wrong."

"This argument isn't worth having," I sighed. "Each time more of God's prophecies are fulfilled, his detractors change their position. They ignore his successes and say that the next prophecy is too incredible to believe. Then when that one is fulfilled too, we go through it all again. I'm sorry, Eliezer, but you and people like you just don't *want* to believe, however strong the proof is."

Eliezer didn't respond. He was one of that class of Jews who firmly believe that they are strong adherents of our religion and worship God faithfully, yet reject his word spoken through prophets.

Phinehas took the opportunity to change the subject. "You were asking about prophets of Yahweh in

Babylon," he said to me. "And that's where we can give you even more news. The prophet we've heard most about is Ezekiel, although some also talk about a prophet called Danel. Perhaps he's the Daniel you mentioned."

"Ezekiel the priest? The son of Buzi?"

"I believe so."

"What's he been saying?"

"He went into captivity at the start of Zedekiah's reign, then started prophesying five years later, and he's been prophesying ever since – for more than ten years now. I read a scroll of his prophecies, and some of them are really strange. Maybe he's gone a bit mad too. After all, he lost his wife very suddenly."[92]

"Where did this scroll come from?" I asked.

"It was brought here by a Levite called Chelub who escaped from the very place where Ezekiel lives, near the Chebar Canal. He noticed that many of Ezekiel's prophecies were directed at the people in Judah, so he decided to do them a good turn and make sure they heard about them. He carefully wrote them all down, then packed up his bedroll and went to Judah."

"Was it really that easy?"

"Not at all," said Phinehas. "Chelub says the Chaldeans don't let their prisoners get away easily, but he managed to escape despite that, then travelled all the way back to Judah without getting caught! Apparently, it took four or five long, dangerous months, dodging soldiers and bandits all the way. An exciting story all round. He's still here in Memphis – you should get him to tell you about it. Anyway, he arrived in Judah eventually, but found it more dangerous than he had hoped."

"Because of the Chaldean soldiers?"

"Yes. Everyone in the land has to have papers proving

---

[92] Ezekiel 24:15-18

that they're allowed to live there, and he nearly got caught several times. He let a scribe copy his scroll, then ran away to Egypt, taking the scroll with him. After crossing the desert and sneaking across the border, Chelub decided to come upriver to Memphis, away from Pharaoh's court."

"So tell me again, what sorts of messages are in the scroll?" I was determined to find that scroll and read it for myself, but I wasn't above getting some snippets of the prophecies earlier if I could!

"Visions of cherubim and flying wheels. Pretending to be an army laying siege to Jerusalem. Cutting off his hair and chasing it around with a sword. All sorts of weird things.[93] And, Jeremiah, you may have had it easy as a prophet: for about seven years Ezekiel couldn't talk at all except when God gave him a special message to deliver! And even then, he could only speak that message, nothing else."

"That would be hard for anyone, but it would have been impossible for me. You see, God told me that I had to stand up for what he said. Argue for his truth at every turn. Just speaking the message once and then staying silent wasn't what he wanted from me."

"Your argumentativeness has got you into plenty of trouble though, hasn't it!"

"Yes," I agreed, "but as you observed yourself when I was travelling upstream, God kept me safe. Nobody has been able to kill me – although some would have dearly loved to do so."

"True. And poor Ezekiel might have preferred to have been killed, but his wife died instead."

"Tell me more."

"He'd been prophesying for about four or five years, acting out all sorts of strange living parables, and she'd stayed faithfully at his side through it all. Then Nebuchad-

---

[93] Ezekiel chapters 1, 4-5, 8-11 and others.

nezzar laid siege to Jerusalem and suddenly God took Ezekiel's wife away to teach the people a lesson.[94] You know, I sometimes wished when I was younger that I could be a prophet of Yahweh – but when I hear things like that, I'm glad I'm not. Prophets may have holier-than-thou attitudes, but they certainly don't have easy lives!"

Was that intended as a compliment?

☙

I unrolled the scroll slowly, my fingers revelling in the soft smoothness of the parchment. The text was clear and black, each character a flowing, though angular, work of art. This was a beautiful scroll, its scraped and re-scraped leather presenting a smooth surface, treated so that a high-quality ink could sink deeply into the leather. Such a scroll allowed a scribe to exhibit his best work. And this scribe had chosen an excellent ink too, so that reading his text was a pleasure. If only such a gift of scribesmanship had been mine! Yet perhaps it would have been a distraction from the work God had chosen for me before I was born. Nevertheless, I can never look at the work of a master scribe without feeling a touch of envy.

Turning my attention from the scroll to its contents, I began to read:

> "In the thirtieth year, in the fourth month, on the fifth day of the month, as I was among the exiles by the Chebar canal, the heavens were opened, and I saw visions of God. On the fifth day of the month (it was the fifth year of the exile of King Jehoiachin), the word of the Lord came to Ezekiel the priest, the son of Buzi, in the land of the

---

[94] Ezekiel 24:1-2, 15-26

Chaldeans by the Chebar canal, and the hand of the Lord was upon him there."[95]

That was all it took. I felt an immediate kinship with Ezekiel. Although he was in a different country, far-off Babylon, he wrote of visions of God, and it took me back to the start of my work for Yahweh when I had seen visions and heard him speaking to me. What an unexpected change in direction that moment had brought to my life! And here was another man – another priest, no less – experiencing the same selection and redirection. I can't really explain how close it made me feel at that moment to Ezekiel, and to God.

My analytical mind had not abandoned me, however, and in the background it had been calmly dissecting the text from young Ezekiel's record. Of course, by this time he must be in his forties – not so young any more. How life moves implacably on!

I must apologise; I'm wandering.

What caught my attention particularly was what seemed to be an insertion by an editor, saying of Ezekiel that "the hand of the Lord was upon him there".

I sat back and pondered the picture these words conjured up in my mind – that of a child standing with his father. A paternal hand resting on a young shoulder, providing companionship, support and direction. The picture entranced me and the description tasted good. Suddenly I could feel God's hand upon me throughout my own life, and it felt delightful.

Later I found that Ezekiel used this description a few times in his own writing, always at times when he seems to have been fighting God's direction – and that too I could take for myself. The life of a prophet is not always easy, and the direction of God not always the path we want to take.

---

[95] Ezekiel 1:1-3

"Do you like it, sir?" asked Chelub, breaking into my reverie.

"Yes, though I haven't read very much. I got distracted. Do you know Ezekiel?"

"A little. I've seen quite a few of his performances, particularly when he lay on his side pretending to lay siege to a clay brick!"

"Lay siege to a brick?" I repeated.

"Yes, he was acting out the siege of Jerusalem. The brick had the city skyline drawn on it and he built siege works and a siege wall around it. Then he held up an iron griddle between him and the city as if he was pressing a siege against it. None of us could make much of it at the time. You can read all about it just a column or two further on."

Looking at the scroll I was poring over, Chelub pointed to a place not far from the start. "There," he said. "It starts with God speaking to Ezekiel, saying 'And you, son of man'."

"Son of man? Does that mean Ezekiel?"

"Yes, God often calls him 'son of man'."

"Hmm," I said, intrigued – God used no special title for me. I read on. God's instructions for Ezekiel's visual parable reminded me of my own performances with yokes, clay pots and loincloths. *"390 days?"* I exclaimed, astonished. "Ezekiel was told to lie down in front of this brick for 390 days?[96] That's a long time! Did he really do it?"

"Yes, he did."

"That's amazing."

"It was, but that wasn't all. Keep reading."

I soon saw what he meant: "40 more days on his right side![97] 430 days all up – 14 months laying siege to a brick!"

---

[96] Ezekiel 4:4-5
[97] Ezekiel 4:6

"You were caught up in the siege of Jerusalem, weren't you, sir?" asked Chelub.

"Yes, I was – and locked up most of the time. It lasted about 18 months from the time Nebuchadnezzar's army came back after scaring Pharaoh away."

"Did you see what else Ezekiel had to do to make it look more like a siege?"

"What do you mean?"

"If you read a bit further, sir…."

Reading on, I learned that, for the duration of his mock siege, Ezekiel was only allowed about 200–220 grams[98] of food each day and about 600 millilitres[99] of water. It triggered memories of my own experiences; Ezekiel's siege rations seemed about right. I remembered the constant feelings of hunger and thirst, how everybody lost weight as time went on. Towards the end of the siege, even royalty became like gaunt scarecrows as food grew harder and harder to come by.

I marvelled at God's attention to detail in showing his people in exile what their brethren in Judah were suffering. Once again, I sat and thought, comparing in my mind's eye the experiences of the exiles and those who remained in the promised land.

Chelub interrupted my musings. "Are you alright, sir?" There was concern in his voice.

I realised that I'd fallen into a reverie again, reliving the horrors of the siege and its climax. Perhaps I'm getting old.

"I'm alright," I answered. "I was just… thinking… – about the siege."

"Was it really as terrible as I hear?" asked Chelub.

"It was worse," I said sombrely. "Whatever you've heard about it, it was worse. I saw… no, I can't say what

---

[98] Ezekiel 4:10. About 7 to 7.5 ounces.
[99] Ezekiel 4:11. About one imperial pint or two-thirds of a US quart.

I saw. Words can't really describe it. I lost what remained of my family, my friends, my associates – even my enemies. Few survived the siege and the fiery judgement of the Chaldeans. And then Jerusalem, and Yahweh's temple, were burned with fire."

But Chelub was not so easily put off. For the next half hour, he grilled me thoroughly about my experiences, his questions showing that he already knew quite a lot about the siege of Jerusalem. I let him ask, although many of his questions stirred memories I had done my best to forget. However, such indescribable barbarism and brutality can never be truly forgotten.

At last I asked him about his own experiences of captivity and exile.

"Life as a captive is hard," he began, thoughtfully. "We have little freedom, and many of us are no more than slaves, whose survival depends on pleasing our masters. Hard work and diplomacy help. But the idolatry makes it hard. Babylon and the other places where we've been spread have so much idolatry that it should shock anyone. Yet many of our fellow Jews happily join in. Some worship the sun, others worship the moon, and a few even worship all the many gods of Babylon. We don't seem to have learned any lessons."

"Do you worship other gods?" I asked.

"No, although I probably don't make as much of a stand against it as I should. The Chaldeans are quick to ridicule Yahweh, and it feels safer not to confront them. I know you wouldn't agree, but that's how most of us feel."

"Did you hear my words from God before you were taken into exile?"

"I did, but at that time I didn't really believe that Jerusalem and the temple could ever be broken down. But they were, and that means you were right."

"*God* was right."

"Yes, God was right."

"Do others agree with you about that?"

"Some do; some don't," Chelub answered. "You certainly shouldn't get the idea that large numbers of people believe the majority of what you said, even though they can't deny that you were right in that detail. You are deeply respected, sir, but I suspect you still wouldn't be happy with their attitude to your words or to Yahweh."

"Then what do people think of Ezekiel?"

"There are many different opinions. Some reject his words out of hand. Others listen carefully but do nothing about it. Overall, though, I think more people listen to him than ever listened to you."

His words hurt, and my face must have shown it, for Chelub hurried on, "Oh, I'm sorry, sir! I wasn't suggesting that they listened to him because he spoke better than you did, or anything like that. Far from it! I believe they listen more *because* of your work and the work of others like you. No reasonable person can deny that your predictions about the destruction of Jerusalem came true. Not only that, but many of your other predictions have also come true. For example, Zedekiah is still alive, although it's hard to understand why. Nobody expected Nebuchadnezzar would let him live after he broke his oath and rebelled."

"I always wondered about that one," I agreed.

"So I genuinely believe that your work has made the work of prophets like Ezekiel easier, sir."

Yet again, I was being reassured. It did take away a little of the pain I have always felt, the pain of forty years spent with so little positive response to show for it.

If my work really has made Ezekiel's work easier, or strengthened Daniel's hand, then all my efforts have been worthwhile.

Chapter 21

Revolution?

March 575BC

That journey to the land of Pathros was my last long expedition.

That statement seems very final, and as I re-read it, I have to admit that I don't know for sure. God gave me my life and God will take it away when he chooses. Until then, I never know when he may give me another job to do! However, a few years have passed since that last expedition and I'm definitely feeling older.

I can't claim that my trip was productive in convincing people to listen to Yahweh's words, but it was very encouraging to me personally.

Meeting Jezaniah again was a complete surprise, his change of heart even more so. He turned to God in such a determined and dedicated fashion, and I was blessed to watch his faith blossom and grow. His outspoken defence of God's messages was the sort of support I had longed for through many years of prophesying, but never really seen. Of my other supporters, Ebed-melech the Ethiopian was the most wholehearted, followed by Baruch. A few more showed half-hearted support, but what a barren landscape I've always seen when I searched for genuine, unambiguous commitment to God's ways!

But Jezaniah was different. He was like a cool breeze at the end of a searing afternoon, or balm on a painful wound. In fact, he even helped me to understand my own messages better, which was completely unexpected.

His life had been unhappy in many ways, but turning to Yahweh when he did, brought him peace and an unalloyed pleasure that was a delight to watch. He returned with me to Tahpanhes and spent two years there becoming a real student of God's word, attending our Sabbath meetings regularly and spending many hours talking with Baruch and myself about the scriptures.

Then one day it all came to an end when he suddenly collapsed as I was reading him a Psalm of David. I called the doctors, but they could do nothing. He was probably dead before they arrived.

I miss him deeply and I treasure the memories of his redirected life. God really will change our hearts if only we let him do so.

Since then, I have stayed in Tahpanhes, working and teaching as best I can, but finding it harder to do many things. My mind is slowing down too; I find it hard to concentrate as I once did. Nevertheless, life is still full of joy and happiness as long as I concentrate on Yahweh, my life-long guide and protector.

It is now nearly ten years since we arrived in Egypt; today is my 67th birthday. If King Josiah had survived, he would be 71 years old today, and perhaps the kingdom of Judah would still exist.

Never mind. There is no point in dwelling on the past, or pondering might-have-beens.

℘

News filters through to me slowly, nowadays. I, who once heard news early because of my constant travels, must now wait with everyone else. News from Babylon often takes a year or two to arrive, and when it does, we have no idea whether it is still true or completely out of date!

Several times over the years I have heard that Nebuchadnezzar's army continues its assault on Tyre. I believe the siege has now been going on for almost ten years – a futile exercise so far.

When will he come to Egypt?

God told me that Pharaoh Hophra will be handed over to his enemies.[100] I naturally assumed he meant Nebuchadnezzar, but Jezaniah cautioned me to think carefully before jumping to that conclusion. What God said was merely that Pharaoh Hophra would be handed over to his enemies – and he has many more enemies than just Nebuchadnezzar. There are the natural enemies one might expect among neighbouring nations like Cush, but there are also enemies within Egypt. When we arrived in Egypt, we heard quiet suggestions that there had been a mutiny in the garrisons along the Nile towards Aswan. It seems the mutiny was put down, but the unrest continued to simmer. This unrest was one of the reasons why there were so many Greek mercenaries in Egypt at the time. Pharaoh Hophra wanted an army he could rely on, and he clearly believed that an army bought with money was more reliable than one inspired by loyalty! Jezaniah knew this and pointed out that God's statement that Pharaoh Hophra would be handed over to his enemies might actually foretell his defeat in a rebellion or civil war.

At the moment, it's hard to know, but I'm glad that Jezaniah's suggestion stopped me blithely telling anyone who asks that Pharaoh Hophra will be defeated by Nebuchadnezzar.

---

[100] Jeremiah 44:30

But how long will it be before Nebuchadnezzar attacks? Will I be dead before it happens?

CR

"Heremyo!" said the distinctive, powerful voice, waking me out of a doze as I sat comfortably in the late afternoon sunshine.

I strove to open my eyes and rouse myself from slumber, knowing that I should recognise the voice but struggling to do so. It took me a while to identify Amasis – though in my defence, it was several years since I'd seen him. As I battled to clear the drowsiness from my brain, he teased me about having an afternoon snooze like an old man. I suppose it was true.

"Amasis," I said finally. "What brings you here?"

"Before I answer that, is there anyone around who may overhear our conversation?"

I glanced around and then motioned him into the house. Baruch and I still shared a house, but I knew that he'd gone to visit a man who wanted many of his financial records copied from arbitrary scraps of papyrus into some more formal documents. Baruch had left before I'd sat down for a short rest, but I checked his work bench in case he had returned and entered the house without disturbing me. It was empty.

"No-one should be able to hear us," I told Amasis as I led him into a windowless inner room, "but can I suggest that you moderate your voice?"

Though I'm sure he tried, Amasis' voice still echoed across the room: "I want to know whether you are still convinced that Nebuchadnezzar will attack Egypt."

"Yes. Nothing has changed. Why do you ask?"

"Have you talked to Pharaoh recently?"

"No. Not for almost ten years."

"Hmm. I'm glad I came to see you by myself, then." Amasis stroked his beard and looked around. This time, he actually spoke quietly. "Pharaoh didn't say so exactly, but he clearly implied that you had come to visit him again, to warn him about Nebuchadnezzar."

"I definitely haven't spoken to him recently," I said.

"Have you noticed that the number of Greek mercenaries in Tahpanhes has been increasing?"

"I suppose so. We don't really have much to do with them."

"The number keeps climbing. And it's not only in Tahpanhes."

"Does that matter?"

"Heremyo, you are not Egyptian, but surely you can see that foreign soldiers can be a mixed blessing."

"All soldiers can be a mixed blessing," I answered. "What do soldiers do if there is no-one to fight?"

"Granted, but foreign soldiers are even more risky. Foreign soldiers have no commitment to the country, just to their own income."

"I can understand that."

"So, what happens if they get upset for some reason? Or perhaps they don't get paid or… perhaps they are actually paid to fight against soldiers who are loyal to Egypt."

"You mean that someone might pay them more than Pharaoh is paying them so that they attack Pharaoh?"

"No," he said wryly. Looking around again, he spoke even more quietly, making sure nobody could overhear his words. "What if Pharaoh was paying foreign soldiers to be ready to fight against soldiers loyal to Egypt? Soldiers perhaps not quite so loyal to a Pharaoh who is selling his country to foreigners?"

"You mean, there could be a rebellion and Pharaoh might try to use his mercenaries to stop it? And you think that is why he keeps getting more of them?"

Amasis pursed his lips tightly and nodded. "Precisely," he said, and now there was no sign of his usual booming voice. Instead, his tone was quiet, conspiratorial.

Perhaps I was slow to catch on, but at this point it suddenly occurred to me that this conversation could be dangerous. Discussing a possible rebellion with Pharaoh's leading general was bad enough, but when it seemed that this general was convinced Pharaoh was trying to hoodwink him… well, the scene appeared primed for unrest, possibly even a full-blown rebellion.

I chose my words carefully. "Amasis, I can only tell you that Nebuchadnezzar will come, although it may still be a few years away. When we last heard, he was…ah, not quite himself. According to Daniel, a prophet of Yahweh in Babylon, that will last for 'seven times', which probably means seven years. His problem started five or six years ago, but he is still king and the attack on Tyre continues, although possibly not pursued with the same flair that Nebuchadnezzar would show."

"What if he stays mad? What if he never recovers? Will that save us from his attack? I always said such an attack was impossible anyway."

"He will recover. And sometime after he does, he will attack Egypt."

"But you still don't know when?"

"No."

"And in the meantime, Pharaoh is ruining the country with mercenaries." Amasis looked thoughtful, but determined. "There are Greeks everywhere," he said with distaste, "and they have no loyalty to great Egypt. We are Egypt, and they are not. We may need to do something."

"I can't comment on that, Amasis. You know that I won't get involved in Egypt's affairs except when Yahweh tells me to. Nebuchadnezzar will come, and any internal struggle in Egypt will probably just make his job easier."

"Perhaps," mused Amasis. "Perhaps. But we can't keep waiting forever!"

Ɔ℞

April 574BC

After that revealing conversation with Amasis, I began to wonder if we were about to see a rebellion in Egypt, led by my old language teacher! He'd been extremely popular when we arrived in Egypt, but I had no idea if this was still the case ten years later.

However, Amasis obviously managed to contain his frustration at Pharaoh Hophra's obsession with Greek mercenaries, because when I next heard of him, it was that Amasis would be accompanying Pharaoh on an expedition to the north. It seemed that Hophra had decided to capitalise on Babylon's apparent lack of direction now their renowned king was mad.

Phoenicia was a desirable target indeed: enviably rich through trade, and better equipped for trade than for battle. Of course, Egypt was not famous for its navy, so Pharaoh would press the attack from land.

I was a little surprised by the news, because assaulting Phoenicia while the Chaldean army was still attacking Tyre seemed rather risky to me. I suppose the move reflected Pharaoh's confidence that Nebuchadnezzar's hand would never again guide Babylon. For me, though, the campaign seemed likely to provide Nebuchadnezzar with the motivation he required to attack Egypt – just as God had prophesied.

The army set off with Pharaoh Hophra at its head and Amasis by his side. It was a mixed army, Egyptian soldiers mingled with large numbers of Greek mercenaries. News from the north arrived regularly thereafter, mostly reporting Egyptian successes. Tyre was bypassed without difficulty and the Egyptians attacked and conquered Sidon, as well as other less important Phoenician towns.

Several months later, the army returned – once again avoiding both contact and conflict with the Chaldean army – to extensive celebration. Reports came to Tahpanhes of cheering crowds lining the broad avenues of Zau to welcome Pharaoh and Amasis, his victorious general.

One evening shortly afterward, Baruch and I sat discussing the political situation of the world as our meal cooked. By that time, we'd been in Egypt for twelve years, and my predictions of trouble for the refugees from Judah were still awaiting fulfilment. I found myself in the same situation as had plagued me in Judah: how could I convince people to listen to God's warnings and change their way of life when such long delays preceded any fulfilment? I had promised that sword and terror awaited them in Egypt, yet most were living peaceful lives with few obvious problems. True, there had been some localised problems where Egyptian mobs had attacked Jewish refugees, particularly following disagreements about money or religion. In general, however, the Jews had fitted in to Egyptian society with precious little trouble.

Even Baruch was becoming a little doubtful, which is why our talk that evening had turned once more to the wider political situation. Having heard some more news that day about Egypt's victories in Phoenicia, Baruch was eager to pass it on.

However, I had heard my own piece of news that I was confident Baruch had *not* heard. Perhaps it was unfair, but I decided before the discussion began that, keen though I was to tell him my news, I would not do so until he had expressed his own opinions.

"Well, Jeremiah," Baruch began, "we're still waiting. Pharaoh continues to reign and win battles, while Nebuchadnezzar doesn't. What's next?"

I shrugged my shoulders and sighed. "I don't know any more than you do, Baruch."

"The enemies of God seem to be thriving, and no-one seems to be suffering as you promised."

"Are you starting to doubt, Baruch?"

This time it was Baruch who sighed. "No-o-o," he said, "not exactly. But I would like to have more evidence to show unbelievers."

"Wouldn't we both!"

"How come Pharaoh can waltz up to Phoenicia, win a few quick conquests and return with plenty of gold in his kitbag when the Chaldeans have been fighting – without success – to defeat Tyre for eleven or twelve years now?"

"I don't know."

"Obed from next door was laughing about it this morning, saying that the next step might be for Pharaoh to invade Babylon! He was sneering at you and your prophecies, calling you the prophet of a doom that never quite comes."

"Has he forgotten what happened to his mother and his brother?" I asked, bitterly.

"I asked him the same thing. It wiped the grin off his face alright – and got him mad!"

"What do *you* expect next then, Baruch?"

"Oh… I don't know. All the simple steps I expected have gone wrong. I expected Nebuchadnezzar to defeat Tyre easily, then move relentlessly on to attack Egypt, spreading terror and destruction. Instead, Nebuchadnezzar's completely lost his marbles and Pharaoh's the one accumulating victories!"

"Do you remember what happened when Hophra's father approached Jerusalem with an army while Nebuchadnezzar was laying siege to it? Remember how everyone was sure that we were saved from Nebuchadnezzar? But it didn't last, did it? Don't you think the same thing could happen again?"

"I *suppose* it could, but really, Nebuchadnezzar's a bit of a lost cause, isn't he?"

"Do you really think so?" I asked, watching him seriously. I needed to hear his answer; to see if he could believe God or not.

Baruch sat in silence for a few moments, thinking. He shook his head once or twice, then drummed his fingers on his knee. His expression kept changing, but it was impossible to tell what he was thinking. Then, finally, he stood up and walked to the door, opening it and staring out into the darkness. Perhaps he was just avoiding looking at me; maybe he was trying to see something in particular. Whatever his intention, he stood there without speaking for several minutes while I sat waiting inside, hardly daring to breathe. I wouldn't pre-empt his decision or make any attempt to sway him with my own words. I wanted him to tell me what he really believed. And I certainly wasn't going to tell him my news. Not yet.

After what seemed like an age, he spoke softly from the doorway. "The stars are beautiful tonight."

"What has that got to do with my question?"

"Nothing. And everything. Yahweh our God told Abraham to look up at the stars and try to count them. Of course, he couldn't, but as he tried, he learned to trust God. And when I look at the stars, I know that God's promise to Abraham about having millions of descendants has been fulfilled. So I have to trust his other promises. Yes, I believe that Nebuchadnezzar will attack Egypt."

I breathed out slowly. I hadn't even realised that I'd been holding my breath!

"I'm sure that you're right, and I'm very pleased that you're convinced about it. You know what? I have a little bit of news for you that makes me even more convinced than I was before. Do you want to hear it?"

"You wouldn't believe me if I said No…."

"You're right," I laughed. "I think it's important news. You know how Nebuchadnezzar was completely crazy and living out with the wild animals? It seems that he's returned to complete sanity! He's back in command of himself and of the kingdom – living in the palace, firmly taking hold of the reins and looking around the kingdom again."

"Whew!" said Baruch. "That *is* important! It's also utterly amazing. How could a kingdom ever wait for their king to recover from something like this? And waiting for so long, too! It really is incredible."

"It might not be long before we see Nebuchadnezzar marching on Tyre and then to Egypt!"

Chapter 22

Kurene

July 572BC

As usual, events didn't pan out as I had expected.

True, Nebuchadnezzar took back the reins of power in Babylon with great energy and before long was back with his army, pressing the attack against Tyre.

Yet even so, his presence and leadership inspired no immediate victory – which was just as well for Egypt, because at that time Pharaoh Hophra was setting off on a campaign against Kurene.[101]

I first heard about it from some of the Greek mercenaries who lived in Tahpanhes. I had become friendly with several of them over the years, which had given me the opportunity to improve my Greek. So when I heard about the bustle in the Greek quarter, I went to find out what was going on.

God has always blessed me with the men he has provided to help me learn languages. They have all been remarkably helpful, far beyond what one might expect, and I considered many of them my friends.

---

[101] Cyrene, Libya.

Zeno was no exception. He had come to Tahpanhes two years before I had arrived, invited – and paid – by Pharaoh Hophra to support his rule. Of course, it wasn't an individual invitation to Zeno, but being part of a company of former Greek warriors who offered their swords to the highest bidder, he was included with the rest.

His was quite a sad story. He had become a mercenary after his wife and only son died while he was away fighting for Greece in the Greco-Punic Wars. Since heroic patriotism had not gained him the acknowledgement he had hoped for from his country, he had looked elsewhere for employment, despite the ongoing wars. His decision to become a mercenary had paid him well, and by the time I met him he was in command of one hundred men and living in a comfortably large house with more servants than I would ever want. Yet he was lonely, since he had neither married again nor taken the easy relationships that so many soldiers fall into.

I can't remember how we met, but we fell into conversation and into a friendship that grew over the years, thanks to a shared interest in language.

When I went to his house that day, I found it a hive of activity. Servants bustled about busily, while soldiers seemed to be coming and going in a hurry, saluting constantly. It suggested to me that the company was preparing to travel.

Seeing all the activity, I was about to turn and leave when Zeno noticed me from a balcony and called out, "Jeremiah."

"Zeno," I answered. "Your household looks very busy."

"Yes," he agreed. "But I'll come down and talk to you anyway."

After a few moments, he appeared out of a doorway on the ground floor, smiling as he greeted me.

"Why so busy?" I asked.

"We're getting ready to go on another campaign with Pharaoh."

"Back north along the coast?"

Zeno looked around at his Egyptian servants and answered in Greek. "Not this time, Jeremiah. Across to Kurene instead. Pharaoh wants to take over the city."

"Kurene is a Greek outpost, isn't it? A fairly recent settlement?" I asked.

"Yes, comparatively recent. It looks like a strategic decision to stop the Greeks getting too much of a foothold in the area. It's a threat to Egypt's borders."

"And so Pharaoh is taking Greeks to fight the Greeks?"

Zeno smiled. "We Greeks have always been good at fighting each other, but mercenaries are a special case. We have no nationality, no home. Sometimes I wish that..."

He stopped. I saw sadness in his face and guessed it reflected a wish that events hadn't driven him so far from home. I must be getting old – I see far more unhappiness or wistfulness in my acquaintances nowadays than I ever used to. At best, life is full of difficulties; often, we are touched with outright tragedy. Even those who *seem* to have easy lives normally conceal past troubles.

Life is never easy, and I'm sure we can sheet home much of the blame for that to our desire for an easy or comfortable life! How ironic it is.

"Do you need to remain in a foreign land, fighting other people's battles?" I asked.

"What other choice is there? Who would welcome me back home if they knew I'd fought for Egypt for so many years? And anyway, what family do I have to return to?"

"You may not have any family, Zeno, but what about the other aspects of home? Language, religion, food, or even just a sense of belonging?" I asked.

"I've lived here a long time now. Language isn't a problem, and I have little time for either Greek *or* Egyptian religion. As for food, I have a Greek cook who makes the dishes I like." He stopped and looked reflective. "I suppose Egypt is home now. Isn't it the same for you?"

I stopped and thought. As usual, I had begun an endeavour with one goal – in this case, looking for information – and been forced into something completely different!

Was Egypt home to me too?

My immediate reaction was a violent denial. How could Egypt ever be my home when Israel was the land promised to my ancestors? Then I started to think about all Egypt had done for me.

Judah and Israel were both in ruins, and Jerusalem, the city of the great king, was burned with fire. My people were in exile in many places: very few remained in the land. I had not chosen to live in Egypt, but it had welcomed me all the same. For more than a dozen years now, Egypt had played host to me and many of my countrymen.

Slowly I asked myself the question again: was Egypt my home?

"No, Zeno, Egypt is not my home. Yahweh, the God of Israel, gave us a land of our own. Israel is still my home and my hope. After 70 years of exile, my countrymen will return – Yahweh has promised it."

"I will never return to Greece," said Zeno. "And Egypt has been good to me."

"So you will go and fight for her?"

"Yes."

"I could not do that," I answered. "Even when my own nation was under attack, I could not defend it because

I would have been fighting against God's plans. If I fought on Egypt's side now, that would also be fighting against God."

"You worry too much about your God, Jeremiah. Life is too short to waste it on worries about imaginary deities."

"I agree with you completely," I said. "We've discussed this before and I'm truly glad that you have abandoned the gods of Greece and ignored the gods of Egypt. They really are imaginary deities. But Yahweh, the God of Israel, is different. Not only does he foretell the future, he *controls* it."

"I wish I had your confidence, Jeremiah, I really do."

"Why don't we talk about it then? I'd love to explain why I *am* so confident. I've worked as a prophet of Yahweh for more than 50 years, and still I see his words coming true. Remember when we heard that Nebuchadnezzar had gone mad? Everyone was sure that he could not possibly remain king, yet God had laid out his future actions with Tyre, Egypt and other nations, so he had to recover. And now he has."

"Sometime I'll take you up on your offer," answered Zeno, "but now I must prepare to follow Pharaoh to Kurene."

" 'Sometime!' " I echoed. "But what will happen if Pharaoh is defeated and you lose your life? Why not listen now?"

"I'm sorry, Jeremiah. I have to go – there's a lot still to do. I'll come and see you when I return."

ॐ

August 571BC

Zeno never did return. The Egyptian attack on Kurene was a complete disaster and Zeno was one of the casualties.

Pharaoh Hophra had intended to limit Greek influence in his neighbourhood, but had ended up bolstering their power instead.

When Pharaoh Hophra and his army finally slunk back to Egypt licking their wounds and counting the dead, there were no celebrations, not even a formal announcement of the outcome of the campaign.

Those who lost their loved ones received precious little explanation regarding their loss, and many responded with anger. In the absence of an official account, the grapevine budded with suggestions and blossomed with explanations. The lifeblood of Egypt's vigour had been spilled and Egypt was not happy.

Timaios was another Greek mercenary I had befriended – a leader and a good friend of Zeno's. He was quite matter-of-fact about the defeat, and even about the death of his friend. He was, after all, a mercenary, used to the costs of war as well as its rewards.

"Welcome, Timaios," I greeted him when he called to me from the door of my house. "I assume that you have just arrived back from Kurene."

"Yes. Zeno asked me to come and see you," he explained.

"Come in and we can talk," I invited, knowing that Baruch would not be upset by me welcoming a foreigner into our house. Some insisted that Jews should refuse any contact with foreigners because they were unclean, but we did not agree.

Entering, we found Baruch bent over a scroll he was copying.

"Baruch," I said, "this is Timaios. You've heard me talk about Zeno, and I think you might even have met him once or twice? Timaios is a friend of his."

"You won't meet him again," said Timaios heavily. He sighed and continued, "Zeno was killed in our attack on Kurene. There weren't many of us killed, but poor Zeno was one."

"That's strange," I said, puzzled. "I heard that there were many soldiers killed."

"Well, yes, there were: many *Egyptian* soldiers were killed as they fled." He looked as if he would have spat on the ground in disgust if we had been outside. "I meant not many of us Greeks died," he finished.

"I see. And Zeno, how did he die?"

"I know you're not a soldier, Jeremiah, but I hope you would expect that Zeno died bravely in battle."

"Yes, I would, although I would have preferred him to have lived bravely worshipping Yahweh, the God of Israel."

"And that's why he asked me to come to see you. Our companies were fighting next to each other and he was badly wounded in an attack by the Dorians. We drove them back eventually, but Zeno got a sword though the chest. He knew he wouldn't live long, and when I tried to make him comfortable, he told me to stop fussing because he had a message for you."

"What was it?"

"That you were right. He should have listened to you more while he could. He said that Yahweh your God was a much better god than the Greek gods he learned about when he was growing up. Now remember, Jeremiah – I'm just passing on his message, it's not what I think myself."

"You and Zeno disagreed about the gods, did you?"

Timaios snorted. "We were soldiers, not philosophers. We didn't talk about religion all that often, but whenever we did, Zeno argued that our Greek gods were sub-human, not superhuman. Like selfish children, he used to say."

"But you didn't agree?"

"I say that it doesn't matter whether they're good or bad. Sneering at them won't make them go away. At least the fact that they're like us means we understand what's happening when they start fighting amongst themselves or picking on successful individuals."

"And you're convinced your gods are real?"

"Of course. My people have known them for hundreds of years, and they've helped or hindered many people and even entire nations."

"Have you ever *seen* any of these gods or demi-gods?"

"No, but others have."

"Have you experienced their interference or help in your life?"

"Of course. Everyone has unexplained successes and failures; times when the only reasonable explanation is that the gods have interfered."

"What did Zeno say about that?"

"He said they were all coincidences; that the gods were all made up by people with good imaginations. He even argued that our stories of the gods were originally written to entertain people!"

"Could he be right?"

"No! After all, many people make decisions based on what we know of the gods. People change the entire direction of their lives to placate the gods. They wouldn't do that if it wasn't genuine!"

"Oh, there's no doubt they *believe* it's genuine. But Zeno obviously wasn't convinced. Why are you so sure?"

"I was a soldier in Ionia, just as Zeno was, and I've fought many battles. It clearly wasn't always the best army that won. Not only that, but skilful and clever soldiers aren't always the ones who do well or gain promotion – or even survive. The only explanation that makes sense is that the gods are interfering in our lives."

"Does that seem good or bad to you?"

"We have to accept life as we find it. After all, there's no point in complaining about things you can't change! But there are ways to work *with* the gods instead of fighting them all the time. If we do things that please the gods, they help us."

"So if you scratch their backs, they'll scratch yours?"

"That's crudely expressed, but I suppose so."

"But if you please one god, you may anger another?"

"Well, yes, that can happen, but it normally only happens to people who become *too* successful. People whose fame begins to challenge the gods. For someone like me – successful as a soldier but not world-famous – it works quite well. I'm still alive."

"Which gods do you worship, Timaios?"

"Ares is the god of war, so I do my best to keep him happy, but Kratos and Hephaestus can't be ignored either, since a soldier needs strength and reliable weapons."

"And yet, if your gods start squabbling among themselves, you could be caught up in it, whatever you do?"

"Possibly."

"So why do you honour these gods when they're not honourable?"

For a moment anger flashed in Timaios' eyes, but it passed and he said mildly, "Some of my fellow soldiers would punish you for saying that, my friend."

"Have you ever heard anything about Yahweh, the God of Israel?" I asked, deciding that now was the time to go on the offensive – or perhaps the time to offer Timaios some consistent hope.

"A little," he answered, looking as if he saw an opportunity to attack. "But I never paid much attention to him. After all, a god whose nation ends up in captivity can't be worth worshipping!"

Perhaps Timaios was more upset about Zeno's death than he appeared. Could it be that he blamed me for it because I'd taught Zeno as much as I had? I tried to be gentle. Blunt, but gentle.

"I'm afraid that you consider all gods as like your Greek gods, Timaios. Yahweh isn't capricious like your gods are, but he doesn't always do what his people want either. He looks after his people in the way that is best for them. Sometimes that means punishing them to teach them to change their behaviour."

"What – even if it makes people laugh at him?"

"Nobody who knows much about Yahweh ever laughs at him, Timaios. He's far more powerful than all the other gods, but he's also better than the best person or god you could imagine. Almost a thousand years ago, the Egyptians thought they could beat him with all their gods and their army, but it didn't work. In the end, they lost their Israelite slaves and took generations to recover from the ten destructive plagues God sent on them."

"Yes, I've heard some of those myths."

For a moment, I felt a flash of anger just as Timaios had done. Perhaps he saw it in my eyes, too. Nevertheless, I smiled and asked, "But why would you call them myths, my friend?"

"They can't be true. There isn't any one god who is so much more powerful than all the others."

"And that, my friend, is judging the living God by the myths of your own gods."

"You win!" grinned Timaios. "I'll try to avoid just dismissing Yahweh."

"Thanks, Timaios. It's a good idea. How can I convince you that he's different from the gods of the other nations? He has requirements for honesty, integrity, justice and obedience. None of your gods are like that, are they? That's why I was trying to tell Zeno about Yahweh. Wouldn't you like to have a god like that?"

"But if you can't control him and he doesn't protect you from the other gods, what use is he?"

"To understand the way Yahweh works, you need to think about him as more like a father – a loving, consistent, generous, protective father, but one who wants to bring up his children to be like him, so he sets rules for them and punishes them when they disobey."

"Who ever heard of a god acting like that?" Timaios scoffed. "Sure, gods like to father children with beautiful women, but they don't seem very attached to them! Anyway, we're getting off-track. I came to talk to you about Zeno, not about your Yahweh."

"If that's what you want, we can do that. What else did he ask you to say?"

He proceeded to repeat what he had already said about Zeno. It was clear that he was just trying to avoid talking about Yahweh, and I decided to let him have what he wanted – for now!

"What happened when Pharaoh attacked Kurene?" I asked.

"We marched near the city and got everything set up ready to attack, but for some reason Pharaoh decided not to immediately surround the city and lay siege to it. Of course, Pharaoh can lead his army however he wants, but it just seemed indecisive. Then again, he left his best general at home, so maybe that's what was wrong."

"You mean Amasis?"

"Yes. Supposedly he was left in Egypt to keep an eye on the borders, just in case something unexpected happened. Some people said he was left for other reasons, but men like me don't get involved in discussions like that." He looked at me in a knowing way, but I had no idea what he meant. Being eager to hear the rest of the story, I didn't enquire any further. Perhaps I should have.

"What happened next?" I asked.

"The Dorians sent out troops from the city – small groups. Just intended to distract us, I reckon. I'd do the same myself. But Pharaoh and his generals seemed to get all hot and bothered about them: dragged the whole army around to meet them each time. We Greeks could have dealt with them easily, but we weren't allowed to. Pharaoh seemed to want to use his Egyptian forces instead of us."

"How did they cope with the Dorians?"

"Not well. It's always hard to tell what's going on in a battle, even small skirmishes like those ones. But the Dorians seemed to cut through their lines easily. From what we heard afterwards, there were lots of casualties right from the start."

"And you and your men were just sitting around watching?"

"Yes – and getting annoyed about it too. The men like to get involved. Without the extra money we get from despoiling corpses and selling captives, the income of a mercenary isn't anything to write home about."

"So you wanted to fight and couldn't, and Egyptians didn't want to fight but had to!"

"Spot on. And it kept going that way for days. We were being jerked around here, there and everywhere, but all we did was watch. Then one day the Egyptian soldiers fought for longer than usual before running. After that, the Dorians chased them right past our division. So we told the men to attack. To be honest, I think they would have attacked anyway – but our commanders aren't stupid, so they gave the order to attack. Quite a few of our men don't consider the Dorians as friends anyway, even though we're all Greeks. Some have old scores to settle. So we attacked."

"Was this when Zeno was killed?"

"Yes. He was unlucky, really."

"Unlucky? How does that fit with those gods of yours?"

"We have a goddess of fortune called Tyche," smiled Timaios.

"Knowing one all-powerful God makes it hard to understand a collection of gods with contradictory and overlapping powers. A god of victory and a god of luck – does it just depend on who's awake at the time?"

"Perhaps. Anyway, you're changing the subject again when I was in the middle of telling you what happened. Where was I? Yes, we were driving them back without much difficulty. A few casualties, of course, but nothing bad. Then some Dorian reinforcements came up just when their troops were about to break and run. Zeno was fighting one of their officers. Well on top, he was, too. I was quite near and had killed my man, so I had some time to look around. He would've killed his man in just a few moments, but instead, he suddenly found himself fighting two. Poor Zeno, I think he got a surprise and slipped. He fell, and quick as a wink, one of the Dorians put a sword through his chest. I knew it was all over for Zeno. Those reinforcements didn't help the Dorians much, either – we soon had them on the run. Then I went back to poor Zeno."

"Could you help him at all?"

"Two of his men were already doing their best, but all we could do was try to make him more comfortable. That was when he told me to stop messing around and listen to that message for you."

"Thanks for letting me know. I'm sorry he died like that, and even sorrier that he never took his opportunity to learn more about Yahweh."

"Whereas I hope his blasphemy didn't cause him any trouble with Charon. Just before he died, I tried to put a coin under his tongue, but he spat it out and told me he wouldn't need it. Stubborn."

"Oh yes, you have some idea about having to pay Charon to take you across the River Styx into the underworld, don't you?" I asked.

"Not just 'some idea', Jeremiah," said Timaios, irritably. "It's a well-known fact that if we don't have that coin, Charon might refuse to take our soul across the river, even if we've been buried. We made sure we buried Zeno, of course."

"Did he seem upset to be dying?" I asked.

"No, not really. He didn't think he had much to live for."

"I wish he'd stayed here and learned more about Yahweh," I fretted.

"He was a soldier, not a priest," answered Timaios. "Like me, his job was killing. And we professional soldiers all expect to be killed in the end. I just hope I'll have my coin to pay Charon."

"Yet there's no way for you to know whether he'll be there waiting for you or whether you've got it all wrong."

"Surely everyone can't be that far wrong?"

"If you Greeks are right then every other nation is wrong. And if Yahweh is right, every other god is wrong. I'll take Yahweh."

"But what if he's wrong?"

"He isn't. I've spoken to him many times. I've heard many of his prophecies of the future – and seen plenty fulfilled. And you can watch some prophecies being fulfilled too. Two examples: firstly, Pharaoh Hophra will be handed over to his enemies, and secondly, Nebuchadnezzar will invade and conquer Egypt."

"It's probably nonsense, but I'll see," said Timaios, grudgingly. "Maybe I owe it to Zeno. He was a good friend."

Chapter 23

Pharaoh's Negotiator

January 570BC

"Pharaoh Hophra killed my brother!" shouted a voice.

"And my son," called another.

"And two of my neighbours," added a third.

Loud cymbal-clashes followed, demanding the attention of everyone in earshot. Yet through the metallic din came faintly a rhythmic chant of "Hophra's a traitor". A few repeats and then silence fell once more. Individual voices began again.

"Loyal Egyptian soldiers died for Hophra."

"But his Greeks are all alive."

"Egyptians fight, Egyptians die; but the Greeks stand by and laugh!"

Once again the cymbals took over, but once again, the chanting could be heard in the background: "Hophra's a traitor. Hophra's a traitor."

The group of dissenters was not large, but I had never seen such action in Egypt before. They were getting support from bystanders, but they were also attracting the attention of Pharaoh's guards.

As I walked along the avenue leading past Pharaoh's

palace that morning, my first warning of anything out of the ordinary had been the sound of cymbals, then I had seen the small group. But as I drew closer and heard the words they were chanting, the event took on a new – and much more dangerous – significance. This was no small group of noisy revellers celebrating near Pharaoh's palace, it was a group of would-be rebels.

Interestingly, the place where they were standing was one where I had tried to get an audience myself a few years before. It was the entrance to Pharaoh's palace, the pavement under which I had buried some large stones at God's command. As far as I knew, they were still there – and I did keep a close eye on the palace over the years, just to make sure.

Nebuchadnezzar would set his throne above them when he invaded Egypt, but that hadn't happened yet. Perhaps what I was witnessing was a step towards its fulfilment.

The strident criticism of Pharaoh continued as almost everyone who came along the avenue stopped to watch. The audience grew rapidly and soon blocked all traffic on the avenue. Nobody seemed willing to join the dissenters, but it was clear that many of them agreed with the criticism of Pharaoh. However, some cast worried glances at Pharaoh's guards, wondering how long this mood of rebellion would be allowed to go unchallenged.

There was no question that the guards had noticed, but since many of them were Greeks and probably had a poor grasp of the language, the period of grace continued. Had Pharaoh been in residence, the protests may have been loud enough for his royal ears to hear the shocking abuse first-hand. Instead, he later heard only a watered-down, but still colourful, report from the chief of his palace guards.

Suddenly, grace exhausted its time of opportunity and cold, unflinching punishment fell on the heads of the rebels.

As the heavy cymbals resumed their clashing and the chanting asserted once more that Hophra was a traitor, the doors of Pharaoh's palace swung open and 50 armed guards poured out. They came with swords bared, ready for action, their approach silent but menacing.

The audience fell back immediately and the sound of the cymbals faltered. Yet the chanters were defiant and the insistent, rhythmic chorus rang out in the sudden quiet:

"Hophra's a traitor! Hophra's a traitor!"

Hophra's guards gave the group exactly one chance to surrender.

"Lie down on the ground," shouted their leader to the rebels. Most obeyed, hurriedly, but one appeared to have an injured leg and didn't move fast enough. The chief of the guards cut him down and left him to die on the pavement. Another turned and ran, but his group's success in attracting a crowd was his undoing. He tried to dodge through the crowd to escape, but there was too little room and the guards were too close behind. He staggered into a group of men, knocking several over, then tripped and fell.

Desperately, he tried to crawl away in the crush, but three guards chased him down. They were careful not to injure any of the crowd, but a business-like sword-thrust brought this mini rebellion to an end as soon as they had the man surrounded.

The dissidents who survived were bound where they lay, then dragged roughly away into the palace. The bodies were left to be dealt with later.

Events moved quickly after that.

Though it was probably an ill-judged display of civic anger, news of it spread across Egypt and we heard of similar happenings in other places, despite the sudden and harsh punishment.

I had already heard of widespread anger in Tahpanhes among the Egyptian relatives of the many soldiers who had died near Kurene. Anger with a ruler normally passes like a storm cloud, but this felt different.

Perhaps the worst aspect of all this was that I suspected, based on Timaios' description, that it was probably all a misunderstanding. Pharaoh Hophra had actually wanted to give his Egyptian forces an opportunity to return to Egypt covered in glory and so had compelled his Greeks to stand by and watch.

Instead, it all went horribly wrong, and Pharaoh and his advisors refused to change their strategy. When the number of Egyptian deaths mounted rapidly, Pharaoh could have brought in the Greeks to help. If Timaios was to be believed, this might even have reversed Egypt's failing fortunes. But Pharaoh stuck to his plan, leaving the Egyptians to bear the brunt of the Dorian assaults – and die in large numbers. Meanwhile, the mercenaries stood by, mostly unscathed.

In war, plans can easily go wrong, rapidly changing the future of nations.

All of those dead soldiers had relatives who were demanding explanations as to why so many Greeks returned alive when the Egyptians didn't.

Pharaoh Hophra was the target of their anger. Had not he knowingly sent their loved ones to the grave? And what explanation could there be except that he intended to strengthen his own rule by eliminating the soldiers he viewed as threats?

Open rebellion spread across the country.

❧

Away upriver in Upper Egypt, far from the presence of Pharaoh and his Greek bodyguard, rumour reported that rebellious troops were gathering, forming an army. It seemed that civil war was brewing, and I wondered what would happen to the Jews in Egypt if war did break out.

Pharaoh Hophra travelled around the delta shoring up support. We saw him in Tahpanhes, but his urgent plea for loyal aid was a far cry from his accustomed leisurely visits.

For me, the next step in the unfolding rebellion came during this visit.

Amasis sent me a letter requesting, or demanding, a meeting with me. As Pharaoh's most famous and popular general, Amasis formed part of the travelling entourage with whose help Hophra was hoping to put down all opposition – preferably without the need for fighting.

Amasis' letter instructed me to meet him at the gates of the barracks in Tahpanhes, not far from Pharaoh's palace.

As the sun was setting that evening, I went there as requested. The entire barracks was on high alert and anyone who stood around outside was being warned and moved on. Obviously, the soldiers were edgy.

Amasis was waiting when I arrived, his personal servant by his side.

"Heremyo," he said, giving me a bear-hug. It was a few years – perhaps five – since I'd last seen him close up, and he looked significantly older. His manner was urgent and he looked concerned. "Can we talk in private?" he asked.

"That's not easy in an open area like this."

"Then come with me in my chariot. We'll go outside the walls for a few minutes before they shut the gates." He dispatched his servant, who returned in a remarkably short time driving a chariot drawn by two horses. There was only room in the chariot for two, so when Amasis climbed aboard and motioned for me to do likewise, the servant got down, his face expressionless. He was probably used to Amasis' abrupt and sometimes frivolous behaviour. I don't know whether he had any concerns about his master travelling with an old, white-bearded foreigner, but if he did, they didn't show.

Amasis drove in his ordinary, reckless way, and soon we had left the city and stopped beside the road. He had excited the horses enough by then that they did not really want to stand still, but he seemed to enjoy their restiveness. There was little traffic and we were able to talk in private.

"Are we still waiting for Nebuchadnezzar to invade?" he asked.

"Yes," I answered. "When I last heard, the Chaldeans were making steady progress against Tyre, so they're unlikely to abandon the attack. However, they aren't finished, so Nebuchadnezzar won't be ready to come here yet."

"And he may never do so..." mused Amasis.

"No, that's not right," I countered. "He *will* come, but I don't know when."

"And you also predicted that Pharaoh Hophra would be handed over to his enemies, didn't you?"

"Yes," I said, wondering if this prophecy – despite having been made several years ago – could get me into trouble if Pharaoh went on a witch-hunt.

"Could that be referring to the current situation, the enemies he has now?" asked Amasis.

"I can't say," I answered, recalling Jezaniah's warning from several years before not to assume that Nebuchadnezzar was the enemy being referred to. "I report the prophecies I'm given. Beyond that, I know no more than you do. Yahweh is the one who knows the details."

"So it could equally easily be rebel soldiers or Nebuchadnezzar?"

"I suppose so."

"You know, Heremyo, you aren't very helpful."

"Helping you to put down a rebellion isn't the job Yahweh gave me."

Amasis looked steadily at me for some time, then smiled and said, "If only I knew whether to rely on your words or not."

"I could give you more specific answers, my friend, but then you definitely couldn't rely on them!"

After a few more moments of thought, Amasis seemed to accept that I could tell him no more. "I must get back into the city, Heremyo. Hophra is like a clucking hen at times. He may start to wonder where I am."

He wheeled the chariot around and drove exuberantly back to the city gates. They had closed, and it took some fast talking from Amasis to convince the guard to let us in. For a while it even looked as if they were going to let him in and leave me outside in the cold. Eventually, however, Amasis' easy manner talked them around and soon I was being dropped off near the barracks and left to find my own way home.

ℭℜ

Hophra left Tahpanhes the next day, taking with him Amasis and many of the Greek mercenaries – including Timaios and his men.

News swirled around perpetually, each day bringing a new harvest of titbits. Unfortunately, these were often contradictory. The rebels had given up and run away; Hophra was dying of some dread disease caught in Kurene. Discerning what was true and what was not was the real challenge.

I won't bore you with all the different ideas I had that were later shown to be wrong. Instead, I will report only the details I found to be true – as far as that's possible! In such a confused situation, one needs the wisdom of Solomon to sift truth from the confections presented as such.

The rebels gathered at Memphis and began to build an army there. The garrisons further upstream all threw their weight behind the rebels, and Hophra could not get past Memphis to alter their opinions.

In the delta itself, most people supported Hophra, but it was by no means unanimous, and the support offered could be ambiguous. From his palace at Zau, Pharaoh sent messages to many towns and garrisons asking for confirmation of their loyalty. Some cities replied with eager loyalty, while others required repeated enquiries to wring from them even an equivocal response. Pharaoh Hophra didn't quite know what to make of it all.

"This reply was received from the garrison at Giza," said Patarbemis, one of the king's most famous advisors. "It reads, 'We will support Pharaoh'."

"Good," smiled Hophra. "An unequivocal statement of support."

"Have a care, sire," said Patarbemis, drily.

"What do you mean?"

"They say they will support Pharaoh. They do not say 'Pharaoh *Hophra*'."

"There is only one Pharaoh, Patarbemis, and that is me: Pharaoh Hophra."

"Yes, sire, but what if you were *not* the only Pharaoh?"

"Are you suggesting there is another Pharaoh?" bristled Hophra.

"Of course not, sire. I am your loyal servant. But what if the rebels name their leader 'Pharaoh'?"

"You are suggesting that this answer is deliberately vague? That can't be true. They support Pharaoh, and *I am Pharaoh*. Surely that is as simple as it gets?"

"I don't know, sire."

Pharaoh Hophra pursed his lips and frowned angrily at his advisor. "I'm not pleased with you, Patarbemis. You don't seem to be giving me the support you promised."

"I am giving you the help I promised, sire. This is not an easy situation and we need to be careful. Act too hastily, sire, and the kingdom may be lost."

"Is that a threat?"

"Of course not, sire. I am doing my best to help you."

"You're not doing very well at the moment! A garrison responds positively and you tell me they're not supporting me. Keep going like this and you won't let anyone support me! Just remember that I'm the one who pays you and lets you work for me. Your prominence – and yes, I know that you're well known as a wise man – comes from my generosity."

"Sire, you are Pharaoh. You are famous as the leader who roundly defeated the Phoenicians, a feat Nebuchadnezzar the Chaldean himself cannot emulate, even though you've weakened the Phoenician forces."

"That's more like it, Patarbemis. Why won't those cursed rebels think like that?"

"Perhaps you should send someone to talk to them? Someone they will listen to."

"But if I go and talk to them they may… they may kill me!"

"You're right, sire. Perhaps it would be better to send someone else – maybe a leader of the army who is firmly on your side and respected by all the soldiers of Egypt."

Hophra sniffed. "But if they won't listen to me, their true leader, who will they listen to?"

"Remember, there's a general who was associated with the successes of your honourable father, and with your successes too."

"General Amasis?"

"Yes, General Amasis. A loyal servant of your father and your honoured self."

"Loyal, yes," nodded Hophra. "Amasis is loyal…" his face darkened a little, "although at times he has tried to tell me that my Greeks are a problem."

"Under your guidance, sire, Amasis has been a most successful general, and the soldiers love him."

"But he wasn't with them on our last campaign."

"No, he wasn't," agreed Patarbemis smoothly, "but they will listen to him all the same." In fact, he added to himself, far more so. Amasis' lack of involvement in the disastrous campaign against Kurene was one of the main reasons Patarbemis had suggested him as a negotiator. The soldiers were much more likely to listen to one who was not tainted by the failure of that operation. They would listen to Amasis in a way in which they would not now listen to Hophra. If the anger at Hophra could be calmed for a while, the urgency of rebellion would diminish and Hophra could gradually work his way back into the army's good graces. Patarbemis was determined that Hophra should be kept in the background for a time. At the moment, keeping him away was the best way for Patarbemis to show his loyalty!

"You are right, Patarbemis," said Hophra, decisively. "Call General Amasis."

ↂ

"General Amasis, you are, of course, aware of the situation in Memphis."

"Yes, sir."

"Patarbemis here is of the opinion that this rebellious rabble may listen to you. I have agreed, so now I want you to go and see them. Take a company of men with you

– enough to give you some protection and prestige, but not so many that you scare them – and talk to their leaders. I have no idea who they are, but you should be able to talk them around for me."

"I should be able to *talk them around*, sir?"

"Yes. Convince them to give up and go back to their stations. Forget this whole rebellion and do what they're told!"

"Ah. Well, perhaps I can, sir, but what if I can't?"

"We will not let your memory be forgotten. We will erect a statue in your honour, and then we will put down the rebellion by force."

"That's a comforting thought," said Amasis, keeping a straight face.

Had I been there, I could have told Hophra that this was pure sarcasm, but he could not conceive of the possibility that his senior General would treat his king with such levity.

"Anyway, I'm sure they will listen to you. If you wish, Patarbemis can go with you. His fearsome intellect might help, but I think your earthy humour is more likely to win the day with soldiers. I have always found my own eloquence a little too… too cultured, too esoteric for soldiers. You won't have a problem like that."

"Thank you, sir." Sarcasm again, but Hophra was blissfully ignorant. Patarbemis, more perceptive, threw a look at Amasis, warning him not to overdo it. "Well, sir, I can do as you wish," continued Amasis, "but I can't help thinking that having an army at my back would be preferable to relying on my honeyed tongue. Have you considered the strategy of assembling the largest army we can command and marching on Memphis? A little extra pressure may make my errand more likely to succeed."

"I have taken your advice on many occasions, Amasis," said Hophra, "but on this occasion I know best.

I don't want a confrontation if I can avoid it. Your achievements are universally admired, and your forceful personality will undoubtedly overwhelm any presumptuous leaders they may have appointed. Bring the rebels back to me and I will spare them all – except the leaders."

Amasis stood for a while, his face impassive save for a faint smile that lurked unnoticed. Hophra, who had expected immediate agreement, was beginning to frown when Amasis finally answered, "Very well, sir. I myself will go to Memphis and take a company of my best soldiers with me. I will speak to the rebels and do what I can to bring about a successful resolution to this rebellion."

"Perhaps you could take some of my bodyguard with you," offered Hophra, generously.

"The Greeks? No, sir. Egyptian soldiers would be best in this situation," said Amasis, decisively.

Patarbemis exchanged glances with Amasis and gave the briefest possible nod of agreement.

As Amasis left the throne room soon afterwards, Hophra was content that the revolution was all but over. Amasis was an exceptional general. In his hands, there was no doubt that Hophra's problem would shortly be solved.

Patarbemis was not so confident. Though he was convinced that this was the best step to take – and with all possible speed – he was still concerned that the rebellion might already have grown so strong that only warfare would solve it. Perhaps, before long, they would be making that statue Hophra had promised Amasis. And then who would lead the army to put down the rebellion?

Chapter 24

An Unexpected Turn of Events

March 570BC

Amasis carefully selected a company of three hundred soldiers and made his way towards Memphis. Having sent a letter ahead to inform the rebel leaders of his coming, he then gave them little time to consider their response.

Early the following day, he neared Memphis. The rebel army was spread out across the open fields downstream from the city. Thus, to reach the gates, Amasis and his company must run the gauntlet of this mass of men, many of whom were angry with the Pharaoh who had sent these visitors.

Seeing Amasis approach the nearest ranks of the mutineers, the rebel leaders trotted out of the distant gates of Memphis. As they advanced, the way cleared before them and shouting troops lined the road, waving their swords and spears high in the air.

Before Amasis, however, the ranks remained closed: an impenetrable wall of spears and unwelcoming stares.

A tense stand-off began; Amasis and his men waiting in silence, while the rebel leaders approached to the acclaim of their massed soldiery.

Then the chant started, near where Amasis sat impatiently on his restive horse: "Hophra's a traitor!" Soon it rose from many throats, a forest of spears waving in time with the chant.

The situation looked grim for Amasis and his men. Their task was beginning to look impossible and the risk to their lives was growing.

However, Amasis was never one to do the expected. Instead of sitting waiting quietly, he suddenly smiled, pulled his helmet from his head, waved it in the air and then threw it away from him. Nudging his horse towards the chanting soldiers, his fist still waving, he kicked his horse's flanks and urged it to rear. Perhaps the animal was used to such treatment, for it reared up, its forelegs pawing the air as Amasis shouted. The chanting of the nearest soldiers faltered.

As the beast sank again onto all fours, Amasis drove it along the crowded road, first at a trot and then at a gallop. Rebel soldiers leaped desperately off the road to right and left to avoid the thundering hoofs.

No longer was Amasis a lesser personage waiting to be granted an interview – instead, he was the initiator.

His company was slow to react, and Amasis was already fifty metres down the road before they began to move. As they followed, thundering two abreast behind their leader, the crowds of watchers – those who weren't having to jump for their lives – were left in no doubt that this was Amasis! Amasis, their leader. Amasis, the unpredictable.

Pharaoh Hophra was forgotten for the moment and approving shouts began to rise: "General Amasis! Amazing Amasis!"

Amasis slowed as he approached the rebel leaders, his horse dropping to a walk. Amasis grinned, and then greeted them. "Egypt is great!" he announced.

"Egypt is great," they agreed, but less confidently. Amasis had the initiative.

"Pharaoh Hophra wants you all to put down your weapons and stop this rebellion," announced Amasis loudly. By this time, his men had caught up with him and the rebel army had closed its ranks behind them.

Though Amasis and his three hundred were entirely surrounded by an army that was willing to bring Egypt to war, he was speaking in favour of the very leader against whom they were rebelling!

"Hophra is a traitor!" growled many voices.

"Let's wait and see what the General has to say," said others.

Amasis was not averse to having such a large audience. When he spoke, he did his best to ensure that as many as possible heard his words.

"Pharaoh Hophra is your king as his father was before him. Royalty and honourable leadership are what a kingdom requires."

"But Hophra led us to defeat," replied one of the rebels' leaders.

"One defeat can happen. He has also led us to many victories, as did his father."

"*You* led the army to victory in Cush!" came a shout from a nearby soldier.

"I led the army. Pharaoh Psamtik led the nation. Royalty is what Egypt needs."

"You led the army against the Phoenicians too."

"True, I led the army – but Pharaoh Hophra, your king, planned the expedition."

"Hophra is a traitor," the chant began all over again. It appeared that Amasis was getting nowhere.

"Hophra killed my friends," called a voice.

"Hophra killed my son," growled another.

"It's true," said another of the leaders. "Hophra saved the Greeks and killed the Egyptians!"

"It is true that Hophra has not always been wise with his use of mercenaries," conceded Amasis, "but he has led Egypt wisely and well for almost twenty years."

"He may have led the Greeks wisely and well, but he deliberately killed our comrades," came a cry from nearby.

"He's no leader of Egypt!" said another.

"He's a traitor, why do you keep helping him?" asked a rebel leader.

"Leading a nation is not easy," argued Amasis. "Experience and a statesmanlike attitude are necessary. None of you can excel Hophra in these."

As he spoke, one of his mounted men sidled up behind him. Occupied in discussion, Amasis did not notice until the man took off his own helmet and put it on Amasis' bare head.

"This helmet will be a sign of royalty. And who has earned the position of royalty more than our beloved general Amasis?"

For a few moments there was silence, then the man's words began to sink in. It was an instant in time in which the course of history could be directed by a single unexpected suggestion.

Amasis – royalty?

The leader of the rebels was quick to see the possibility and seize it.

"Pharaoh Amasis!" he cried.

The cry was taken up by Amasis' men and the other rebel leaders. It took some time for the idea to spread, and many soldiers looked utterly astounded. This was an idea that had never occurred to anyone.

Amasis, Hophra's representative, was now being presented as Hophra's replacement.

Pharaoh Amasis? Was it possible? Would the man himself agree to it?

The leaders of the rebels gathered around and spoke quietly with him. Then two of the rebel leaders took a position, one on either side of Amasis, holding his arms aloft and shouting, "Hophra's a traitor! Hophra is not Pharaoh! Amasis is Pharaoh! Long live Pharaoh Amasis!" A pause between sentences left each to echo across the field as it finished.

"Long live Pharaoh Amasis!" echoed the cry, until the field and even the city itself rang with it.

What would Amasis do next?

Chapter 25

Who is Pharaoh?

Amasis prepared to march against Pharaoh Hophra in his royal city of Zau, but there were more twists yet to negotiate in this tortuous struggle for power over Egypt.

When Pharaoh Hophra heard the news that the rebels had appointed Amasis king, he understood clearly that he needed to act straight away.

He called his advisors and asked for advice. In short order, almost as many suggestions as there were advisors assailed his ears, most of which had little to recommend them. But as he sat on his throne listening half-heartedly, he suddenly stumbled on the perfect solution to his problem.

He would send Patarbemis to negotiate with Amasis! Patarbemis was wise. Patarbemis was convincing and persuasive. Patarbemis was an exceptional negotiator. If anybody could end this rebellion without bloodshed, it was Patarbemis.

Hophra leaned forward and opened his mouth to announce his plans – and then a tempering thought occurred to him: Patarbemis was also popular.

When he had sent Amasis, he had been confident that the man was wise, convincing, persuasive and an outstanding negotiator. He had been fully convinced that if anyone could end the rebellion without bloodshed, it was Amasis.

Pharaoh pursed his lips and stroked his smooth-shaven chin, several more outlandish suggestions drifting past his ears unnoticed. How could he make sure Patarbemis would not follow in Amasis' footsteps, or – horror of horrors – perhaps even join him as a counsellor?

"Silence!" he said, frowning and waving his hand irritably in front of his advisors. It annoyed him that so many of them were seeking only the personal fame that would accrue to them if he took their advice. Couldn't they see that this was a serious problem – so serious that they should forget their self-interest and pull together to ensure his continued reign?

At least Patarbemis was taking it seriously, waiting quietly for him to continue. He asked himself again: did he need to worry about Patarbemis' loyalty or could he rely on him?

He looked steadily at Patarbemis and pursed his lips again. Being Pharaoh was no easy task, and choosing what advice to take was far more difficult than merely offering the advice!

"Should I trust you, Patarbemis?"

"I'm afraid I can't give you advice about that, sire," answered Patarbemis, irritatingly reasonable. "But, sire, have I ever let you down?"

"No, you haven't. Would you let me down if I sent you to command Amasis to return to me in Zau as my faithful general?"

"If you commanded me to do so, sire, I would do my best, but I cannot advise such action."

"Why not?"

"Amasis can never again be your faithful general. No man who has allowed himself to be flattered into rebellion once could ever be trusted again."

"I suppose you're right," said Hophra slowly. "But he's such a successful general…. Alright then, would you let me down if I sent you to command Amasis to give himself up to me in Zau?"

"Once again, sire, if you commanded me to do so, I would do my best, but I would recommend a slightly different course of action."

"Explain."

"Just imagine, sire, if Amasis were to agree to your demands and march towards Zau with his army. You could not know whether he was genuinely surrendering or deceiving you with the intention of attacking you when you least expected it. I suggest instead, sire, that you demand that he give himself up immediately and return with me to your palace."

"That sounds good, Patarbemis. We will do what you recommend." Hophra waved toward his other advisors dismissively, ejecting them from his presence. Once they had left, he continued, "You, then, Patarbemis, will proceed immediately to Memphis to meet this rebel, Amasis. Take him alive and bring him to me here at Zau. He has caused more trouble than all of the rest of the rebels and must be punished."

"Very well, sire."

"Take some armed men with you, and hurry."

"Yes, sire."

"Bring him back with you or I will be very angry. Remember: if your mission fails, there will be no way to avoid warfare."

"I will do my best, sire."

"You must not fail!" warned Hophra, punctuating each word with a tap of his pointing finger on the armrest of his throne.

CR

As Amasis had done before him, Patarbemis approached the rebels at Memphis backed by an armed guard. The army was still camped in the fields around the wall, but their numbers had swollen still further.

Now that Amasis was in command of the rebels, he at least made sure that Patarbemis was welcomed on arrival – and instructed to wait where he was. Accordingly, he sat on his horse at the extremity of the camp, wearing a patient air, while Amasis made his way out from the city.

"Welcome, Patarbemis," said Amasis when he arrived. "Have you come to join us?"

"Of course not," retorted Patarbemis. "I am a faithful servant of Pharaoh."

"I am Pharaoh now. Will you be faithful to me? You are a wise man; your advice would be valued."

Patarbemis screwed up his nose and almost snorted. "You! Pharaoh? Hophra is Pharaoh, as you acknowledged yourself just a few weeks ago."

"Times have changed," said Amasis, mildly. "Wise men change with them."

"Pharaoh Hophra commands you to surrender, Amasis, and to return with me to Zau, where you will be punished for your rebellion."

"Hophra's commands no longer have the power they once had in this neck of the woods. Instead, I have agreed to serve the faithful soldiers of Egypt as their Pharaoh. And soon I will be Pharaoh over all Egypt."

"This is treason, Amasis."

"Treason is in the eye of the beholder. At Kurene, Pharaoh saved Greek lives in preference to Egyptian. Is that not treason? Should not Hophra be punished for that? I have with me the men to enforce this judgement."

"You swore your allegiance to Hophra, Amasis. Come with me and make your peace with him."

Amasis spat on the ground. "So much for Hophra," he said. "If he wants to see me, why doesn't he come here?"

"No, Amasis. It is not the servant's place to command. The servant must do his master's bidding, and Hophra your master says: Surrender, and come alone to Zau."

Up to this point, I was able to put the story together in detail, but at this stage the narrative becomes a little contradictory. I can't be sure exactly what Amasis did in response to Patarbemis' demand. There are several stories, none of them fit for polite retelling. What I heard of Amasis' crude response did not really shock me – in my experience, Amasis was prone to silliness at times, and even to tastelessness and irreverence.

But whatever he did or said, it seems to have angered Patarbemis, who repeatedly insisted that he must obey Hophra's commands and return to Zau.

"If Pharaoh wants me to, I will return to Zau," responded Amasis finally, "but when I do, I will bring others with me." His waving arms, encompassing the entire army, made his meaning clear.

"Have you no loyalty to Egypt?"

"To Egypt, yes – but not to Hophra. I have planned to do this ever since the day Hophra betrayed the citizens and soldiers of Egypt by bringing in mercenaries from Greece. Hophra rules Egypt for himself and the Greeks. I plan to rule Egypt for the Egyptians. If Hophra is a true servant of Egypt, he will welcome my plans."

As they spoke, Patarbemis had been scanning the army spread across the fields around Memphis. His rough estimate of the size of the army gave him pause, and the extensive preparations for battle convinced him of Amasis' determination to take over Egypt.

Wisely, he decided to leave while he still could. Hophra must hear the news as soon as possible, before this army arrived on his doorstep!

Patarbemis and his men hurried back to Zau to recount the bad news. Pharaoh Hophra must have had his scouts out, because when the party arrived at the gates of the city, Pharaoh was awaiting them in his chariot.

"Patarbemis, you traitor!" he raged. "I sent you to bring Amasis, but you have not obeyed."

"I…"

"Silence!" roared Hophra. His chief executioner and some assistants stood close by, Hophra evidently having intended to execute Amasis on the spot had he been foolish enough to return. Instead, he told them, "Patarbemis does not listen to instructions, so cut off his ears."

A gasp went up from the crowd at the gates, but it all happened too quickly and there was nothing they could do. Patarbemis was unceremoniously dragged from his horse and flung onto the roadway. Several men held him down while the chief executioner produced a sharp knife and obeyed Hophra's instructions. Blood spurted horribly as the severed ears were presented to Pharaoh, who was still fuming.

Patarbemis lay still in pain and shock, but Hophra was not yet finished. "I appointed this man to a position of honour in my court, yet he turns up his nose at my commands. Cut off his nose."

The executioner did so.

Patarbemis survived the ordeal, but spent the rest of his life ruing his choice of master.

This unexpected event having taken place in public, there were many horrified witnesses to spread the news across Egypt. Anger can lead men into foolish errors, and Hophra's rage against Patarbemis cost him dearly.

Patarbemis was held in high esteem in Egypt for his wisdom and loyalty. This cruel and arbitrary punishment of such a man turned many Egyptians against Hophra immediately. Until that time, the opposing sides in the conflict were probably more or less evenly balanced, but from then on, Hophra could only count on the support of his mercenaries. His Greek guards numbered 30,000, but what was that against the massed and angry soldiery of all Egypt?

℞

From that point on, civil war was inevitable and the result predictable.

Pharaoh Hophra called all of his mercenaries together and prepared to march against Amasis.

Of course, Amasis was in no hurry to join battle. This cruel treatment of Patarbemis had inflamed a situation already dangerous for Hophra. Every day brought extra soldiers flocking to Amasis' banner, and his messengers made sure that the horrific news spread upstream also. Amasis' star was in the ascendant and he had no need of haste.

Timaios may have been right that the Egyptian army was poorly led, but that was without Amasis. When Amasis met Hophra's largely Greek army, he had a great numerical advantage, and his experience and extensive preparation paid off too.

Hophra had 30,000 Greeks, Ionians like Zeno and Timaios, and Carians as well. Yet despite knowing full well the size of the force he was confronting, he was confident of victory. Yes, he was certain that he had been appointed Pharaoh by the gods and could not possibly be removed, even by the gods themselves.

Nevertheless, Amasis was an experienced general and his leadership of the Egyptian soldiers was effective. Under his skilled leadership, the outcome was never in doubt. Whenever the Greeks advanced, they were met by far greater numbers of Egyptian soldiers who held up their advance while other divisions outflanked and even surrounded them.

Despite the Greeks' valiant efforts, the battle was lost. I never met Timaios or any of his men again, so I assume that they were all killed along with so many others.

Hophra, however, was not killed. As his forces dwindled under Amasis' onslaught, he made one last desperate effort, throwing all of his troops into the battle, in an attempt to force a wedge through the Egyptian defences to attack Amasis himself.

The attempt failed and his men were thrown back. Hophra tried unsuccessfully to flee the battlefield but was caught. Surrounded by angry Egyptian soldiers, he was brought before Amasis as the man relaxed in one of Hophra's own buildings in Memphis.

"Hophra, your Greeks failed you," sneered Amasis. "And your cruelty cost you the kingship."

"I am still Pharaoh. It is I whom the gods appointed. Your so-called reign will be short-lived, and then my vengeance will be beyond your imagining."

Amasis laughed. "I could kill you tonight, and then where would your vengeance be? Instead, I am going to take you back with me to Zau. You will watch as I take over your palaces, your temples, your wives and your children. You will witness my reshaping of the city to suit my own taste and see me rebuilding temples as I choose. You are nothing, Hophra."

"I am Pharaoh…"

Amasis laughed again. "No," he said gently, "you are not Pharaoh any more. As Pharaoh, you were dedicated to the soldiers of Greece, not Egypt, and when the challenge came, they couldn't protect you. When I fought for your father, Egypt won battles on its own. Now that I am Pharaoh, Egypt will be great again."

Brave words – but words that boasted against God. Amasis should have known better. Egypt had nothing to look forward to but God's judgement.

CR

Amasis didn't keep Pharaoh Hophra in Zau for long. Hophra's enemies were demanding that he die, but apparently Amasis didn't want to kill him. Perhaps he could see that killing Hophra would set a precedent he might regret if he ever became unpopular himself.

Instead, Amasis resisted their demands, ordered ex-Pharaoh Hophra into exile and weathered the limited protests. It seemed that the change of dynasties had been achieved with comparatively little trouble or long-lasting enmity.

Amasis threw himself into his new job as if he expected to be ruling for a long time. I was surprised to hear that he was taking an interest in Egypt's agricultural output and encouraging the development of new farming methods that could increase the quantity of food available for the kingdom. It seemed inconsistent with the light-hearted, almost happy-go-lucky soldier who had taught me his language so many years before – including at times trying to trick me into using completely inappropriate or informal words in polite conversation.

I was disappointed to hear that he was already providing support for capital works on some of the temples in Zau and along the Nile. My hope that he would reject idolatry and worship Yahweh instead had obviously been too optimistic.

By that stage, I had been in Egypt for sixteen years, and my patience was being tested again. Or perhaps it is better to say that God's patience and kindness were being shown all over again.

When the survivors of Nebuchadnezzar's devastation of Judah had first come to Egypt, God had promised that the sword would follow us and that we would meet a terrible end – perhaps even worse than that suffered by our countrymen who had died in Nebuchadnezzar's invasion.

Sixteen years later, though, most still lived in peace, often a deeper peace than they had ever seen in Judah during the last sixteen years of its existence. True, there had been times of anti-Jewish sentiment, normally as a result of their involvement with money. The most recent had been during Amasis' rebellion, when all foreigners had been targets of nationalistic fervour. Jews in particular were associated with Hophra because he had been Pharaoh when the largest group of Jews had entered Egypt. Naturally, nobody remembered that the welcome had been extended on Amasis' recommendation! But though this had led to quite a few deaths, it was nothing like the last few years of life in Judah. Back then, the daily death toll due to war, famine and disease was so high that everybody had genuinely felt that their life hung in doubt before them, as God had threatened in the Book of the Law that it would.[102]

So, once again, I was left waiting for disaster to strike and wondering why it didn't. It was an uncomfortable mindset, looking, almost longing, for disaster to strike. Yet

---

[102] Deuteronomy 28:49-57; 66-67

without the disaster, more and more people began to doubt Yahweh. It's tragic and incomprehensible, but God's work in the past is quickly forgotten if his latest promised work doesn't hasten to its end *now*. With time, the certainty of earlier prophetic fulfilment seems somehow to lose its conviction. Self-examination showed that even my confidence and contentment were taking a battering.

Each day I woke up with questions in my mind and found myself irritable and impatient. I tried to pass it off as part of becoming a grumpy old man, but it wasn't that. The fact was that the problem that has plagued me throughout my life had resurfaced: I wanted God to fulfil his promises in *my* time, not his!

Having talked to many people over the years, I've found that we all seem to suffer from the same fundamental difficulty: if we have a problem or weakness when we are young, it never seems to leave us. We can often master it with God's help, but that mastery is only temporary unless we actively keep it under surveillance and control, acknowledging our need for ongoing help. It is so easy to believe that we have overcome once and for all, but such overcoming never seems to be truly complete until death stops the problem from recurring!

In this case, I was working through the same lengthy steps as usual: avoiding, worrying, excusing, arguing, complaining, and then finally accepting that God knows best – just as he did last time.

I had slowly overcome my initial reluctance to acknowledge that it really was a long time since the prophecies were made, got over worrying that something had gone wrong, stopped excusing the delay to others, given up arguing with God that he should get on with it, and finished complaining that he was putting me in a difficult position. All that over, I was finally tentatively exploring the idea of accepting that God was following his plan and had no responsibility to meet my demands, when I heard a knock on my door.

Happy to be able put off my final self-abasement for a while, I went and opened the door. A man accompanied by several servants stood at the door. From an Egyptian point of view he was well dressed, but I still can't get used to seeing high-ranking officials wearing next to nothing! It just doesn't seem right. Anyway, he began to speak in stumbling Hebrew, paying me a major compliment in doing so. For an Egyptian official to speak to a foreigner in his own language was almost unheard of. However, I took pity on him and interrupted in Egyptian: "You can speak to me in Egyptian, I understand it."

Looking relieved, the official said, "Thank you, sir. The great and noble Pharaoh, Amasis, requires your attendance at the palace." He named a date five days ahead.

"Which palace?" I asked. Egypt had many palaces, but Hophra had spent most of his time in the largest, most comfortable one – the one in Zau which I had visited when we first arrived in Egypt. Would Amasis do the same? And if so, did he expect me to visit him there?

"Ah, yes, which palace. Well, Pharaoh will be arriving in Tahpanhes in four days' time and will expect you in his palace at midday the following day."

☙

Those extra few days before Amasis arrived gave me the time to take that final step of humbly admitting that God really did know what he was doing, so when I walked along the pavement towards the entrance to Pharaoh's palace in Tahpanhes, I was properly prepared.

As I approached, I tried to remember the exact place in the pavement where the stones had been buried all those years ago. Changes to the walls and entrance of the palace, as well as to other parts of the pavement, made it difficult to determine, but I took some time to study the slope of the pavement and worked out where the most fill would have been required to achieve the graceful curve that still led to the elegant palace entrance. It fitted with my memory of the location, and as I continued on towards the entrance, I was confident that I knew exactly where the hidden stones lay.

The guards at the gates quizzed me and demanded proof of who I was, but one of the older guards seemed to recognise me, although I didn't recognise him.

"Pharaoh will see you soon," said a younger guard, stiffly.

The older guard was more relaxed. "Yes, Heremyo, he's just finishing a… a breakfast feast with some of his old officer-friends from the border battalions."

It was obvious that the younger guard was meant to be in charge and preferred more formality. He frowned and said, "Follow me, sir. I'll take you to the waiting area and then Pharaoh's throne-room staff will look after you."

Following, I found myself in a large, mostly empty hall with high ceilings and ornate decorations everywhere. In just a few moments, I would be seeing my old tutor again, but now, incongruously, he would be Pharaoh. What did he want from me?

It wasn't long before I was hustled into a banqueting hall where a large number of men were feasting. At the highest table, I saw Amasis. He must have been watching for me, because our eyes met and he immediately put down his cup and called, "Heremyo! Come up here." I walked up to the table and he patted the seat beside him. "Sit," he said in Hebrew.

No wonder people were already calling him unconventional!

I sat down and we talked about the weather for a while before he asked about farming in Judah. Neither subject was my specialty, so when I had a chance, I changed the subject and asked him how often he spoke Hebrew nowadays.

"Very rarely," he laughed. "Can't you tell?"

"You don't speak as well as you used to," I admitted, still using Hebrew, "but you're not bad for a Pharaoh."

"Knowing a language or two that your advisors don't know is essential, I find," he responded in Hebrew, looking around, "and, as far as I know, none of them speak Hebrew. We can talk freely."

Taking pity on his struggles to express himself, I offered, "We can speak Egyptian if you need me to."

"No, Hebrew it must be, awkward language though it is. I have questions. I am a new Pharaoh, so will your prophecies of Nebuchadnezzar's invasion lapse?"

"Why should they? They are prophecies for Egypt, not for Pharaoh."

"I thought you would say that, but wasn't there a prophecy directed at Pharaoh Hophra? I can't remember what it was, though," he said, a gleam in his eye.

I stopped and thought, working my way through the prophecies I had told him. "You're right," I said. "God said that he would be handed over to his enemies."

"That's it," he smirked. "It didn't work, did it!"

"It hasn't yet," I protested, then, seeing the gleam in his eye, asked, "Is that why you sent him into exile instead of handing him over to be executed?"

"Don't you believe that I couldn't remember it?"

"How could I say that Pharaoh was lying?"

"Maybe you would deserve more respect if you could."

"Whatever the truth of that is, Pharaoh Hophra will still be handed over to his enemies just as God said," I answered, "but…"

"…you don't know when it will be," Amasis finished for me. "I've heard that so often, I know when it is coming, but surely eventually you'll have to admit that it's just not going to happen."

"No," I said confidently. "God will do exactly what he says. The only way that could ever change would be for Pharaoh and his whole nation to repent and worship Yahweh instead of the idols whose temples line the Nile."

"There's no chance of that, Heremyo," said Amasis, shaking his head. "I wouldn't last long as Pharaoh if I told my people to ignore their idols. I'll listen to your prophecies, but not to suggestions like that."

"You might get a surprise if you were willing to trust Yahweh."

"Yes, I might be surprised by just how quickly my supporters could find another Pharaoh."

"Nebuchadnezzar will surely come," I warned him.

"But you can't tell me when, and Nebuchadnezzar is still busy fighting against Tyre."

"Yes."

"I'll have to take my chances. Let me know if you hear any more prophecies, Heremyo – particularly if you can tell me when they're going to happen."

"Yahweh sets the time, Amasis. You may be Pharaoh, but you can't control God's timing any more than I can."

Chapter 26

Hophra Returns

March 568BC

Amasis had been reigning for about two years by the time I heard from him again.

My seventy-sixth birthday had passed, but I didn't seem to be able to slow down much. My desire to make sure that our worship continued despite the destruction of the temple kept me very busy. It may seem incongruous, but although very few would listen to the words of God that I delivered, everyone expected me to take a hand in leading their worship. Attendance at Sabbath assemblies had decreased greatly over the years as more and more Jews left Tahpanhes for other parts of Egypt, and many assemblies had merged with others or closed for good. Worship had settled into a time of comfortable reminiscing and far-fetched nostalgia. My memories of the last years of the kingdom of Judah bore little resemblance to the descriptions I heard during Sabbath worship or the discussions that followed our assemblies. When the temple in Jerusalem was available for God's people to freely meet with God, they filled it with corruption and lifeless idols, yet to hear people now describing their lives in those years, one would imagine that visiting the temple had been their chiefest joy and that few days had passed without them celebrating the sovereignty of Yahweh their God.

It was nonsense, of course, but it seemed to comfort many who had lost so much of their family and their reason for living. Did it result in a more genuine worship of Yahweh in the assemblies of Tahpanhes than had been common in Jerusalem? Maybe, but I doubt it.

Baruch remains as reliable as ever. Since God told him to abandon his ambition, he has tried hard to do so. Humility is a difficult goal, but he has pursued it with admirable determination. And now I can report that his growing humility has brought him more success than his ambition ever did. Not only is there a waiting list for his work that will probably outlast him, but he is preferred over all other scribes as a consummate teacher of the art of penmanship. Parents of aspiring scribes all seek the great Baruch to teach their sons.

In fact, I have the distinction of being perhaps his only complete failure in teaching. He has tried diligently to improve the legibility of my handwriting, but without any notable success. Poor Baruch – he frets about it.

Overall, our life is quite comfortable, and that worries me, since I know it must come to an end sometime.

Judgement will come, and the destruction promised by Yahweh for all those who disobeyed his word and went to Egypt.

Hints that our peace might be about to come to an end began to appear shortly before Amasis once again visited Tahpanhes. Some spoke of Hophra building a force of Egyptian supporters and Greek mercenaries, and it seemed that they might be right. However, it wasn't until I met Amasis again that I discovered the true situation was far more dire for Egypt.

As usual, Amasis acted as if we were still friends with frequent communication when he arrived in Tahpanhes, sending for me to meet him at the city gates. I wondered if he had made enquiries first about whether I was still alive! After all, I've already lived more than 20 years longer than my father or my brothers. Surely my life must come to an end soon? Yet apart from having some difficulty with remembering fine details of recent events and feeling a little more tired in the afternoons, I feel healthier than I did during my last few years in Judah.

I keep expecting to get old, but it doesn't seem to happen. What a blessing this is! I feel that I am slowly healing from the horrific experiences I shared with so many in Jerusalem as Nebuchadnezzar poured out God's judgement there.

Perhaps I am getting old, though. I seem to wander more in my writing.

Be that all as it may, I made my way to the gate in the middle of the morning as Amasis had demanded. There I found him in his chariot, surrounded by guards mounted on what seemed to me excitable, highly-strung horses that wouldn't stand still. Amasis seemed to revel in their skittish behaviour. When he saw me, he suggested with a laugh that I join him for a ride beyond the wall. He seemed to find the idea so appealing that, without waiting for an answer, he began to arrange for two of the most skittish horses to be made available for us.

"Join me for a gallop, Heremyo," he shouted again, even going so far as to mount the horse he had taken from a young guard.

"Have you ever seen me galloping, Amasis?" I asked.

He looked disappointed, but agreed to take me with him in his chariot. "After I've had a quick gallop myself," he added, wheeling the horse around and galloping out through the gate as people scattered to left and right in front of him. It was hard to imagine any other Pharaoh behaving in such a way, but his guards didn't look particularly surprised.

The young guard whose horse was out galloping beyond the walls led me to Amasis' chariot and bade me climb into it.

"Are you really Heremyo the prophet?" he asked, as I did so.

"I am," I replied.

"My father was a guard in Pharaoh Hophra's throne room when you first arrived in Egypt. He tells me of the great respect shown you and says that you have met most of the kings around the world!"

"Oh, no!" I laughed. "Most of the kings I've met were reigning twenty to fifty years ago. Most of them are now dead, or deposed and exiled, like Hophra."

"But you *have* spoken with kings in many countries, and, from what I hear, given them orders from your god."

"True, Yahweh did give them orders, but none obeyed his commands. Pharaoh Hophra would not listen, and even your lord, Amasis, will not listen to Yahweh."

"Oh, but he does, sir. He tells us that we must expect trouble from Nebuchadnezzar because you told him he would invade Egypt. He does not forget your words."

I was surprised to hear that Amasis was willing to mention my words to his men. Perhaps he was more devout than I thought. As I considered this, Amasis swept in through the gate, causing pedestrians to leap for their lives once again. His hair was blowing in the wind and his face wore a wide smile. He pulled up the horse in front of me as I stood in his chariot and slid to the ground, breathing hard. Giving the reins to the guard, he looked at me reproachfully and said, "Heremyo, our discussions would have taken place best at a gallop, but now we must travel sedately with no excitement at all."

"Yes, sir. I'm not as young as you."

"Nonsense, Heremyo! Your god keeps you young, and he would keep you safe at a gallop if you would only let him."

"I will hear you better with us both in the same chariot," I said firmly, speaking in Hebrew.

"Very well," he answered in the same tongue, and climbed into the chariot.

Immediately, we were off, his beautiful horses eager to run, but always running smoothly in perfect unison. They covered the ground at a remarkable pace, and soon we were well away from the city walls.

"Is Nebuchadnezzar still going to attack?" Amasis cried to me as the wind blew at such hair as I still possessed.

I looked at him without answering.

He looked across at me and smiled again. "Yes, yes, I know you'll tell me nothing has changed and all that, but something *has* changed."

"What has changed?"

"Hophra has joined forces with Nebuchadnezzar."

"What do you mean?"

"Ever since I defeated him, Hophra has been gathering an army ready to attack me, hoping to take Egypt back. And now he's gone to Nebuchadnezzar for help."

"Isn't Nebuchadnezzar still busy with Tyre?"

"No. He's done what he can in defeating and sacking the city on the mainland, but he can't overcome the massive walls surrounding the island just offshore. All of Tyre's wealth and power is now safe on the island, and Nebuchadnezzar is tired out and fed up."[103]

"So now he's looking for an easy victory, is he?" I asked, slyly.

---

[103] Ezekiel 29:18-20

Amasis frowned and turned sharply towards me, but relaxed when he realised I was smiling.

"Taking Egypt is never an easy victory, Heremyo, but what will happen now?"

"If Nebuchadnezzar comes with Hophra, I suppose Hophra will win."

"I was sure you'd say that. Am I to be ousted from my position as Pharaoh?"

"I can only tell you the future…" I began.

"…as far as Yahweh tells you," Amasis finished for me.

"That's right. I know the general picture, but I don't know all the details. I know Nebuchadnezzar will come to Tahpanhes, but whether he will come with Hophra or not, I can't say."

"You know, Heremyo, your information about the future is always just enough to worry me, but never enough to give me the answers I need!"

ᘒ

It wasn't long before I, and everyone else in Egypt, heard plenty more about ex-Pharaoh Hophra. True, the details were sketchy and a little confused, but all reports agreed that Hophra had indeed received help from King Nebuchadnezzar and was now approaching Egypt with the intention of invading and reclaiming his 'rightful' heritage.

Amasis had already begun preparing to defend his kingship and was asking all 'loyal' Egyptians for help.

The contest for the hearts and minds of the Egyptians was fierce, but in Tahpanhes at least, there was no doubt that Amasis was winning. Elsewhere, though, some suggested that Hophra had a sizeable following, and that he had sent many representatives to woo back his former subjects.

Accordingly, Amasis hurried around Egypt, Patarbemis at his side, sometimes giving him advice and at other times standing as mute, disfigured testimony to the fickle loyalty of Hophra. Amasis posed the question: should Egypt return to a leader such as Hophra? He urged his people to trust him and reject Hophra as an arrogant, self-serving leader, all too firmly convinced of his entitlement to the kingship.

Some left Egypt to join Hophra in his march against Amasis and these, we heard, were rewarded handsomely. Where the gold came from to fund such largesse I don't know, but many suggested bitterly that it came from Nebuchadnezzar. It made sense to me that a foreign king could advance his own cause by helping warring factions in a nation he hoped soon to overcome himself.

In a short time, Hophra was at the borders of Egypt and Amasis had mobilised the army and was marching to meet him.

Hophra's army was surely not as large as he would have hoped, and his movements suggested that he was not looking for an immediate engagement with Amasis. A game of cat and mouse on a grand scale followed, but it was hard to tell which was the cat and which the unfortunate mouse. Amasis seemed to be looking for direct confrontation as quickly as possible, but Hophra took advantage of his smaller, nimbler force to avoid the conflict. The experts who like to comment on these things suggested that any delay in forcing a pitched battle on the invading force played into Hophra's hands because it suggested that Amasis was unable to decisively crush the invading force. Each day that Hophra avoided a confrontation, they argued, strengthened his position.

Personally, I wasn't convinced, because it seemed to me that the argument was just as valid in reverse: if Hophra was unable to inflict a swift, crushing blow with his invading force, surely that indicated that Amasis had his measure and would be in an increasingly secure position, as Hophra must soon run out of supplies.

Be that all as it may, Amasis finally managed to corner Hophra and his army and force them into mortal combat.

The battle was brief and decisive. Amasis' forces quickly overwhelmed Hophra's men and the danger was over.

However, victorious Amasis continued his eccentric behaviour by resisting his supporters' demands that Hophra be executed. Instead, he hosted the former Pharaoh in his palace in Zau, feeding him delicacies and clothing him in fine robes.

For some time, then, Hophra was given comfort and relative freedom, while his supporters across Egypt were crushed and his men of war punished severely.

Since Amasis had become Pharaoh, his people had often admired and appreciated his eccentric behaviour, but this situation was different. Such an action gained him little support or approval.

Deputations were dispatched from many parts of Egypt to demand that this favoured treatment of Hophra cease immediately. What justice could there be in allowing Egypt's worst traitor and most dangerous enemy to live? Were not his supporters being executed all across Egypt? Yet the man himself was enjoying the comfort of the royal palace.

Perhaps Amasis wanted to keep Hophra alive to give Nebuchadnezzar less justification for an attack on Egypt in retaliation for the death of the leader of an invading force supported by Nebuchadnezzar himself.

Whatever his reason, when the pressure continued to mount, Amasis wisely gave in.

Hophra was removed from the palace and delivered to a group of his most vocal critics. They quietly strangled the former Pharaoh and buried his body in the burial-place of his fathers.

Many rejoiced at the death of Hophra, confident that Egypt was out of danger once more – for the moment at least.

Would the defeat of Hophra be enough to deter Nebuchadnezzar from attacking Egypt, or would it cause him to attack? Only time would tell. Egypt held its breath, waiting to learn the answer.

Chapter 27

What Next?

May 568BC

This time it was I who initiated contact with Amasis. It was all very well to give him answers when he asked, but God had made me a prophet to the Gentiles, and that included Amasis. I had a job to do and my conscience demanded that I do it. I must warn him again – even though I was sure he had not forgotten my message.

I made my way to Zau, to the palace I had not visited since Hophra was Pharaoh. After fighting my way through the usual stifling blanket of minor, intermediate and major underlings, I finally found someone who assured me that he would tell Pharaoh I had called. Then I waited.

No doubt Amasis was very busy. I'm sure that any leader would be busy when his country was under threat from a nation that had invaded and overrun most of the inhabited world! Nevertheless, in just three days, I received a message that Pharaoh would meet me in one of the many temples in the city. I don't even remember which one it was now. It didn't matter which it was: I refused to go.

My contact in the palace looked almost as if he was going to die of apoplexy. It was obvious that he could not begin to imagine how anyone could ever conjure up such a refusal, let alone how a faithful servant such as he could convey it to Pharaoh! It took a lot of fast talking from me to convince him that, since the answer was mine, Pharaoh would be angry with me, not with him. I think it was true of Amasis, although it might not have been of Hophra.

This response to my refusal reminded me once more of God's command to me almost sixty years ago, when he told me that if I faced up to opposition as if my forehead was made of iron, I would never be overcome. It has always worked, and now it worked once again in Egypt.

The very next day, I received a visitor at my lodgings, dressed as a servant of Pharaoh. "Come," he said. "Follow me."

I did, although I had no idea what was about to happen. Death must eventually come to all of us, and I seriously wondered if it was to be my turn to meet it. However, the servant had not come to execute me, but merely to lead me to Amasis. The entire time I have lived in Egypt, he has never wanted to talk to me in front of anyone who could understand what we were saying. Perhaps he is wiser than I have given him credit for as a somewhat unpredictable and thoroughly unconventional leader.

I was led to a jetty jutting out into the Nile River, with royal boats tied up on either side, loading and unloading cargo for the palace. The servant walked with me to the end of the jetty, where a large boat with royal markings was moored. A troop of guards stood guarding the gangplank, and their ranks opened reluctantly before us to enable me to descend to the boat's deck.

In the middle of the deck was a small, roofed compartment, and inside I met Amasis and a few advisors. I recognised two of these as men who had been with Amasis when I met him at the guard post as we waited to enter

Egypt after the destruction of Jerusalem. Obviously he still wanted to have men around him whom he trusted from olden times. However, unless they had learned it since that time, they did not speak Hebrew.

"Heremyo!" Amasis greeted me. He smiled faintly, but it was not his habitually enthusiastic greeting.

"May Yahweh bless you," I said. I suppose it was a pointed greeting, given my refusal to meet him in one of his temples. Nevertheless, I have always found it better to face up to confrontations sooner rather than later.

"Thank you," he said, distractedly, then switched to Hebrew. "I need your help, Heremyo."

"I came to see you to give you my help," I answered, also in Hebrew.

"What shall I do when Nebuchadnezzar attacks? You have always told me that he will defeat Pharaoh. Now I am Pharaoh. Should I fight him?"

"If you fight him, you will not overcome him."

"If I refuse to fight him, my army may rebel and fight him anyway!"

"The choice of what you do is yours, but if you want to do what is best for your nation, concentrate on avoiding conflict with Nebuchadnezzar."

"But what if he is determined to fight me? Must I give up?"

"Yes."

"In abject surrender?"

"Yes."

"Hmm. You've always been a hard taskmaster, Heremyo. From teaching Hebrew to teaching about Yahweh your God, you've always insisted that you're right."

I smiled, but disagreed gently. "In teaching Hebrew, you may be right, I can be stubborn. However, when it comes to teaching about Yahweh, he has given me no choice."

"Is that why you refused to come to the temple?"

"Yes."

"I was just trying to find a place where we could be quiet together – paradoxically, a busy temple is one of the best places to find privacy."

"Privacy, perhaps, but not holiness."

"You know I'm not very good at holiness," he answered.

"It's a pity," I commented. "You could easily lead Egypt to worship the God who controls the world and all nations."

"Don't fool yourself, Heremyo. It may seem as though Pharaoh is in control of Egypt, but if I went against the gods of Egypt, you'd soon see that Pharaoh is only king if the people want him."

"Why don't you try?" I urged.

"My people like what they call my 'eccentricity', but I know how far to push it and when to stop. I won't go beyond that. What do you think I should do when Nebuchadnezzar arrives and my people want to fight him?"

"Stay quiet. You know I told you Nebuchadnezzar would put his throne above that pavement near your palace in Tahpanhes."

"Yes, I remember. Do I have to be there?"

"Perhaps that will be up to you, but Nebuchadnezzar is a king, and kings always seem to want victory. He's sure to want you there to acknowledge his triumph."

Amasis frowned and shook his head. My advice was not welcome.

We talked for a little longer about what he might do, then he closed the interview and I was led back to the palace. I wondered what he would choose, feeling some sympathy for him. Personally, I believed Amasis' best path was to send a message to Nebuchadnezzar making it clear that he, Pharaoh, would not fight and that Egypt would accept Nebuchadnezzar, king of Babylon, as king over Egypt also. I was confident that Amasis could convince his nation to stay with him in the surrender.

Well, Amasis didn't do what I wanted, but he did tend towards it. Perhaps it saved some Egyptian lives, but I think he was mainly interested in saving his own life.

June 568BC

Nebuchadnezzar's invasion of Egypt was much more direct and incisive than Hophra's had been.

Likewise, Amasis' response to the invasion was correspondingly less direct than his response to Hophra. Pharaoh remained quietly in his palace in Zau, quick to send messages, but slow to mobilise the army.

Nebuchadnezzar was looking for a "winner takes all" confrontation. Amasis, it seemed, was not.

I cannot say exactly what was going through the mind of my former instructor in Egyptian language and culture, but it appeared to me that he was listening to Yahweh's words to at least some extent. Yet his response was crafty and careful, endeavouring also to avoid confrontation with his own people. The chatter around Tahpanhes continually suggested that Amasis was busy gathering an army, preparing to march to put the foreign invader in his place as he had done with foreign armies on several occasions while a general. It was coming… it was coming… but it never came. From the position of an almost unbiased observer, it struck me that these were really delaying tactics, played out to satisfy the local audience without risking a real confrontation with Nebuchadnezzar. Perhaps I'm wrong, but that's how it looked to me. Amasis never did gather an army to meet Nebuchadnezzar, although he did gather regional forces in their local areas, where they did plenty of marching around, presenting the glory of Egypt to a doubtful audience. Old successes were paraded before the populace, but Pharaoh seemed to skilfully avoid any attempt to reproduce them.

Nebuchadnezzar had no such qualms. He wanted to add Egypt to his empire, and his men wanted plunder.

I don't know what messages went back and forth between predator and prey, but apparently Amasis was able to convince Nebuchadnezzar to slow down – pause even – and not attack the royal cities.

Then one day I was talking to one of the Greek mercenaries whom Amasis continued to maintain in Tahpanhes, despite his objections to Hophra enlisting them in the first place.

"Amasis keeps avoiding conflict," mused Meliton, a Lochagos[104] I met from time to time near the palace while doing my work as a prophet to the Gentiles, "but he may be leaving himself open to a general rebellion."

"Why do you say that?"

"There are plenty of Egyptians who want to fight Nebuchadnezzar, and they're not happy with Amasis."

"Do you think they'll rebel against Amasis? But surely that would be playing into Nebuchadnezzar's hands. What better way for him to defeat them than to attack while they're in the middle of a civil war?"

"You could be right. Nevertheless, parts of the army are *very* unhappy with Amasis. Many of the leaders are looking for any excuse to openly condemn Amasis and make their own decisions."

---

[104] A Greek army rank equivalent to a Roman centurion.

"Yahweh has warned that Nebuchadnezzar will attack Egypt and defeat her. Amasis has heard this warning – perhaps he is listening to Yahweh." Meliton was used to hearing me talking about Yahweh. I had explained the power of Israel's God to him on more than one occasion and referred to Yahweh often. Meliton had even come along to one of our Sabbath meetings to find out more. Unfortunately, he had not embraced Yahweh as his God because he still suffered from the common delusion that mankind is in control of his own destiny.

"Surely no ruler would listen to such a weak message?" Meliton asserted. "A leader must fight for his kingdom or he'll lose it! Amasis must know that."

"We'll have to wait and see what happens, won't we? I don't know what Amasis will do, but I'm sure he'll get a better result for Egypt if he avoids a confrontation with Nebuchadnezzar."

"But surely that would mean he'd have to acknowledge Nebuchadnezzar as his master."

"Of course, but he'll have to do that anyway. Yahweh has already said that Nebuchadnezzar will bring destruction to Egypt."

"Then why not get it over with?" smiled Meliton. "Why not meet the Chaldeans in battle and win or lose as the gods allow?"

"There is only one god: Yahweh. He controls the nations, and when he warns that a nation will suffer, they will suffer. The only way to change his judgement is for a nation to change its behaviour. It seems to me that Amasis might be trying to do that – at least in part," I argued, well aware that Amasis was not following God's words completely.

"You can believe what you want about your god Yahweh, Jeremiah, but mark my words, there are plenty of men in the Egyptian army who want to fight Nebuchadnezzar."

ℭ℞

August 568BC

Meliton was right. Amasis continued to *sound* active in the defence of Egypt, but after his third rejection of his generals' advice to attack the Chaldeans, they ran out of patience. Withdrawing to Memphis, they set up their headquarters there and sent messengers throughout Egypt.

"Stand up and prepare!" they proclaimed to any who would listen. "We call Amasis, king of Egypt, 'Noisy one who lets the hour go by!' "[105]

We even heard from them in Tahpanhes. I think what surprised me most about the whole affair was that many of the Greek mercenaries marched off to join the rebellion. Then again, I suppose if you fight for money, what does it matter who pays you? The rebels presumably offered enough gold to convince the hired men to march. Meliton did not go with them, nor did his men.

Units of the army from areas around Zau and most of the delta ignored the call to arms, but others from upper Egypt were eager to fight – although I should point out that not all of them were antagonistic towards Amasis.

Nevertheless, having gathered the biggest army they could, the disgruntled generals led it off to war, denouncing Amasis as a traitor to Egypt. Nebuchadnezzar was quick to oblige their desire for war, and once more Memphis was the scene of a decisive battle.

Nebuchadnezzar's approach was cold and clinical. His army swept away the Egyptian army as a servant-girl might clear drifting leaves: sweeping them up before gathering them and dropping them in the fire. Why was

---

[105] See Jeremiah 46:17.

their defeat so complete? Yahweh pushed them down, just as he had the army of Judah.

I was glad that I was not there to see what happened in the town of Memphis – I had seen more than enough of such horror in Jerusalem. The sword devoured.

The Chaldeans are a nation feared near and far, and with good reason. They learned their craft from the Assyrians even as they defeated them, then added cruel twists of their own. As Jerusalem was emptied of people, so too was Memphis. In Jerusalem, the houses were centres of idol worship, places where incense was burned to false gods. Memphis was no different, and as Nebuchadnezzar had cleansed the city of Jerusalem with fire, so he did with Memphis.

Yet surely such wanton savagery cannot go unpunished. Truly Judah and Jerusalem were guilty, and Memphis and her people likewise, but Babylon herself is not free of guilt. Surely the time for her punishment will come too? Must their remorseless, relentless, ruthless hate really last the full 70 years that Yahweh has warned me of? How can the world bear it?

℞

Nebuchadnezzar's first battle in Egypt was not his last, but it was the only one in which he met a large army.

From that time on, news was hard to get, but I learned all I could, with help from my friends, including Meliton the Greek.

When Nebuchadnezzar fought the generals who had lost patience with Amasis' stalling, he also fought some of the Greek mercenaries initially brought in by Hophra. Amasis had not dismissed them, and many had finally joined the rebels. When Nebuchadnezzar overcame them, few survived to consider returning to their native lands.

I've said before that I often don't understand Yahweh's predictions for the future when I announce them. Now, I can go one step further and say that I'm sometimes still not sure when the predictions have been fulfilled.

For example, God said about the defence against Nebuchadnezzar's attack on Egypt:

> "He made many stumble, and they fell,
>   and they said one to another,
> 'Arise, and let us go back to our own people
>   and to the land of our birth,
> because of the sword of the oppressor.' "[106]

I suspect that this refers to these Greek mercenaries, but I can't be sure. Fortunately, some words a little later in the same prophecy make me more confident:

> "A beautiful heifer is Egypt,
> but a biting fly from the north has come upon her.
> Even her hired soldiers in her midst
>   are like fattened calves;
> yes, they have turned and fled together;
>   they did not stand,
> for the day of their calamity has come upon them,
>   the time of their punishment."[107]

Nebuchadnezzar was very much like a biting fly attacking Egypt, the beautiful heifer. He continued a nagging campaign until all his adversaries were defeated. Yet a gadfly only causes inconvenience and discomfort, whereas Nebuchadnezzar spread death and destruction up and down the Nile. Does the picture reflect the fact that there was no doubt that Egypt would continue as a nation?

Fascinatingly, Nebuchadnezzar's actions destroyed Amasis' foes on every hand. Amasis remained quietly in Zau while his opponents went out to fight, and by the time

---

[106] Jeremiah 46:16
[107] Jeremiah 46:20-21

Nebuchadnezzar finished his rampaging crusade, Amasis had no surviving opponents. Should he continue to live, I expect he will reign over Egypt for many years, probably quite successfully. He has bent his neck to the yoke of Nebuchadnezzar just as God commanded Egypt and so many other nations to do. Perhaps he alone, of all the rulers I have met, has truly listened. True, he has struggled and fought against God at times, but overall, he has been willing to do what none of Judah's kings did: avoid fighting the Chaldeans.

I like to dwell on such questions because they are more pleasant than the thought of what Nebuchadnezzar's campaign did to my own people.

Before we left Judah, God warned that destruction and vengeance would come upon those who disobeyed him and fled to Egypt:

"All the men who set their faces
to go to Egypt to live there
shall die by the sword, by famine, and by pestilence.
They shall have no remnant or survivor
from the disaster that I will bring upon them.
For thus says the Lord of hosts, the God of Israel:
As my anger and my wrath were poured out
on the inhabitants of Jerusalem,
so my wrath will be poured out on you
when you go to Egypt.
You shall become an execration,
a horror, a curse, and a taunt.
You shall see this place no more.
The Lord has said to you, O remnant of Judah,
'Do not go to Egypt.'
Know for a certainty that I have warned you this day
that you have gone astray at the cost of your lives."[108]

---

[108] Jeremiah 42:17-20

These were the people I spoke to at Chimham's Inn almost 20 years ago. Some died on the way to Egypt, others died of disease or community unrest in Egypt. Yet many survived until Nebuchadnezzar came to mete out the final punishment. Through Nebuchadnezzar, Yahweh poured out his anger on those who had fled to Egypt, just as he had promised. From what I hear, very few are left.

What would Moses say if he was here in Tahpanhes with me today? He dedicated 40 years of his life to leading our people out of Egypt, and at the time God promised that they would never return here again. If only we had followed God's instructions!

Over the years, people from Judah have spread throughout Egypt, congregating mostly around the Nile. Ironically, many left lower Egypt because that was where they expected Nebuchadnezzar to attack.

In the circumstances, however, Nebuchadnezzar marauded up and down the Nile, seeming, from what I can gather, to single out any Jews he met for punishment and death. No longer would many of my countrymen exercise their skill with money to earn a comfortable living in Egypt. Instead, they lie dead, mute symbols of what happens when mankind resists God.

Reports told me of the deaths of some I knew. Johanan the son of Kareah had laughed at God's warnings when he wasn't busy getting angry about them! Now he was dead – another life wasted.

In the end, what had their obstinate determination to worship the gods they preferred earned them? For almost sixty years, I have been warning people against this stubbornness, yet without visible success. Nevertheless, God has never told me to stop telling people. My life as a prophet has seemed incessantly busy, but I'm sure God would have liked me to have done even more. Could I have done better? Have people died because I haven't tried hard enough?

When I mentioned this fear to Baruch, he laughed. "More?" he scoffed. "How could you have done more?"

Gratifying though his words were, I'm still not completely convinced. I can remember times when I sat around waiting, even asking for God to bring punishment, eager for those who attacked me to get what I considered was their just deserts. Could I have saved lives if I had worked harder?

My father: if only I could have convinced him to use that delightful voice of his to woo people to God! Now it's too late. He's gone, and both of my brothers are dead as well.

Baruch could tell that I was dubious. "Jeremiah," he said sternly, "you've worked as a prophet to your own people and to the Gentiles for longer than Moses did. You've probably spoken about Yahweh to more people than any other person who's ever lived. With his help, you've travelled the length and breadth of the world warning everyone you met – whether they wanted to hear it or not!"

In some ways I'm reluctant to even report his words, but they did strike a chord with me – not because they exonerated me, but because they highlighted the fact that I have indeed been blessed by God with a strength and determination far beyond my natural abilities. He told me to be an iron pillar and a bronze wall, and then when I tried, he made me able to stand up against godlessness when I was just too tired to do it by myself.

From my early youth I've also been blessed with an awareness of God that none of my family – except my mother – was ever blessed with. Yet on top of that divine awareness, God has poured out upon me the blessing of his constant presence, his clear instructions, his gentle guidance.

Why have I been so blessed when so many struggle to even be aware of God in any way? How can I respond but with gratitude? And what can I do but ask myself if I could have cooperated with him better?

Baruch does much of my research for me now. I'm feeling tired, and it's hard to travel far. He tells me that Nebuchadnezzar is now making his way back downstream, his endless tale of slaughter finally winding down.

You can imagine my wonder one afternoon when Baruch said, "Jeremiah, they say that Amasis is coming to Tahpanhes to meet King Nebuchadnezzar."

"That's amazing," I said, unable to keep a smile off my face. "Whose idea was that?"

"We may never know. What I *do* know is that you've done your best to tell Pharaoh about Yahweh's plans and the futility of fighting them."

"Perhaps. Anyway, I can't wait for them to arrive here. I think I know what's going to happen."

"I hope you're right."

Chapter 28

Vindicated

September 568BC

Amasis arrived in Tahpanhes as expected, but it was a very low-key arrival. Normally when Pharaoh visited, prior notice was given so that the local authorities could ensure an appropriate welcome. But not this time. No crowds lined the broad avenues, and at one intersection, Pharaoh's cavalcade even had to pause while a large cart pulled by a long line of leisurely oxen made its way over the cross road.

By chance, I saw him arrive at the palace.

It may seem silly, but I had returned to look at the pavement outside the palace and pray. Over the years, the appearance of open spaces gradually changes, even those that are not actively renovated or remodelled. Extra murals may be added or faded ones painted over; decorative statues are added, moved or removed; torch mountings are modified. They may be small things, but they all subtly change the overall appearance. As I studied the pavement leading to the palace doors, I tried once again to work out exactly where I had enacted the parable I was hoping to see fulfilled. After a while, and a deal of prayer, I felt that I had the location worked out quite accurately:

exactly halfway between two torch mountings on the wall – mountings that had not been there at the time.

Having located the place, I crossed to it and stood a while, turning my mind once more to prayer. My request to Yahweh was that his prediction would have its fulfilment very soon. Nobody nearby could have had any idea that I was praying, but perhaps I looked distracted.

"Time to go home for a rest, old man," said a sudden gentle, but business-like voice in my ear. I felt a hand under my elbow with a gentle pressure to suggest where I should move.

I started in surprise, turning to look at him and stuttering a bit as I answered, "I–I–I… I'm sorry, I was deep in prayer."

"Prayer, was it?" The man looked a little apologetic. "I thought you might be… but never mind, Pharaoh has just arrived. See, here he is, coming along the pavement. I need you to give him space."

He clearly thought that I was either senile or drunk, but as I began to object, I followed the direction of his gesturing arm and saw Amasis, walking right towards me.

"Heremyo," he greeted me, his voice the most subdued I had ever heard it. The attentive servant who had tried to move me on bobbed his head at Amasis and stepped back, leaving us to talk.

"Greetings, Amasis," I answered. "You're here to meet Nebuchadnezzar?"

"Shush, shush," he said, looking around quickly. "I am, but we're trying to keep it fairly quiet."

I was struggling to understand what he said. I was tired and I'm finding Egyptian harder and harder to understand. Hebrew is still easy, but I'm losing the other languages I once knew. Amasis saw my expression and repeated his words in Hebrew.

I smiled my thanks and replied, without considering that I was addressing Pharaoh, "I don't think you'll be able to keep it quiet, my friend."

" 'Friend', you say, Heremyo? Yes, you are my friend, but I think that's the first time anyone has genuinely called me 'friend' since I became Pharaoh."

"I've known many kings to a greater or lesser extent, Amasis, but you are the only one I would call a friend."

"Have you met Nebuchadnezzar?"

"Yes, twice, but only briefly."

"What is he like?"

"Proud, ingenious and very intense. A brilliant general, too."

"That fits with what I hear. On a professional level, I would love to meet him in battle." His eyes lit up. My dismay must have been obvious, for he held up a hand and said, "Don't worry, Heremyo, I'll try to avoid it."

"If you fight, Egypt will lose," I said.

"Egypt was great before Nebuchadnezzar came along. And she will be great long after he is gone."

"She will only be great if you listen to the words of Yahweh."

"Well, I don't have any more time to talk now," Amasis said dismissively. Then he looked more closely at me and added, "You should go home and rest, Heremyo. You don't look very well."

"I am a bit tired," I admitted, "I'm getting older. When is Nebuchadnezzar coming?"

Amasis looked around carefully. There were few people near us, and none looked even vaguely interested in what we were saying. Presumably they couldn't understand Hebrew.

Nevertheless, Amasis leaned towards me and spoke quietly. "Tomorrow afternoon, I believe, but don't tell anyone. I want to get through this with as little fanfare as possible."

"I don't like your chances," I answered, wearily. "I told you what Nebuchadnezzar is like."

"I'll do my best, anyway."

☙

I went home and collapsed into bed and slept until morning. For some reason, I've been very tired for the last few days, so I've taken the opportunity to bring this diary right up to date. Several times recently, Baruch has offered to write it for me, but I still feel the need to write it myself. I don't think I could organise my thoughts enough to dictate it.

I felt better in the morning and told Baruch as much as I could about the previous day's events.

"You should come with me to the palace this afternoon," I said.

"When?"

"I don't know, exactly. I was planning to go early and stay there until the action finishes."

"What action?"

"You have heard that Nebuchadnezzar is coming?"

"Yes."

"Then take your best guess. I can't say anything more. I think Amasis asked me not to."

Baruch looked at me with furrowed brows. I wasn't completely sure of what had happened, and thinking about it was making me tired again, so I stopped. This afternoon was important and I had to get to the palace to watch the show.

I've waited a long time for this.

"How about I go to the palace and see what is happening," offered Baruch. "I'll find out when everything is ready to go and come back and fetch you. Do you think you can walk that far?"

"Walk that far?" I scoffed. "Of course!"

So now I'm sitting here, waiting for Baruch to come back. He's a good friend and has been a great help to me over the years. He's not so young himself, but he's still a hard worker. All those letters he's written for me in that neat handwriting of his. If only I had been blessed with such a skill!

Baruch has written out all of my messages from God, and recently he's been on at me to order them for him, but how should they be arranged? If I put them in the order God gave them, there will be lots and lots of repetition. I've already arranged them so that there isn't much repetition, but Baruch would like to go through and remove even the repetition that's left. He tells me he's already done a rough copy of it, but he won't show me until it's 'ready'.

I still have that box of scrolls that we brought from Judah, too, but I've always been too busy to get them organised. There are lots of short scrolls, and some longer ones too, but most of those aren't in the right order. I've always made sure to write down God's messages, but sometimes the latest scroll wasn't available where I was and so I wrote a new message at the end of an older scroll. I should also explain to Baruch the code I used to write the dates for each entry. At least if he knew that, he could put them in order better.

I don't know.

It's too hard, today.

I'm tired and excited – if one can be both at the same time!

Perhaps I can get back to it tomorrow.

C&R

Amasis may have hoped to keep Nebuchadnezzar's visit low-key, but Nebuchadnezzar didn't cooperate. As he approached Tahpanhes, his army continued to burn, pillage and collect captives. True, the wanton destruction had been more widespread in Upper Egypt, where more resistance had been shown, but the Chaldean army left its mark on Lower Egypt too.

Many of their targets were the temples in which the Egyptians worshipped their multitude of deities. Nebuchadnezzar demolished and burned many of these, often triggering a violent response from disgruntled worshippers. The Chaldeans seemed almost to welcome these confrontations, which gave them good reason to litter Egypt's sand with more corpses and to lead away yet more captives in Nebuchadnezzar's train. As a result, ever-growing lines of chained and humiliated Egyptians stumbled sullenly along behind the Chaldean army.

Amasis didn't seem to care much about the assaults on Egypt's temples, though, despite the fact that he had renovated several of them earlier in his reign.

Obelisks are scattered throughout the land as common celebrations of Egypt's greatness, and Nebuchadnezzar's men threw many of them to the ground, shattering them, just as God had said he would. Sadly, I find that I can no longer remember God's exact words.

In the morning, news came that Nebuchadnezzar's army was almost at the gates of Tahpanhes and that the land behind it looked like a charred wilderness. I began to wonder if Amasis would succeed in retaining his position as Pharaoh. After all, he was allowing Nebuchadnezzar to wreak widespread suffering and destruction without resistance – official resistance, that is. I had heard various rumours of confrontations where the resisting forces seemed surprisingly well equipped despite their limited size, and used strike and run tactics that seemed to me to bear the hallmarks of Amasis' leadership. Perhaps despite everything he was indulging – in a stealthy, limited way – his desire to test his mettle against Nebuchadnezzar.

Amasis can be a bit of a puzzle at times.

Nevertheless, Nebuchadnezzar wanted a royal welcome at the gates of Tahpanhes, and Amasis had no choice but to accede to his demand.

Despite a night's rest, I still felt exhausted and even a little muddled. When Baruch offered to watch the morning's events and report back, leaving me to rest at home, I accepted gratefully. We agreed that if he had not returned by about noon, I would go to Pharaoh's palace to see what was happening.

So Baruch departed, and I rested on my bed, still working to get this diary completely up to date. I also slept. As a result, I was not present at the gates when Nebuchadnezzar's approaching army spread out and encircled the city. It was a show of force that left no question as to who was in control. Amasis welcomed Nebuchadnezzar at the gate attended by nothing more than a guard of honour. Had Nebuchadnezzar chosen to openly humiliate, imprison or kill him, the guard would have been no protection at all. Yet Amasis welcomed Nebuchadnezzar graciously, and the Chaldean empire-builder treated him with equal grace and politeness in return.

Baruch returned a little before midday to report all of this, arriving just as I was preparing to struggle out to the palace. Already I wondered how I was going to endure hours of standing. I still felt weak and shaky, but I couldn't resist the attraction of seeing an expected fulfilment of prophecy.

Baruch observed that although Amasis had delivered a short speech of welcome, he had not been very well, coughing frequently and speaking gruffly, in little more than a whisper. I may be unjust, but I couldn't help wondering whether the cough might be a convenient way of making sure that few people heard Pharaoh's words acknowledging Nebuchadnezzar as his master – after all, I had seen no sign of any cough when I spoke with Amasis the previous day!

☙

"We should go to the palace," I said wearily to Baruch after a while. I struggled to stand up and grabbed quickly at the doorpost to steady myself. "I need to watch Nebuchadnezzar's presentation at the palace."

"Don't worry, Jeremiah, it's not happening today. You can sit down again. Or would you rather lie down?"

Without waiting for an answer, he helped me over to my bed and I sank onto it.

"Why isn't it happening?" I asked, concerned.

"Amasis' steward began to announce that King Nebuchadnezzar would be presented to the people at the palace this afternoon, but Nebuchadnezzar waved him to silence and called Amasis over, much as one might summon a young child or a junior servant. After a while, it was announced that Nebuchadnezzar would be presented tomorrow morning instead. I don't know what the hold-up was, but Amasis didn't look very happy."

"Perhaps Nebuchadnezzar has planned a different presentation from what Amasis wanted," I guessed.

"You could be right," agreed Baruch, "but whatever the reason, you can rest again this afternoon. Perhaps you'll feel better tomorrow morning."

"I hope so."

After resting all afternoon, I felt a little better. Baruch prepared our evening meal and I ate my share to keep him happy, but it seemed like hard work. Although I felt tired, I also felt like reminiscing.

"Remember when you went to read all of my prophecies to the people in the temple?" I asked.

"Yes. I expected it to be a simple job, but it ended up a terrifying day."[109]

"Hiding behind a small screen in a dark, locked room while they searched every other room in the temple, at last making their way to ours. Is that how you remember it?"

"Exactly so. When they finally brought the key and opened the door, I was almost sure they'd find us."

"But they didn't. God really cared for us that day, didn't he?"

"And he's cared for us ever since, too. So many of our family members and acquaintances have died, but we keep on living," marvelled Baruch.

"And now most of those who dragged us down to Egypt, where they thought they'd be safe, have died at the hand of Nebuchadnezzar and his men. They thought they could escape God's judgement, but no-one can do that." I sighed, wishing that reminiscing could bring happy memories rather than the memories of terror on every side that have filled my service to Yahweh.

Perhaps Baruch sensed my sadness and overpowering desire for happy reflections, for he said suddenly, "Wasn't Ebed-melech a good example of trusting God? A foreigner, but so faithful."

"And so grateful when Yahweh promised to keep him safe through the destruction of Jerusalem. There was no

---

[109] Jeremiah 36:4-26

doubt that he believed it completely. His faith was inspiring."

"Yet God's own people wouldn't believe."

"They considered Yahweh as helpless as the gods they claimed to worship. That day when I called our people together to watch me bury those stones under Pharaoh's pavement, I remember one of them said I'd been wrong with all my prophecies. He sneered at me."

"Was that Rapha the Lazy?"

"I… yes, I think it was," I said, cautiously.

"Well, guess who I met at the gate today?"

"Rapha, you mean?"

"Yes."

"But he left Tahpanhes years ago."

"True. Apparently he went upstream. This morning he told me he was in Memphis when Nebuchadnezzar attacked. What he saw reminded him of the Valley of Slaughter."

"The Valley of Ben Hinnom, you mean?"

"Yes – that's how much gruesome butchery there was."

"Yet he survived?"

"Somehow, yes. He sounded quite bitter at times, but at other times he just sounded resigned. He said most of the Jews he knew in Memphis had been killed, and the reports from further up the river were just as bad."

"So why did he come to Tahpanhes?"

"I asked him the same thing, but he said he'd tell me tomorrow. He was asking about you, too. He assumed that you'd be dead by this time and seemed glad to hear that you weren't."

"Glad? He must have thought up some new words of abuse to throw at me." Did I sound bitter or resigned?

"Perhaps. But he looks quite different – for a start, he's lost a lot of weight. I didn't recognise him until he introduced himself."

"Well, I suppose I'll have to see him tomorrow and find out what he blames me for now. You know, Baruch, this work as Yahweh's prophet doesn't get any easier with time."

ℭℜ

After a good night's sleep, I felt much better – better than I had felt for some time. I even woke early enough to indulge my life-long love of watching the sun rise. Leaving my bed, I went outside and climbed the ladder up to the roof. It was still cold and the blackness of night had only just begun to lift.

Sitting on the parapet, I revelled in the beauty of the clear, star-filled sky as the nearly-full moon set in the west, departing almost as if to leave the sky clear ready for the sun to fill it with splendour in an hour or so. I guessed that tonight would be a full moon and thought of Moses and Aaron leading the Israelites out of Egypt under a full moon so many centuries earlier. A generation of slaves experienced new life as Yahweh gave the gift of freedom to his people. Yet now God's people have been driven into captivity out of their Promised Land because they rejected Yahweh, the God who led them out of Egypt. Many returned to Egypt, and most of these have since died in this foreign land.

I wondered when my own time in Egypt would come to an end. It wasn't a morbid thought: I do not seek death, but am content that God's work for me is probably nearly finished. Today, I hope to see something I have waited many years to see, but in the meantime, I rejoiced in the beauty of another dawn, the first I have seen for some time.

Slowly the sky in the east lightened and the dimmer stars began to flicker out. From the point on the horizon at which the sun would soon edge its way into view, a band of deep grey light spread slowly around the horizon in both directions until it met in the west, completely encircling the sky. A dark red glow followed, slowly swelling in the east and transforming the greyness. I can't properly describe just how deep a red it was. It was as if an enormous blaze in the heavens had exhausted itself, its fading embers dying moments before, leaving only the faintest echo of their last glimmers. This indescribable red glow steadily filled almost half the sky, its deep melancholy achingly beautiful. I longed to share this moment with someone, but as usual, I was alone – except for the presence of God. It was a time to relax in the strong, loving arms of my maker, who has always caught me when I fall, strengthened me when I need it, and taught me whenever I will listen.

The ever-growing light of sunrise gave me strength, and I felt the intense closeness to Yahweh that I have felt on several occasions during my inexpressibly privileged life.

By the time I descended the stairs in the full light of day, I was content. In the house, I found that Baruch had recently risen and was about to go out in search of me. I described the sunrise to him and he suggested that I include a description in my diary. When I read the description now, it feels feeble and inadequate, hopelessly incomplete and lacking in beauty – but that is always the way when humans attempt to describe God's handiwork!

Amasis was to present Nebuchadnezzar to the Egyptians that morning at the entrance to Pharaoh's palace. I was eager to watch everything that might happen, but Baruch suggested that I husband my strength and wait until the presentation was about to begin. Dissatisfied, but wise enough to accept that he was right, I remained at home, getting this diary completely up to date. Not only is my writing very untidy – as it has been all my life – it is now also the spidery writing of the old: jagged edges everywhere.

Still waiting.

Finally, the news has come that preparations for the royal presentation are complete. Nebuchadnezzar's men are making their way through the city with Amasis' men, encouraging Egypt's citizens to come and see their conqueror. I don't think Amasis will be very pleased, but I hope he'll accept that he can do nothing but indulge Nebuchadnezzar's rampant self-promotion.

Baruch has finally agreed that it is time to leave for the palace.

Chapter 29

Nebuchadnezzar's Throne

Baruch is a good chap. Although he's getting old himself now, he walked slowly with me to the palace and was quick with a hand on my elbow once or twice when I stumbled.

As we neared the palace, we began to meet more and more Chaldean soldiers, standing about in twos and threes, dressed in fine uniforms. Most were chatting and joking in Aramaic. However, despite their cheerful, carefree appearance, they were also carrying shields and spears, and looked quite alert. The Egyptian citizenry showed no desire to go near them, but from time to time a soldier would wave his arms at the pedestrians and point towards the palace – though their satisfied announcements that Nebuchadnezzar would soon be welcomed to a banquet hosted by Pharaoh meant little to a populace who knew nothing of Aramaic.

No Egyptian soldiers or Greek mercenaries were anywhere to be seen. It was as if the city had been completely taken over by the Chaldeans. I wondered if the situation would last or was just temporary.

Ahead of us, I could see Pharaoh's palace, and then for the first time that day I saw some Egyptian soldiers –

just a few, standing close together in silence. They looked subdued, possibly even a little frightened.

I, meanwhile, felt excited. This was quite different from seeing prophecy fulfilled in the destruction of one's own city and country. Despite having lived in Egypt for… well, quite a few years, it is not my home, and seeing it taken over by the Chaldeans hurts much less than did the fire and slaughter meted out in Jerusalem.

Baruch found us a place to stand where we would have a good view of proceedings outside the doors of Pharaoh's palace, but where I would have a wall to lean against, and even a low retaining wall to sit on if need be.

We had been there only a short while when a man approached us who seemed to know me.

"Jeremiah, man of God," he greeted me. "It's a long time since we met, but I wanted to apologise for the way I treated you then."

I looked at him closely but couldn't recognise him at all. I looked across at Baruch to see if he expected me to recognise this man. To my puzzlement, he was smiling.

"This is Rapha," Baruch said. "Remember I told you that I met him yesterday? And also that I didn't recognise him, just like you don't!"

"Ah, Rapha." I looked closely at him, but I still don't think I really recognised him. "You left Tahpanhes quite a while ago," I said to him. "Where did you go?"

"I went upriver, into the Land of Pathros. I was there when you came to warn us about the impending disaster, but I didn't go to listen to your message. I was too lazy. You might remember that everyone called me Rapha the Lazy." He smiled crookedly and added, "In fact, I was proud of that name and lived up to it until about two years ago."

"You mean you've stopped being lazy?" I asked, surprised.

"Yes… well, mostly. Sometimes I find old habits hard to break."

"True. So what made you want to change?"

"Everything in my life started to fall apart, and it all arose from my laziness. My wife left me because she was fed up with me never doing any work in the family. My children told me that they didn't want anything to do with me because they were ashamed of my laziness. And there were many other things as well."

"Did you just wake up one day and decide to change, then?" asked Baruch.

"No, it was only gradual. At first, I wouldn't admit to myself that the problems were my fault – I blamed everyone else. I know it's ridiculous, but I even blamed you two for setting a good example that highlighted my failures."

"What made you stop blaming us?" I asked.

"When everyone had left me alone, I had to start doing things for myself. I had to work; I had to cook; I had to clean; I had to do all sorts of things I'd always avoided. And I began to find satisfaction in work – and to feel ashamed of my earlier behaviour."

"Did any of your relationships start to mend?" asked Baruch.

Rapha bowed his head, looking sad. "No," he answered. "I had begun to hope that things might improve, but then Nebuchadnezzar and his army arrived. Somehow, I survived the massacres, but the rest of my family is all dead. My wife had gone to live with another man who, quite honestly, looked after her much better than I ever did. However, they were both killed by Nebuchadnezzar's men. And I believe that my four children and their spouses are all dead too. Even my grandchildren are dead, I think, though nobody can confirm it for me."

"That's a tragic story," I said, "but surely they can't *all* be dead. Nebuchadnezzar hasn't been killing everyone. Surely some of your grandchildren must be alive. If you've learned how to work hard, why not work hard at looking for them?"

"I've already done that," Rapha answered flatly. "It's true that Nebuchadnezzar hasn't killed everyone, but there were very few survivors in some areas. That's what it was like where my family was. They all died except for me," he said bitterly. "I, the useless one, am the only one who escaped."

"Then perhaps you now have a chance to make up for your earlier behaviour."

"That's why I'm here, Jeremiah. I came first to apologise, and then to ask for your advice."

"Apologise?"

"Yes. I remember laughing at you in this very place; asking you why you kept working for Yahweh. I'm sorry. If I'd learned the value of working for Yahweh earlier, perhaps my life wouldn't be so bad."

"I don't know about your particular case," I answered, "but I do know that if you want to please God, you have to work hard."

"I've slowly learned how to work hard, but too late to fix my problems. It won't bring back my wife, children or grandchildren."

"No, it won't, but it's still worth doing, Rapha," I said. "Doing the right thing is always worthwhile, however much you may already have lost by delaying."

"I guess you're right, but it seems a bit unfair that I get an opportunity to get my life in order while the people I caused so much trouble to don't."

"Don't worry, they had the same opportunity as you did to change at any time. After all, they criticised you for how you behaved, so they knew it was wrong. They can't blame you if they then made bad choices themselves."

"You may be right, but I'm still not happy with the example I've set and the things I've done – which is why I came to apologise."

"If you decided to change and are genuinely working on doing so, I'm very pleased," I said, and I was: changes like that are pretty rare.

"You said you had a question, too," observed Baruch.

"Yes, I did," said Rapha, "and it's a genuine question, too. Jeremiah, you warned us that we shouldn't come to Egypt, and that we would all die here. Back then I thought you were just making it all up, but now I'm convinced, and I expect to be even more convinced by the end of this afternoon. So I need to ask: now that I believe I shouldn't have come in the first place, should I go back to Judah? I don't really want to go because I'm afraid of what Judah will be like and I've lived here for so long, but I want to do what God wants me to do. So should I return? Or is it too late for that?"

For a few moments, I stared at him. No one else had ever suggested this to me, and I hadn't even thought of it myself for many years. This was a man who for years had laughed at my message and ridiculed the idea of anyone working for Yahweh and doing whatever he said. Finally, I smiled at Rapha and answered, "I suppose you should. I don't have any direct blessing from God for you, and you're right that originally he said everyone who had set their hearts to go to Egypt would die. However, he also talked about a few fugitives returning, and I suppose you're a fugitive from Nebuchadnezzar's rampaging army."

Over the past few days I've been finding it frustratingly difficult to remember God's past words, but suddenly, I could remember them again clearly. I read them hungrily as fiery letters on the wall of my mind and re-membered my experiences of the burning fire of God's voice speaking within me. It was a fleeting but joyous re-living of the most fulfilling times in my life, when Yahweh, the Creator, spoke directly to me and made life worth liv-ing – whatever suffering his word brought to me.

Baruch looked at me with sympathy, knowing that in the past I would have easily reeled off the words of God, but aware that this was no longer true.

So I grinned at him triumphantly, then turned and said to Rapha, "I can tell you just what God told me to say in the Land of Pathros – the message you avoided. He said:

"…none of the remnant of Judah
who have come to live in the land of Egypt
shall escape or survive or return to the land of Judah,
to which they desire to return to dwell there.
For they shall not return, *except some fugitives*."[110]

"You said none shall return," pondered Rapha. "Is it worth me going or should I just give up?"

"Is it laziness asking that question, Rapha?" prompted Baruch.

"I don't think so. It's more asking whether God will accept my repentance or not. What do you think?"

"Remember Jonah?" I answered. "He said that Ni-neveh would be destroyed. Yet their repentance changed that. King Ahab also repented and God delayed the pun-ishment of his family until after he died. God accepts re-pentance, although he doesn't always change everything to make our life easy."

"Will you pray for me, Jeremiah? I've repented for my sins in rejecting God's commands, and I think I should show my repentance now by returning to Judah."

---

[110] Jeremiah 44:14

"I can't say for certain whether you should go or not," I replied. "However, I think you're probably right to go. God hasn't commanded you to stay here."

"Then I suppose I'll go. But first, I want to watch what happens here with Nebuchadnezzar."

"Well, it looks like they've set up a throne for him," said Baruch.

"Where is it?" I asked.

"Over there, between those two torches on the wall," he answered.

"That must be near where you buried those stones, Jeremiah," said Rapha, excitedly.

"Yes," I agreed. "I worked out recently that they were exactly half-way between those torches. As Yahweh said,

"Behold, I will send and take
Nebuchadnezzar the king of Babylon, my servant,
and I will set his throne above these stones
that I have hidden,
and he will spread his royal canopy over them."[111]

"That's amazing!" said Rapha, shaking his head, eyes wide.

"And the final, utterly staggering, detail is the awning they've set up over the throne!" said Baruch. I'd never seen him so excited by fulfilled prophecy before.

"Yes, 'his royal canopy'," I agreed. I felt as if a weight that had been dragging me down for years had been lifted from my shoulders. I felt as light and free as a gliding eagle. Prophecy was my life's work, and now I saw a prophecy coming true in exact detail. The most satisfying part was that this prophecy was being fulfilled without me being overcome by mourning over the slaughter of my peo-

---

[111] Jeremiah 43:10

ple. This time, the slaughter had already happened elsewhere, and I had written my laments – but this was something new, exact and inspiring.

The three of us looked at each other and laughed like children as we celebrated our wonder at Yahweh's command over world events. The audience nearby must have thought we were completely mad!

As we rejoiced, many servants began to emerge from the palace. Some were dressed in Egyptian garb, while others wore the clothes of the Chaldeans.

"This must be what we've been waiting for," said Baruch. "Amasis and Nebuchadnezzar must be about to arrive."

⟩⟨

All the reports about Nebuchadnezzar agree on one thing: he's very proud of his achievements. Of course, he has a lot to be proud of, but the level of self-aggrandisement I heard from him years ago and everyone reports about him is surely over the top.

Yet I've been intrigued to hear that this self-conceit appears to be less marked since his episode of insanity. When I learned that Pharaoh would be presenting him to the crowd in Tahpanhes, I was eager to see for myself what he's like now.

I've often wondered what our own King David was like as a leader and how much he promoted himself rather than God or his nation. After all, in the end a shepherd is judged on the health and strength of his flock, not his own confidence, eloquence, presentation or appearance. I've met many kings over the years – Baruch says probably more than anyone else alive. At the start, I used to keep count, but after a while I grew out of that. Now I don't think I could work out how many there've been even if I wanted to, and so many of them are dead now anyway – not a few at the hand of King Nebuchadnezzar and his ever-expanding empire.

That experience has taught me that kings are generally proud. Very proud. Yet there are some who seem genuinely to view themselves as servants of their nation rather than leaders who deserve unquestioning adulation. Josiah was such a king, and perhaps he inherited his attitudes from King David, the greatest king-shepherd.

There were a few others – foreigners – that I met over the years who were a little like that, and they were much more likely to listen to God's messages than others were. Yet even they never really listened. Serving your nation is good as far as it goes, but for a king to achieve the best possible outcome for his nation, serving God has to be an even higher priority.

I'm rambling a bit about this, but there is a reason.

King Nebuchadnezzar's servants are good at presenting their king as invincible, omnipotent and even omniscient, but as I watched the events of the day unfold, I thought that I perceived a difference in him from my earlier experiences with him. It was a difference that surprised me, given his sensational success as Babylon's ruler, so I'll try to describe it as I observed it.

It must have been time for the festivities to begin. Baruch, Rapha and I saw a sudden flood of attendants pour out of the palace doors, dressed in traditional Egyptian clothing. These took their place in the corners of the courtyard and anywhere the assembled crowd looked a little thin. Suddenly, the entire area was full of attentive people ready to celebrate.

The sound of approaching trumpets was heard from within the palace and then trumpeters marched out through its wide-open doors with measured stride. They also took up their stations where they would be heard by not only the still-growing audience, but probably the entire city. A sudden silence fell as a senior official walked alone through the door and continued about 20 metres towards the two thrones, then stopped and turned. A few trumpeters moved up to stand behind him and, as he bowed deeply towards the doorway, sounded a long blast on their trumpets.

Out strode Amasis, and the massed crowd of Egyptians welcomed him with cheers – a little subdued by the presence of so many Chaldean soldiers, but cheers nevertheless. Amasis smiled, waving and shouting greetings in his unorthodox way. I couldn't help smiling at his performance, and he seemed to throw a special wave in my direction. Had he seen me in the crowd?

After this frivolous performance, he became a little more serious, turning and facing towards the palace doors, holding out an inviting arm towards them as he did so.

For a moment, it was almost as if Amasis was the commander, the central figure of the event. The audience looked on in fascination, craning their necks to get their first view of the conqueror of the world as Pharaoh presented him.

Yet this time when a figure strode down from the palace there was no flippancy. Instead, a serious, forceful, challenging presence came to meet Amasis. Perhaps some would have chosen Amasis' performance over the quietly commanding presence of Nebuchadnezzar, king of Babylon and conqueror of Egypt, but to me, it seemed Nebuchadnezzar had the best of it.

Silence fell. I suppose I wasn't alone in my opinion.

In the sudden quiet, I found it hard to take my eyes off this man who had wreaked God's vengeance on my nation and the city of peace. He looked subtly different from how I remembered him. Not just older, but more complete.

He strode across toward Amasis, slightly lifting his left hand in acknowledgement of the crowd's respectful silence.

As he arrived, Amasis began one of his most important presentations ever.

"Welcome to the Beautiful Land, my lord Nebuchadnezzar," announced Amasis, clearly still suffering from a cold, but obviously doing his best. I wasn't completely convinced by that cold, but Nebuchadnezzar probably was. One up for Amasis: a silent and unnoticed victory that would probably salve his ego a little. What did I say about kings?

"King Nebuchadnezzar is not only king of Babylon, but king of kings and lord of lords." Amasis' voice was fading as he spoke and he broke down in a fit of coughing. He pushed on bravely, but his voice was so quiet that few could have heard his words. He waved to an official standing nearby, who had obviously been primed for the situation and smoothly took over, speaking with a powerful, pleasing voice. He recounted the great achievements of Nebuchadnezzar and welcomed him as the guardian of Egypt – a more palatable word than conqueror, while still clearly ceding authority to Babylon's triumphant leader.

The crafting of the speech that followed almost took my breath away. As it listed Nebuchadnezzar's achievements, the words suggested that Egypt was somehow positively associated with his numerous victories!

Once again, I couldn't help smiling, and this time I found Nebuchadnezzar looking straight at me. His eyes narrowed, and I wondered if they held some recognition. Whether they did or not, I thought it best to school my face into solemnity.

Amasis listened to this speech without any sign of a cough, but as it finished, he dissolved into another coughing fit which left him doubled up with pain. It was clear to everyone in the audience that he would be unable to undertake his next choreographed task, so no-one was surprised when he signalled once again to the official that he should lead Nebuchadnezzar to the grand throne prepared for him. Slowly the coughing subsided, and Amasis was able to sidle over to the smaller throne and take his place upon it while Nebuchadnezzar was still being settled into his splendid chair.

Knowing Amasis, I couldn't help noticing this little bit of byplay, but really it was unimportant compared with the incredible events I was witnessing that day.

Unlikely though it was, Nebuchadnezzar was sitting on a throne flanked by brightly burning torches mounted in special holders on the wall. There was no doubt about it: he was exactly above the stones I had buried under that pavement. When I'd buried those stones so many years before, I had announced to a doubtful audience the very happenings that were now taking place in front of me. I stole a glance at Rapha and found him looking at me with excitement in his eyes. As our eyes met, a huge grin spread across his face, and I couldn't help it: I grinned back.

God's words were being fulfilled. *Exactly*. To my original audience they may have seemed impossible, even laughable, yet here it was. Nebuchadnezzar was there and Egypt was his footstool!

Words can only do so much. I couldn't really describe how I felt in this situation. Humility, joy, awe and amazement were all mixed up inside me, and all I could do was shake my head in wonder.

Yahweh really *is* in control of the nations, and I was privileged to see yet another proof of this.

I looked at Baruch and found him grinning too.

"Is there anyone else here today who was here when I buried those stones?" I asked them quietly.

My question wiped the grin off Rapha's face and he replied sombrely, "I don't think so, Jeremiah. I think all the ones I remember are dead."

"But they wouldn't have believed it anyway," said Baruch. "They would have explained it away as A Coincidence."

"I suppose you're right," I agreed, sadly.

Nebuchadnezzar sat comfortably on his throne above the pavement while his attendants announced his achievements and qualifications to rule Egypt. As they finished, a group of about eight or ten servants stepped forward holding some glittering material, neatly rolled up. They attached it to a fitting on the wall and began to unfurl it above Nebuchadnezzar and his golden throne. Clearly it was a symbol of Nebuchadnezzar's control being spread out over Egypt, with Nebuchadnezzar sitting at the apex of this unfurling banner. Amasis was seated to one side, lower and clearly of less importance. I was sure the implication would hurt.

However, as I considered this, Rapha grabbed my arm, somehow managing to look even more excited than before.

"It's happening!" he said. "Just as you said it would."

I probably looked blank, so he explained.

"You said that Nebuchadnezzar would set his throne over those stones, is that right?"

"Yes."

"And you also said that he would spread his royal canopy over them! It's happening right in front of us. Every detail is exactly right!"

Chapter 30

An Extraordinary Ending

I'm sure nobody else in the crowd watched with as much excitement that day as Rapha, Baruch and I did. Others may have found a thrill in seeing two great kings together, but for us there was the incomparable thrill of seeing the invisible hand of the king above all kings as he displayed his power over these two kings in the world of men.

The reception continued with speeches of welcome and acknowledgement, some traditional Chaldean music being played along with Egyptian music. Displays of some of the spoils taken by Nebuchadnezzar from other lands were presented for all to admire, but to me, the important part had passed.

Or so I thought.

With a final blast of trumpets, the grand presentation came to an end and Nebuchadnezzar rose from his throne. He waved to the crowd, then gathered a few bodyguards around him and beckoned to Amasis. Amasis deserted his own, less grand throne, and crossed to where Nebuchadnezzar stood. After speaking together for a few moments, Amasis laughed and turned to look out at our section of the crowd. As he scanned the crowd, our eyes met and he pointed exultantly towards me.

Signalling for Nebuchadnezzar to follow, Amasis began striding towards me, forging a path through the crowd.

Baruch and I looked at each other. What was going on? We had little time to wonder because Amasis was soon within easy earshot and called, "Heremyo! Prophet of Yahweh, the king of kings."

"Yes, my lord," I stammered, surprised to hear such an acknowledgement on Amasis' lips – surprised, that is, until I guessed that it was intended to make the point that Nebuchadnezzar also had an overlord. Amasis would get himself into trouble sometime!

Amasis greeted me with his customary bear-hug, although it was a little gentler than in times past.

Nebuchadnezzar was only a few strides behind, accompanied by his closest bodyguards, who looked nonplussed. Amasis turned to him and spoke in Aramaic, "This is Heremyo, my lord. He is a prophet of Yahweh, the God of Israel. Have you heard of Yahweh?"

"Oh yes! If you knew Daniel, who is another prophet of Yahweh, you wouldn't bother asking. I have learned much about Yahweh. However, I know that he's not only the God of Israel, he's the King of heaven and earth. Everything he does is right, and he taught me a painful lesson I'll never forget. A lesson about pride."

I wondered whether Amasis would handle the subject of Nebuchadnezzar's madness sensitively, but I shouldn't have wondered. Amasis was Amasis.

"Was that when you went mad?" he asked.

Nebuchadnezzar looked at him, a bit surprised and clearly not pleased: people never spoke to him like that! Nevertheless, he recovered his poise very quickly and answered, "I suppose that's the best description of it. Yes, I lived out with the animals for seven years until I learned my lesson. How did you know about it?"

"It's big news when the empire-builder everybody is terrified of is suddenly taken out of the picture. Your situation was kept very quiet for a few years, but then people began to hear about it and everyone breathed a sigh of relief. Nobody believed you could ever come back to the kingship after something like that. Nobody, that is, except Jeremiah here."

"I had some doubts when I first heard of it," I admitted, "but they didn't last long."

Nebuchadnezzar looked at me hard, and the man's powerful character was almost palpable.

"Yes, you are Jeremiah the prophet," he said. "I thought I recognised you in the crowd from our earlier meetings. I'm amazed you're still alive. You spoke to my father the king before he died, and now I've reigned for 37 years. How old are you?"

"75… no, 76," I answered, struggling to remember.

"Your God must have cared for you to survive all the disasters you've lived through. How did you know about my sickness?"

"I talked to some Israelites who escaped from Babylon, and they also brought some scrolls with them."

"After I recovered, I knew that there were a lot of wild reports going around about the situation, so I wrote a detailed report of my own," said Nebuchadnezzar. "I wanted to make the point that it was not an ordinary madness, but one brought about specifically by Daniel's God, just to stop me from being so proud."

"Daniel predicted it, didn't he?" I asked.

"Yes, inasmuch as he interpreted a dream I had. He also warned me that his God would punish me if I didn't get my ego under control.[112] I did try to behave better and be more gentle for a while – Daniel is very convincing, you

---

[112] Daniel 4:19-27

know – but gradually I slipped back into my old ways. Then one day, twelve months later, I was in the middle of boasting about my greatness when a voice from heaven told me that my kingdom had been taken away from me and that I would live among animals until I acknowledged the God of heaven."[113]

"What did it feel like, my lord?" asked Amasis.

"Terrifying. Immediately I felt as if I couldn't think straight, and that everything in my palace was too much to cope with. Simple things that we expect of a child were beyond me, so I was put outside to live. I was aware of what was going on, but I couldn't analyse anything or even talk to people. Everything was frightening and oppressive. Yet I clung to my memories, proudly remembering what I had been and determined to reclaim it. For seven long years, I refused to accept God's decision."

"Then you recovered?" asked Amasis.

"Oh, no. It wasn't just that it was the right time for me to recover. I stayed sick until I finally acknowledged that Yahweh was the king of heaven, and once I did, my recovery was instantaneous. Straight away, I felt as if I must get on with things. I could think and start planning."

"O king, did you thank God for the healing or the lesson?" I asked.

Nebuchadnezzar smiled. "I was just about to say that, Jeremiah. I really had learned my lesson, so I stopped myself; stopped my planning, stopped my assessing and stood there in the park near my palace and praised and thanked God. Then I went inside and went back to being king again. Since then, I've tried to remember my lesson, but it's not easy when there are presentations like today. These were the things I used to live for, and they drag me down very quickly if I'm not careful."

---

[113] Daniel 4:29-32

"I thought that I noticed a difference in you, O king," I said. "You seemed a little more… restrained."

"I'm glad you could tell. Now I like to extol and praise the King of Heaven and acknowledge that he is much greater than I am. Daniel is still a great help…"

Amasis interrupted him, asking, "Could you really just take over as king again? I'm not trying to be rude, sir, but surely no kingdom would just unquestioningly welcome back a king who had been mad for seven years?"

Once again, Nebuchadnezzar smiled. It was as if he was remembering something that still gave him great pleasure. "I know what you mean, Amasis. It does seem impossible, doesn't it? And that's part of what made it so amazing, and convinced me even more completely of the power of Daniel's God. You see, Daniel was there keeping the kingdom on an even keel as he always does, ready for my return, which he was so confident about. As the seven years drew to an end, he began to tell everyone that I would be coming back to work soon, just as well as before or even better. He warned them all not to think they'd be able to pull the wool over my eyes or expect to get away with anything because of my 'condition'.

"I knew nothing about it at the time, but Daniel had set up a sort of countdown so that when I came inside, my servants were all waiting for me. My bedroom was unchanged, as if I had walked out only a few minutes before. Everything was just how it had been, except that the national coffers were in a better state!" He added with a self-deprecating smile, "I wasn't there to spend money on self-aggrandisement."

I was utterly amazed. I could never have imagined Nebuchadnezzar smiling a self-deprecating smile, but there it was. Amasis also seemed thoughtful, and I wondered what he might learn from this.

"Now I try to hold on to the humility I've learned. Pharaoh Amasis, perhaps you have even helped a little today."

"What do you mean?" asked Amasis.

"I observe that the terrible cough which stopped you from announcing my achievements has suddenly got better."

Amasis looked as if he was about to cough, but after a glance at Nebuchadnezzar, thought better of it. He smiled and said sheepishly, "I didn't think you would notice, sir."

"In my earlier years, I'd have had you executed for less."

"Oh," said Amasis, looking utterly abashed. He had been caught out. I wonder, will he ever learn not to play mind games with great men? He is still convinced that such people are blind.

Turning from the discomfited Pharaoh, Nebuchadnezzar put a hand on my shoulder and said, "Jeremiah, you have been blessed to live a full life and to see God's hand at work."

"Yes, your majesty, I have, and this afternoon is one of the greatest examples. Many years ago, shortly after I came to Tahpanhes, Yahweh told me to bury some stones under that pavement over there, directly under the throne you were sitting on, O king. He told me that you, Nebuchadnezzar, would come and set your throne over them, and spread your royal canopy over them. You can't imagine just how much joy I've had watching you doing exactly what Yahweh said. Rapha, here, was present when I spoke the words of the prophecy to the people of Judah."

"Yes, I was mocking you, wasn't I? I'm glad God has showed me how wrong I was."

"I must say it gives me goose-bumps to think about it," said Nebuchadnezzar. "Did you write this prophecy down? Can I read it?"

"Yes, I wrote it down. I've always written down God's instructions and his prophecies."

"Could you show it to me?"

"I don't have the scroll with me. It's in my house."

"I'll come with you, as long as it's alright for these bodyguards to come too."

"My house is not exactly a palace, my lord."

"I lived in the field for seven years, Jeremiah, rain, hail and shine. Any house is a palace compared with that."

Nebuchadnezzar then turned and asked Amasis, "Did you know about this prophecy, Pharaoh?"

"I knew that Jeremiah kept insisting you would come to Tahpanhes."

"Is that why you tried to stop me coming here?"

"I suppose so. I didn't want him to be right, otherwise I knew he'd insist I listen to Yahweh's words more. I could have argued harder, though, but to some extent it suited me to have it here, so when you insisted, I didn't fight it."

"I guess you were happy to keep me away from your main palace, hey?"

"Well, yes."

"And I was happy to stay away from the larger crowds my advisors told me would attend there."

Baruch had moved to stand by my elbow and we were ready to leave. Nebuchadnezzar signalled to his men to follow him and we set off together. I did my best to hurry, but, what with hours of standing and the excitement of watching prophecy fulfilled, I was quite shaky on my feet. Baruch did his best to support me without making it obvious, but Nebuchadnezzar noticed anyway.

"Fetch my palanquin," he commanded a bodyguard.

"Will you be safe while I am away, my lord?"

"Don't worry about that, just hurry and get my palanquin – and the bearers."

Nebuchadnezzar got his way: I was carried home in King Nebuchadnezzar's litter.

When we arrived, I went in to find the scroll and Baruch lit some lamps and did his best to make the main room a little more presentable. The two of us are generally tidy men and our scroll collections are well-organised, but even so, I had to admit after a while that I couldn't find it, and Baruch took a while to identify the right scroll and track down the prophecy Nebuchadnezzar was interested in.

"What language is it written in?" asked Nebuchadnezzar as it was produced.

"Hebrew, your majesty," I said. "Do you want us to translate it for you?"

"No need," said Nebuchadnezzar. "I can read a little Hebrew."

This announcement amazed me, and it must have shown. Nebuchadnezzar looked a little embarrassed.

"Daniel convinced me that I needed to learn more about the God of heaven," he explained, "and that the only place to find him was in the Hebrew scriptures. So I read them sometimes. Not as often as Daniel would like me to, I'm sure, but I do find them inspiring."

What an astonishing situation this was. I had spent my entire life trying to convince my own people – *God's* people – to listen to his words, and they had refused to do so, yet here was a powerful foreigner who not only acknowledged the God of Israel but read his word!

Baruch passed him the scroll, opened to the section we had just seen fulfilled.

How many people get to read a scripture which they themselves have fulfilled?

Nebuchadnezzar read the text out loud in his clear, strong voice, his Hebrew surprisingly good:

" 'Thus says the Lord of hosts, the God of Israel:
Behold, I will send and take Nebuchadnezzar
the king of Babylon, my servant,
and I will set his throne
above these stones that I have hidden,
and he will spread his royal canopy over them.
He shall come and strike the land of Egypt,
giving over to the pestilence
those who are doomed to the pestilence,
to captivity those who are doomed to captivity,
and to the sword those who are doomed to the sword.
I shall kindle a fire in the temples of the gods of Egypt,
and he shall burn them and carry them away captive.
And he shall clean the land of Egypt
as a shepherd cleans his cloak of vermin,
and he shall go away from there in peace.
He shall break the obelisks of Heliopolis,
which is in the land of Egypt,
and the temples of the gods of Egypt
he shall burn with fire.' "[114]

He stopped and stood in silence for a few moments.

"Amazing," he breathed. "It's like reading a report of our campaign here in Egypt. When were you told to bury those stones?"

I looked at Baruch for assistance and he answered, "About 17 years ago, your majesty."

"That's right, O king," said Rapha. "Jeremiah called us all together to listen to the prophecy so that we would know what to expect." Rapha was still a complete surprise to me – a reminder that sometimes, just occasionally, people really do change.

---

[114] Jeremiah 43:10-13

"Well, that is amazing," continued Nebuchadnez-zar. "Completely astonishing. One detail in particular amazes me, although you may not notice it. Yahweh calls me 'Nebuchadnezzar the king of Babylon, my servant'. I can assure you that I wasn't his servant when you wrote this. Yet now, it's just another part of the exact fulfilment you watched today. I used to boast about great Babylon, the city *I* built, but now I could boast about fulfilling the words of Yahweh – except that I didn't know I was doing so!"

CB

What a day!

This really has been the day of a lifetime.

After reading the prophecy he had personally fulfilled, Nebuchadnezzar stayed for a while in my home, chatting to us and praising the God of heaven. It was inspiring, and I hope it inspired Amasis to learn more about Yahweh and listen to his commands.

By the time they left, the open area outside our house was crammed with people. Nebuchadnezzar's guards had called in reinforcements and Amasis' guards had finally caught up with their eccentric charge. Many, many others were there too, crowded around the door, and Baruch seized the opportunity to go out to the crowd and read the prophecy they had seen fulfilled that day. He read it in Hebrew, Egyptian and Aramaic, so that everyone present would be able to understand what a great event had happened that day.

Nebuchadnezzar and Amasis both wanted me to accompany them to the palace so they could honour me and honour Yahweh, but I was just too tired. I hope they were able to praise God well enough without me. What a delightful evening it could have been.

Once everyone had finally left, I was tempted to lie down and rest, but I felt that I had to write everything down while I still remembered it. My memory is failing me, I'm afraid.

So I sat and wrote. And as I wrote, I revelled in the wonder of worshipping a God with such foreknowledge, power and love. My life felt vindicated; my work complete; my joy beyond bounds.

I sang praise to the God for whom nothing is impossible.

Epilogue

A Great Man

Jeremiah, the great prophet and priest, died during the night.[115]

He lived a long life; a life of service that few in the history of the world will ever outshine. This man will stand with the great – with Abraham, Isaac and Jacob, the twelve patriarchs, Moses and Aaron, and the judges Yahweh sent to lead his people.

Among the prophets he can stand with head unbowed because he always saw his work clearly and never flinched from doing it – whatever the cost. He gave up so much in the hope of saving his people. And he genuinely hoped to save them.

At the command of God, he travelled widely as a prophet to the nations. He met more kings and leaders than anyone alive; possibly more than anyone who has ever lived.

By the order of Yahweh, he never married – acting out a parable for his people. It was a parable ignored, but did that make the sacrifice vain? No, because God rewards sacrifices made in his service.

---

[115] The Bible does not tell us where, how or when Jeremiah died.

Also by command of Yahweh, he could never attend either celebrations or funerals, and for this he suffered constant, carping criticism.

Of all the strict requirements that Yahweh put upon his willing servant, the one Jeremiah found most difficult to obey was the command that he should not pray for his people. Despite the hatred and abuse he suffered from them, he longed to pray freely for his people, yet he could not do so.

He endured the hatred of his family and his tribe, including beatings from evil, self-centred priests who were not fit to tie his sandals.

Although born into a rich family, he searched out those who needed help and gave away his riches. Nobody has ever acknowledged this – perhaps few even realised it – but Jeremiah chose to love his neighbour, even to the extent of making himself a pauper.

With him a good deal of history has died also. He began his work in the thirteenth year of good king Josiah, almost sixty years ago. Persistently, tenaciously, resolutely, unwaveringly, he tried to persuade all he met of God's commands – not only the nation at large, but also the four kings of Judah who followed Josiah.

Jeremiah would have said that he failed in those things. I say that it was not he who failed, but those to whom he spoke.

The priests denied his message and rejected the God they were committed – by an eternal covenant – to serving. The same priests despised Yahweh's temple and degraded its holiness. They traded on their position, exchanging holiness for riches.

The Levites failed too. On occasion through our history, the Levites have shamed the priests into fulfilling their responsibilities. Yet in the days of Jeremiah, the Levites were no better than the priests. They joined the priests in treating religion as a business. Could a tally of the Levite dead ever be made, it would be clear that they have paid for their sins.

The people – those sheep who were to be led to righteousness by the sons of the house of David – these were the ones who ultimately brought disaster. Even when their kings were righteous, the people still rushed headlong into depravity unless held back with a very firm hand; when their kings led them into vice, they followed enthusiastically.

And the kings: what can I say of the house of David? Would not David – the shepherd of the nation, the sweet Psalmist of Israel – have hung his head in shame at the behaviour of many of his descendants? How he would have wept could he have seen the temple he was so eager to build, filled from one end to the other with idols and altars to other gods.

Judah, the kingdom of two tribes, is finished.

Jerusalem, the city of peace, is burned with fire. Its walls lie broken. Its gates are ruined.

The derelict temple courts are empty; the dedicated treasures carried away; the holy places demolished.

Perhaps the rains of 70 years will wash away the blood shed within the city. Perhaps the evil of my people can be washed away too. May lizards and sparrows tread lightly on the ruins of King David's dreams until his descendants return from captivity. Oh, Jerusalem!

Jeremiah, the prophet of Yahweh, gave his life to God against the will of his family, his fellow priests, his fellow prophets and his nation. Jeremiah is dead. There will never be another prophet like him, and no lamentation can describe the loss that comes with his death; however, few now remain to mourn.

His words from the Lord were so often words of un-remitting but well-deserved condemnation. What a testing time he faced in delivering them! Yet some of his happier words also paint a glorious future for the nation of Israel and the whole world. Abraham, our forefather, is to be a father of many nations, and the temple in Jerusalem a house of prayer for all nations. Jeremiah the great prophet was blessed to hear the words:

"Behold, the days are coming,
declares the Lord,
when I will fulfil the promise I made
to the house of Israel and the house of Judah.
In those days and at that time I will cause
a righteous Branch to spring up for David,
and he shall execute justice and righteousness in the land.
In those days Judah will be saved
and Jerusalem will dwell securely.
And this is the name by which it will be called:
'The Lord is our righteousness.'
"For thus says the Lord:
David shall never lack a man to sit
on the throne of the house of Israel,
and the Levitical priests shall never lack
a man in my presence to offer burnt offerings,
to burn grain offerings, and to make sacrifices forever.
"Thus says the Lord:
If you can break my covenant with the day
and my covenant with the night,
so that day and night will not come
at their appointed time,
then also my covenant with David my servant
may be broken,
so that he shall not have a son to reign on his throne,
and my covenant with the Levitical priests my ministers.
As the host of heaven cannot be numbered

and the sands of the sea cannot be measured,
so I will multiply the offspring of David my servant,
and the Levitical priests who minister to me."[116]

I counted Jeremiah as my friend as well as my mentor and guide. He explained to me, as far as he could understand it himself, what those words mean, and reminded me that Abraham was promised the land but had never received it. Abraham's hope was a hope for the future, and Jeremiah joined in that hope. God will keep his promises.

Only yesterday I was with him as two powerful kings sought his company and his advice. What a scene it was, to see him carried to his house in a litter as they walked beside him like servants! It was deserved recognition for a great prophet I was privileged to know well. I wish you could have known him too.

Now I must follow the path he trod without his guidance – and without his encouraging smile. I will miss him. Yet he will stand again on the earth with the Righteous Branch Yahweh told him about, the son of David. Jeremiah will stand with that great cloud of witnesses who have lived and died in faith.

"Precious in the sight of the Lord
is the death of his saints."[117]

The work of Jeremiah, the son of Hilkiah, servant of the Most High God, is ended – for now.

---

[116] Jeremiah 33:14-18, 20-22
[117] Psalm 116:15

Timeline

We do not know how old Jeremiah was at any stage. However, he began to prophesy in the 13th year of King Josiah and was taken to Egypt 41 years later. If, as assumed in this timeline, he was 17 years old when he began to prophesy, then he was 58 years old when taken to Egypt.

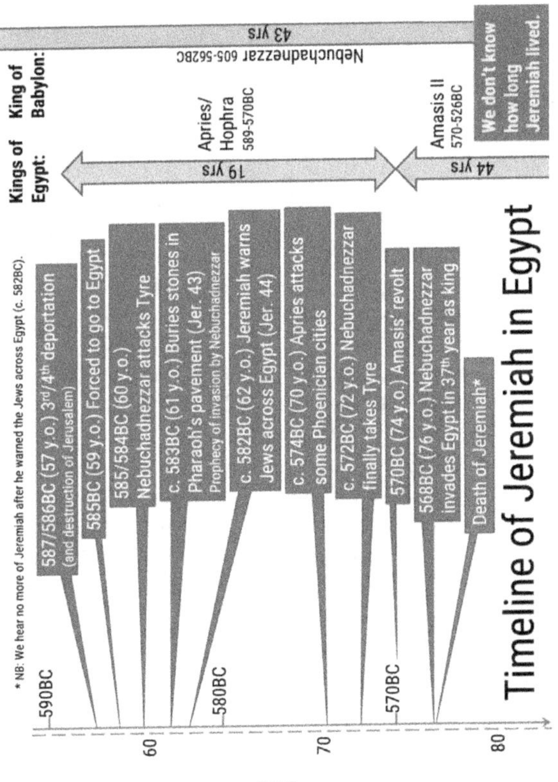

Historical Note

Volume 5 – No Remedy ended with the survivors in Judah planning to flee the country following the assassination of Gedaliah, Nebuchadnezzar's appointed governor. Up until then, the story is based on the many details of the time recorded in the books of Kings, Chronicles, Jeremiah, Lamentations, Ezekiel, Daniel and other prophets, as well as some historical information from outside the Bible. At that point, however, most of the Biblical sources fall silent.

This sixth volume attempts to retell events in the life of Jeremiah from that time on, a time and place in history about which the Bible says very little – directly. However, there are still many hidden nuggets of information that help us to imagine what might have happened to Jeremiah in Egypt as he came to the end of his life as Yahweh's prophet to the nations.

The book of Jeremiah does include some messages from God after his arrival in Egypt, and these are all included in the story. The books of Daniel and Ezekiel also provide some background information regarding the reign and military activities of Nebuchadnezzar, as well as some prophecies regarding Egypt.

As a Christian, I take history written in the Bible as fact. I know that the Bible is not intended as a history book, but it does provide plenty of historical information that most history books do not record. Whereas most nations only record their good news (and sometimes wildly exaggerated at that), the Bible tells the good and the bad, victories and defeats, joys and sorrows.

Given this limitation of written history from outside the Bible, I treat it with much less confidence, although at times other records of history can help us to understand what the Bible is reporting.

The ancient Greek historian Herodotus (c. 484BC to c. 425BC) wrote over one hundred years after the events in this book. He gives details of the actions of Pharaoh Hophra (Apries) and his successor Amasis II. They are discursive, but quite interesting to read. Some of the events he reports have been included in the book, including Hophra's failed attack on Kurene,[118] the appointment of Amasis as Pharaoh,[119] the mistreatment of Patarbemis[120] and Hophra's kind treatment but later execution by Amasis.[121]

Some of the character and unconventional behaviour attributed to Amasis in the book also have their basis in the writings of Herodotus.[122]

For many years, the invasion of Egypt by Nebuchadnezzar was denied by historians and archaeologists. However, the acquisition by the British Museum in 1878 of a Babylonian clay tablet[123] that describes the invasion in the thirty-seventh year of Nebuchadnezzar's reign (~568BC) overcame this denial. Nevertheless – due to a lack of *supporting* evidence rather than the existence of any evidence *against* it – historians still widely believe that Nebuchadnezzar's invasion was not as cataclysmic and destructive as Jeremiah and Ezekiel had prophesied that it would be. Perhaps evidence will come to light in the future, or maybe Egypt responded to Yahweh's warnings sufficiently that God lightened the punishment he had promised. We do not know.

---

[118] Herodotus 2.161
[119] Herodotus 2.162
[120] Herodotus 2.162
[121] Herodotus 2.169
[122] See Herodotus 2.162, 2.172-174
[123] See https://www.jhalsey.com/jerusalem-book/standard/egypt/bm33041.html and https://www.britishmuseum.org/collection/object/W_1878-1015-22.

The events surrounding Amasis' ascension as Pharaoh and Nebuchadnezzar's invasion of Egypt are not clear. It appears that Amasis rebelled against Pharaoh Hophra (Apries) and took over as Pharaoh, but that Hophra subsequently returned to Egypt, either with Nebuchadnezzar or with some support from him. However, he lost a battle, was taken prisoner by Amasis and was later killed.

Josephus also states that when Nebuchadnezzar captured Egypt in the twenty-third year of his reign, he carried away Jews from there.[124]

It is not known from either scripture or history how, when or where Jeremiah died.

---

[124] Antiquities of the Jews, Book 10, Chapter 9.7.

About the author

Mark Morgan was born in Australia during 1963; the youngest son of Peter and Meryl Morgan. Deeply involved in religion all of his life, he has worked as a lay preacher, Sunday School teacher and missionary – trying to balance the many demands of spiritual life with those of family and paid employment.

After graduating, he worked in engineering for several years before concentrating on software development. Happily married and blessed with eight children, he has spent many years reading the Bible and learning to teach its lessons.

Writing Bible-based novels now fills much of his time.

Free Download

Paul in Snippets

A 109-page PDF novelette by Mark Morgan.

The life of Paul painted from the Acts of the Apostles.

Get your free copy of *Paul in Snippets* when you sign up for the Bible Tales mailing list. As well as the eBook, you will receive a weekly email newsletter with micro tales, informative articles and special offers.

Visit **https://www.BibleTales.online/free-pins**

Bible Tales Online

Other books by Mark Morgan are available from Bible Tales Online.

Terror on Every Side!
THE LIFE OF JEREMIAH

From a family of priests in the peaceful reign of good King Josiah, came a young man Jeremiah, bringing words from God to his people. It was no message for the fainthearted, either. It was a message of *Terror on Every Side!*

Volume 1 – Early Days
Volume 2 – As Good As It Gets
Volume 3 – Darkness Falling
Volume 4 – The Darkness Deepens
Volume 5 – No Remedy
Volume 6 – That Broken Reed

Available in paperback, hardcover and eBook with audiobooks for volumes 1-5 and volume 6 in production.

Micro-tales

Collections of short stories about Bible characters or events, available in paperback, eBook and audiobook.

Fiction Favours the Facts
Fiction Favours the Facts – Book 2
Fiction Favours the Facts – Book 3

Other novels

Joseph, Rachel's son
The King's Armour-bearer

Bible Tales Online continues to publish books. To find the list of currently available books, visit

https://www.BibleTales.online/books

Bible
Tales

www.BibleTales.online